Achilles Heel

Robert Chessar

Grosvenor House
Publishing Limited

This book is published by
Grosvenor House Publishing Ltd
Link House
140 The Broadway, Tolworth, Surrey, KT6 7HT.
www.grosvenorhousepublishing.co.uk

This book is a work of fiction. Any resemblance to
people or events, past or present, is purely coincidental.

A CIP record for this book
is available from the British Library

ISBN 978-1-80381-296-0
eBook ISBN 978-1-80381-342-4

Jane.
Without you, this book would not
have been completed.

The test of a first-rate work,
And a test of your sincerity
In calling it a first-rate work,
Is that you finish it.

(Arnold Bennett)

CONTENTS

Introduction

Because humans are fallible, everything they do is liable to have errors. Some are small and can be fixed; some are large and can't. Somewhere in between these two conditions is the occasional small glitch, for which the perpetrator will not accept blame. This story centres on such a one. It tells of a seemingly simple pipework heating system to be installed in a Royal Naval Armaments Depot in Scotland for the Ministry of Defence. The name of the depot, its location and the characters in the story are fictitious. This is, nevertheless, a dramatized version of a similar event.

A junior consulting engineer is forced by his client (the M.O.D.) to reduce the estimated costs of his design. He is up against time constraints and is bullied by his superiors. Under intense pressure he makes an error that is not noticed till the project has already started on site.

When the installation contractor finds and reports the technical fault, those above him in positions of power, refuse to accept the evidence and use their authority to protect their reputations. If the fault is not addressed, a major environmental disaster will occur. The strength and resources of Messrs Franz Liseur, an international mechanical services contractor, are brought to bear in the attempt to convince the four antagonists, the Ministry of Defence, the Consulting Engineers, the Supervising

Officer and the Main Building Contractor, to relent and alter the design before it's too late. If this fails, there will be enormous financial penalties. Can Liseur's Scottish engineer, Douglas Fairbairn, find a way to prevent that?

The reader will not require a degree in physics to understand this story. It turns on errors made at the design stage of this massive external heating system. The drama of the people and authorities engaged before, during and after the construction is intimately exposed.

Worry not that this is about an engineering installation. There are no fancy formulae to confuse you, dear reader. My mentors did ask, however for a couple of thumbnail sketches to help them understand the story. I give you the secrets of *flanged joints* and hairpin shaped *expansion loops*. You will need no more that these.

Flanged Joints.
Pairs of welding flanges are bolted together to join two pipes.

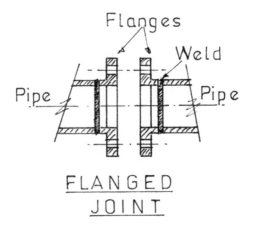

FLANGED
JOINT

Expansion loops (Hairpins)

These absorb the thermal expansion of the pipe. Two anchors hold the pipe and force the hairpin legs to bend inwards as the pipe expands. Tubular guides keep the pipe straight. The biggest pipe is 250mm (10 inches) in diameter. There are powerful forces to accommodate.

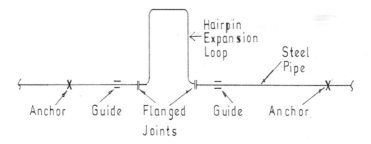

The three lists that follow will be useful for quick reference as the story intertwines the diverse cast.

THE PLAYERS:

The Client	The Ministry of Defence (M.O.D.)	
	James Briggs	Top man in Scotland
The Supervising Officer (S.O.)	Norman Keen	
The Consultant	Building services designers	
	The Clark Chisholm Partnership	
	Dean Chisholm	Senior partner
	Sean O'Casey	Senior Engineer
	Torquil Knight	Design engineer
The Builder	(The Main Contractor)	
	Jarvis & Craig Ltd	
	Hugh Jarvis	Owner
	Joe Hadshaw	Project Manager
	Terry Cordwell	Site Foreman
Heating Engineer	(The sub-contractor)	
	Franz Liseur Ltd	
	Tony Surtal	Scottish Branch Manager
	Douglas Fairbairn	Contracts Manager
	Mark Trumann	Senior Engineer
	Mark's assistant	John Logge
	Labour Manager	Archie McGregor
	Site Foreman	Angus MacLauchlan

THE OTHERS

George Yeoman	The Clerk of Works (C.O.W.) Employed by the M.O.D.
John Smith	Indemnity Protection Ltd Consultants Insurance Company
Colin Thompson	Scottish Institute of Mechanical Engineering Research, (S.I.M.E.R.) The hydraulics expert
David Young	Young's Valves Ltd Pressure Regulating Valve supplier
David Pringle	Torquil's flatmate
Phillipa Grant	Torquil's girlfriend

THE HIERARCHY

Client
The Ministry of Defence

Supervising Officer
Norman Keen

Design Teams

Services Consultant
Clark Chisholm Partnership

Structural Engineer
Keen Parr Felt Partnership

Builder / Main Contractor
Jarvis & Craig Ltd

Services / Sub-Contractor
Franz Liseur Ltd

1. The Client employs a Design Team
2. The Structural Engineers design the structural requirements
3. The Services Consultant designs the mechanical and electrical systems
4. The Client appoints a Supervising Officer
5. The Client engages and pays the successful Builder / Main Contractor.
6. The Builder engages and pays the Sub-Contractor
7. The sub-contractor is at the bottom of the heap

Power is strongest at the top and reduces with each step down.

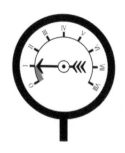

CHAPTER ONE:

Concession

Part 1
Mid December1988:

Clark Chisholm offices ~ Consultants Glasgow
He sat at the third floor window with his arms folded,
staring out at the disappearing day. The rain had stopped.
The big sash window rattled in complaint at the gusting
westerly wind that was blowing low, black and grey
clouds across the darkening sky; their ominous creep
seeming to scare the blushing sun, forcing it to hide
below the sombre western silhouette of the city skyline.
His office, high up on Woodlands Terrace, overlooked
Kelvingrove Park. In a wistful reverie, he visualised his
parents' house in Forres overlooking Findhorn Bay up on
the east coast. He recalled many bright dawns rising out

of the North Sea. Those mornings always cheered him as a youngster when he rose to get fed and ready for school. This dismal, mid-December, Glasgow sunset was doing nothing to lift his spirits. He had a problem. It had troubled him for over a year. An answer was proving elusive. His job was to find a solution. Failure to do so could bring the sun down on his short career. He spun his chair round to look again at the calculator on his desk. All his revised numbers had been entered but fear of the result prevented him from pressing the answer button. If the wrong figure came up he was surely sunk? He decided *it's now or never.*

A tentative tap on the 'equals' sign revealed the bottom line. *Just below seven hundred thousand pounds.* He allowed himself a thin smile as he wrote the figure into his notes.

"I hope this will satisfy Mister Briggs?"

His chair squeaked as he spun round just in time to glimpse the disappearing sun. He stood up, lifted his calculation file, headed past his four young colleagues and went out of the drawing office for his lonely journey down one stair to Sean O'Casey's office. On the gloomy landing he paused and looked upwards. In summertime the impressive glass atrium on the roof of this terraced Victorian town house gave the stairwell warmth and brightness. This afternoon it merely reflected the cold light from the single central chandelier. He gripped the bannister and moved down the spiral stair. The revised cost was to be reported next morning at a meeting with Mister Briggs. This evening, all he wanted from his senior mentor was some encouragement and advice. He doubted whether O'Casey would be different from his customary ill-disposed self.

Three years earlier Torquil Knight began his career as a mechanical services designer with the Clark Chisholm Partnership of consulting engineers. He knew his way around the complexities of design and costing of heating and ventilation systems. In his first couple of years he had already designed and managed, four minor projects quite successfully...on time and within budgets.

This current commission from the Ministry of Defence was however, causing him some embarrassment. Negative signals from his boss had him doubting his ability to get it finalised. At the meeting last week with the Ministry of Defence in Edinburgh, James Briggs had again thrown out Torquil's budget cost saying that it was still too high. He rejected Torquil's urgent attempt to explain, *you just can't keep cutting costs*. The integrity of the design was bound to suffer. Briggs was adamant; the costs had to be cut to the bone. He directed Torquil to get back to his office and not to return until he had a much lower figure. Now he had that figure. He hesitated outside O'Casey's office door, took a slow intake of breath, knocked and entered.

"Hello, sir."

O'Casey was at his desk, with a blue biro pen, marking corrections on a report. He looked up. Torquil ignored the senior man's audible sigh of annoyance and got to the point,

"I've worked out a revised figure for tomorrow's meeting in Edinburgh."

"Just remind me? What project are you talking about?"

"The one at Bluff in Morayshire; the armaments depot at Findhorn Bay. I've got my meeting at ten tomorrow with Mister Briggs of the M.O.D. I told you last week that he demanded a lower figure."

"And what are you going to tell him, Torquil?"

"I've reduced the last figure from eight-hundred and fifty thousand to just below seven hundred thousand."

Sean raised his eyebrows,

"That's a substantial drop. Have you included a contingency sum?"

"No."

"Well, don't you think you'd better?"

"I wanted to see what you thought."

"Torquil, you should know by now; we generally add about seven per cent for the unforeseen. Make it seven hundred and fifty thousand. Knocking off a neat hundred thousand quid might get you through. Are you in agreement with that, Torquil?"

"Not entirely. I have maintained the design brief but to get the cost down I've had to omit things."

O'Casey dropped his pen on the desk with a little force, as if to emphasise his exasperation with the young man's naivety. He sat back, clasped his hands behind his neck and gave a soft laugh that fell short of being scornful. He shook his head from side to side and whispered with pointed sarcasm,

"Well *naturally* you omitted things. That's what *sensible* people do. Enlighten me?"

Torquil didn't read the subtle body language of the senior man but he did note the seemingly softer response and the indirect compliment about *sensible people*. He relaxed a little and continued,

"This job mainly comprises steel pipes. I've reduced the specification for the steel tube, the steel fittings and thermal insulation."

Sean exclaimed,

"You saved that much on pipes alone?"

Picking up on his boss's surprise, Torquil blushed. Doubt crept into his mind. *Did this man know something he was not aware of?* He forced himself to believe his own numbers and gave his best answer,

"The project has fourteen kilometres of big diameter steel pipes. I was surprised at the saving but I have checked and double-checked my estimate. What I have told you is quite real, sir."

"Please Torquil. Stop calling me sir! You're not in school now. I'm not your teacher."

Torquil felt the rebuke. It was just one more indication of his inadequacy from O'Casey. His whispered *sorry,* was not acknowledged.

"Call me Sean, like everyone else does. Now, don't you think it's getting late in the day for any more discussions with this man, Briggs? Will he give you the green light this time?"

"I don't believe they have any option, sir, eh...Sean. I can't see any other way to get the costs down without involving a re- design."

Sean had some respect for the young man's determination; continuing to pursue a final agreement with his difficult client. He had no misgivings about the lad's ability to finalise the design and get the project out to tender, but he was making quite a meal of it. From January to December Torquil had kept his head down, battling with this awkward Ministry of Defence man who seemed to be bullying him into submission. This was the way a young rookie consultant got the tough, sharp-end experience needed to stand up to obdurate clients like James Briggs. Torquil was expected to rise to the opportunity.

The partners had felt the job was ideal for Torquil since it was in Forres, his own hometown. After all, he was a Bachelor of Science honours graduate mechanical engineer from Glasgow University; qualified way beyond Sean O'Casey. Sean came up the hard way through the contracting side of the construction business. His position as a senior engineer in this partnership was as high as he would ever go. He could never become an associate or partner. Torquil might well be his boss in the near future; with his name and qualifications emblazoned on the firm's letter heading. Until that happened O'Casey felt it was his job to treat Torquil as a subordinate. He picked up his pen and resumed his scrutiny of the report on his desk.

Torquil waited for his boss's final word. Sean looked up with an expression that said, *are you still here?* He gestured him away with another curt admonition,

"Don't be late for your meeting tomorrow and don't come back without an agreement."

"Right, Sean. I will do my best."

He turned to go but O'Casey could not resist a final stinging orison,

"I pray your best is good enough, Torquil."

Torquil stiffened but remembered his good manners. He bit his lower lip and managed,

"Thank you Sean. Goodnight."

Sean didn't reply. Torquil was hurt by O'Casey's lack of warmth. This was another unkind hint and implicit threat to his job if he came back without the go ahead. He felt that all the odds were against him. Like a salmon swimming upstream towards a line of hungry bears he must win this trial of his ingenuity.

As he cycled the short distance back to his flat near the park, he still had some hard thinking to do. *What would he do if the client rejected the latest figure?* That would present a huge problem. It would not be possible to return to his office having failed three times to reach agreement. The outcome surely would be the sack. He had no idea how he would react if the M.O.D. still insisted on further cuts.

Just as he rounded the corner into Bentinck Street, he spotted his flatmate, Davy, strolling along the pavement on the opposite side of the road; his arm nursing two fish suppers wrapped in newspapers. Tuesday night was David's turn to fetch their dinner from the chip shop in Dumbarton Road. They kept a kitty to pay for the necessary food and rent for their ground floor flat they had shared for the last four years. A quick shout got his pal's attention. Torquil caught up with him at the close to be greeted by David's usual sobriquet,

"Hi Torky! You're early. Don't tell me you've been sacked?"

"Not yet, Davy; but it might be soon."

David turned the key and held the door, allowing Torquil to get his bike inside.

"The fish suppers smell great, Davy. My mouth's watering."

"Me too. The vinegar's soaked through the paper. Can't wait to get these out on a plate. What's with all the drawings? Still having problems designing that job up north?"

"Not the design; it's the client. I'm going back to Edinburgh in the morning to meet James Briggs."

"Oh yeah, *the Devil from the Ministry*. I remember you telling me about him after your last encounter. How about forgetting the plates and just eating these out the paper, Torky? You can fill me in as we scoff. Want a beer?"

"Sure. I'll switch on the fire. It's bloody freezing in here!"

David Pringle got his BSc. the same year as Torquil. His first job with a small family firm was boring him stupid so, he was just about to give them four weeks notice. He was hopeful that his career would take off next February when he joined a Civil Engineering firm of consultants, the Peurova Partnership in North Queensferry. It was unlikely that he and Torquil would ever again cross paths, but they agreed to keep in touch somehow. The two had become good friends and for reasons of economy, had settled into the habit of spending their weekday winter evenings at home, eating and chatting, playing at cards or listening to their combined collection of records.

Tonight was different. For a couple of hours they talked about Torquil's problems; firstly about his boss but more importantly about the obduracy of Mister

James Briggs. David became concerned at the possibility of his friend being fired or having to resign.

"Torky. It seems to me you are caught in a cleft stick; between a boss who doesn't help you and a client who won't be satisfied no matter what you do. It's only my opinion but you should find a way to stand up to both of them."

"That can't happen. Briggs is the top man in Scotland. There's nobody above him except the Minister of Defence in London. O'Casey is too well in with Dean Chisholm, the guy who owns my firm. Either way I'm done for. If Briggs says no tomorrow, that's it. These guys are all-powerful. I'll have to resign before I get kicked out. It's the only way I can think of to get me out of all this."

"But your firm will still be stuck with the problem; don't you see? That could be to your advantage."

"How's that? Briggs would give the job to another firm."

"I don't think he can. You've now got the cost down so low that another firm might not take the commission. He needs you more than you need him. You are in a stronger position than you think."

"That's easy for you to say, Davy. I'm afraid I don't see the way out."

They both sat in silence; staring at the floor; clasping their beers; searching for the answer that would disentangle

Torquil's difficulty. David was first to raise his head and introduce what he thought was a promising notion,

"Torky. He keeps telling you to get the cost down, doesn't he?"

"Yeah. What are you getting at?"

"Well, he can't keep doing that if you ask him a simple question."

"You'll have to explain that, Davy?"

"If he won't accept *your* cost, just ask *him* what figure *he'll* accept."

Torquil looked at the floor to think about that idea. It didn't take long to dawn on him what Davy had just proposed. He smiled. It was so simple. Why did he not think of it? His smile broadened as he turned to face his friend,

"Yes! Oh! That is so clever, Davy. That will be my get-out move. Game, set and match! Mister Briggs."

Davy corrected him,

"Check Mate! Mister Knight."

Torquil smiled at David's clever metaphor. He relished the idea of turning the tables on Briggs. His mind raced with positive thoughts. *That's what I'll do. It's bound to work. I'll re-design the job to that figure, I'll convince Sean O'Casey that I can get it out to tender and I'll save my job.*

"Right Davy! If James Briggs continues to be awkward...I'll do it! I only hope I can pull it off."

"You'll be fine, Torky. You never know, he might *accept* your new figure. Be confident. Keep your head. Look Briggs in the eye. Picture him standing there in his undies; but try not to laugh out loud!"

Torquil giggled like a schoolboy at the mental image.

"You'll get me hung if I burst out laughing. Thanks for listening to my tale of woe, Davy. I really appreciate your help."

"As you said Torky, it's easy for me. You're the one who has to do the business. Good luck."

The chat with his pal helped imbue Torquil with renewed resolve for his meeting. He slept well and rose early to get to Queen Street to catch the nine o'clock train to Haymarket.

Part 2
Next morning:

M.O.D. Offices ~ Edinburgh

The Chairman of the M.O.D. held the absolute conviction that the authority he wielded was his by right. He was the epitome of those insufferable people in positions of power who take sadistic delight in dominating their juniors. His choicest anecdote for a dinner party, always delivered using extravagant language, was to recount his success in humiliating an office boy. *The pathetic fellow trembled visibly and augmented his humiliation by performing the most wretched spectacle I have ever witnessed of ignominious micturition!* For those who did not catch his meaning he added an emphatic punch line; *the bugger peed himself in public!* Without a doubt he was clever at his job but it was clear to everyone within his sphere of influence that James Briggs was also a bumptious, arrogant bully. No one near him would dare to question his conduct. His masters were based far away in London. None of his staff was aware of the tough directive Briggs had received the previous day from the Defence Minister's Personal Private Secretary...

Get the costs for the Bluff armaments base agreed. Get the work started on site as soon as possible. The project is way behind schedule. The existing district-heating system is falling apart. The annual repair and maintenance bills are soaring. The minister wants the whole project completed within eighteen months. The final statement was short but not sweet; *if you cannot manage that, the Minister will find someone who can.*

Still shaken from the undisguised threat to what he assumed was his safe position in Edinburgh, Briggs made his way to his conference room, fully determined to pin Torquil Knight to the wall. No matter what budget the consultant reported, it would not be accepted. By forcing the cost down as low as possible he might regain favour from London. Faced with sinking or swimming, he intended to ensure it would not be James Briggs who drowned.

Exactly on time, Torquil entered the room. Seated on the long sides of the table were the usual dozen or so officials, all members of the technical staff. Briggs looked imperious. Even when seated, his six-foot seven-inch frame was impressive, wrapped in his House of Bruar, Harris Tweed jacket, tartan waistcoat and matching woollen tie. A flamboyant royal-blue handkerchief cascaded from his breast pocket. There was no suggestion of his personal unease. He waited while the young man took his seat at the far end of the table and with his customary dominance, opened the meeting,

"Good morning gentlemen. Introductions are superfluous. Be it sufficient for me to welcome, once again, our esteemed consultant, Mister Torquil Knight from the Clark Chisholm Partnership. We all know why you are here, Mister Knight. Will you kindly advise your amended budget for your installation at Bluff?"

Torquil felt it best to waste no time on civilities to the assembled throng. This was between him and the man at the other end of the room. He got to his feet and spoke slowly,

"Good day, Mister Briggs. At the last meeting I reported a figure of eight hundred and fifty thous..."

Briggs practically spat out an angry riposte that cut him short,
    "That is not what I asked you, Mister Knight. I want to know your *new* figure?"

Visibly shaken by the abrupt interruption, the young man sat back to gather his composure. He had not expected this meeting to be friendly but this undeserved salvo from Briggs was blatant belligerence. Torquil had planned to state clearly, before giving his new figure, that he would not be to blame should the integrity of his design suffer by any further reduction in cost. The silent spectators had to be made aware it was their chairman who was jeopardising the quality of the work. Still determined to get his point over, he tried again,

"I *will* tell you the new figure, Mister Briggs; but first of all I must advise that the saving made is due entirely to my reducing the specification and quantity of the major materials. The design still complies with your brief but the quality of the design is basic. I trust with that in mind you will allow the project to proceed to tender with my revised sum of seven hundred and fifty thousand pounds?"

Torquil lowered himself onto the edge of his chair. All eyes turned to Briggs. He moved his broad shoulders forward from his half-reclining posture and placed his palms downwards on the impressive surface of the stout oak table. Torquil sat back. He had said all that was necessary. He mentally willed Briggs to give the answer he so badly wanted. The next few silent seconds seemed like an age until Briggs began to speak in an unexpected and cordial voice.

"That is indeed a most welcome reduction in your assessment of cost, Mister Knight."

Torquil blurted out a grateful but premature response,

"Thank you Mister Briggs. I'm glad it meets with your approv..."

But he was cut off once again by his smiling adversary, still using the same conciliatory manner,

"Please, Mister Knight. Kindly do not rush to congratulate yourself. I am afraid your cost estimate is still too high."

Torquil was open-mouthed. He mumbled a babble of awkward words in a vain attempt to augment his genuine advice. Briggs would not listen. He raised a hand for silence, like a judge about to pass sentence and continued with an intense diktat,

"Let me be clear for the final time. The future of this project has been put in jeopardy by your failure even to finalise this cost. The on-site work should have commenced by now. You have had this on your desk for over a year. You seem unable to satisfy my simple and straightforward requirements. You will depart from here and reconsider your design. The cost must be reduced to an acceptable figure. Continuing to fail will compel me to seek to engage another firm of consultants."

With growing horror, Torquil watched Briggs raising both fists, slamming them down on the table and growling his final, vicious mandate,

"Do I make myself clear, Mister Knight?"

All eyes turned to Torquil. The young man swallowed hard. This dreadful level of aggression was almost more than he could withstand. If his firm lost the project he would definitely be out on his ear. Losing his first job in these circumstances would end his career before it got off the ground. There was no other option; he had to attempt his last-ditch gambit. He coughed, took a sip of water, stood up and fixed his eyes on Briggs. With as much control as his trembling voice would allow, he spoke,

"Mister Briggs. I have failed on three previous occasions to get you to accept my estimates. I believe it would save us time if *you* were to tell *me* the figure *you* have in mind. When I know that, I should be able to tailor my design accordingly. Thereafter, I will get the project to 'tender stage' by early February."

He sat down, aware of the redness on his face and his shallow breathing. His eyes remained on the chairman and his future lay on the line. He had thrown down the gauntlet. Would Briggs accept the challenge or would he have Torquil thrown out of the meeting? He noticed a change in the chairman's demeanour. Briggs was sitting back; smiling. In a quiet voice he intoned,

"Thank you, Mister Knight. I do so savour an offer I have difficulty in refusing. Just allow me, for the sake of absolute clarity, to recapitulate your proposal. I believe you intend to produce a new design within a matter of weeks? One that not only will satisfy my brief but also will be within the figure you have most eloquently requested me to give you. That figure will be officially recorded in the minutes as the final figure for the whole mechanical services contract. Is that what you have just offered, Mister Knight?"

The young fellow gulped. This cunning man had him trapped. He attempted to visualise him in his underwear but Briggs would not get undressed for him. His only possible answer was *yes*. Torquil couldn't know what sum Briggs would demand but he had to accept what was bound to be the last word. Cornered and alarmed meant backing down now was not an option. His only hope was for Briggs to be reasonable.

"I'm waiting, Torquil."

The use of his first name tempted Torquil to believe that Briggs intended to be even-handed. He was outnumbered anyway. Fighting with this man seemed pointless. After all, it was he who asked Briggs for a figure. To accept whatever Briggs had in mind would settle the impasse. He was out of choices. The die was cast but it was loaded in favour of his opponent. He rose to his feet and, with as strong a voice as he could summon, he yielded,

"Yes sir. I will accept your figure."

The trap had been set. Briggs wasted no time to spring it.

"Then Mister Knight, the minutes of this meeting will show the final cost of the project to be five hundred thousand pounds."

The noise of Torquil dropping into his chair startled the lethargic witnesses. Briggs continued,

"Furthermore, I want your final design drawings on my desk for my approval within say, eight to ten weeks. After that I want the installation completed, running, commissioned and handed over within eighteen months. Do you understand, Mister Knight?"

Briggs had him where he wanted. It was impossible. He felt cold.

"Yes sir."

Briggs stood up and slapped his palms together; satisfied at having bullied his way through another tight situation. There was no compassion in his parting words as he swaggered out,

"This meeting is over, gentlemen. Goodbye, Mister Knight."

The others got up and shuffled to the door. Torquil sat alone and wretched in the empty room. He closed his eyes for a while. *By trying to outwit Briggs, I placed a rope around my own neck. How could I be so stupid as to let Briggs trap me like that?* He cursed his lack of experience. He had hoped for guidance from his senior colleague but had been hung out to dry by the Irishman. O'Casey would see the minutes of the meeting within days. *It's best to tell him as soon as I get back to the office. He won't be pleased.*

Torquil gathered his papers and left the building. It seemed a good idea to walk to the wee Italian café in Torphicken Street. Their strong coffee had bolstered him on his previous visits. He ordered his favourite capuccino. It tasted good but did little for his confidence. He left and walked round to Haymarket station.

The journey back to Glasgow relaxed him. In the minutes it took for the train to reach the station at Gyle, the trauma from his fearful encounter with Briggs had diminished. His mind was able to concentrate on the main components of his design for Bluff. In his typical systematic manner, he considered all the elements of his scheme that had been cut to the bone. *How can I possibly get the costs down any further?* That was the difficult bit. Between the Gyle and Falkirk High, he had his eureka moment; the answer flitted momentarily across his brain like a butterfly almost escaping the net. He sat upright, grabbed it back and to the annoyance of an older man in the almost empty carriage, he yelled, *that's it!*

Back at the office he paid the taxi driver, rushed upstairs to his desk and pulled out the cost file. A quick examination had him clenching his fists in silent victory. He was saved. He grabbed the roll of design drawings and ran back downstairs. At O'Casey's room on the first landing he stopped, composed his statement, knocked and half opened the door,

"Sean; I've done it. I've got an agreement with Briggs. I'm going home with my stuff to sort out the design. See you tomorrow. Bye."

He was closing the door even before O'Casey had lifted his head to mutter,

"About bloody time!"

Part 3
That afternoon

Torquil's flat ~ Bentinck Street ~ Glasgow
For the rest of the afternoon Torquil sat at his dining table and concentrated hard. On tracing paper overlaid

on his original drawings, he sketched some ideas for amendments that began to make sense. His draughtsman would easily transform these scribbles into professional drawings. As soon as Briggs approved them, they would be issued to a number of building firms for competitive prices for the work. He looked at his watch...*half five already*! David was due in at six. His jacket was half on as he shut the door of the flat and began his sprint round to Dumbarton Road to pick up two black-pudding suppers, two pickled onions and a bottle of Irn Bru.

During their meal his pal was impressed on hearing Torquil's account of the dramatic meeting. David wanted to know more about the ingenious solution to the impossible problem of cost. He was also a bit lost on the details of the new design; it was a bit too technical for him.

"What's the main difference between your old scheme and this new one? Doesn't matter whether you use water or steam to do it, Torky. Heating is heating isn't it?"

"The client's brief is ambiguous. It says *replace* the existing dilapidated steam heating system. My approach was based on *copying* it. There's a lot of sophisticated paraphernalia required to control and deliver piped steam at high pressure and temperature to thirty-five separate buildings. It proved to be very expensive, hence the aggro from Briggs. I'm *replacing* it with a water system. Simple and cheaper."

"Yes...but...eh...What will they say when you tell them you're using hot water instead of steam?"

"It's really only semantics. *Replace* doesn't necessarily mean *duplicate*. Briggs won't care about that detail as long as the cost is kept down and the job works."

"That's fine but where is all this big saving coming from?"

"That's the clever bit, Davy. For the safety of personnel, armaments buildings on site are heated with low-pressure hot water. The present system sends steam through heat exchangers in separate outhouses. The steam indirectly heats the water like the hot water tank in your house only more complex and therefore, relatively expensive."

"How expensive?"

"Roughly eight thousand pounds per building."

"So, just explain to me how you save a quarter of a million, Torky?"

"Ah! Sorry Davy. There's a heat exchange plant room *for each building*. There are thirty-five buildings. If you do the arithmetic you can see the saving is nearly three hundred thousand. Am I clever, Davy?"

"I never doubted it my boy! What's next?"

"I'll phone Briggs tomorrow and confirm his five hundred thousand budget.

"Then what?"

"Changing the drawings and specification will take time. I also need to redesign the main boiler house; but I'm confident this job will be out to tender before or by the end of February.

"That's great, Torky. If it all works out then you are some smart operator. Fancy a beer?"

"Yep!"

Torquil felt contented with his day's work but in his head, one of Davy's phrases lingered in his mind...*if it all works out.*

CHAPTER TWO

Conference

Part 1
Feb 1989

Jarvis & Craig offices ~ Govan

Hugh Jarvis, a portly man in his mid-fifties, leaned forward on his wing-backed armchair and puffed out a plume of cigar smoke as one of his managers entered his office. Joe Hadshaw, summoned to discuss future workload, laid three sets of opened tender documents on his boss's desk. Jarvis pushed two of them aside in favour of the one from the Clark Chisholm Partnership. Joe was intrigued to know why that one was of particular interest, but remained silent.

Clenching a long cigar, Jarvis tapped a stubby finger on the covering letter. A roll of ash toppled onto the polished surface of his desk. He noticed it, as well as the slight whiff of whisky from Joe who was stifling a grin.

Jarvis, with an angry flourish, used the heel of his hand to brush the dust onto the carpet,

"Where exactly is this site, Joe?"

Pleased to be asked, Joe was eager to show that he had read the paperwork,

"It's up at the Moray Firth, Hugh. The drawings show it located in the forest at Culbin where the North Sea enters Findhorn Bay. The town of Forres is just a mile or two inland."

"Why the hell does the Ministry of Defence always put their buildings in out-ae-the-way places? Don't they know it costs more to get men and materials away up there? It's in the middle ae bloody nowhere. Maybe we should give this one a miss? What do you think, Joe?"

Once again keen to shine, Joe gave that extra morsel of data that Jarvis would perhaps not know.

"There arnae many nuclear establishments near major populations, Hugh. If anything happens up there, you only lose a wee bit of Scotland. And the North Sea gets slightly warmer."

It pleased him to watch Jarvis lean back in his chair and smile at the cryptic humour. Joe pressed home his advantage,

"You're right enough, Hugh. It's a fair distance but our work's just a brick-built boiler house. The big money is in the mechanical sub-contract."

"Sounds good, Joe. Tell me about it?"

"They've to do the new boilers and all that, but I reckon their hardest bit is fitting about four miles of heating pipes along the sand dunes to heat each of the isolated armament buildings. We get our two-and-a-half per cent main contractors discount from their work just to stand and watch them. That could be a good few grand. It's a quick turn round to be completed within a thirty-five-week programme. It could be done and dusted by Christmas."

"That's what they said about the First World War, and you know what happened then, don't you, Joe?"

Joe didn't know. He smiled as if he did but kept his mouth shut. His boss took another lungful of smoke, stroked his chin and considered Joe's comments. Hugh Jarvis had a good nose for any quick and simple contract that had the chance to return an easy profit. Jobs like that don't come often. There had been a few baddies but in twenty years in charge, Hugh Jarvis now controlled a multi-million turnover. He promoted talented managers, surveyors and accountants who ensured most of the selected contracts made money and he lived very well on it.

Joe on the other hand, was proving to be a bit of a disappointment. He used to be top notch but recently his judgement was a muddled mixture of eagerness to please and low self-esteem. Hadshaw tended to paint rosy pictures. Hugh felt that if he gave him time he might overcome his present personal problems and get back to the man he used to be. Hugh would give him that one chance, but was not hopeful.

On the plus side, he had done work with these consultants before. Dean Chisholm and he had played the odd round of golf. He ensured that Dean Chisholm always won. He recalled some good times. He made up his mind,

"Alright, Joe. We'll take a punt at this one. Since it's programmed for 35 weeks, we'll put in a penalty clause. You know how that works, don't you?"

"Yes Hugh. We can tie the sub-contractors in knots if they screw up. I'll get enquiries sent out to them in tomorrow night's post. There are lots of drawings and documents to be copied. Are we asking the usual four firms for prices?"

"No Joe. On this one it's better to have six prices. Make sure they get all the documents. I want no excuses from any of them."

"Will do."

"Get onto the agency and hire those two quantity surveyors we used on that M.O.D. job at Beith. Tell them to pick at least two sub-contractors we haven't used before and make sure to include the *Government Contract Works* documents. I want the mechanical sub-contract sewn up tight."

"Understood, Hugh. The one that gives us full control of them?"

"Correct. *We* employ *them*. They can only deal through *us*; not allowed any direct contact with the design team.

They will be *under* us, and if there's any delay, I want to pin the blame on *them*."

"Catch them on the hop, Hugh...and stay one jump ahead?"

Hugh didn't laugh,

"Exactly. And not only that...we control the money."

"I don't get involved in that. Does that give us an advantage, Hugh?"

"Yes Joe. It's obvious; we get the money from the client but pay the sub contractor as little as possible. It's all within the rules. That way we can scrape a few extra shillings."

"Ah don't understand that. Is keeping their money not illegal?"

Hugh Jarvis smiled and tapped the side of his nose,

"Listen and learn, Joe. I'll let you into a wee business secret. In Government contracts there's a standard clause that says the MOD will pay us *'from time to time'*. They're legally obliged to pay *eventually* but you canny hold them to a date. We'll tell the subs that we've not been paid yet and they'll just have tae sing for their cash. Meanwhile it's gathering interest in our bank."

Joe Hadshaw was surprised to be given this financial lesson. This glimpse behind the curtain of devious dealing by his boss, skimming as much profit as possible from the contracts, flashed a pleasing thought across his mind. *Maybe Hugh is signalling that I'm in line for promotion?* He dispelled the thought in an instant but his greedy reflex caused an unwary smile to flash across his face. Jarvis spotted it,

"Why the sudden happy smile, Joe?"

"Oh! Nothing, Hugh," Joe lied. "It's just that I enjoy these talks with you about our workload and I appreciate the guidance you give me to get things done. It's nice to get tae know some of the stuff that goes on behind the scenes and how you're running the company so well."

While Joe spoke, Hugh puffed on his cigar, saying nothing but mentally he was weighing up his long-term employee. *Bloody little crawler's soft-soaping me again. I wish I knew what it was that made him suddenly smile like that. All these years I've worked with him and I still don't know how his daft wee brain ticks. He'll be in a hurry to get away home tae his empty house for his nightly snifter. I hope he sorts himself out. This job could be his swan song if he disni get off the bottle.*

"Well, that's very nice of you to say so. The feeling's mutual. Now off you go and let me get on with doing my job, like you said...so well. Goodnight Joe."

"Right, Hugh. I'll away then. Goodnight."

It just dawned on Joe as he left, that all the time he was in Hugh's presence, he was never invited to sit down.

Part 2
Apr 1989

Franz Liseur offices ~ Clydebank

Tony Surtal took some time to study the priced tender document on his desk. It had been a long time since Franz Liseur had received an enquiry with the *Clark Chisholm consultant's* name on the drawings, let alone one for the Ministry of Defence. He mused; *these ministry contracts can be a pain in the arse*, but that's not what he said to his chief estimator.

"This one looks quite simple; a boiler plant and some extensive heating pipework. Nice timing too. It'll keep our team in Aberdeen busy."

Willie Spence nodded in agreement.

"I think we should go for this one, Willie. I'm told they store small nuclear armaments there as well as ordinary ammunition. Be nice to get back into Ministry work that doesn't involve impossibly complex nuclear shelters and bloody blast-proof monstrosities like that one near Fort William two years ago. How much did we lose on that Willie?"

"Not my job to know that, Tony. Talk to the project engineer who ran it."

Tony laughed at the estimator's practiced impertinence. He was under no illusions about Willie's capacity to absolve himself of blame if a contract lost money. He was, of course, first to step forward for praise if a contract 'washed its face'.

"Aye, Willie, your estimate was bang on; every penny covered you said at the time?

"As always, Tony. As always."

When he took over as branch manager ten years ago, Tony Surtal had inherited this unlikeable man. Willie Spence was a self-seeker. Always ready to slide out of trouble and blame others. To his credit, he ran his department quite well. Keeping him in the branch was a case of better the devil you know than some new guy. Tony never missed any opportunity to tease Willie about his mistakes, some of which were minor but one in particular was rather costly.

"Was that not the job with two boilers and you only priced for one? Just a slip of the pen you said at the time, Willie. A wee slip of the pen that cost us ten grand?"

"It wasn't me, Tony. It was the comptometer operator."

"I know that Willie. That's what you always say?"

"You also know that I always tell the truth, Tony."

"And you know that I always believe you, Willie. I don't expect you to let that happen again. Now, let's see what we'll do with this little baby. I think we will go in with a cost plus two per cent. Scrub the overheads for the office."

Willie Spence inhaled through pursed lips. Tony ignored him and continued,

"Take out all travelling time and allow for a couple of caravans for our Aberdeen squad to kip on the site. That saves us paying them 'dig' money."

Tony smiled at his estimator's usual uncomfortable reaction to an unwelcome instruction. Willie took a step backwards, put his left hand over his mouth in an imitation of shock horror and pointed with his pen at the estimate sheets on Tony's desk. Then came out with his safeguard speech putting the onus on the boss,

"Tony! I've priced this job at over half a million! If you cut those bits out you're going in at about four hundred and sixty thousand. It's madness. There is *no way* you'll make any money!"

Willie Spence was partly right of course, but Tony was the boss. Tony made the final decisions on overheads for tenders. It was always prudent to offer a protest. Willie would be able to say it was not he who cut the price to the bone; nothing he could do about it; above his salary level and all the stock get-outs that had kept his head on his shoulders for years. Tony gave an audible sigh of exasperation,

"Yes, Willie. Let me worry about that. I wouldn't want you to be losing any sleep over this. Go and finalise the price and we'll get it out the door. There's a good chance we'll win this and get our faces back in with the M.O.D."

Part 3
June 1989:

Jarvis & Craig offices ~ Govan

Tenders from six mechanical services contractors lay in front of Hugh Jarvis. The director had spread their letters out and was looking puzzled. A glass coffee pot sat, half empty beside the milk and sugar on a tray at the end of his impressive polished rosewood desk. Two cups, stained and empty, were parked out of the way of the papers.

Joe Hadshaw liked this boardroom. Being invited into it gave him a sense that he was part of the inner sanctum of the firm. He wasn't. He was only there to discuss the six tenders for the Bluff contract. This was Hugh Jarvis's office and it was only on occasions like this that Joe Hadshaw was allowed to be in it. He was feeling quite relaxed until Hugh fired a question at him.

"Are you positive you sent all the documents to Franz Liseur, Joe?"

Joe winced at the implied criticism. The direct question reminded him that Hugh was the boss and Joe was merely his servant.

"Positive, Hugh. I checked them all myself as you instructed. They definitely got all the documents we had because they've returned them all with their tender. Is something wrong?"

"We've got six prices. Five are way over five hundred thousand. The one from Franz Liseur is only four fifty-seven. What do you know about them, Joe?"

"Nothing much except that they're a French outfit. Dae ye think they've made a mistake?"

"Could be. Maybe they've priced it in French francs Joe?"

Joe didn't pick up on Hugh's joke. Hugh shook his head, sighed and carried on,

"Okay, Joe. Get the QS to look over it and if it's kosher, we'll build it into our bid. Tell him to phone Liseur's manager for confirmation of his price. If he says it's correct, get a registered letter of provisional acceptance sent to them. We don't want a last-minute withdrawal."

Part 4
Jul 1989

Clark Chisholm offices ~ Glasgow

Torquil Knight and his boss, Sean O'Casey were seated on one side of the long ebony conference room table that was surrounded by fourteen leather-bound and studded ebony carver chairs. On the other side sat Dean Chisholm. In front of him lay five unopened, sealed, addressed, A4 envelopes from five building contractors. The labels showed that these were the tenders for the nuclear armaments establishment project at Bluff.

To avoid collusion, the rules of *bona fide* tendering require all of the offers to be assembled and opened at the same time and in the presence of a partner of the firm. The amounts must be written down and verified by the signatures of a partner and a witness. Any late arrivals must be disregarded and disqualified.

Torquil was edgy. A substantially higher price than half-a-million pounds for the mechanical services work could sign his death warrant with this firm. He sat with his knees together, pressing his clasped hands. He said a silent prayer as he watched Dean Chisholm, the senior partner open five envelopes, scan the prices and without a word, enter them on the standard form. He carried the three highest priced packages over to his desk, put them in a side drawer, locked it and pocketed the key. The two lowest, together with the standard form, he slid across the table to Sean O'Casey,

"Just witness my signature on the form please Sean, then you and our young friend can get away and check those two offers. Let me know by lunchtime tomorrow which price you find to be the winner and in compliance with the specification. That'll allow us to issue the necessary letter off to our friend James Briggs at the M.O.D. in Edinburgh,"

He turned his attention to Torquil. Chisholm was oblivious to the trauma the boy had undergone in the last two years. O'Casey, for his own personal reasons, had not made him aware of the James Briggs affair concerning the costs, the time lost and the recent redesign. The young fellow was on his feet ready to leave when Dean Chisholm spoke to him,

"I believe this is your first significant tender, Torquil. I can understand why you're looking a little tense. It is always a worry whether your probable cost estimate is on the right side; but I hope that you might now be able to relax. We've all gone through it, haven't we, Sean? I'm sure you will enjoy managing the project, which I believe, is next to your own home territory. Forres, is it not?"

"Yes it is Mister Chisholm. My family have lived there for nigh on a hundred and fifty years. My dad is the fifth generation."

"Will you leave us and be the sixth generation to spend your life among your ancestors, Torquil?

"I haven't really thought that far ahead, sir. I want to make a career in this business first. Perhaps I will retire there."

"I see. So, you will marry a lowland lassie Torquil. Then when your career down here is over, you will steal her away up North?" Chisholm teased.

"Oh no, Mister Chisholm, I have a girl in Forres. I expect to marry her if she'll have me, but I haven't asked her yet," Said the boy who was beginning to feel a little uneasy and had become conscious of his face reddening.

Seeing this, Chisholm decided to take pity on him, "Alright, Torquil. We are finished here. How are things downstairs? Everything to your liking I hope? Is Sean keeping you on the straight and narrow?"

Torquil was non-plussed. He smiled and nodded. He was struggling to find a simple answer to the well-intended questions from the senior partner. He began to mumble something about one or to things that concerned him but it was okay so far, when he felt a hand pressing on his right shoulder.

O'Casey was gently steering him to the door to stop the lad being tempted to start a longer conversation. That might create difficulties for them both...but more particularly for him. He smiled at Chisholm in the way a mentor does when leading his pupil away from a busy professor who really was only trying to be polite. Chisholm nodded in acquiescence.

On the way downstairs Sean referred to the senior partner's point about Torquil's estimate of the cost for the project. "He's right you know, Torquil. It's always a worry with your first big one. From my quick look at the standard form when I signed it, I think, you are home and dry. One builder has your cost just under and the other is just over your budget. For my money that is bang on, son."

"Wow! That is the best news I've had in a long time. I have to admit I've had more than a few anxious months. Jim Briggs of the M.O.D. is a real tough cookie. When he nailed me to a cost of half-a-million I thought I was done for."

"Were you really so worried?"

"Yes Sean. You'll never know what I went through on this job."

"Well laddie, you rose to the occasion. You've been tested with your feet to the fire. You did well to get your design finalised and out the door, and here's the result. One of these two companies is going to build your design. How does that feel?"

"Superb, Sean. I never felt this good in two years. It's like a great weight has been lifted off me."

Torquil was rightly happy. Sean O'Casey and James Briggs had almost pulled him apart by his head and feet. Now he felt the thrill of success. Getting close to the start of his very first major contract was starting to make him feel good. Even better, he could now talk to his mentor more confidently. Sean patted him on the shoulder,

"I know you were stressed out this afternoon upstairs with Dean Chisholm. How are you now, Torquil?"

"Honestly, Sean, I feel pretty good."

"So you should. You will feel a lot better in about a year from now when it's done and dusted and working like a sewing machine, eh?"

"Yes, I hope so.

"Okay, Torquil, what do you say we get these two tenders checked out right now and find the winner?"

"Okay...Sean."

They first made a separate note of the two lowest prices from the standard form filled out by Dean Chisholm.

Price (i)

Bowen Builders Ltd		£325,000.00
A.1 Heating Ltd		£532,000.00
	Total	£847,000.00

Price (ii)

Jarvis & Craig Builders Ltd		£340,000.00
Franz Liseur Heating Ltd		£493,750.00
	Total	£833,750.00

O'Casey smiled at his colleague,

"Well Torquil, now you see who is likely to be doing your project. There's a fair difference. I don't expect it will be A.1 Heating who'll win after we've checked their arithmetic."

"Doesn't seem like it Sean. I hope it's Jarvis & Craig with Franz Liseur."

"So do I, Torquil. So do I."

They sat in Sean's office to study a tender each to establish that both were arithmetically correct and complied with the specification. O'Casey was first to finish. As he sat back patiently to await Torquil's result, his thoughts turned to his own position. He was going no higher in this firm. This youngster however, was now on the first rungs of a good career. As long as Chisholm relied on Sean to ramrod the young engineers, it would be in O'Casey's best interests to keep Torquil away from the boss and slow the boy's progress.

The lower price *was* from Jarvis & Craig. They had used Franz Liseur's price for the mechanical services. Torquil was relieved to discover the cost for his system was noted as £493,750.00 pounds including Main Contractor's overheads and profit. He blew air through pursed lips thinking, *God! I can sleep tonight.*

CHAPTER THREE:

Contract

Part 1
Early Sep 1989

Jarvis & Craig offices ~ Govan

Hugh Jarvis called Joe Hadshaw for a quick meeting, telling him to bring along young Terry Cordwell whom Hugh had earmarked for promotion to site agent. They walked in through the open door of his office. Without looking up from reading a document that lay on his uncluttered rosewood desk, he gestured them toward the chairs in front of him. He continued jotting down some notes. They waited for some minutes, enveloped in swirls of Jarvis's pungent but pleasing cigar smoke. While screwing the cap back on to his fountain pen, he looked up and smiled,

"Morning lads. We've just been awarded the contract for the armaments depot at Bluff. You'll know the one, Joe; remember we tendered for it a couple of months ago?"

Joe nodded,

"Yes Hugh, I recollect saying it looked like a quick and simple bit of work for us. Just a boiler house and a few concrete bases for the mechanical contractor's pipes. If my memory's right you used that French firm's price?"

"That's right, Joe. The Franz Liseur crowd are big in France but in Scotland they only have a main branch here in Glasgow and a small branch up in Aberdeen. I think they'll do a good job. What I don't want, because they are well resourced, is for them to get the better of us. I spoke to our quantity surveyors this morning. We'll start a delay file as soon as Liseur sign the order this Friday."

He looked at Terry Cordwell,

"I'm putting you in charge of this project, Terry."

"Thanks, Mister Jarvis."

"Not necessary lad, you've earned a chance to run your own site. This is a wee bit special though. It's a job for the Ministry of Defence. Anything you'd like to ask?"

"When does it start? What's the timescale? What's its value? Am I getting more money?"

"Hey! Slow down laddie. I admire your enthusiasm but you've nae need tae show off wae me. These are good questions and Mister Hadshaw here will answer most of them all in good time. As for money, you will get an acting site-agent's rate plus there are bonuses to be had under our incentive scheme. Joe can explain all that. OK son?"

"Yes, sorry Mister Jarvis."

Hugh was impressed by the young man's boldness, a reminder of himself at that age, eager and straining at the lead. He noted that Joe was smiling at Terry. *Perhaps Joe also sees some of his own 'old self' in the young man's attitude.* Hugh liked that. He picked up his notes and continued,

"Right lads. I want the site compound to be established four weeks from today...or earlier if possible. Both of you should work together on this and don't waste any time. The procurement guys are placing orders for materials as we speak. Talk to them this afternoon about your huts, site plant, tools, machinery and whatever else you need."

"Can I have a set of documents and drawings?"

"Yes, Terry, your set is over on that table just behind you. You can get delivery dates from the buyers. The quantity surveyors will give you the estimated labour hours for your on-site team and how much money has been allowed for setting up the site. I want a draft programme for our work the day after tomorrow; Joe will help you with that, Okay?"

"No bother, Mister Jarvis. Where's the site?"

"It's on the Moray Firth coast near a wee town called Forres. You'll find a map in the documents. Joe can fill you in with the rest. I think that's all you need, Terry. Off you go and get started. Remember... draft programme, two days. Joe, you hang on here please."

Terry got up, gathered his bundle of papers and left. He was feeling pleased with himself. As for Joe, he was trying to guess the reason why he had been asked to wait. He admired Hugh's clear decisions and the speed at which he worked...leaving nothing to chance. Hugh pulled a sheaf papers from his desk drawer. Joe remained quiet.

As if about to say something of importance, Hugh hesitated for a few seconds, placed the papers on his desk, leaned on them, clasped his hands under his chin and looked squarely at his old workmate.

Joe said nothing; it was not wise to speak until the boss was ready. He merely returned the look, slightly lowered his head while maintaining eye contact with the boss and raised both eyebrows in a silent question. He had no idea that Hugh had been keeping tabs on him for some time and was pondering a dilemma about whether Joe's future still lay with the company.

He was either to be got rid of due to his drinking, gambling and sad home life, all of which could harm the firm, or he might be given a chance to improve his unhappy lifestyle; a divorcee living alone with his two current hobbies; Nancy whisky and Lady Luck. The firm would certainly benefit if he got back to being the capable manager he once was.

As these few silent seconds elapsed, Joe seemed to sense that Hugh was preparing to say something of importance to him. *I hope this isni bad news for me. He's not said anything recently about any promotion. Maybe this is it?*

It had been a difficult quandary for Hugh. He had known Joe Hadshaw for many years. His mind was made up to try to save Joe by boosting his morale. It was worth a last effort to encourage the man to turn his life around; give him a reason to quit the bottle, get back some self-respect. It would be up to Joe to respond and grasp the chance to get his life back on track. The sudden opener from Hugh startled Joe from his musing,

"Right, Joe! This is how we're going to play it. As one of my senior managers I want you to be the front man on the Bluff contract. Phone Liseur today and get them in here on Friday morning to sign the contract. When they come in on Friday I want you to deal with them. You can use my office here."

Joe's face reflected his uncertain thoughts as he absorbed these strong instructions *I'm no usually pushed to the front like this. What's Hugh's game? Maybe this is a test. Is he making me walk the plank, on my own, sink or swim?*

"Will you no be here, Hugh?"

His response seemed to Hugh like a cry for help. He needed managers who had the confidence to rise to challenges. It was clear that this man, Joe needed more than he thought was necessary. Hugh would not go back on his decision to help the man and so he answered using his practiced persuasive voice.

"Listen Joe, you don't need me to hold your hand on this. I'm giving you your head...you're ready for it. You know I'm right behind you if needed. You'll be the one they deal with. I'm confident you can handle it."

Joe was astounded. He knew this could have gone another way but it did seem like a promotion...of sorts. He started to feel more like a man who was valued and decided to try and act like one. Although in the back of his mind he still did not understand from what angle Hugh was coming, he brightened up and spoke with what he hoped was a new bravado,

"What's the trick, Hugh?"

"There's no trick, Joe. I'm giving you full authority to manage this contract from the word go. Your first meeting with them is important. Using my office will give you style and confidence. They'll see you as the manager with the big impressive desk. Unless you need me to step in, you will be in sole charge of all decisions. Don't worry. I'll be somewhere in the office if you need my help."

"How will I ask you if you're not there, Hugh? Will it no look a bit silly if I have to phone you?"

Hugh was expecting more from Joe. It was looking like his decision may have been the wrong one. He decided to persevere,

"I've got every confidence in you to carry this off, Joe. If you get stuck, just say you're going to check something with your quantity surveyors. I'll keep you right. You'll still have the initiative to keep Liseur in their place."

"Okay, Hugh. Thanks for showing confidence in me. Ah know I've slipped a wee bit recently but ah'll give it my best shot."

"That's the spirit, Joe. Remember, these are our domestic sub-contractors with no access to the client's design team. They are big players in their field but they are below us in the pecking order on this contract. If these boys get their toes in the door they could run rings round us. That's the first part, Joe."

Now, greatly relieved, Joe Hadshaw was fully alert and raring to go.

"I'm up for that Hugh. Let me guess. You're setting a trap for them?"

Hugh saw this as a sign that his decision about Joe appeared to be the right one. He relaxed and leaned back into his chair with his hands clasped behind his head,

"Something like that, Joe. The second part goes like this. I want to make life as difficult as I can for Franz Liseur. This is where the two quantity surveyors come in. We'll begin by logging all the key dates from Liseur's detailed day-by-day programme. If they miss a date we send them a registered letter stating our intention to claim loss and expense for their delay.

"Sounds fairly standard so far, Hugh. We always do that. "

Hugh unclasped his hands and got up. In a practised movement of informality he walked round his desk and placed his right hand on Joe's shoulder.

"You asked where the catch was, Joe. Well I'll tell you. I think you'll like it."

"I'm sure you're right, Hugh."

Hugh proceeded to walk round the room pushing his hands deep into his trouser pockets and swivelling from heel to heel in a kind of slow, triumphant dance while explaining his cunning plot to confuse Liseur, his unsuspecting sub contractor,

"I want you and Terry to draw up our programme in two parts. The first part is to show the boiler house being built between now and the end of December. The second part will show us starting to pour the concrete supports for Liseur's pipes starting at the beginning of January."

"I can do that, Hugh but I still don't see the advantage for us."

Hugh swivelled again, stopped abruptly and stooped to look right into Joe's face,

"Liseur will need concrete bases for their pipes. The site is seven thousand metres long. If they need a support at say every three metres, there will be about two-and-a-half thousand bits of concrete for us to pour. The concrete bases will need at least a month to set."

As Hugh again turned away to motor round the room, Joe, who was still not actually getting what his boss was driving at, attempted a mollifying response,

"Well, Hugh, if we pour a hundred bases a day most of them will be cured during February. Liseur will be able to begin fitting their pipes by mid March. How does that hold them up?"

With another spin, Hugh turned to Joe and laughed as he gave the solution Joe was still failing to figure out,

"We'll not be holding *them* up, Joe. *They'll* be holding *us* up. We canny start pouring bases on the first of January *without Liseur's drawings*. We wait till the last minute and demand their drawings first thing in January. If they have slept on this they won't have *done* any drawings. That means they will already be in delay; plus it takes at least another two weeks to get them approved by Clark Chisholm. With a whole month to cure the concrete bases, Liseur will probably create a delay of at least six weeks or more. We'll have them on toast; don't you see? We can take them to the cleaners."

Joe decided to act like the penny had dropped at last... but it was not the case,

"I like it, Hugh! That is so devious. We can eat them alive!"

Hugh was pleased that Joe had got the plot and his former confidence was returning.

"Well remember this, Joe...it's dog-eat-dog out there... and vice versa!"

Joe laughed for the first time in a long time but still hadn't quite grasped Hugh's plan to trap Liseur. He asked a leading question,

"There's one thing I don't get, Hugh. When I make up our programme with Terry, where do we show Liseur's starting date?"

Hugh Jarvis was delighted to hear this. He spun round again, crouched down a little lower and pointed straight at Joe's face, yelling,

"Aha! Now you've got it. We're not obliged to tell them when to start. They can start at any time within our eight-month period. More than likely they'll want to start working as soon as the boiler house is wind-and-watertight. They'll see from our programme we intend to pour the concrete for their pipes at the beginning of January. *They* will think that *we* are the ones in delay, not realising that it's their responsibility to produce *drawings* for us before we can start on their bases."

Finally Joe had the veil lifted and could see how Liseur were to be caught with their pants down.

"Oh I like that. That's so clever. I've got to hand it to you."

"Thank you, Joe. And it's all within the rules too. The game's afoot. Let's hope the *game's-a-bogey* for Franz Liseur! If you have any doubts, shout now. If you are okay, then you'd best get going and organise the Q.S.'s. And Joe, we have to do this right. I don't want this screwed up!"

Joe respected his boss but once again he was hurt to hear what was an apparent threat. He absorbed the disappointment and forced a confident answer,

"You can rely on me, boss. Ah won't let you down."

Hugh Jarvis didn't respond; just smiled, waved him away to get on with the job and thought; *I hope you don't let me down, Joe, your jaiket's on a shaky nail.*

Part 2
Mid- Sep 1989

Franz Liseur offices ~ Clydebank

Tony Surtal was a typically busy branch manager. On top of lining up several golf meetings and sales drives to bring in more enquiries from builders and consultants, he was anxious to leave his office for, hopefully, a final meeting to entice Douglas Fairbairn to re-join Liseur as contracts manager. Morgan Pegler, his commercial manager, was in Tony's office discussing a number of new orders that had come in. None looked particularly urgent.

"Morgan, I want you to give these a look over. Let me know if there are any gaffes from our pal in the estimating."

"Do you mean the comptometer operator or Willie Spence?"

"Aye, Morgan, it'll end up at her anyway but I'd still like to roast the wee beggar if you find anything to worry us. If they are okay then just leave the files in my office. I'll deal with them when I get back from my meeting but don't expect me back tonight.

"Sounds like a boozy do, Tony?"

"So, you've noticed I'm going in by taxi?"

"No, but that explains a lot. Is it anything to do with the boss coming up from London?"

"I can't tell you what it's about but you're right, Jules is coming to lunch with me. I'm in a rush to meet him at the airport. The shuttle is due to land within the hour. I don't want to be late. I'll fill you in tomorrow morning, okay?"

"I've heard a rumour, Tony. About a week ago I spoke to a sales rep who said he saw you last month in an Edinburgh pub talking to Douglas Fairbairn.

"You shouldn't listen to idle gossip, Morgan."

"I am sure of my source, Tony. You know you need a good guy as contracts manager. Douglas is a shoe-in for that space. Are you getting him back? I for one would welcome the stability he would bring. Can you not give me a clue?

"It could be one of several people, Morgan, but you are not far off. This one may not be able to come. His firm is very wealthy and may be determined to keep him. You will be one of the first to know. Keep it to yourself. Now, I really do have to get going."

Morgan touched his nose with his forefinger and mischievously ended his interrogation with,

"Okay. Have a good lunch. And Tony - give Douglas my best wishes."

On his way to the airport, Tony had a little time to reflect on his pursuit of Douglas Fairbairn. It had taken almost three months and several meetings trying to persuade his former contracts manager to return to the fold. They had shared four good profitable years together before Douglas Fairbairn decided to leave contracting and join a prestigious firm of consulting engineers.

Tony and he had worked well together, having fun solving many complex contractual and financial difficulties with an assortment of clients. The work was mostly for public bodies; local authorities; the National Health Service; shipyards; engineering works and the like...plus, of course, the Ministry of Defence. Government jobs were lucrative but hard to finalise. Red tape and obduracy from MOD personnel often delayed agreement that hindered progress of the work and payment of accounts.

Tony knew, in spite of his warm recollections of working with this man that it was not going to be easy persuading him to leave the 'consulting' life-style and jump back into the roller-coaster-ride of 'contracting'. Especially since Douglas was a high-flying earner. The Peurova Partnership paid their best men well. He had enjoyed six years working with them in North Queensferry.

Their setup was superb. Their office was situated in an idyllic setting in the grounds of an old country estate within what used to be the walled fruit-garden covering nearly an acre. It was a very smart, ultra-modern single-story building forming a hollow square. French windows from the library gave the staff access to a central garden area furnished with tables and chairs and shaded by apple, pear and plum trees. To any onlooker it must have looked as though they lived like princes.

Tony's task was not simple. He had to proceed carefully when attempting to paint a similarly enticing scenario that would tempt his friend to come back to Liseur. He had spent time and employed great patience during his recent clandestine meetings with Douglas. It was vitally important to win his trust. Those discussions took place in neutral territory to avoid detection and spread of rumours. They were both confident the secrecy had avoided being spotted by any one from Liseur or the Peurova partnership. Morgan Pegler however had just revealed that their attempts had not been entirely successful. The cat was almost out of the bag. Today's meeting had to be concluded one way or another.

An hour later, Tony, Douglas and Jules Dispard were sitting chatting over an aperitif in a private room of *The Rogano* in Glasgow's Exchange Square. The next three pleasant hours were spent eating elegant food while covering the whole range of items associated with an important change in Douglas's career. During coffee, liqueurs and cigars, Tony signalled the waiter for the bill, then, hoping to impress Jules Dispard, he proceeded to summarise the lengthy and adroit discussions,

"It has taken a while but I hope we have satisfied all of your requirements, Douglas; the company car of your choice; the bonus scheme; pension provision; holidays; your own office; the present and future workloads; terms of reference; the present team of engineers; your management title etcetera. All that remains now is for us to agree your salary."

Douglas laid down his Drambuie glass and sat back in his chair. He was no stranger to this level of magnanimous coercion by a prospective employer. This was the ticklish point at which the whole thing could founder. He would either go away without succeeding in returning to the job he had enjoyed so much last time he was with Liseur or, it would be his for the taking. He knew the form and made his gambit,

"Yes, Tony. First of all, let me thank you and Monsieur Dispard for a very splendid meal. I trust that my salary will not be a stumbling block?"

Tony raised his whisky in a gracious gesture,

"You are welcome to the food, Douglas. I am glad you are happy with the prospect of being welcomed back to the fold. Do you have a figure in mind for your salary?"

Douglas had served the first ball and Tony had skilfully returned it with his direct question. The rule of this game was to resist being first to give a figure. A nimble, non-committal response was needed. He reached for his glass from the table, looked at Tony and suggested,

"I am quite happy to negotiate so, please feel free to open the bidding."

Jules Dispard interrupted their game. Adopting his most charming French accent, he demonstrated his considerable diplomatic skill by removing any possible bargaining arguments,

"It will not be necessary for Liseur to bid. We want you to join us as soon as you can. Regardless of what you are presently being paid by Peurova Partnership, we shall give you three thousand pounds more per year. If that is not enough, then this meeting is over, Mister Fairbairn."

With a warm smile he held out his hand. Douglas grasped it firmly.

"Can I take it that you accept my offer, Douglas?"

"It is quite acceptable, Monsieur Dispard. Thank you. I am required to give three months notice. If you will kindly confirm all this by the end of the month, I shall tender my resignation on the first of October. That means that I shall be free to join you, Tony, on the first working day of January next year."

Grinning broadly, Tony jumped up, grabbed Douglas's hand and bawled,

"Fantastic! I'm so pleased you're coming back. You won't regret this, I promise."

Jules Dispard took the bill from the Maître de, smiled and said,

"It is ironic that we are in this fine seafood restaurant, Tony. We have landed a fine catch of our own today. Douglas. Let me shake your hand. Welcome back to Franz Liseur."

The next day Tony wasted no time in making the important announcement known to his key men. His secretary, Helen came into his office with Morgan Pegler and Mark Trumann. They saw Tony lounging back in his chair, hands clasped behind his head and wearing a huge smile.

"Take a seat chaps and chapess. I have good news for you all."

Morgan Pegler offered a suggestion,

"Don't tell us that you got lucky last night, Tony?"

Helen tittered at the immodest joke while Mark looked as if he had missed the funny bit. Tony responded with a giggle, sat forward and began to tell them his news,

"Well, Morgan, in a way I did get lucky but not in the way you're suggesting. I think *you* might be able to guess what my news is. You're all about to be reunited with an old friend. Douglas Fairbairn is re-joining us in January."

"That's wonderful." Said Helen.

"Oh I like that, Tony." Said Mark.

Morgan was impressed and went over to shake Tony's hand,

"I was sure you were up to something yesterday, Tony. I just knew you were fishing for Douglas, a very smart move. He'll make a difference here. Well done, laddie!"

"Thanks Morgan and I'm glad you all approve. Now here's how he will be accommodated. I'll get an office built for him at the end of the drawing office. He'll have a glass window to watch the guys sleeping at their desks. He'll have peace and quiet to work some of his mysterious magic with the team out there. I expect if he hasn't lost his touch he will in no time have the place running like a Singer sewing machine. Douglas also carries an innate tendency to be lucky. He instinctively seems to know how to get out of tight spots, especially with obstinate clients. I am personally very chuffed to have got him to come back to the fold."

"You and me both, Tony," said Morgan. "What do you want from me."

"Not a lot for the moment. I want any new contracts that don't start till next year to be left in his office. He'll no doubt want to adjust some of the present working arrangements with you guys and your lads so, he'll have a good body of work and a short honeymoon period to get the swing of the system here. You can take that on and I'll do the rest. Okay?"

"What about the mail that goes with these jobs? Do you want me to read it and give you any feedback?"

"No, The jobs will be starting well into next year, Morgan. On that basis I'll just get Helen make up a folder for each job and file the letters. There should be enough time for Douglas to take care of any problems arising. Is there anything else you guys need from me?"

Mark asked if he needed to do anything.

"Yes, Mark, you will have the pleasure of telling the boys out there that their lives are going to change for the better in January. If they ask why I'm certain you will be able to satisfy their curiosity?"

"You bet, Tony. This is the best news I've heard since he left us six years, four weeks, three days and sixteen hours ago."

They all laughed. Mark's arithmetic was disgracefully untrue but his sentiment was sincere. One thing was clear. They all felt comfortable with the news that a star performer was about to re-enter their lives.

Part 3
Late Sep1989

The Peurova Partnership ~ North Queensferry
Douglas Fairbairn was leaning over his drawing board scrutinising the architect's drawings for a forthcoming project for the Royal Air Force at Machrihanish. Without knocking, his boss, John Pammis breezed in.

"Douglas, I think you're going to like this. I got the partners' agreement to raise your salary."

He handed over a headed letter addressed to Douglas. It simply stated that his annual salary was to be increased as of the date of the letter by £3,000.00. *This is quite a coincidence*, thought Douglas but he decided to play dumb,

"I don't understand, John. I never asked for a raise. What's going on?"

"You're one of the good guys, Doug. Our client for the hotel refurbishment in Edinburgh is very impressed by your management of their project. There's talk of more of the same throughout Scotland and possibly a couple south of the border. They want you on board for all of them. We are enjoying splendid fees. I wanted to make sure you got your share, that's all."

Douglas smiled. Having caught his boss in perhaps telling a white lie, it was time to yank the rod and reel him in."

"Then why not just give me a bonus? I could understand a one-off payment, John. But increasing my salary is unusual. I can only assume you've had your ears to the ground." He smiled and gave the line another pull, "Heard a rumour, have you?"

John Pammis drew his head and shoulders back; the way people do when they are asked a direct question that might demand an honest but incriminating reply. Douglas held out the net to land him,

"So, have you?"

John was well aware of Douglas Fairbairn's perspicacity. He should have known better than to try to finesse a smart move on him. He shrugged, regained his smile and came clean,

"Okay. I'll be honest with you, Douglas. I've heard a whisper that you're thinking of going back to contracting. I want you to stay with us. You have been an out-and-out safe pair of hands. We like you; the clients like you; the lads below you in the team are in awe of your skill with the projects you've handled. That's not to mention your valuable insight from your contracting experience. You can't buy that, Douglas; it just happens with some people. You are one of those people. That's the reason for the offer. The Peurova Partners and I don't want to lose you. Please stay with us?"

Douglas had developed a fondness for John Pammis, the man he met six years ago to discuss joining the

Partnership. John had extolled the virtues of Peurova. It seemed to Douglas that the job was his even before he came to the interview. That was why he had insisted on a second interview; to make sure John Pammis was under no illusions about his actual skillset.

The consulting side of the building services industry required certain attributes that he was not entirely sure he had. It was important to tell what he felt he was weak on *before* he joined Peurova. If John Pammis was expecting too much from him it would be too late after he got the job. Working with one of the biggest, most respected consulting practices in the world demanded openness and honesty. Douglas had no intention of joining them without laying down some caveats. It transpired that he had nothing to fear. John was impressed by his 'no bullshit' approach.

During their six years working together, they maintained a rewarding level of mutual respect. They 'said it straight' with each other. There was rarely any doubt about what the other was thinking. Douglas's determination to get things done 'right first time' had made him a valuable leader of the project management team in the Building and Engineering group of this global firm.

In that same spirit, having enjoyed a bit of mischief with John, it was now the moment for Douglas to make his future intentions crystal clear,

"John, I can't stay. I am not going to say sorry. It's just that I have a strong desire to get back to the cut and thrust of contracting. My years here have been wonderful but I feel that I am getting a bit too comfortable and it's the right time to move on. I have already accepted a position with Franz Liseur. I will give you a letter confirming this?"

His boss half folded his arms. With his right thumb and forefinger, he pressed his bottom lip into a pout and sighed,

"Oh dear. I was afraid of this. I am obviously too late, Douglas. It seems you have made up you mind. Are you giving me the usual three months' notice?"

"Yes of course, John. Tony Surtal expects me to re-join them in January in my previous role as Contracts Manager. In these circumstances, having given my word, I can't accept your very generous offer, not even if you were to offer twice as much. I will part company with you at Christmas."

John Pammis put out his right hand and it was warmly grasped. He knew he was never going to persuade this trusted, talented engineer to remain. With an air of sad dejection he conceded the inevitable departure,

"I understand, Douglas. It's a pity we are unable to tempt you to stay. Did they give you a better offer?

Douglas thought for a moment. He had assumed that John Pammis already had got wind of Liseur's offer but, just in case he hadn't, he decided to play it cool. That was for him to know and John to find out. His salary was a secret that he never discussed with anyone but his employer. The obvious answer was simple and honest,

"No, John."

"Then why go? Surely money is the reason for getting out of bed in the morning?"

"Maybe for you John, but not for me. The money *is* important but it is secondary to the kick I get from solving problems that seem insoluble. I love sailing close to the wind; every day; looking over the cliff edge. Feeling the fear, that's where I get my buzz."

John Pammis stood for a moment absorbing Douglas's surprising philosophy before capitulating to the inescapable departure of his colleague,

"I thought you got that here with us, Douglas but I respect your decision and wish you the best of success when you return to your old home. Good luck. We will miss you. I will miss you. Take care, my boy. We'll have a snifter or three before you depart."

He turned and left. Douglas felt sad but relieved that he had got that bit out of the way. He folded the letter and put it in his pocket. It would not become official now but it would be fun to show it to Tony Surtal in January.

Part 4
Mon 8th Jan 1990

Franz Liseur offices ~ Clydebank
It was the first working day of the New Year. Tony spent a pleasant hour wandering round the office with

Douglas to allow him to reconnect with his old colleagues and the new engineers who now made up his team of nine. The next couple of hours were spent in the privacy of Tony's office discussing the work-in-progress and some contracts that had arrived since their meeting with Jules Dispard last year. That done, they left for an early lunch in a restaurant up at the top of Kilbowie Road where they could take their ease and chat about old times and the future.

"So, you'll have noticed a few changes in the set-up Douglas?

"There are a some new faces augmenting the old team that I remember and your order book is healthy. Seems secure for the future. I'm looking forward to having good fun with the lads I know and getting to know the youngsters. The office hasn't changed that much since I've been gone."

"That's true. I hope it's not too much of a comedown from the swanky Peurova set up?"

"Not at all. In some ways it's more comfortable for me to be out of the rarefied atmosphere at Peurova. Those guys are all high fliers; hugely qualified graduates. It was quite scary for me, a self-taught youngster out of the Glasgow slums, to have been head-hunted by them."

This was great news for Tony. It was highly unlikely that his new man would change his mind any time soon to return to the high life of consulting engineering;

especially with a firm like Peurova. They now have the problem Tony had and would be at pains to replace Douglas Fairbairn. Tony grinned,

"That's great to hear, Douglas. They stole you from me six years ago. I'm delighted to have nicked you back from them. They'll know what they've lost. If they try any funny business, I hope you'll let me know?"

It was Douglass's turn to produce a broad grin. He reached into his inside pocket and withdrew a white envelope.

"It's funny you should say that, Tony. You might be interested to read this letter John Pammis handed to me. It was just days after I shook hands with you and Monsieur Dispard and confirmed my acceptance of your offer."

Tony took a few seconds to digest the implications of what he was reading. He looked at Douglas, whistled, folded the letter and gave it back to him without a word. Douglas took it, tore it twice and dropped it on the ashtray on the table.

"Nuff said, Tony?"

"Nuff said, Douglas!"

They proceeded to enjoy their lunch and nostalgic pleasantries before eventually returning to the office to get on with the real work for which Jules Dispard was paying them.

One hour into the afternoon, Douglas shot out of his office, strode across the corridor and, ignoring Helen's waving arms, barged into Tony Surtal's room without knocking,

"Tony! Have you read the file for this contract at Bluff?"

"Oh! Hello again Douglas. Am I to assume you are unhappy about something?"

"No. I'm bewildered. This contract was awarded to us in September last year!"

"I know that, Douglas. It's due to be done this year. Is there a problem with that? It's only a short programme."

Douglas adopted a posture of amazed surprise and retorted,

"Only a short programme! It's the first thing I've looked at. We should have been on site weeks ago. The file hasn't even been opened by anyone."

Tony sat back thinking, *I love this guy. One hour behind his desk and he is already firing on all twelve cylinders. I'll humour him and have a bit of fun.*

"Not *quite* true, Douglas. Morgan Pegler checked the finances for me. This time at least Willie Spence has priced it correctly. So it might make a copper."

Douglas was not amused and intended to make his argument as strong as possible without actually shouting,

"It's not going to make any money if we start late. We'll always be behind Jarvis & Craig. I'll bet there's a loss and expense claim from on file already. We'll not get this done on time, Tony. Did you read their letter that came in this morning?"

Tony of course had read all the mail but just glanced at those for his contracts manager's direct attention and action. His answer was a little brittle but tinted with humour,

"Briefly; among the other seventy-five that came in."

Douglas either didn't notice the jest from Tony, or he chose to ignore it. He continued to force the issue of the project going into delay, implying that someone had not done his homework,

"The builders started on site late last year? They're asking us to give them our working drawings for the external pipework supports by next Tuesday. The boiler house is built waiting for our plant items and not a screw or nail's been ordered yet! Did you not know that?"

Having felt that his point was made, Douglas fell silent. Tony put down his pen, sat back and folded his arms. He grinned,

"Eh, no I didn't know that, Douglas. What would you like me to do?"

"I want someone to take responsibility for this hopeless and potentially very costly situation with the drawings and the programme. We'll get hammered, Tony."

Tony maintained his boyish grin while absorbing this dire news from Douglas. In his head he mused, *this is the man who left his safe job with the Peurova Partnership. This is the man I knew was a firebrand, a dedicated problem solver. This is the man who usually causes problems with obstructive and uncooperative clients. It has only taken Douglas an hour to revert to type before barging in, red faced to spit out the tacks. Now's the time for a bit of friendly sport with this man for whom I have the utmost respect,*

"Douglas. I've hired a guy to sort this out."

Douglas fell for it.

"And who might that clever dick be, Tony?

Tony yelled a loud guffaw,

"My new contracts manager."

Douglas froze, turned his head to the side, and held up his hands in surrender,

"You bugger, Tony. I give in. I should have realised that coming back here would be just one big bundle of fun."

"Yes my friend. I appreciate there's been a bit of a slip up. I should have spotted that but I'm sure you can handle it."

Douglas shrugged. Tony's apology had done the trick. It was up to him to get his head round the problem and find a solution. He fired a caveat,

"You must think I'm a bloody miracle worker."

"No I don't. I know it's hard; but I also know you can wriggle and win. So, tell me, what are you going to do?'

"First thing is for me to read the whole file to find the bombshells. Then I'll get Mark Trumann in and allocate the job to him and John Logge. They can start by placing the orders. I'll shut my door and read through the documents for anything that'll give us an edge. I need to find some way of slowing the job down."

"Good man! If I know you Douglas, you won't be long doing that. Now that we've cleared that up, why don't you get back to your own office and get a move on with what I'm paying you for?"

"Okay, Tony. Since there's no good reason to stay..."

He had pursed lips and wore a pensive smile as he sauntered back to his office. The big problem was time. It would not be long before the main contractor applied the penalty clause. The costs against Liseur would soon escalate. Franz Liseur was big enough to absorb any such losses. Here he was, right from day one of his tenure with them, in the state he loved best; wrestling with an impossible problem, He was being squeezed by the main contractor who was miles ahead of them at the site and his boss expecting him to dream up a way to get Liseur out of trouble.

Through the internal window of his office, he watched the peaceful activity of his staff; making phone calls; working on drawing boards; reading specifications; swapping stories; laughing. All of them working to achievable programmes, making rational decisions, solving problems...achieving.

Sitting at his desk he pondered how to solve *his* problem. *It'll probably take about a month to issue all the general equipment orders for a project. To set up the sub-contracted works will take a bit longer...maybe another two weeks.*

Jarvis & Craig, by sleight of hand, had grabbed the advantage and put Liseur behind. He had to find some way to stall the project for about six weeks to catch up with the builder. Somehow, he had to win back time to have any hope of curtailing the consequential financial losses. He leant out of his door and shouted for Mark Trumann in the drawing office,

"Mark! Can you give me a minute of your time please?"

A quick summary of the situation brought Mark up to speed.

"Douglas, if I'm guessing right, this means we're in the shit before we start?"

"No need to guess, Mark. From what I've read on the builder's programme I suspect that Jarvis & Craig have been laying a trap for us. I'll have to find a way to stall them and win a breathing space."

"What do you want me to do, Douglas?"

"Work on this and put in as much overtime as needed to have everything placed on order by the end of the week after next."

"That's a big ask. We've not even seen the file."

"I know it'll be difficult, but it's important. I'll hold your hand if you get into trouble on this one We must try hard to save our skins from those predators, Jarvis & Craig. Take the files and set up meetings with the sub-contractors for sometime next week. There's only two, Automatic Controls and Thermal Insulation. I need these orders placed tout-de-suite. You along with one of the new engineers will front the discussions. Call me in if a push is needed to get their prices down, okay?"

"Right, Douglas, but what about the rest; boilers, pumps and all that?"

"Start phoning today to get their quotes validated for all the major plant items. Push for at least five per cent off the top. We're going to need all the spare cash we can get. Call in Freddie from Brown & Tawse and place a bulk order for all the pipes, fittings and valves on a sale or return basis. That will get another two or three per cent if we are lucky. Oh, give me all the Jarvis & Craig letters out of the file. That's all I need."

"Okay Douglas. I'll get cracking with this. I don't envy you your problem. What are you going to do to make up for this amount of lost time?"

"Two things, Mark. First I'll get the Labour Manager to collect a ten-man team of welders and fitters ready for a start on site in ten days. Who is in charge of labour nowadays? Is it still Jimmy Wolfe?"

"No. He retired two years ago. Archie McGregor's been promoted. Do you remember him?"

"Yes, I recall he was a very clever senior foreman. Give him a call to come in and see you and me tomorrow or Thursday. Oh, and print a set of drawings for him, Mark. Archie will have to get moving on this little baby of ours. Don't you think so?"

"Oh yes. This one is a cracker. I hope he can go as fast as you. You mentioned two things Douglas. What's the second?"

"I'm going to close my door for the rest of today to study the contract and Jarvis & Craig's letters. I'm looking for a chink in the builder's armour. I'll also read the Clark Chisholm specification. Keep your eyes peeled for any errors on their design drawings. There's bound to be a mistake or two that could be to our advantage."

"You should know, Douglas, you've been a consulting engineer for the last six years. I bet you made a few errors during that time, eh?"

"You're almost right, Mark. I did make a big mistake once."

"Are you going to tell me what it was?"

"Yes, of course. One day I *thought* I had made a mistake...but I hadn't! Now scram and get moving on this. By the way, Mark; use that young guy, John Logge as your assistant on this. I've read his CV and he seems quite useful. Maybe he could run the project with you in the background. What do you think?"

"I agree. I've watched him working, Douglas, but the politics of this job might be a little bit beyond him. I'll let him do the donkeywork and see how he shapes up. He's made some smart moves on his projects. Maybe he's after my job?"

"He's not clever enough for that...not yet anyway. If he ends up handling this baby at Bluff maybe *then* you should start looking over *your* shoulder. Reassure young Logge that Tony and me will do the politics. Let's see how it goes. Meanwhile Mark, maybe you should be after *my* job, eh? "

"No chance! I saw what you went through last time you were here. It looks to me as if things haven't changed much either. We've all missed you and I for one am really happy to see you back again 'coz I've no desire to be in your position."

"Thanks Mark. Now I'm closing my door to do some detective work. So, enough of this foolish lovemaking, let's see what you can do, okay?"

"Sure boss. I'll get right onto it and leave you in peace."

Douglas pulled out the GC/Works 1 domestic sub-contract document and settled down to scrutinise it for any lifeline he could grab. As usual with government papers the document was a pest to read. Each main clause had a number followed by a myriad of sub-numbers and sub-sub-numbers, all supposed to produce absolute clarity of meaning. It was the typical hotchpotch of gobbledegook. It seemed like only a short time later when he heard a knock on his door. Douglas looked up and was glad to see Mark at his door with a cup of coffee and some biscuits,

"Oh, coffee time already, Mark? Thanks, I can use that right now."

"It's half four, boss. Thought you had fallen asleep. How're you getting on?"

Douglas giggled,

"This contract is murder to read. I'm only at clause eleven but I'm on page thirty-two. It's doubtful if there's anything here that could help us."

"Yeah, I know that contract. It's not worth the paper it's written on."

"It is if you're the government. All I've read up till now is stuff that protects them; nothing I could use to create a delay in our favour. It's all about saving the necks of the client and his professional team."

"Sounds a bit brutal for us, boss?"

"You're right. Give me a Royal Institute of British Architects contract any day. This is like suicide for us. Anyway, I will read it through to the end just to be sure I've turned every stone. Cheers for the biscuits."

Mark closed the door with quiet respect. Douglas sipped his coffee that by now had gone cool. He gulped the rest down, laid down the cup and with dwindling hopes turned to page thirty-three. Clause12.1 was a short, clear sentence that made him sit upright and bang his fist on his desk and yell,

"Christ! This could be the answer."

It read, *'The Supervising Officer shall provide the contractor with setting out details.'*
   To be sure, he re-read it and sat back to think of the best way to use this little bombshell to his advantage. It took him a minute or so to form a plan of attack. He would get a letter out in the post that very night. He called Helen in and dictated a letter to the builders, with instructions to post it by registered mail.

Jarvis & Craig

8 Jan 1990
Attention of Mr J. Hadshaw

Dear Sirs,   R.N.A.D. Bluff (No 001)

We acknowledge and thank you for receipt of your Mister Hadshaw's letter dated fifth inst. in which you

request our working drawings for the external pipework installation at the above site.

In that regard, we respectfully advise we will be grateful to receive setting out details from you. These should, in our opinion, have been issued to us some time ago. Since you have not yet done so, we regret to advise our inability to provide you with the drawings you require.

Might we suggest that you approach the Supervising Officer on our behalf to solicit these details in accordance with Clause 12.1 of the Government Contracts Works 1 Domestic Sub-Contract that we mutually agreed and signed last year?

When we receive those details, no effort will be spared to have drawings issued to you within the four-week period we normally allow on our programmes for such drawing office work.

Please appreciate the need for your timeous response. We are anxious to make a start on our external works. We shall of course try to mitigate any delay to our work, created outwith our control by your failure, so far, to provide these important details in accordance with the aforementioned Clause in our contract with you.

Yours Faithfully,

Douglas Fairbairn,
Contracts Manager
For: Franz Liseur, Scotland   Ref HT/DF

Douglas knew this initial salvo could be the start of an all-out war between him and the builders, not to mention the M.O.D.; just what he was good at. In these matters he did not have a nerve in his body. It would be stimulating to know that for a change, it was the *builder* who squirmed. Contracting is a devious business of subtle moves, not unlike the game of chess. Douglas had an arsenal of cunning moves and wasn't afraid to deploy them to gain an advantage, but only if such manoeuvres were within the rules of the game. No illegal move would be made in his attempt to rescue Liseur from the risk of serious delay created by Tony.

He reckoned on having about a week or so before Hadshaw reacted. The builder would brand his smart letter as 'the height of impudence' to suggest that the client would provide these details. He expected that, but he had other ploys to keep the builders busy. This breathing space at least allowed him to instruct the office team to progress the procurement of men and materials. Tomorrow he would initiate the site construction team. He would also talk to Tony about Jarvis & Craig's letter from Christmas 1989 citing Liseur for five weeks loss and expense damages of £14,000.00.

Part 5
Thu 11th Jan 1990

Franz Liseur offices ~ Clydebank
First thing in the morning the Labour manager, Archie McGregor arrived at Douglas's door and light-heartedly announced himself,

"Excuse me. Is the new contracts manager in?"

"Archie! Come in. Long time no see. Last time we met you were in a boiler suit. I'm pleased to meet the new Scottish Labour Manager. How the devil are you young man?"

"I'm good, Douglas. How are you these days? Canny stay away from the old firm, eh?"

"Something like that, Archie but I came back for less money because I missed you so much."

Archie laughed out loud,

"Now that I don't believe. We hardly know each other, and you'd better know that I don't kiss on the first date. As for your cut in wages...you'll have to pull the other one. I didni come up the Clyde wae a perforated bus ticket."

It was Douglas's turn to chuckle. He lifted the phone, asked Helen to bring in some tea and biscuits and invited his colleague to have a seat. When comfortably settled, he set about providing the information that Archie would need. That involved a brief description of the location of the site and the broad outline of Liseur's mechanical services responsibilities. Then he got down to specifics about the establishment of their site compound and accommodation for the tradesmen.

"Here's a copy of the estimate sheets. You'll note the amount allocated for the wages and lodging allowances.

It also shows the number of man-hours allowed. The builder's programme is tight. Here's a copy. You'll note it shows no time for us."

He sipped some tea and nibbled on his digestive while Archie considered this information.

"There's not much money shown for the men to travel to the site and back. Why is that, Douglas?"

"Well spotted. We'll need to use the guys from Aberdeen. They'll be accommodated in a caravan park just outside Forres, close to the site. We'll pay the cost of that for duration of the job. If the men can agree to go home once a month they will get to work three weekends out of four. The extra cash will cover their travelling time. A bonus will be awarded at your discretion for good production."

Archie looked pleased. He trusted Douglas from his past experience. Discussing these important items directly with the new contracts manager was reassuring. Douglas told it like it was: no flannel just the facts and no attempt to pull the wool over his eyes or skin money from the site operatives. He ventured a comment,

"I like the way you work, Douglas. I'm happy with all that so, I'll shoot up to Aberdeen tomorrow and rustle up the men we need."

"Good man. Give me a call to keep me in the picture.

"Okay. This looks like a nice wee contract. Handled right, we should '*scoosh*' it."

Douglas was glad to hear this response from Archie but felt it prudent to rein in the young man's enthusiasm,

"Much as I like a positive attitude Archie, let's just be careful with this contract son. It'll be a fight from the start with this builder. Don't underestimate Jarvis & Craig."

"Why are you so sure we'll get problems from them, Douglas? I've never been afraid of any builder. Why is this one different from the rest?"

"Because their reputation is well known. They're only in it for the penalty clause. I'm sure of that since I've already spotted their first trick to put us in delay. We'll have to be on our toes. They'll throw in every spanner they can to screw us. It's important that we keep our noses clean, get the work done efficiently and get off the site as soon as we can. Now Archie, what do you need from the boys in the drawing office?"

"I'll ask Mark for drawings and some help with placing orders for the caravans. I'll set a provisional start date for two weeks from Monday coming, that will be, let me see my diary, the twenty-ninth of January."

"Right. That's good Archie. Agree a delivery schedule with Mark for the site material and boilers etcetera. Talk to him soon about setting up a programme of work. I want to approve it before it's issued. That's it. Have you anything else?"

"Just to say it's good to see you back here, Douglas. Things have been a little different since you went away. I look forward to working with you."

"It's mutual, Archie. Let's get this job done and dusted before the Jarvis & Craig mob realise what's happened. If these bandits are trying to fleece us, they'll have to be up very early in the morning."

"Thanks Douglas, I'm up for that. Cheers."

They shook hands with strong friendly grips and Archie dashed off to confer with Mark and the boy, Logge.

Douglas was content to feel that his team was gathering momentum. He turned to look again at the drawings lying open on his desk. Something he saw earlier had set him thinking. His designer's instinct had been tweaked. There was a certain relish in looking for glitches or minor design errors made by the Consulting Engineers. It was pleasing to expose these and watch their blushes. Consultants are congenitally indisposed to admitting errors. More especially when they are told the cost for putting them right.

As he searched, Douglas allowed a couple of idle thoughts to cross his mind, *contracting can be fun; Maybe that's the main reason I left consulting and came back to Liseur, the adrenalin rushes are addictive. Could it be I suffered withdrawal symptoms for the last six years? This might be my first good 'fix'.* The raucous ringing of his phone dispelled his reverie. He lifted it to take his first call.

"Hi, Douglas Fairbairn."

"Hello, Mister Fairbairn. I'm told you are the Contracts Manager. Is that correct?"

"It depends who is calling. If you are my wife's lawyer then I'm somebody else. Where did you get my name?"

"From the insolent registered letter you sent to me. I'm Joe Hadshaw. I don't have a sense of humour."

"It would seem so, Mister Hadshaw. I apologise for my levity about my wife's lawyer, but I assure you that my letter was anything *but* a joke."

"It's not a joke. It's a piece of barefaced cheek. You obviously don't know much about contracting. You're ignorant of the meaning of the conditions of contract. They're no there for your benefit. They're there to protect the client's interest. How do you expect the client to give you drawings? That's your job so, I'm telling you now Mister Fairbairn, you'd better get on with it or face the consequences!"

"Well Joe, now that you've got *that* off your chest, are you done?"

"What do you mean?"

"I just wanted to know if you were ready to hear my reply or are you just going to shout at me for a while and then hang up. If that's the case then you'd better know this, you won't get any drawings from me until I have your response to my letter. And it will have to be in writing."

"You will get a letter. It's being typed as we speak."

"Can I suggest you save yourself a stamp?"

"What are you getting at now? Are you trying to be clever again?"

"Listen to me, Joe. I am always clever. I *do* know a lot about contracting. I also know a lot about Consulting. Something else I know a lot about is the GC works 1 contract for this project."

"Okay, so you're clever. What's that all about?"

"I'll tell you if you want to learn."

"Don't get smart, Fairbairn. Say your bit and get off my phone!"

"Well now, that's kind of you. You just said we would not get the client to do our drawings. We have not asked the client for drawings."

"Yes you have. You asked for setting out details from the Supervising Officer. That's the M.O.D. and the M.O.D. is the client!"

"Not *our* client, Mister Hadshaw. *You* are our client. We are asking Jarvis & Craig for these drawings since we are your domestic subcontractor. We have no contractual connection with your client. Furthermore, the document we signed last year states that the Supervising Officer for this contract is Mister Norman Keen of the Keen, Parr Felt Structural Engineering Partnership. That firm is decidedly *not* the M.O.D."

There was a silence at the other end.

"Mister Hadshaw...are you still there?"

"Yes. I'll get back to you."

He hung up.

Douglas now had a brief moment to go and speak to Tony,

"I read the files yesterday and note that the builder has issued a loss and expense letter."

"Oh dear, I didn't know that. How much are the talking about?"

"Fourteen grand. Their saying we've cost them five weeks of delay."

"What's the script for dealing with that, Douglas?"

"Keep it on file till the end of the job and then we will probably be ahead of them. Otherwise, we'll just spend the whole time arguing and fighting with them and losing more money than the job's worth."

"Let's assume you're right. Just ignore it for now and see how you get on with your ferreting through the files and the contract. Anything so far?"

"Yeah, Tony, I gave them a letter yesterday that will cause a wee flurry. There's a half-chance we'll get a bit of time back with it."

"Okay, Douglas. Well done for now. We'll keep our eyes on these buggers. You know I'm here if you need heavy artillery. Anything else I need to know about?"

"No, but I need to concentrate on this if we want to beat them. I'll keep you posted."

Part 6
Fri 12th Jan 1990

Franz Liseur offices ~ Clydebank
The phone rang.

"Hi, Douglas Fairbairn here."

"This is Joe Hadshaw. You are required to attend a meeting at the M.O.D. offices in Edinburgh at 11.00 a.m. on Tuesday coming. Please make sure that you attend."

"Not until you tell me what it's about."

"You know fine well what it's about."

"I can guess but that's not a good basis to agree to attend a meeting with someone as antagonistic as you, Joe."

"You will do as you are bid, Fairbairn or I will talk to your boss."

"Okay, Joe. When you've done that, I expect you'll call me back. Bye now."

He gently replaced the receiver and sauntered through to Tony Surtal's door, knocked and went in. A short appraisal to Tony was all he had time for before the phone rang.

"Hi, Tony Surtal here. How can I help you?"

"Mister Surtal, this is Joe Hadshaw of Jarvis & Craig. I want to complain about your contracts manager. He has been very insolent on the telephone this morning and has refused to attend a meeting with the client on Tuesday."

Tony responded brightly,

"Hello Joe. I remember you from the contract signing last year. Happy New Year by the way; did you have a good time over the festive season?"

"Listen! I'm not on here to swap civilities with you Mister Surtal. I want you to reprimand your boy."

"Oh I don't think that will be necessary, Joe. I know this man very well from years of working with him as a colleague and as a consultant. He is always civil. I understand that you refused to tell him of the purpose of this meeting and told him just to guess. Is that correct?"

"I never said that! He knows fine well what it's about. He wrote a stupid letter demanding setting out details from the Supervising Officer. You are not going to get these unless you come to this meeting with the client on Tuesday. Are you going to be represented or not?"

"I'm not sure, Joe. You said it's for a meeting with the client. Correct me if I'm wrong, Joe, but according to the documents I signed on your beautiful big desk, last September, in your very smart office, we are your domestic subcontractors."

Joe had become frustrated,

"What's that got to do with anything?"

"Well, Joe, in case it has escaped your mind, our client is actually your good self. So, is Douglas to come and have a meeting with you?"

Hadshaw was less than amused at being played with. Tony sensed the man was out of his depth and about to turn ratty. He was not wrong,

"Listen carefully, Surtal. Your boy has set the cat among the pigeons with his letter. We have spoken to the M.O.D. and they have asked for our attendance to discuss your letter."

Tony put his right hand over the mouthpiece, smiled and winked. Douglas remembered that mannerism whenever his friend got the better of an opponent. Tony sat back in his chair; looked up at the ceiling and responded in a nonchalant way that suggested the belligerent Joe Hadshaw had come second.

"Well Joe, that sounds like a very civil approach from your client. I guess you will read our letter to them and tell them it is perfectly clear what we have asked for. I also expect to be protected by you, since you are, legally and contractually, *our* client."

"I need your guy there with me to argue your case if you've got one!"

"But I've read our letter. It states our case perfectly lucidly. Seems to me Joe, that you don't actually need Douglas there to hold your hand. All you need to do is advise our inability to give you the drawings you need and ask them to provide the setting out details in accordance with the contract. Unless of course you don't feel competent to do that?"

"You're as bad as Fairbairn. You are just being obstinate when all that's needed is a bit of come and go."

"But Joe, you *demanded* our presence and would not tell Douglas what it was about. That doesn't seem to me to be come and go. It sounds like an order rather than a civil request. I suggest that unless you practice what you're preaching, I will instruct Douglas not to attend. I'll leave you on your own to get what we need from *your* client."

"Are you refusing to come to the meeting?"

Tony sat forward, thumped his fist on his desk and spoke with a harsh and commanding tone,

"Now listen carefully, Joe. Phone Douglas now and *ask* him to attend. I can tell you that you will not succeed by trying to bully him. He is very experienced. If you approach him the right way you will get the best of his skill. He manages the contracts, not me. With the right approach I am sure Douglas will give you all necessary help with your problem. Bye now."

Tony quickly hung up, denying Hadshaw the chance to say any more. Douglas smiled and waited. Tony spoke softly,

"I don't blame you for playing games with him, Douglas but the fun is over. These are dangerous people. We don't want them giving the M.O.D. the wrong signals about how we operate. He will phone you and he will tone down a bit and you'll agree to attend the meeting. Get the best out of it that you can. Your letter may have gained us some time. It may yet get us more. I know you are on a good wicket with this approach. But don't milk it; you don't want to push them too far."

Douglas nodded sagely. He was grateful for Tony's solid support and impressed by his skill in playing Hadshaw like a trout. Joe was swelled headed; acting like he was the boss of his firm but had shown little or no finesse. He was a jumped up foreman trying to act like a director. He had lost a battle and would be looking for revenge. His type usually failed, given sufficient time. This time he had no other option but to eat dirt if he was to persuade Douglas to attend the meeting. Back in his own office the phone rang,

"Hi, Douglas Fairbairn here."

"Hello Douglas I spoke to your boss and explained the purpose of the meeting at the M.O.D. next week. He assured me in the circumstances, that you would be able to come along and assist us to get the setting out details we both need. Will you be available?"

"Sure, Joe. I look forward to hearing what they have to say. I don't expect they will give you what we need but it's better to get it cleared up. Don't you think?"

"Absolutely! See you there. Don't be late!"

Part 7
Tue 16th Jan 1990

M.O.D. Offices Edinburgh
Jim Briggs sat in his magisterial position at the top of a long narrow table. The usual dozen other representatives of the M.O.D. filled up most of the seats down each side. Douglas was there with Mark Trumann. Joe Hadshaw had brought along his site agent, Terry Cordwell. They had arrived on schedule but it was evident the client's men had been there for some time. The table was untidy with scattered contract drawings and abandoned coffee cups. Several photocopies of page thirty-three of GC/Works 1 conditions lay around. Clause 12.1 was highlighted in red. They had evidently been discussing ways to re-interpret the wording that had suddenly become awkward for them. Douglas knew fine well that the M.O.D. had no intention of issuing setting out details. It was not something they ever did for pipework. He was nevertheless relishing the mischief he had created, using the contract wording to gain time. Briggs spoke first.

"My name is James Briggs, Principal Controller of the M.O.D., Scotland. Starting from my left, all present will kindly state their name, title and the body they represent."

One of those round the table identified himself thus: *Norman Keen of the Keen Parr Felt structural engineering partnership and the Supervising Officer for the Bluff project.* After Joe Hadshaw timidly named himself and sat down, Briggs read a statement to clarify the positions of both the M.O.D. and the Supervising Officer in the matter of setting out details.

"It is not the policy of the Supervising Officer on behalf of the M.O.D. to issue setting out details for pipework installations in any Ministry of Defence buildings. On this contract at Bluff this obligation falls on the builders, Jarvis & Craig. The floor is yours Mister Hadshaw."

There was silence. All heads turned to look at Hadshaw. Douglas had expected Joe to speak on his behalf but he just sat looking bewildered. He appeared to be overawed by this august assembly. Douglas decided he had no option. He got up to speak,
    "Good morning, gentlemen. Clause 12.1 states that the Supervising Officer will provide setting out details. Mister Briggs is correct in stating that the pipework *inside* buildings does not require setting-out details."

Before Douglas could continue, Briggs was on his feet,

"And who might you be, sirrah!"

"I am Douglas Fairbairn of Franz Liseur, Mister Hadshaw's sub-contractor. He asked for my attendance at this meeting to assist him in presenting my arguments. May I continue?"

"You most certainly may not continue. I do not hold with domestic sub-contractors like you barnstorming my meetings. Sit down, sirrah!"

Douglas remained standing.

"I said sit down, damn you! You do not have permission to address this gathering. Sit down or I will have you removed."

Douglas smiled and returned to his seat. Briggs turned his attention to Joe,

"Mister Hadshaw, I offered you the floor to state your piece. Will you stand up man and tell us what this is all about?"

Joe stood up with a jerk and his chair fell backwards with a clatter. He twisted round to gather it up and almost fell over it. Briggs was not amused but said nothing...only stared disbelievingly at this caricature of a man looking such a fool. Joe turned to face him. In a mild subservient voice he apologised,

"Sorry about that, sir. Douglas Fairbairn knows what needs to be said and I would like you to let him speak for me."

He sat down. Briggs coughed a loud 'ahem', looked at Douglas and stated the obvious,

"It would seem, Mister Fairbairn, that if you do not proceed to unfold the mysteries of your undoubtedly spurious arguments, then there will be no point in any further continuation of this charade of a meeting. You are invited therefore to kindly take the floor."

"Thank you, Mister Briggs. As I was saying, you are correct that internal pipes do not necessitate the SO providing setting out details. The pipes I am referring to are not within a building. They are shown running along the side of a hill in the open air. There is no indication of their intended *location*. He emphasized the word 'location'. That gap in information clearly requires setting out details as stated in the contract. Without these, my company will be unable to provide our client, Jarvis & Craig with working drawings. Jarvis & Craig will consequently be unable to construct the required concrete stanchions to accommodate our pipe supports."

Douglas sat down. Jim Briggs at last stirred his large body and rose to his feet. His right forefinger stabbed at the table in a steady, forceful rhythm as he delivered his seemingly final and incontrovertible deliberation,

"There is no requirement in this contract for the Supervising Officer to give you the location of your pipes."

Douglas got up again while Briggs was still standing. He knew fine well that this would be the argument they would put up. He reckoned that they probably did not read past clause 12.1 that was so graphically highlighted on the copies of the contract conditions scattered around the table. This was his opportunity to pull his proverbial rabbit out of the hat,

"Forgive me, Mister Briggs. I'm afraid I must disagree. Allow me to read Clause 12.2 of the contract conditions. '*The Drawings are the graphic and pictorial portions of the Contract Documents showing the design, intent, location, and dimensions of the Work, generally including plans, elevations, sections, details, schedules and diagrams.*' I am drawing your attention to the word 'location'. There are no defined locations for the pipework on any of the contract drawings."

Someone else jumped up and angrily leant over the table, flung back several of the contract drawings and slammed his hand down on one of them, shouting...

"There is your setting out information. The drawings have ordnance survey contour lines; they show where you pipes should be located! What is your problem Mister Fairbairn?"

Douglas was not intimidated,

"Since you ask, sir, there are several problems. Firstly you will notice the pipes pass over several different contour lines. You seem to be inferring that the pipes have to rise and fall along these lines. In my experience the pipes require to run in straight lines; otherwise the heating system will not function.

His antagonist yelled,

"Utter rubbish!"

Still undeterred, Douglas turned over to another drawing and continued,

"Secondly, sir, please look at this pipework drawing and note that in any case, there are no such contour lines shown."

His attacker scoffed,

"He's clutching at straws now! It's about time...."

Ignoring his invective, Douglas cut him off and spoke with increasing volume,

"And lastly, sir, since you insisted on knowing if I have a problem with your contour lines, I have to point out, that in any case these contour lines are not actually drawn on the ground at the site and thus are not able to be regarded as setting out datum marks or locations. I rest my case, gentlemen."

Douglas thumped the table as a final gesture of defiant argument and sat down. The loudmouth sank deeper into his chair, with his mouth open and huffed indignantly towards Briggs. No other sound came out except for a hiss as he drew in a gasp and shook his head in disgust.

Briggs realised that Douglas had made such a good case that it might actually embarrass the M.O.D. This *prima facie evidence* could allow the contractors to go to court and Franz Liseur could possibly win their argument. Firm action was needed to prevent this. The builders had to be bullied into backing down. It was clear that the obvious weak link was Joe Hadshaw. Briggs decided he would have to come down heavily on Jarvis & Craig in order to scare them off.

He was however, reluctant to do that with Liseur's men present. One reason was that the M.O.D. had no contractual ties with Liseur. He also preferred to get them out of the meeting while he ladled into Joe Hadshaw. Briggs desire was to physically kick Douglas and his colleague out of the room but duplicity was needed. He was good at that. He increased the drama by banging his first on the table.

"Right gentlemen. I have heard enough of this contractual argument. In my opinion the representative from Franz Liseur has been argumentative, obdurate and disrespectful to this meeting. I must insist on his departure. Mister Fairbairn, please absent yourself and your colleague from the room and wait outside."

Without argument, they left and sat in the corridor. Mark spoke first,

"That guy with the drawings was a real clown, I'd love to see him on a hill looking for contour lines."

Douglas liked the levity. It lightened up the mood.

"Yeah, how do these guys get the jobs? They sit a civil service exam and then think they rule the world. As long as he's got a hole in his bum he'll never be a leader of men. Briggs on the other hand; he's the one to watch, Mark."

A few minutes later, a white-faced Joe Hadshaw emerged with his colleague. He tried to force a note of menace into his short speech,

"You are to produce the base details for your support within two weeks. If you refuse, Jarvis & Craig will lose the contract and so will you. Costs for our loss and expense will be down to you. Understood?"

Mark Trumann pursed his lips and took a swift intake of breath. Douglas smiled,

"Nothing new there then, Joe. Don't you worry yourself; by the time this job is over you'll be paying *us* for losses. I've filed your loss and expense letter...in the bin!"

"You think you're very cool! It'll cost your firm a fortune."

"No chance, Joe. It's only bluster. Briggs has abused his power. I saw how strong you were in there, Joe. You let him intimidate you into submission. We'll do a set of drawings. Don't worry; we will not be getting sacked from this job. They don't want any trouble. The best thing now is to stick together and get it done without any further arguments or disputes between us."

Joe's face was ashen. It was clear he had been very frightened and well out of his comfort zone. Without another word he whirled round and made to leave. He pulled open the exit door, hesitated and turned round,

"I hope you're right, Fairbairn, or my boss will be talking to your boss."

Douglas got the last word in,

"Sure Hadshaw! I hope they say more than you did in there matey."

When the door slammed, Douglas turned to Mark,

"Fucking coward! He hasn't caught on yet that Briggs has just given us a two-week breathing space. Hadshaw won't give us any more trouble on this job. Let's get back to the office and get some drawings done. I've got more mischief to invent before we are out of the woods."

"Like what?"

Douglas chuckled,

"You'll see."

On the way back to the office Mark noted that Douglas seemed to be a bit withdrawn, quietly musing over something. Years before this he had got to know something of the way his boss's mind worked. Sometimes he was blasé about a big problem, tending to laugh it off while wrestling with how he was to solve it. Today though, he seemed to be struggling to find a solution to something else entirely, something that was not going to be easy. A personal matter perhaps. He broke into their silence,

"Why the studious look, Douglas?"

"Oh, sorry, Mark, it's just these buggers at Jarvis & Craig. He's hired a couple of guys to ram us with letters claiming damages for loss and expense."

"Already! We've not even started yet. What's their game?"

"It's main contractors bashing their sub-contractors. It's an old trick. They can make a lot of money by fooling us. They didn't ask us for drawings till it was too late. We've unwittingly been holding them up but they deliberately didn't push us. They gave us enough rope. Now they choke us. It's too late to make up the time. We are on a hiding on this Bluff contract and I'm not sure how we can extricate ourselves. We've been hit with a claim for fourteen grand for four weeks delay."

"Jesus, Douglas, we're not due to start on site for at least another three or four weeks. That means they could take us for the same again before we are even on the site."

"You're right, Mark. We are preventing them from pouring the hundreds of concrete plinths for our pipes. Even if we give them drawings next week it takes at least month for their concrete to cure before we can position our pipes. Do you see the problem?"

"Yes, Douglas, now I see why you've been a bit quiet. What's next?"

"I'll think of something. Who knows...maybe a good fairy will wave a magic wand."

Part 8
Wed 17th Jan 1990

Franz Liseur offices ~ Clydebank
Douglas was in the office early to get a bit of quiet. He was sitting at John Logge's desk going over the drawings for Bluff. Something had caught his eye. He had great trust that his brain could often notice things that *seemed* normal but somehow triggered a nerve somewhere; a kind of warning but not an alarm; just 'unusual'. What he had seen was eluding him and he was testing his theory, scrutinising each drawing to rediscover what that elusive 'thing' was. The young engineer came in just before nine to find the boss at his desk. He offered a joke,

"Hello Douglas, are you swopping your office with me today?"

Douglas was so engrossed that he missed the boy's attempt at levity. What he was looking for was still eluding him. He looked up.

"Oh, morning John. I wanted a quick look at your drawings. Something's bugging me about this design but I can't quite bring it to the front of my brain."

John smiled and listened. He realised that it was perhaps disrespectful to try to be jocular. His boss was concentrating hard, searching for something important but indefinable. Douglas stood up and gave the lad back his chair.

"I'm sure it will come to me. In the meantime, I want to get you started on some details for the brackets for the external pipes. The drawings show the new heating pipes running along beside the old worn-out steam pipes. Do you see that?"

"Yes Douglas; all the way along the site for about eight kilometres. There are twelve drawings in a row to show all that. What would you like me to do?"

"The M.O.D. gave us a hot reception yesterday. We have to produce drawings or lose the job. Do twelve new tracings of the existing steam pipes. Show them with a single, heavy dotted line. Draw another solid single line alongside the existing pipes. Make the distance between them two metres. Add a prominent notice on each drawing clearly stating that the centre line of the new pipes is two metres from the centre line of the existing steam pipes for the full length of the site. Is that understood, John?"

"Yes, Douglas. I'll do twelve tracings with a big note on each. What's this all for?"

"It's to show the builder where to build concrete bases. Talk with Mark about adding details of what we need from Jarvis & Craig. The bases only need to be every three metres along the pipe. Mark will keep you right on this. These are simple location drawings and all the bases will be the same size and design. Okay son?"

"Yes Douglas. When do you need them done by?"

"The drawings don't have to be works of art, just simple details. Get them checked by Mark, let me see them, get them printed and hand delivered to the builders on Friday or, without fail, on Monday morning. Can you manage that in two days son?"

"Yes Douglas. I'll get started straight away."

"Good lad."

On his way back to his office Douglas stopped dead in his tracks. He spun round and went back up to the drawings on John's desk. He flipped to one showing a branch connection to one of the thirty-five buildings and exclaimed,

"Got it! The consulting engineers are idiots! Now we've got them."

John Logge looked at his boss running back down to his office and grabbing the telephone. He was intrigued but resisted the temptation to go and ask him ask what he had found.

Douglas had picked up the scent and was off and running; looking for blood. In these circumstances the young man thought it wise not to get in the way or he would be trampled. He would wait for Mark to come in. Then his curiosity might be satisfied. He pinned tracing paper to his drawing board to begin the process of setting out the pipe details.

Douglas flipped open his telephone number index at 'Y' and fired the number into his phone. A sweet feminine voice answered,

"Good morning. This is Young's Valves Ltd. Elsie speaking. How can I help you?"

"Hi Elsie, let me speak to David Young please?"

"Who's calling?"

"Tell him that it's Douglas Fairbairn."

A hearty voice came through the phone.

"Hello Douglas! How the devil are you? I hear you are back with Liseur now. To what do I owe the pleasure?"

"Hi David, I am settling in quickly and there are a few problems with a job at Culbin Forrest. Do you know it?"

"Ah! Glad you're back in contracting getting your feet wet my boy. Good luck. Yes I am aware of the Bluff Depot project. I was in on the design with a boy called Torquil Knight of Clark Chisholm. Must be well over a year since I was in to see him. I assume you've landed the contract. I suppose you want a good price for my lovely pressure-reducing valves?"

"Not just yet, David. I want to ask you why there are P.R.V.'s on the pipework?"

"That's an easy one. I get some difficult queries about our valves but this is simple. The valves lower the steam pressure to gain more latent heat before passing through the steam-to-hot water heat exchangers at each building. The buildings are then heated by the hot water, not the steam. But Douglas, why the question? I assume you would already know all that?"

"David, listen very carefully. What would you say if I told you that the main pipes are not carrying steam but medium pressure hot water?"

"I would say I am bitterly sorry to have spent the best part of a couple of years trying to get my P.R.V.'s specified by Torquil Knight. My valves will only work on steam and condensate systems. They simply will not function on any closed-loop water system. I suppose you will not require them now the job is no longer steam?"

"David, you have made my day!"

"Well, Douglas I'm glad you're happy. That order was worth about five grand to my company! A grand of that is my profit margin."

"Don't worry David. You will still get your order. Just don't deliver them to site unless I say so. The P.R.V.'s are still shown on the drawings. If they cancel these valves you can hit me with a twenty per cent cancellation charge and I'll ask for a variation order so you will get your profit.

"Nice one Douglas. Thank you for that. It's a shame because I quite liked that young fellow, Torquil Knight. That's a bad bloomer on his part."

"I suspected that was the case, David. The main reason I am calling you is mainly to ask you what happens if we fit these valves in a closed medium temperature hot water system?"

"Any water system that operates above boiling point, say maybe a hundred and twenty degrees Celsius or more will react violently. As soon as the pressure falls, the water flashes to steam; you get explosions in the pipework; the pipes start to dance up and down. Coupled with that problem, it is impossible for the water to get back into the return pipe and get back to the boiler house. It's madness to use these valves! I don't know of any text book that has a system like that in it!"

"Thanks David. I will have to talk this over with some of Liseur's technical people. It seems we have found a basic design fault. I'm duty bound under the contract to bring it to the attention of our client."

"Do you mean the M.O.D.?"

"Not this time. We are domestic subcontractors to the builders, Jarvis & Craig. We'll have to ask them to pass on the news. We met the M.O.D. boss, Jim Briggs, yesterday on another matter. He's a bully and will not take kindly to hearing from us so soon after he unceremoniously chucked my engineer and me out of his office. The builders, Jarvis & Craig were no help to us. They just rolled over and licked Briggs' arse."

"Well, Douglas, I wish you luck. I know Jarvis & Craig. Watch out with that bunch; they are very cost conscious and cutthroat with their sub-contractors. They put Ayrshire Heating into bankruptcy two years ago on the M.O.D. job down in Greenock. I had valves on that one and it cost my three grand in the end."

"Right David. I will be very wary. Liseur can buy and sell this builder. We are not about to go bust with these guys. Thanks for your help."

"Douglas. Before you go, let me warn you also about Clark Chisholm. They don't like their designs being queried. Just expect some flack from them. They are extremely high-handed when it comes to anyone questioning their design capability."

"So would I be in this situation. Don't worry, I'll be diplomatic."

"I'll be happy to assist you with any technical arguments you may need. I don't like being used for a year and then not even getting the courtesy of a *thank you but we are not using you.* Let me know if you need me."

"You are a gentleman and a scholar, David. This information has helped me enormously. I was certain this valve thing was a mistake but just wanted confirmation. I will take it from here and if I require more help I'll give you a bell. Cheers for now and thanks a lot. "

"Goodbye, Douglas. Good luck my boy. Oh! And welcome back to the how-de-do of contracting...in at the deep end straight away, Eh?"

"Yep! I hit the ground running and I'm loving it already. Cheers, David."

He replaced the phone and looked up to see Mark standing in his office doorway.

"Good morning, Mark. It looks like we have another letter to write to our esteemed friends Jarvis & Craig."

"Morning boss. How's that?"

Douglas explained the design error. Mark was taken aback.

"Are these consultants off their nuts? It's obvious to a dog in the street that this won't work!"

"It might be obvious to many people but the onus is with us alone to prove it is wrong.

Douglas lifted the intercom and called Helen through. She came in and sat down.

"Take a seat Mark, while I dictate these two letters. A short letter about the drawings first."

Douglas began,

Jarvis & Craig

17th Jan 1990
Attention of Mr J. Hadshaw

Dear Sirs,   R.N.A.D. Bluff (No 002)

Further to our attendance at yesterday's meeting with the M.O.D. we advise that detailed drawings showing the positions of the bases you are to build for our pipes will be in your hands on or before Monday 22nd January.

In line with our promise to mitigate delays, our normal four-week drawing programme has been shortened by three weeks and four days.

Accordingly we record a saving of contract time of three weeks and three days that we will use to nullify those delays you have levelled against us.

When you have these drawings, please oblige us by having these bases ready for our work to commence on site on Monday 29th January.

Yours Faithfully,

Douglas Fairbairn,
Contracts Manager
For: Franz Liseur, Scotland   *Ref HT/DF*

Mark was stunned at the gall of his boss,

"Douglas, they are going to love you. Do you seriously believe you will actually get away with a move like that?"

"Listen carefully, Mark. I'll try any move that saves us the big end of fourteen grand. Our good fairy has smiled on us but Joe Hadshaw will not be smiling when he gets this next one. I'd love to watch him telling the Supervising Officer that Clark Chisholm have made a mistake. Listen to this."

Douglas dictated his next letter.

Jarvis & Craig
17ᵗʰ Jan 1990
Attention of Mr J. Hadshaw

Dear Sirs,   R.N.A.D. Bluff (No 003)

Due to our summary ejection from yesterday's meeting, we advise that we will not be available for any further meetings involving direct contact with your client, particularly if that is in the presence of Mister James Briggs. We must therefore request that you advise your client of our suspicion as follows: -

Clause 2.0 of our mutual contract conditions requires that the Supervising Officer must be advised with alacrity of any suspicion of an error or omission relating to the drawings or the design of the systems.

In that connection Clause 2.0 obliges us to advise you that we have noticed a possible technical problem in respect of the design of the pipework systems shown on the contract drawings from Messrs Clark Chisholm.

Accordingly, 'in our capacity as a contractor and not as a licensed design professional', we state our belief that the use of pressure reducing valves on the medium temperature water heating pipes is technically wrong and will prove dangerous, if not fatal, to personnel or property.

We rely on this letter to free our company from any responsibility for any hazardous results from the failure of the Supervising Officer to rectify this error. Failure to so inform the Supervising Officer may place Jarvis & Craig in breach of contract.

We will carry out your instructions as required by our mutual contract but please be aware that we shall not install any system we consider dangerous as stated above.

Please advise your instructions within fourteen calendar days of receipt of this letter. In the absence of a reply we shall stop our work on the pipework systems until this technical issue is resolved.

Any delays resulting from your inability to properly instruct us in this matter will be recorded by us as part of a loss and expense claim against your company. Those delays will begin to be recorded after the expiry of fourteen calendar days from the date of this letter, viz. 31st January.

Yours Faithfully,

Douglas Fairbairn,
Contracts Manager
For: Franz Liseur, Scotland   *Ref HT/DF*

cc   Franz Liseur Lawyer, McMeikle & Huggett
cc   Jarvis & Craig Company Secretary {Hand delivered with receipt}

Douglas asked Helen to get the letters ready for signing by lunchtime. She left. Mark's face held a look of admiration. He shook his head and spoke,

"Well! Bugger me Douglas! You don't miss them and hit the wall. These drawings will put them right on the hot seat and this P.R.V. thing... that's really going to knock them for six. How did you spot that?"

"Don't know, Mark. Sometimes you notice that something is unusual but your brain doesn't pick up on it. It only gives a little flash in your head that's too quick to identify what it was. You're left to try figure it out. Maybe my few nights sleeping on this project made the old grey matter work overtime. Anyway, it's now out in the open. We've run it up the flagpole so, let's see if they'll salute it or shoot it?"

"It'll be them that's up the pole. And up shit creek if they ignore your warning!"

"We'll keep piling on the pressure. No pun intended. I want you to hand deliver these two letters this afternoon. Get the lassie to type receipts for each of them quoting their reference numbers. Don't leave without getting our pal Joe Hadshaw or someone from Jarvis & Craig to sign for them. They may be needed for the court case. Keep young Logge's nose down on his board to get the drawings over by hand to Joe on Friday if possible, but Monday at the latest. Let him work over the weekend if you think he's struggling."

"I'm on it boss but isn't it a bit early to talk about court cases; suing the builders?"

"No, we have to move fast. We're not ahead of them yet. The builders have set out to trap us. It's up to us to make them feel insecure if we are to get ourselves out of trouble."

"I get it. Is this the mischief you told me about yesterday, Douglas?"

"You could say that but there's more to come, Mark. When are those two sub- contractors due in? Is it today or tomorrow?"

"The controls guys are coming in today at two thirty. I already have five per cent off them so it should be a formality."

"What about the Ayrshire Insulation people?"

"They're due in at four this afternoon. Their guy Peter refused to give a discount. He told young Logge they want to *increase* their price because it's outwith their three months acceptance period."

"Oh did they? Right, Mark, use my office for your meetings. I'll be popping out at lunchtime but I'll sit in when you meet these guys from Ayrshire. Don't tell them who I am and don't agree anything with them. Keep them talking till I get back."

He got back just before the Ayrshire Insulation guys arrived and went over to sit beside Mark in the drawing office to explain the plan of action,

"When you're in my office I'll come in a few seconds later. I won't speak. You can introduce me as your colleague if you need to. If they offer you any papers I'll make a noise. That's your signal to refuse to take it. If they refuse to withdraw their higher offer I'll make another noise. That means thank them but kick them out the door...fast! Okay?"

"Yes boss!"

Helen phoned Mark at his desk to announce their arrival. Mark and John Logge ushered the two men into Douglas's empty office. Douglas sauntered in and sat in the corner as an observer thus giving his senior engineer the desk and the authority that went with it. The insulators had no idea of the reversal of positions and that was just how Douglas planned it. He did not know this particular company and kept a low profile while Mark went into his opening gambit.

"Thank you for coming in Alec and Peter. My name is Mark and my colleague is Douglas. This is my assistant, John, whom you spoke to recently on the telephone."

They all shook hands. Mark continued,

"We want to discuss your quotation with a view to giving you the order for this prestigious Ministry of Defence project at Bluff in Morayshire. In our call to you the other day, John asked you to look over your tender seeking ways to bring it to a lower figure. How did that go, Alec?"

"Well Mark, we noticed that our tender was issued to you in May of last year. It was open for acceptance for three months after which it would be subject to confirmation or adjustment."

"Yes I know, Alec. It's not unusual for a longer time to elapse between us tendering and being in a position to pass you an order. I hope you are not about to tell us your price has risen?"

"I am sorry to say that we have not been able to hold the cost down. An order from you today would have to be the subject of a new quotation from us. I have taken the liberty of bringing the revised tender for your consideration."

He slid an envelope over the table towards Mark. Douglas unfolded his arms, leant forward, placed his elbows on his knees and rested his chin on his hands. His feet made a clatter on the floor. The two visitors turned to stare at him because of his sudden and noisy movement. Mark responded strongly at the signal,

"This is not a new project. You are bound by your offer and I can't accept a tender higher than your first one which you quoted to us on a "fixed price" basis."

He pushed the proffered envelope back across the table and waited for the response.

"Eh, I know that we quoted a fixed price to you, Mark. But the acceptance period has expired."

Without hesitating, Mark spelt out his clear rebuttal of this silly argument,

"Alec, you know that is nonsense! Your quotation is for the work to be done in the summertime this year and this was made abundantly clear in the documents we sent you with our enquiry. If I had given you an order last July, surely your fixed price would include for the work being done a year later? Surely you must have allowed for that in your first offer?"

Alec looked shocked and struggled to find fault with Mark's reasoning. Maybe he thought he was fairly good at negotiating with clients but this was different. He was under instruction to get the order without giving any discount. Alec fully expected Liseur to say they would accept his original tender price but they were holding their ground. He forgot the standard reply. The smart argument was to say *if I got the order last year I could have purchased all of the expensive materials and put them in storage at last year's prices.* In his confusion he blurted out the wrong response,

"I hear what you're saying, Mark, but my instructions are to get you to accept my new price or we cannot accept your order."

He had missed out an important step in the negotiating process. He should have withdrawn his new quote, flung it in the bin and said he would accept an order for the full value of his old quote. That may just have been acceptable. But he didn't. He had blown his last chance. Douglas stood up, shook hands with Alec and Peter and left the room. Mark took Douglas's cue, got up, shook hands with both of them and left followed closely by young John Logge who had learned a lot about negotiations just by listening. He held the door open indicating their departure was required. Mark fired a parting shot,

"Thank you for your attendance chaps but we will go elsewhere for the insulation for this project."

They left. Over at Mark's desk Douglas stood smiling.

"Right Mark. I believe the second lowest price was Clyde Insulations. Get John here to phone them and ask for Mister Smith. Say we are offering him the job on a plate and the price is...that's where you put in Ayrshire's price, less five per cent."

"Douglas, how do you know he'll agree that?"

"Because, my young friend, I went to visit my mate, Gordon Smith after lunch. He agreed to accept our order on that basis."

Part 9
Thu18th Jan 1990

Franz Liseur offices ~ Clydebank
Douglas Fairbairn knew that at that moment both of his letters would be burning holes in Hadshaw's desk. Joe would probably have no clue how to deal with them; he was not a chess player. Douglas was right. Joe was

sitting fuming. *That smart bastard from Liseur is at it again, playing his sneaky childish games.*

Joe was never really sure if the setting out nonsense from Liseur was just a trick to gain time. This time though, he was certain this new technical rubbish about P.R.V.'S was one of Fairbairn's stupid ruses. Unable to see beyond his hatred of Douglas, Joe couldn't appreciate the dangerous legal minefield in which he would find himself if he ignored these letters. His reaction was that of an ordinary bricklayer, promoted beyond his skill level; jumping up and down in an ignorant rage; *why is this Liseur mob giving me all this hassle?*

He was determined to have their respect. After all, he was their client...not the other way around. *Have these so-called engineers no regard for their betters? Do they think I'll believe some daft story that a clever, university-trained, professional consultant had somehow made such a big mistake in his design that it could stop the project in its tracks? There's no way I'm going to be fooled again by such an out-and-out lie from this troublemaker, Fairbairn. It's time he was sorted out once and for all.*

By this time smoke was coming out of Joe Hadshaw's ears! He grabbed the phone,

"Get me Douglas Fairbairn!"

"Hello. Douglas Fairbairn here."

"You taking the piss, Fairbairn?"
    "That all depends who's at the other end."

"It's Joe Hadshaw. Now you listen to me, Fairbairn. You are in delay on this job, not us. Your drawings are late and it's going to take a month for those bases to cure ready for your work. That's all down to you. And now you want me to tell the client that the consultant has made a mistake and you intend to stop the work on site. It's daft. How can you stop the work on site if you've not even started yet? Listen you to me, Fairbairn, you've got another think coming if you believe I'm going to fall for any more of your stupid, hare-brained scams!"

Douglas studied the fingernails of his right hand while waiting for the rant to abate, and then adopted a pointedly amicable manner,

"Oh, hello Mister Hadshaw. You've got my letters then?"

The effect created a more irate harangue,

"Yes! And don't bother thinking that's the end of it. Believe me Fairbairn; there is no way I'm passing your crazy theories to my client. I'm telling you now that you're contractually bound to install this work as detailed on the drawings so, I hereby instruct you to get on with it!"

"Oh dear, Joe, I think you are being a bit hasty. Please understand, in the circumstances dictated by our contract that I can't comply with your verbal instruction; not even if you put it in writing and deliver it by registered post."

"You'll get nothing in writing! The contract is the only writing you'll get. You've signed it and you will get on with it or I assure you, there will be big trouble!"

"Well that's not quite correct. My letter to you states that unless the client advises me how to eradicate the error and avoid a dangerous event, then under current health and safety legislation, to avoid injury to personnel, I shall be *forced* to stop the work."

"You are tying yourself up in knots, Fairbairn so, you can just go ahead and hang your fucking self!"

"Well Joe, I'm afraid that's not quite right either. First of all, the rope is not round *my* neck, it's your responsibility now if something goes wrong. Secondly, you're using a mixed metaphor.

"Stick your mixed metaphor up your arse, Fairbairn! How's it my responsibility?"

"Simple. You are *my* client. I have no legal connection to *your* client. I've told you there's a serious technical error in the design. You are bound by the same contract as me and if you don't pass that information on to *your* client *you* will become liable. If that is not clear to you then you should read my letter again. If I don't get clarification in fourteen days I will be legally obliged to stop the work. You will be asked to explain that. Don't expect me to bail you out this time, Joe."

There was a notable silence from Hadshaw. Douglas kept the phone to his ear waiting for a reply. All he heard was Joe Hadshaw's laboured breathing. He continued to listen, rather than hang up. That would be a pointless display of superiority. *Hadshaw obviously feels well out of his depth. It would be churlish of me to rub salt into*

Joe's bruised ego by slamming down the phone. He smiled at his *own* mixed metaphor. Joe's heavy breathing continued. Douglas coughed to let him know he was holding on. A quavering voice whispered back,

"I've read your letter again. You are one smart bastard, Fairbairn. I'm going to show you just how smart I am. You will not get a reply to this letter and I have no intention of passing your mind games on to my customer. The shit will hit the fan if you dare to withdraw from the site. Your letter is now in the bin. Let me see how smart you really are? You'd better have good lawyers ready!"

Before the irate idiot could slam down his phone, Douglas quickly interjected,

"Okay, Mister Hadshaw. If you want to play silly buggers, that's entirely up to you. I'm pleased you read my letter again. Perhaps before you binned it, you should have read the codicil?"

Hadshaw evidently had no idea of what a codicil was and simply snarled a question,

"What dae you mean?"

"Our letter informs you, at the bottom of the page, that our lawyers in Glasgow already have a copy of it. As we speak, I am looking at a receipt for the other copy, duly signed by your company secretary. Take my advice Mister Hadshaw; do what I advise and you will avoid being sued."

Douglas now felt superior enough to hang up before the guy could respond. He was satisfied that he had convinced Jarvis & Craig's man of the importance of telling the their client of the error.

Just in case they acted like dopes and still refused, he had a fall back strategy. He had to ensure that the Clark Chisholm people were made aware of this serious blunder. Although he relished a bit of contractual mischief, Douglas also had a high regard for safety as well as a desire to avoid any major embarrassment to the consulting engineers.

Having worked in three consulting firms he had experience of similar situations. You had to be a bit subtle when advising professional designers of their mistakes. As often as not it would be something fairly easy to fix and not too costly if found early; perhaps only requiring minor alterations to a set of figures or some dimensions.

This error on Bluff was more serious than that. There would be dire implications if it was ignored or if his firm were to be coerced and bullied into installing the system as designed. Douglas suspected that waiting to fix it much later in the project could be costly and time-consuming for all concerned, not just Franz Liseur. His primary aim was to make sure it didn't cost Liseur anything.

It was time to disclose this design error to Tony Surtal. If this became bigger than Liseur's Scottish branch office could handle, help would be needed from the head honchos in London, Paris or even the research and development boffins in Switzerland.

A quick explanation was all that was needed to persuade Tony to call London, alerting them to a possibly protracted and costly contractual wrangle. Tony Surtal agreed with Douglas's idea to involve the P.R.V. supplier, David Young; asking him to make a courtesy visit to Torquil Knight. In that way it would give the young consultant a chance to review the P.R.V question. Then he could start to prepare some kind of face-saving solution before it became expensive or cost him his job...or both.

A quick phone call to Mister Young got him to come in for a brief meeting that afternoon. David was eager to make such a visit to Clark Chisholm and explain why these valves should never be used in a closed-water system. He had nothing to lose. He had Liseur's official order for the expensive valves. It was looking fairly certain that the consultants would be content to issue an instruction to omit them from the design. David would then get cancellation costs as promised by Douglas. By a call from David to Torquil Knight an appointment was arranged for the following Monday at about eleven o'clock.

On Monday afternoon, Douglas would learn the consultant's reaction and more importantly, what the decision might be to rectify the glaring mistake with the minimum of fuss. The main thing was that Douglas wanted to start on site on the following Monday. Everything was being geared up for that. It would be a pity to have to stop the contract a week after starting. This was not a game anymore.

The work had to be done. After all, they *were* in business to make money. The hope was, they *would* make some money, not lose it. A little time had been gained to get Liseur's preparations underway.

More time was definitely needed to obstruct Jarvis & Craig's delay notices under the penalty clause. Liseur had to overtake and stay ahead of the main contractor. Otherwise they would be unable to avoid huge charges being levelled against them. That was not an option and Douglas knew he must ensure that it did not happen.

Part 10
Fri 19th Jan 1990

Jarvis & Craig's offices ~ Govan
After he had calmed down, Joe Hadshaw had second thoughts about Douglas's letter about the P.R.V.'s. He decided to sleep on it and get hold of Hugh Jarvis. It would then be up to his boss to choose to ignore it or pass it on to the Ministry of Defence.

Jarvis read the letter and didn't attempt to hide his exasperation,

"What's the matter with you, Joe. Of course you must pass it on, otherwise we will be left holding the hot end of the poker. This is a game of pass-the-parcel. Jim Briggs won't hold on to it for any longer than it takes to phone Clark Chisholm. It's their mistake, not the MOD, not ours and, more importantly, it's not Franz Liseur's."

Hadshaw was utterly deflated. He hoped Jarvis would agree that Liseur's were playing silly buggers. Instead he seemed to be taking their side. He reigned in his thoughts of revenge on the two who made him to feel like a junior schoolboy in the big boys' playground. He whispered,

"What do you want me to do?"

"Christ, Joe! It's simple. Phone Briggs and read him the letter. Then send him a copy with a compliment slip signed by you. Get permission to send a copy to Clark Chisholm for the attention of the guy whose name is on the drawings. I seem to remember it was an odd name."

Joe was happy to inform him that the name was Torquil Knight.

"That's it! Torquil...damned funny name, it's his fault. He's the designer but I want his boss to see this letter before it gets to that fellow. Is that quite clear?"

"Just what I was thinking. Thanks for your help, Hugh!"

Jarvis dropped his eyebrows and pursed his lips. Joe turned and hurried towards the door. His boss's scowl said it all. Hadshaw's days at the front of this project could very well be numbered. Hugh halted him in his effort to escape, and queried Liseur's letter nullifying the fourteen thousand damages claim.

"Yes, Hugh, they did their drawings about four weeks early."

"Bollocks! Send another one for six weeks for January and February."

"Yes Hugh, I was just going to see the two surveyors to get that done."

"Well don't let me stop you. Do it now Joe. Tonight's post!"

Part 11
Mon 22nd Jan 1990

Clark Chisholm offices Glasgow

Torquil Knight was at his desk. He took a moment to reflect on why he was feeling so good within himself. The past twelve months had proved less traumatic. His flatmate had secured a position with the Peurova partnership in North Queensferry. He was delighted that David had decided to stay in their flat. He bought a second-hand, 650cc, T100, Triumph Bonneville motorbike and rode it to his office in Fife every day.

Another reason for Torquil's current euphoria was that the Bluff project was still in that quiet, post-tender stage during which the mechanical contractor was not yet underway with the work on site. Also, for almost a year, there had been no need to subject himself to the mercy of that ogre of the M.O.D., James Briggs. Soon he could enjoy attending site meetings up there in Forres and took comfort from the knowledge that his torturer would not be at those gatherings. His real joy though, was the prospect of travelling up the day before each meeting to stay the night at his parents' house and to spend the evening with his girl friend.

Phillipa Grant and Torquil had hardly had a relationship since he left Forres to attend the university in Glasgow. She had gone to St. Andrews University to study business law and economics. Her future career would be to work as an accountant in her family firm of biscuit manufacturers. The company, *Forres Flake Fingers,* was famous throughout the world. This year she would become the fourth generation to enter the management group of the biggest employer in the town. Her dad, Gregory Grant, had suggested that Torquil might be his chief engineer one day; looking after the myriads of mechanical apparatus and services in the huge factory complex overlooking the town.

That prospect held some attraction for the young man but he wanted to gain experience in the hard world of building services down south in the central belt. It was natural though, for him and Phillipa to talk about their plans for when they might get married and settle down. He mused on their recent tête-à-tête by phone when they talked about that again. The strong bond that had sustained their long relationship from schooldays till now was clearly helping them to make abiding promises to each other, rather than rushing into juvenile, love-struck decisions. He felt the warmth that radiated from her; the reassurance that their distance apart was nothing more than a space filled with their mutual respect and love.

His loving thoughts were soon dispersed when, just before ten o'clock Sean O'Casey appeared at his side and handed him a letter. While his junior read it, Sean hovered over him, watching the boy's face turn red as he realised he was once again in trouble. Torquil turned to look up at his boss's face and an unspoken question refused to dislodge itself from his larynx. O'Casey took the letter back. To Torquil's surprise, Sean displayed an unusual level of affection by patting him on the shoulder and speaking in a whisper,

"Relax son. The contractors are playing games. Don't worry your head about this. You got the job out the door. It's now up to those comedians to get it sorted out.

You concentrate on your other projects. You just let Dean Chisholm and me worry about the one at Bluff. We don't make mistakes in this firm. Okay?"

The young man relaxed. In spite of his relief at not being publicly castigated for this alleged error in his design, he did feel a bit odd that his boss was taking it so well. His voice returned,

"Yes, Sean. But there might be something in what those Liseur people are saying. Maybe I should take another look at the calculations...just to be certain?"

"Not necessary Torquil. I've discussed this with Mister Chisholm. We will not be railroaded by *any* contractor, let alone this French mob. These valves are not pressure *reducing* valves, they are pressure *regulating* valves; do you understand?"

"Not really, Sean. I would say that those are both the same thing. Are they not?"

Sean O'Casey had simply invented the two names for the P.R.Vs. As an ex-plumber he had no idea what either of his valve descriptions meant. *Reducing* and *regulating* seemed to him to be opposites therefore if one was wrong then the other was correct. He had no technical knowledge of the purpose of this type of valve or in what circumstances it should or should not be used. Blind to his ignorance and using his position of seniority, he continued to reinforce his erroneous statement by assuring his young colleague that there was not a problem with his design,

"They're not the same son. They're two different valves. Just remember that you are innocent till proved guilty. There is no way this Fairbairn guy can show we have made any mistake. He is not a designer like you. Liseur have no authority in this contract. This nonsense will peter out, I assure you. It will be their nose that gets bloody. Don't you waste any time on it. You forget about this project, including the site meetings. The supervising officer will keep us fireproof if there's any more mischief from Liseur's man."

Little did O'Casey appreciate Torquil's predisposition to learn for *himself* if there was any suggestion of an error in his work. The more the man spoke to him, any respect Torquil had for O'Casey due to his seniority in the firm, lessened. He had no intention of just accepting this implausible cover story without revisiting his files,

"I hear you Sean, but if you don't mind, I still want to review my calculation file?"

"Please yourself but don't waste any of the *firm's* time on it. Remember, you've spent all the fees getting it out to tender. Checking your paperwork will have to be done in your own time, lad."

"Yes Sean. Bye the way, David Young is coming in this morning at about eleven to ask me about the P.R.V.'s. Do you want to be there when I talk to him?"

O'Casey, with charm completely dissipated, reverted to type and bawled at the youngster,

"Bugger me, Knight! Are you totally stone fucking deaf? Why are you seeing this guy? "

Torquil flinched,

"He phoned on Friday for an appointment."

"You're not to see him! Tell the receptionist to send him to me. Don't get involved in this. I will deal with him. Is that understood?"

Torquil wilted,

"Yes, sir."

O'Casey growled,

"Sean!"

Torquil looked away, "Yes, Sean."

O'Casey shook his head, tutted his annoyance and strode back to his office. Once again Sean O'Casey had figuratively skelped Torquil's backside. And had done it in full view of his other colleagues. The lad was no longer the happy boy who came to work that morning. But neither was he stupid. He was sure the letter had made a valid point but could not check it out till after work. He thought it strange that the boss could just brush something like that under the carpet. *Surely a check was called for to counter Liseur's assertion?* Sean's words were ringing in his brain; *we never make mistakes in this firm.* He shivered. *Am I going to be the first one to be guilty of that?* He decided to take his files home. One way or another, he was going to find out. *If I find I've made a mistake then that know-all, Sean O'Casey will be a fool if he ignores it!*

Back at his flat, he told David he had some homework and after tea he was going to shut himself in his bedroom to concentrate on it. He had to figure out why Liseur said that it was wrong to use the P.R.Vs.

He settled down to study his files and cross-refer to his university notes, in particular his submitted thesis dealing with the properties of steam as a heating medium and energy carrier. Few people on his course had any interest in the subject. Steam was expensive to produce and complex to control. Because of that it was being used less and less in the heating industry. His specialist knowledge had figured highly in the Clark Chisholm decision to take him on.

After some solid investigation he began to believe that Liseur might be right. There was no sudden flash of inspiration. It had taken a considerable time to dawn on him that he had been guilty of a schoolboy error. It was just over a year since, in his panic to find an answer to the cost restraints set by the bullying Briggs, he had clutched at what seemed a brilliant lifesaving solution. He sat back in his chair, grabbed his face with widespread fingers and sucked in air between his two pinkies pressed over his lips. Just as Davy came in with a tray holding two jam doughnuts and two mugs of cocoa, Torquil shouted at the wall,

"I...am...such...an. Idiot!"

Davy put the tray on the table and stood still beside his pal,

"Hey, Torky! Has it taken you two hours to find out what I could have told you at tea time."

Torquil didn't laugh. He just turned to his friend and burst into tears. David was shocked to witness his friend's breakdown. He flushed with embarrassment at his thoughtless levity. It was crystal clear that Torquil was in bad trouble. In an effort to console his sobbing friend, he pulled in a chair, sat down and put a comforting arm round his shoulder. In part to apologise and also to reassure Torquil that he was there to support him, he spoke in a low, sympathetic voice,

"The last thing you need is my silly joke, Torky. Tell me what this is all about? Maybe I can help?"

Torquil pulled out his hankie to wipe away his tears and compose himself enough to look at David. He managed a grin that was more of an apology than any attempt at humour. In indirect proportion to his mental trauma, his reply was quiet and understated,

"I'm sorry, Davy. I've got a bit of a problem. I've made a bad mistake on the ministry job I designed a year ago. The contractors have spotted it and a letter has come in to my boss. He assured me that the problem is not for us and said it's up to the contractors to fix it. He told me I've not to handle the job anymore or discuss it with anyone. I can't even go to the site meetings. I'm scared, Davy. I don't know what to do."

David listened closely, trying to understand Torquil's personal difficulty. He could see that Torquil's bosses were most likely attempting a whitewash; coercing their inexperienced colleague into colluding with them and trying to compel him to keep his mouth shut to preserve the firm's reputation. He thought it best if he could persuade his friend to defy the pressure from his boss. They would have to allow him to find a way to sort it. It was tenuous but he gave it a try,

"Come on Torky, it can't be that bad. Now that you understand the problem, it's sure to be easy to fix. It would be worse if you hadn't found out in time. Tell O'Casey that since the job hasn't started yet, you can just instruct a change of design. The cost is bound to be minimal."

"No Davy, it'll need more than a simple change. My whole design is screwed up. I'll have to explain to the boss tomorrow morning. Major alterations will be needed to put it right and it *will* prove costly. It's all a bit technical and I don't want to bore you with it."

One thing that David had learned in his own short career was that a problem shared was a problem halved. He wanted more information so he could fully grasp how serious this thing was. Then he would be able to help with the solution or at least assist Torquil to reason it out. It would allow his friend to feel confident when he confronted Sean O'Casey with the magnitude of the blunder. He grabbed a doughnut and cocoa, sat back in his chair, adopted an attitude of rapt attention and said,

"I can do 'technical', Torky Knight. So, try me."

Five seconds later Torquil had a jam doughnut in one hand and a mug of cocoa in the other. He spent a few more seconds to consider how to fulfil his pal's request. *This isn't going to be easy. How can I explain to David if I'm not even sure how I fell into the trap; rushing into such a stupid decision; never mind figuring out how I'm going to put it right? David is a structural engineer so; maybe I'd better start from first principles,*

"David, have you ever seen steam coming out of the spout of a boiling kettle?"

"Yes."

"Wrong! You saw condensation. If you look carefully at the spout there is a bit just at the outlet of the spout that you can't see. It is steam. It's an invisible gas. Got it?

"Yes."

"Now then, you must know that the temperature of boiling water is a hundred degrees centigrade?"

"Yes, it's then that the water turns into steam."

"Right. Now why does the steam come out of the kettle so fast?"

"That's easy. It's because when the steam expands to a greater volume the pressure increases and forces the steam out of the spout. Where are you going with this, Torky?"

"You'll see in a minute. Now tell me what would happen if the spout was sealed while heat was still being applied?"

"That's easy too. The kettle would explode as the pressure built up."

"Correct, David. Now you can understand that steam, being a gas, can be compressed. Held in a kettle, pressure builds up. That's how a steam heating system works. Pressure pushes the steam along the pipe to where it is wanted. Are you still with me?"

"So far."

"Okay, that's good. Now, this is the clever bit about steam. It takes a lot of energy to turn boiling water into steam. That extra energy is called *hidden or latent heat,* because when all the water is turned into steam the temperature is still a hundred degrees. The latent heat is stored in the steam, like a battery storing electricity.

"I understand that, Torquil, but what's the connection with steam?"

"When you want to get the heat from the steam at a hundred degrees you just allow it to condense back into water inside a radiator. It gives you back its *hidden* heat and becomes water again at a hundred degrees. You see?"

"Ah! Now I get it. It's so simple. You recover the latent heat by letting the steam condense back into water. How is that a problem at Bluff?"

"I'll come to that. First you need to appreciate that to condense the steam you need to reduce the pressure. To do that you use a use a pressure-reducing valve fitted to the pipe. The water goes back to the boilers at a hundred degrees.

"Okay. I get all that. So what went wrong?"

"The old and dilapidated steam pipes at Bluff had to be removed in their entirety. My plan was to install a new steam system with many improvements but it was going to cost over a million pounds. Briggs killed my solution by demanding lower and lower costs. You can't argue with a man like that, he's a bombastic bully and uses his power like a gun to your head. If you oppose him, he'll find a way to get rid of you or make you run away and hide. My only option was to put in a cheaper scheme. I chose high-pressure water as the heating medium."

"But, Torky, a year ago, did you not say high-pressure water was a brilliant design idea to fit his cost demands? What's happened to change your mind?"

"I didn't see it at the time. The thirty-five separate buildings on the site are all low-pressure water systems. My mistake was in keeping the pressure reducing valves."

"Maybe I'm being thick but why does that not work?"

'For one thing, David, you can't put high-pressure water into a low-pressure-system because the high-pressure water will immediately flash into steam. Secondly, the return water from the low-pressure system will not flow back into the high-pressure return pipes."

"Oh, now I see what you mean.

"Yes, and now so do I. It is so utterly simple that I didn't see it at the time."

"Jesus, Torquil. How can you fix it? Am I right in thinking there is a solution?"

"Nope. I have no idea how to get out of this. But it has been useful trying to explain it to a layman, David. Much obliged."

"Think nothing of it. I think the best thing for you is to get to bed. It might look a bit better in the morning. Maybe you'll get a brainwave after a good night's sleep?"

Davy sat still; watching with concern as Torquil adopted a worrying stillness. *The talking seems to have calmed him but was he any nearer to finding a way out than when they began their chat?* Torquil had sat back, closed his eyes, clasped his hands on his lap, rested his chin on his chest and sighed deeply. It was in that state that his brain gave him another jolt. *Oh no! How can I tell Phillipa that I'm off the project and won't be making regular visits back home to see her before my site meetings. That's another weight for me to carry but I won't be sunk. I'll sort it all tomorrow.* He opened his eyes, looked at his friend and tried to project his bravest smile of decisiveness,

"I don't think it's going to be like that, David. Tomorrow I'll have to make a full confession to Dean Chisholm. Thanks for listening to me. I'll sit a while and get my mind ready for tomorrow. You get off to your bed, Davy."

Behind his closed eyelids Torquil had visions of a dole queue. He regretted that he had been bullied. Sean

O'Casey and Jim Briggs had both hounded him to get the Bluff tender down in price and out the door. Under that pressure he had missed the obvious. His panic had forced him to clutch at any straw. On reflection he wished he had the courage at the time to stand up to the M.O.D., even if it meant the sack.

Now, sitting alone again, eyes closed, without his friend, Torquil's mind drifted into a very difficult mental place. Although O'Casey had told him to ignore the problem, he knew instinctively that it was best to admit such a costly error. *Most likely O'Casey will just dismiss my confession. The power to correct this lies with those men above me. I'll always be at their mercy. If they stall my attempts to put this to rights it will drag on and on till they finally get caught out and then there will be hell to pay.*

His depression deepened. Although his thought processes were pristine, he had no idea then how near to the truth his prediction was. His negative thoughts were powerful but he overcame the urge to descend further into his gloom. He rallied, sat up, opened his eyes wide and with his brain alert, made his decision. It was clear what he must do. He rehearsed in his mind how he would address the problem,

First thing in the morning I'll insist on talking it all over with Sean O'Casey. Then Dean Chisholm must be advised to make a call to Mister Briggs to make him aware of the problem. They must stop the project and allow it to be redesigned. This is their last chance to help me and save the firm from embarrassment. If after that they refuse to act and allow me to stay with the project, then I'll take matters into my own hands. They won't do that to me again. I won't give Briggs and

O'Casey the gratification of hurting me. O'Casey won't get the pleasure of sacking me.

He opened his notebook, took the cover from the top of his parker fountain pen and in his best handwriting began to compose a letter,

Dear Mr O'Casey,

Due to the catastrophic error I have made in the design of the Bluff project, and your refusal to rectify it, I wish to tender my...

His plan was to spend tomorrow morning making copies of all of his files and drawings to take home at lunchtime. That way he could work on the design problem without being accused by O'Casey of wasting any of the firm's time.

In the afternoon he intended to demand a meeting with O'Casey and Dean Chisholm to explain the seriousness of his design error.

Should this approach be refused, he would leave his letter on O'Casey's desk just prior to his quiet and dignified exit. He would not say goodbye.

Part 12
Tue 23rd Jan 1990

Franz Liseur offices ~ Clydebank
"Hello. Douglas Fairbairn."

"Hello, Douglas. David Young here. I need to warn you about the consultants. They are not going to do anything about these P.R.V.'s.

"Come again? I thought you were in to see them yesterday morning. Did you tell them their design wouldn't work if they used your valves?"

"I had an appointment to see their young engineer, Torquil Knight, but I was diverted to a very irate senior engineer, Sean O'Casey. He told me in no uncertain terms to stop wasting their time with spurious ideas concerning their design."

"Is that so?"

"Yes, I was only in his office for about a minute. He made it clear that there were no mistakes in their design and ushered me out into the street. I've just had the equivalent of 'the bum's rush'! These people are in the early stages of a cover-up. On the way to the exit they threatened to remove my firm from their list of favoured suppliers. What should I do now, Douglas? I'm afraid I'm at a loss as to how to assist you without putting my firm in jeopardy."

"Well, David, I admire your attempt to save their skins but it would seem there is no way you can do anything for them. It's a pity they are being pig-headed. I won't expect you to go there again but your product technical data may be required if this goes legal."

"That's not a problem. I'll give you all the help you need."

"Thanks for that. I've had a closer look at the design. It's not just a case of taking out your P.R.V.'s; the whole system is wrong. I expect they will come to realise that. A few changes in the drawings now, before we start installations, would be costly but the design could be saved. If they leave it too late then it will be much harder and more costly to fix."

"Is that so, Douglas?"

"Yes David, you said it started out as a steam installation. Now they've changed it to a sealed water system. Why do you suppose they did that?"

"I never thought about that. There is no reason I can think of, unless maybe the M.O.D. wanted the capital cost brought down?"

"That's exactly what I think happened David. I've met the big guy, Jim Briggs in the M.O.D. Edinburgh. I bet he has put the consultant through the wringer. Torquil Knight has panicked and done a quick hatchet job on his design to get the costs agreed and the job out to tender. Remember you said that it took you about two years to finalise your discussions with them? I'm guessing it took Torquil Knight that kind of time to *get* the costs agreed."

"It all seems plausible Douglas. What are you going to do now?"

"Only one thing I can do. I'll discuss this with Tony and make a suggestion to him."

David Young chuckled down the phone,

"What might that be if I may be so bold as to enquire?"

Douglas Fairbairn didn't smile,

"I'm going to ask Tony's permission to bury these fuckers!"

"Good luck with that, Douglas."

Tony Surtal wasn't keen to do what Douglas suggested,

"It's not a good idea to make the consultants look silly. They can deny us access to new work; especially in Scotland's two *big smokes;* the central belt and Aberdeen. I'm not a friend of Clark Chisholm as a firm but I've played golf with Dean Chisholm at his club in Troon. That gives me an excuse to phone on some pretext and discuss the design bloomer as a side issue."

Tony fully understood the severe implications of doing nothing. Not that he was worried for Liseur's reputation. If Tony played the game correctly, only the *consultants* would suffer embarrassment by trying to hide their error. Douglas had put their letter of warning exactly in the right places to protect Liseur if this went too far to be stopped, and it all ended up in court.

Liseur's lawyers were top notch. They had phoned Tony soon after reading their copy of Douglas's letter. Their advice was sound. Tony should go to the head of Clark Chisholm and advise them that they could be at risk. Then confirm the conversation by registered letter copied to the builders and to them. Tony should allow the installation to continue at site only when they get permission in writing from their client, Jarvis & Craig.

Douglas was content with this new information. Having strong legal muscle meant he was being guided and protected by people he could trust. It was no longer a game. He watched with quiet respect as Tony picked up the phone and dialled.

"Can I speak with Mister Chisholm please? It's Tony Surtal of Franz Liseur here."

"Tony! How the devil are you old boy?"

"Oh, you know? Keeping the wolf from the door. Making a crust and all that. How are you after our last wee battle at my club at Cowlairs?"

"I put it down to the weather and my new clubs. I don't usually win by so much but I suppose you just don't play so well in the rain, Tony?"

"Come off it, Dean! I let you win. After all... you are the consultant and I'm only a poor contractor."

"Ever the diplomat Tony. I take the win in the spirit it was meant. Thanks for the game. Do you want to try your luck again?"

"Yes, early next Tuesday morning would be good. How's your diary. I've got a slot for Troon, King's Course for 10:30. We could have some lunch down there if you have the time?"

"Let me look at my diary. Yes, my afternoon is tied up but I'm free all morning. I'll be happy to do nine holes. Winner pays for lunch. I'll see you there at ten. Okay?"

"Fine. I've marked that in. Just a wee point before you go. There is a slight problem with the job at Bluff Armaments Depot."

In an instant, Dean Chisholm's affable manner changed

"Oh? Tell me more?"

Tony eased the Clark Chisholm senior partner into the knowledge of a possible need for some alterations that if not addressed fairly quickly, could be very costly and time consuming for all parties. Dean listened without a word, ensuring he was fully informed of the implications for his firm. His response was short but not sweet,

"I don't like the sound of this, Tony. Let me talk to my colleagues. I'll call you back shortly."

Tony hung up. His teeth were biting the right-hand side of his lower lip. He looked at Douglas and sighed,

"Dean Chisholm is *not* a happy chap."

"Not surprising. I hope he can talk sense to his underlings."

They spoke for a few minutes about Bluff and a couple of other jobs. Tony was content to see that his Contracts Manager was relishing all of the various challenges but most especially this one at Bluff. He had only been back in the firm for twelve days and already there was the mummy and daddy of a problem with the very job Tony thought was going to be quick and easy. He was starting to think that cutting the tender price to ensure he got the contract might, in hindsight, have been unwise. From a cash-flow point of view it was ominous to be at the start of a potential financial disaster. The phone rang.

"Tony Surtal here."

"Tony. It's Dean Chisholm. Listen to me very carefully. Do nothing. Say nothing. Get on with the job. Get it finished. I am assured it will work. I will put this in writing. Golf on Tuesday is off I'm afraid. I have had an urgent call to attend the M.O.D."

"Short and sweet, Dean. I need a letter of instruction from our client, Jarvis & Craig, or I'll be forced to stop the project?"

"I'll see that you get one but you are making a very big mistake. My firm will never admit to your spurious allegation of a design error. Let me remind you that you are a domestic sub contractor to Jarvis & Craig. I have instructed all my team to refuse any further interaction with you on this project at Bluff. Farewell Tony."

Dean hung up. Tony very slowly replaced the receiver while he considered his next move. He turned his chair round and looked out of the window to the tree-lined park outside. He was still wincing from Dean Chisholm's brevity...*nothing nice about that call.*

Douglas sat patiently, watching and waiting. Tony realised Franz Liseur now had a tricky problem to navigate. The battle lines had been drawn. They were being challenged to prove their theory that the design was so faulty that it would not work. Otherwise, they would be branded as troublemakers. They would more than likely be removed from the MOD lists and probably many consulting firms' lists as well. Not a good prospect for future business in Scotland.

Douglas had certainly made a name for *himself* by pinning a target to his back. The builders, the M.O.D. and Clark Chisholm would be out to make his life, and Liseur's business, as difficult as possible.

Tony pondered two options. Tell Douglas to ignore the problem and just to get on with it or hide behind the barricades in a battle of attrition that was bound to ensue if they stood up to the bullies. He didn't like the former. It was the coward's way out. That was what Dean Chisholm was doing; hoping some miracle would save his firm's reputation. The latter meant assembling Liseur's big guns and attacking the enemy's weakest point; the faulty design. It *was* wrong and it was up to Liseur to find a way to *prove* it. He spun his chair back round, looked Douglas in the eye and smiled; decision made.

"Right Douglas! I agree with you. Let's bury these fuckers! And we might as well shove Jarvis and his mob into the hole with them."

"How's that?"

"I was reluctant to show you Jarvis's latest letter on damages. They say that the concrete takes time to set and won't let us onto it with our pipes till the end of February. That means six weeks delay costing us twenty-one thousand quid. How are we to nullify this one, Douglas?"

Douglas smiled,

"Oh, I expect I'll think of something, Tony."

But Douglas felt sure he'd have to do more than rely on his good fairy.

Part 13
Tue 23rd Jan 1990

Jarvis & Craig offices ~ Govan
Hugh Jarvis got Joe Hadshaw to sit and listen while he read out the letter that had come in by fax from James Briggs.

Jarvis & Craig
Attention Mister H. Jarvis
23 Jan 1990   *Contract at R.N.A.D. Bluff*

You are hereby instructed to advise your sub-contractor, Franz Liseur, that there is no question of changing the design of the mechanical installation at the R.N.A.D base at Bluff. You must proceed to install the mechanical installations in accordance with the contract drawings and specifications.

You are further instructed to inform your sub-contractor that we shall ignore any further unsolicited opinions concerning the design for this project from them.

Yours etcetera,

James Briggs
M.O.D. Edinburgh

He handed the letter to Joe Hadshaw whose face was a picture; it lit up with a wide grin of satisfaction and he let out a sigh of perverse pleasure. He spoke through clenched teeth,

"This will sicken them. This will shut them up. Those guys at Liseur think they're clever bastards but the consultants have done their homework. What's the best way to deal with this, boss?"

"It's entirely up to you. Personally, I would just send them a copy under a covering letter without any comment except, *let us have no more nonsense from you about P.R.V.'s.*"

"That's just what I was thinking. I'll get that off in the post tonight."

Jarvis was not impressed. He had altered his opinion of Joe Hadshaw's capabilities to run this project. Not only was Joe not confident enough to handle the smart personnel at Liseur, but also these recent letters were ominous. *It looks like this simple project could turn into a bit of a battle. I must make sure we end up on the winning side.*

"No, Joe. Get the letter typed and delivered by hand tomorrow morning; and get a receipt signed by Surtal or Fairbairn. And another thing Joe, I will attend the site meetings with you."

Joe Hadshaw shuddered, turned and left without a word.

Part 14
Wed 24th Jan 1990

Franz Liseur offices ~ Clydebank
Tony signed the receipt for the Jarvis & Craig letter with the attached M.O.D. letter. He read these and immediately called Jules Dispard to inform him and discuss a strategy. He called for Douglas to join him, waited while he read the letter, then joked,

"We are not going to need big shovels to bury these people, Douglas."

"So it would seem, Tony. This is getting serious but contractually it's also very interesting. What's our plan now that they've decided to help us by digging their own graves?"

"We will comply. This is a crystal clear instruction from the very top. We will not react in any way by phone or by letter. Just get the work started on site."

"Okay, Tony. We're starting on Monday."

"Fine, Douglas. The backroom boys in our company are on the case. We are into the early stages of building our Defences. Jules Dispard is assembling our best team of engineers, lawyers, and accountants. Our in-house hydraulics experts have already begun a technical appraisal of the Clark Chisholm faulty design. Out of that we'll devise the best legal and contractual strategy."

"That gives me great satisfaction, Tony. In Peurova we had a similar arsenal of big guns to back us up when occasions like this occurred. Sometimes you wonder why some authorities believe they can get away with anything just because they have power over you. It'll take time, but I'm sure we'll come off best in the end."

"I agree Douglas but it seems that every one is against us. We must build arguments that can't be refuted by our client, Jarvis & Craig, or indeed any one above them; up to and including Mister James Briggs."

"Absolutely, Tony. I'll keep my hands on this project and take the site meetings. I can't allow them to bludgeon Mark and gain any ground."

"I agree. If you want me at the meetings then just ask."

"Sure, Tony. We might need all our troops to beat this lot. Jarvis just want to steal our money. The consultant is blinkered to a simple design error and I don't know why. That bumptious bastard, Briggs' only reason for being is to shit on people from a great height and boost his already overblown self-image. There won't be many meetings. You should attend them all if we are to be sure of winning."

"Okay. I'll play it your way, Douglas. Let's go get them!"

CHAPTER FOUR

Contention

Part 1
Mon Jan 29th 1990

Bluff Depot

Liseur's site foreman, Angus MacLauchlan, arrived at the depot with a squad of fitter- welders. Their first job was to erect four timber site huts inside the armaments depot. The security men would not let Liseur's lorries enter their gates with the huts, tools and equipment. Angus tried to reason with the two guards in navy uniforms,

"My instructions are that our site set-up has to be built *inside* the perimeter fence."

"Listen mate! My orders are that you are not allowed to do that. Your huts and gear will be erected beside the main contractor's cabins over there behind the new boiler house. All the other huts are there."

"But that means all our pipes and fittings will then be on the inside of the perimeter fence, but the huts are gonnae be outside. That disnae make any sense tae me."

"That's not allowed either. All your equipment will be outside. There will be no pipes, fittings or any other stuff stored inside the security fence. That's always been the rule here. There are no exceptions. Just move over there where you're told."

Angus was about to get angry with this obstinate guy when he felt a hand on his shoulder. He turned round to see a man with J & C printed on his site safety helmet.

"Excuse me." He said. "Are you Liseur's man?"

"Aye. Ah'm Angus MacLauchlan. Who might you be?"

"'I'm Terry Cordwell, site agent for Jarvis & Craig. There's nae point arguing with the security guards. Get your lorries away from the gate. You've to build your site huts in the space we've marked out for you in the site compound over there."

"Listen Terry, my boss told me to build our huts inside the perimeter."

"I don't know who your boss is in *Glasgow* but I'm your boss on this *site*. Just do as you're told. And another thing, don't call me Terry. In future you call me Mister Cordwell. Understood?"

Now, Angus MacLauchlan was an old hand at debunking petty dictators. He learned from his early apprenticeship experiences that bullies are balloons that needed to be burst. It can be done suddenly by force or craftily with guile and subtlety. Angus chose the latter for his first foray with this arrogant wee tin-pot,

"Please yourself...Terry,"

Terry Cordwell scowled at this show of insubordination but as is usual for his type, he turned and walked away just as Angus finished speaking,

"Just as long as you call me Mister MacLauchlan."

Cordwell didn't turn round but from the sudden pause in his stride Angus knew that Jarvis's man had felt the sting of the virtual arrow in his back. They were not going to be friends on this job. Angus had met worse than Cordwell in his time. He had skill in deflating his sort but was man enough however, to accept the instruction he had been given. His protest had been overruled. There was no option but to get on with building Franz Liseur's accommodation beside the Jarvis & Craig huts.

The main contractor had wasted no time. Their squads of men had started to pour the first of many hundreds of concrete bases for Liseur's pipes. It would be another two weeks at least before the concrete was cured to allow Liseur's pipes to be laid on them. Angus had planned for that. Part one was for his men to install pipes and heavy equipment in the boiler house. The other part was to use a forklift to move the heavy steel pipes onto the site and place them adjacent to the not-yet cured concrete plinths. That way gave him a modicum of production from his squad.

Angus was however very far from happy with this rate of progress. Much of their time was being wasted by the restrictions on entering and leaving the site. Every time they went in and out with a piece of pipe they had to go through rigorous inspection by the armed security personnel. As they were not even allowed to take in food or drink, each tea or lunch break involved the same laborious inspection process. Forced to walk increasingly longer distances back and forth to their huts outside the security fence was also having an adverse effect on his men's morale.

The boiler house, being located outside the secure area was easier on them all. Angus was sure that in about a month the boiler house installation would be well underway.

One of the larger items was being moved on rollers into position in the plant room. It consisted of a series of pumps, a complex control panel and valves and pipes, all contained within a steel framework. One of Angus's gang scratched his head,

"Whit's this big thing for, Angus?"

The big man smiled. He loved being asked a question like that since it gave him the chance to display his technical knowledge, although it was limited.

"It's to maintain a high pressure in the heating pipes, Tam."

"How does it have to be pressurised, Angus?"

"This heating system operates at over a hundred degrees centigrade. At a hundred degrees water boils intae steam. This pressurisation unit raises the pressure so the water can be heated to a hundred and thirty degrees without boiling away. It works fine until somebody opens a drain cock."

"How come?"

"Well Tam, as soon as the water hits the outside air pressure, it instantly turns to steam."

"Is that a problem on this site, Angus?"

"No really, Tam; if it's just a wee drain cock. But if one of the main pipes is fractured in any way you'll get thousands ae litres ae water suddenly turning to steam. It would be like a geyser in Yellowstone Park in the USA."

"Whit wid we dae then, Angus?"

Angus turned and sauntered away. Over his shoulder he flung the best piece of advice he could muster,

"Ah don't know about you, Tam, but ah wid run like buggery."

In spite of his levity with Tam, Angus had spotted something about the big unit that seemed odd. He had installed many of these units before but this one had no sign of an expansion tank. In his mind he tried to figure this out, *in a closed, pressurised system like this ah would have expected to see a tank to collect the expansion when the water is heated. I'm only a site foreman. The smart people above me probably know best. Ah'm no very happy about asking a design question. Ah could look a bit silly if the answer's obvious.*

He decided to let that go and worry more about another thing that was causing him concern. A fearsome amount of welding was needed for joining the external pipes. Angus was always on the lookout for ways to save time. Welding out on site in all weathers was a lot more difficult and thus time consuming, especially on cold and frosty winter weather on a muddy hillside facing the North Sea. It was also onerous for the men using forklift trucks to drag half-ton diesel-electric generators through the gate and into the security area for each of the welders...and out again at the end of each day. Angus phoned Mark Trumann to discuss an idea to speed up production,

"Hi Angus what can I do for you?"

"We're gonnae be losing a lot of time carting these welding machines in and out of the secure area as well as having to weld in there in the cold and wet."

"If you have a better idea then spill it out, Angus."

"Could you persuade the powers that be to allow me to erect a covered enclosure for my welders outside the security area next tae our huts? The guys are getting really narky. They're only carrying in the pipe at the moment. They'll lie on the ground tae the plinths are cured but already the guys are knackered. The prospect ae welding pipes in the rain under wee plastic tents and gettin' their balls frozen off wae the cauld up here isnae somethin' tae look forward tae.

"That sounds sore, Angus but am I missing somethin? You'll have to do all of welding inside the perimeter fence."

"Aye, you are, Mark. What I'm sayin' is, in our welding compound outside the security fence we could weld flanges to each length of pipe. Then we just carry them into the secure area and bolt them thegether. That would save a fortune in labour costs because of the time saving and the welding would be...."

Mark butted in rather sharply and cut Angus off in mid-sentence,

"Hold on, Angus! Hold on. That would not be cheaper and it would be contrary to the specification."

How dae you figure that, Mark?"

"Well, for a start it takes two flanges plus a load of bolts and nuts to make a flanged joint. That means two welds instead of one. Secondly there is no provision in the price or the drawings for flanges. Sorry; but that's a non-starter."

"Mark, I think in the long run it would save time and money."

"Sorry, Angus. I see the way you're thinking but there's most certainly no chance of us paying for twice the number of welds, never mind all the thousands of flanges, bolts and nuts to join them all up. It's tough on your guys but you will have to keep doing it the way it's been priced. Just forget it and concentrate on keeping within our budget. If you have a problem with that you'd better talk to my boss; but I already know what he'll say so, you'll be wasting your time.

Angus put the phone down thinking, *Christ, I'm glad ah didnae mention the expansion tank*. He was later to learn that he would have been *better* to raise that particular concern.

Part 2
6th Feb 1990

Franz Liseur offices ~ Clydebank

During Angus's call about the flanges, Mark Trumann had coincidentally been looking at the Clark Chisholm's drawings and specification details concerning the pressurisation unit. He too had spotted the absence of an expansion water spill tank. Disbelief set in as he tried to understand how, when a hundred thousand litres of water was heated up to one hundred-and-thirty degree Celsius, the huge expanded volume of the water was going to be accommodated.

His tentative guess was that a fairly large spill-tank was needed. The contract documents were quite clear. The heating system was required to run continuously, twenty-four hours per day for every day of the year. As the water heated during the initial start-up, something like five cubic metres of expanded water would have to be captured and contained somehow, otherwise it would just have to be run off to waste! When shutting down for maintenance, the system would cool down and the water would contract. The same volume of new water would be needed to replenish the loss. Mark had a thought, *four or five thousand litres lost once a year during maintenance is a small amount on this job. It would be no trouble to discharge that amount of relatively clean, cool water down the drain into the Moray Firth. And refilling would be easy and cheap.*

On that basis he had decided, because the designer probably knew best, that he should just forget his concern. That thought lasted only until he read the supervising officer's first variation instruction of the contract. He realised it was imperative to speak with Douglas Fairbairn.

"Yes, Mark. What's up?"

"I hate to be the bearer of bad tidings, but I think we have another design problem at Bluff."

"Like we need another one! I'm already wrestling with the P.R.V. problem at the moment. What's this new one, Mark?"

"Look at this variation order. They want to run the heating only during working hours and switch it off overnight using frost protection during the night to switch it on if there is cold weather. The heating was designed to be on all the time"

"I saw the instruction. So what? It's just a matter of setting the time switch. I bet it's another attempt by Briggs to save more money. The system already has frost protection I assume?"

"Yes, but that's only the electronic frost protection for the boilers. They want us to frost-protect the pipework exposed on the hillside by adding twenty per cent glycol."

"I told you I have read the instruction. Maybe I'm just being thick today, Mark. Why is there a problem with the use of glycol?"

It's like this, Douglas. Losing *clean water* to waste *once a year* would be a pity, but every day is disgraceful. On top of that, losing something like a thousand litres of *glycol* to waste every day is profligacy on a massive scale. It's expensive; it's flammable; it's heavier than water; it will sink to the seabed in the Moray Firth and it will kill anything it touches that lives down there."

It won't run to waste. They will have specified a spill tank to take the expansion."

"No, Douglas. There's no spill tank."

Douglas's eyes widened. His reaction was passionate,

"You're pulling my leg!"

"No I'm not. There is no facility in the specification or the drawings to cater for the expansion and contraction of the water."

"Jesus! These people must be out of their minds. They're lurching from one disaster to another."

"Couldn't agree more, Douglas. What do you suggest we do?"

"You phone the Moray Firth Water Purification Authority right away. Ask them to fax us a letter forbidding this nonsense. Get your lad, John Logge, to phone the pressurisation unit makers for a firm quotation and best delivery promise for supplying a suitably sized tank complete with all necessary controls and pipes to comply with this new instruction. Tell them to design it for size and function. Okay?"

"Right away. What about the glycol?"

"Good point, Mark. We'll probably never use it but get onto a water treatment outfit and find out what this amount of glycol will cost. Find out the cost of whatever kit is needed to dose the system. Probably into the suction side of the pumps I suppose. I'll finalise the costs with you. Keep our esteemed estimator away from this."

"Right boss, I'm on it."

"Mark, how's the pipework progressing at site?"

"Seems to be going well. The client wants to carry out ultrasonic testing on the welds. Our welders are all certificated so I don't expect many joints will fail."

"Fine. Let them get on with that. The client's examiners, like the rest of their design team, will probably make an arse of it. Tell Angus to keep a close eye on the welders. Let me know the Moray Firth Water people's comments on the glycol as quick as you can. And chase that tank price. I want to ram this right up them. It's time for us to fire off another couple of letters to our pals at Jarvis & Craig. What do you say, Mark?"

"Yep! This should shake them up again. Thanks Douglas. Bye the way, how's the P.R.V. thing going?"

"Well, I'm waiting for a call from the Scottish Institute of Mechanical Engineering Research."

"That's a mouthful. What do you want from them?"

"Yeah, you're right. Let's call them SIMER for short. Last week I asked them to do a computer check on the dynamics of using the P.R.Vs. on a sealed water system. They're having a wee problem running a programme to mimic the performance of the Bluff pipework under working conditions. They keep telling me the pipes jump up and down!"

"That's what David Young *said* would happen."

"I know. I told them we expected them to find that but they insist it shouldn't happen. They are checking and double checking their algorithms and won't let us use their findings till they are certain they are correct."

The phone rang. Douglas picked it up, switched on the loudspeaker and waived Mark to stay with him,

"Douglas Fairbairn here."

"Hello Mister Fairbairn. It's Colin Thompson from the SIMER. We've agreed your theory about the pipework at Bluff. We ran your system ten times and it was always the same result; the pipes danced off the brackets. We tested the software on a stable set of temperatures and pressures and nothing happened. This tends to verify the reliability of the software. You can confidently show your clients that their system will eventually 'self-destruct'. When would you like us to set up a demonstration for them?"

"That's great news, Colin. I'll call you in a couple of days. Sometime next week is probable. Is there any day best for you chaps?"

"No, we are here every day. If you give us an hour's notice we can accommodate you whenever you wish."

"Grand. Thanks Colin. See you next week."

Mark shook Douglas by the hand and congratulated his inventiveness in getting that august institute to deliver, so quickly, such damning evidence of the consulting engineer's faulty design.

Tony Surtal was equally ecstatic when Douglas went through to his office and let him know the great result.

"I love it, Douglas. Now we're in a position to make these buggers pay attention. I'll send a private and confidential letter to Dean Chisholm inviting him to come and witness the simulation at SIMER.

"What about the builder, Tony?"

"I don't give a hoot about the builder, Douglas. This is between Chisholm and us. This is his last chance to use common sense and save his firm's reputation before it's too late. If he insists on burying his head in the sand after seeing proof like this then I will personally sink my size nine boot where Dean Chisholm will feel it most and like it the least!"

"Hold on now, Tony. Surely he'll have to come to heel?"

"I doubt it. He's 'old school'. They don't admit mistakes...ever. That's what scares me. He'd rather go down with his ship than get into our lifeboat, and I don't want us all to go down with him. We must *bring him* to heel, Doug."

"Well boss, with the help of SIMER, I just might have found Chisholm's *Achilles heel*."

"Now you've got me, Douglas. What would that be?"

"It's what we'll use to bring him down, Tony. Even the high-and-mighty Dean Chisholm can't argue with *The Laws of Physics*. That will be his weak point."

"Oh, I see what you mean, Douglas. Nice analogy."

Part 3
Tue 13th Feb 1990

Scottish Institute of Mechanical Engineering Research ~ (SIMER)

Tony and Douglas arrived at ten o'clock. Colin gave them a preview of the computer simulation an hour before any of the invited guests were expected to come. They sat quietly and watched the pipes sitting stationary at first. As the effects of the P.R.V.'s came into play the pipes visibly moved sideways. After some seconds the movements became more pronounced; the pipes started to lift and fall.

Colin explained that the dynamics of the system altered dramatically as the temperature rose. Added to that, the effect of the P.R.V.'s attempts to reduce the pressures to the branches was even more dramatic. These reductions in pressure made the water flash to steam. The computer simulation was not able to simulate sounds but he said these noises would be very alarming. When he said it would sound like gunfire, Tony remarked,

"I've heard that sound Colin, it's called 'steam hammer'. It's rather scary, not unlike gunfire. That's the last thing you want to hear in an armaments depot. The sound of gunfire for God's sake! It'll cause panic!"

"That's may be the least of your worries, Tony. Watch the screen carefully. It's about to get much more exciting."

After some minutes the computer began to show the pipes wriggling out of their supports and then twisting and turning in a wild and frightening dance. Upwards and sideways they went as if being pushed and pulled by some irresistible phantom hand.

Although the screen only showed a diagrammatic representation of the pipes it was clear that they were bound to fall down the slope of the hill towards the outbuildings. Then the computer simulation showed the pipes breaking into pieces. The simulation showed the high-temperature water flashing to steam. Tony yelled,

"Holy smoke! There is no way the M.O.D. should be instructing this installation to continue. The consultants are going to love us for saving their arses! They must stop it now. When they realise their design will end up like this, the only option is for them to get back to their drawing boards."

Colin invited them to his office where coffee was laid out. They sat waiting for whoever was going to turn up for the official demonstration. They didn't wait long. Dean Chisholm arrived with Sean O'Casey. The builders and the M.O.D. team never attended. Tony welcomed them, introduced Douglas and invited Colin to show the computer simulation. The consultants sat in stony silence watching the disaster unfolding on the screen. Tony and Mark used their discretion to observe them for any reaction but there was none. The show ended and Sean O'Casey spoke.

"Is that it?"

"Yes." Said Colin

"Mister Surtal, you brought us all the way out here to look at a few minutes computer simulation showing some make-believe system tearing itself to pieces?"

"This is no make-believe system, Mister O'Casey. Colin Thompson is one of the foremost experts in Scotland in the field of computerised investigation in fluid dynamics. The system is as accurate a mimic of your system at Bluff as it is possible to achieve. It has taken nearly four weeks to prepare this demonstration. The safety and cost implications of taking this installation to completion on site are frightening!"

"Mister Surtal, the only frightening thing for you to consider is your cost for producing it. It is only a crude computer mimic. It has no real or practical relationship to my engineer's design concept."

"I disagree strongly!" Protested Colin. "What you have just witnessed is what is likely to happen if you put this flawed hydraulic system into operation. The chance of failure occurring is ninety-five per cent. You would be wise to consider our suggested modifications to prevent the system from destroying itself. Apart from time and cost penalties, there are also health and safety considerations."

"What a fine speech, Mister Thompson." Said Sean O'Casey. "I would do the same if *my* client was beside me and I expected to get paid my fee."

"Now just hold on!" shouted Tony, stepping towards him. "We are here to show you and Mister Chisholm something that has cost us time and money to bring to your attention. It is disgraceful for you to accuse our accredited expert of ingratiation. You will take that remark back now O'Casey, or I will be forced to do something rash!"

Dean Chisholm interjected his body between the two.

"That will be enough, gentlemen. I am sorry for my colleague's hurtful remark, but it is clear to me that what we've seen is only a simulation. I am responsible for all of the work we do. We are also paid very well for what we *know*. Now I want my senior engineer to tell me whether this system of ours falls within the ninety-five per cent or the five per cent of your stated probability?"

Tony, Douglas and Colin looked at Sean O'Casey. It depended on him now. Either he would defend Torquil Knight's design or, in front of his firms owner, admit that the chances of the system failing were high.

Sean recalled the young man handing in his letter of resignation. Torquil insisted that his design was wrong and the P.R.V.'s were the problem. Because Sean would not listen or do anything to start to put it right, Torquil had left the firm in disgust. The young man had shown that he would not sacrifice his principles for something as serious as this. O'Casey was on the spot and his mind was searching for an option that would safeguard his job and his career. Since Liseur's men didn't know that Torquil Knight was no longer an employee of the firm he decided there was nothing to lose by throwing the boy to the wolves.

"I spoke to our designer. He has a BSc Honours Degree in Environmental Control from Glasgow University. He assured me that his system is not unsafe. Liseur's have referred to pressure *reducing* valves as being the problem. The designer did not have these items in his design...

"Yes he did!" Shouted Tony cutting him off. "They are clearly on your drawings *and* in the specification. You cannot deny that they are in the contract, O'Casey!"

"Not true, Mister Surtal. What are specified in the contract are pressure *Regulating* valves. There is no five or ninety-five per cent to be decided; these items are one hundred per cent properly functional and safe. I rest my case gentlemen."

Tony was dumfounded. He could not believe what he had just heard. The consulting engineers were hiding behind the difference between two words that in fact meant the same thing. He said so very loudly,

"That, Mister O'Casey, is pure nonsense! You will regret what you have just said. Tell him, Colin."

Colin switched off his computer screen and turned to Dean Chisholm.

"Mister Chisholm. You have witnessed a grave error of judgement on the part of your senior engineer. In my opinion you would be advised to pay attention to what you have seen here today and take action to avoid a serious event at this site."

"Thank you for your opinion, Colin. I respect it but it is after all just that...your opinion. I will stand by my engineer if you don't mind. There will be no more discussion between Franz Liseur and us on this topic or, I fear any other topic to do with this installation at Bluff. I shall make this decision known to our client at the M.O.D. You, Tony, will be well advised to keep you team's heads down and get on with this contract without any more spurious allegations of this kind. Good morning gentlemen."

Tony was not for letting Dean Chisholm leave the meeting without giving him a stern warning.

"Just a minute Mister Chisholm. I want you to know that in the fullness of time you and your so-called engineer will pay a heavy price for what you have decided today. I will also record this with my client and Jim Briggs at the M.O.D. You will regret this. You will pay! Make no mistake! You will pay dearly for this high-handed, pompous and patronising abuse of your consultant's powers."

Dean Chisholm and Sean O'Casey stormed out of the door, slamming it shut. Douglas, who had listened, open-mouthed to Tony's parting speech, gave a rueful smile and said,

"So! That's what you meant by your size nine boot?"

"Yes, Douglas. I don't miss the target at times like this. The way he banged that door meant he really must have felt it. Now we've got a humdinger of a fight on our hands. The builder, the consultant and the M.O.D. are lined up against us. I love it! Let's go for lunch. Come on Colin, Douglas is buying."

Part 4
Thu 15th Feb 1990

Franz Liseur offices ~ Clydebank the same afternoon
Tony called Douglas and Mark into his room for a chat.

"Tell me why this design is wrong? There must be more to this than meets the eye. These clowns are scared of something and I want to know and understand what it is. Then we'll be in a position to muster stronger help from down south."

Douglas put forward his best theory.

"I've had a good look at the overall picture of this site at Bluff. Here are my notes for what I believe went wrong during the time the consultants were preparing the project for tender. It is quite scary to read and if it is anywhere near the truth of what actually happened then we will be up shit creek if we don't make them understand the danger they are in!"

Tony and Mark read quietly for a couple of minutes. Mark spoke first,

"This all makes sense, Douglas. It's hard to credit they could make such an error in the design and still be defending it."

Tony nodded his agreement and added,

"I can't think of any closed loop system that uses one pressure on the flow and another on the return. That only works if it's gas in one pipe and water in the other i.e. steam and condensate. I agree with you, Douglas. Chisholm's man must have found the steam system too expensive so he changed it. But why use medium pressure hot water when the buildings only need low pressure?" All they had to do was change it to a low-pressure and they'd have no need for P.R.V.'s. Surely it's as simple as that?"

"No it's not, Tony. To carry the amount of heat required for the buildings would have meant pipes twice the size. He needed to keep the pipes within budget so he blithely raised the temperature and pressure to keep the pipes the same size. He made the schoolboy error of keeping the pressure reducing valves to connect to each building system."

"Why would he do that?"
    "He was being pushed and he wasn't thinking clearly, Tony. It's forgivable. We've all done similar things in the past. I know because I once made a mistake."

Mark laughed and so did Tony, but before he could respond, the phone rang. It was Helen to say a Mister John Pammis was on for Douglas.

"Thanks, Helen, put it through to the phone in his room. Douglas, it's John Pammis of your old home on a personal matter so, take it on your own phone."

"Thanks Tony, I'll try to be quick."

He headed across to his office wondering what on earth his old boss was after. Probably it would be about one of his unfinished projects for Peurova and a couple of quick answers would be all that was needed.

"Hi John, to what do I owe the pleasure?"

"Hello Doug. Nothing serious, I need you to sign off a couple of non-disclosure forms. I should have done this last year but the shock of losing you put it out of my head."

"Very droll, John. But I take the disguised compliment in the way it is intended. Why not send them to my house. You know the address. I'll get them back to you by return, okay?"

"Yes Douglas, that's what I was going to do but I wanted to just let you know to avoid any stress when you got a letter out of the blue."

"Be truthful John. You really just wanted to hear my voice."

"Yes, of course I did my young friend. I knew you would see through it. Tell me, how are things shaping up? Had enough of the rough old contracting game? Coming back soon?

"Very funny. I'm having great fun at the moment. Some really good jobs but one in particular is totally hilarious.

We are kicking the consultant to death and they are not liking it at all."

"Anybody I know, Douglas?"

"Probably but I don't want a libel suit. Suffice it to say it's a nice wee ministry project up in Forres. A design fault and we are winning."

"Sounds like you are in your element with that. Take it easy on the consultant. Remember how hard it is for us consultants to make a crust?"

Douglas laughed out loud and so did Pammis, who after some slight hesitation asked another question,

"Excuse me for asking, Douglas but that job in Forres wouldn't be for the armaments Depot at Bluff, would it?"

"How would you know about that, John? Am I treading on your toes up there?"

"Absolutely not. I heard a whisper round our office about that project. A new structural colleague has a friend who used to work for the Clark Chisholm consultants in Glasgow. I believe they are handling that project. Could it be that one?"

"That's interesting, John. It is the Bluff Depot but I'm sure there is only one project going on there just now. The name on our drawings is Torquil Knight. Your colleague says Knight *used* to work there but we're under the impression he's still there?"

"No he isn't. That's the name his friend told me. Davy Pringle started with us in January. David shares a flat with him in Glasgow. Torquil found he had made a major error but the boss wouldn't listen so, he just walked out in disgust one day and went home."

"John, this is astounding. What was the mistake? Can you find out?"

"I already know he designed a steam system..."

Before he could finish, Douglas gave the rest of the answer,

"But because the cost was to high he changed it to a medium pressure hot water system?"

"Yes. So it's the same one. Glad to be of assistance. My fee will be with you shortly, Douglas."

"Listen, John. I owe you a fine dinner for this. Name the place and time and I'm your man, Okay?"

Accepted. See you soon. Take it easy on old Dean Chisholm. My lips are sealed but keep me posted. Bye for now Douglas."

He hung up. Douglas dived across to Tony's room; Tony wanted to know why his man was wearing a wide grin.

"You will not believe what I've just found out."

"I know." Said Tony. "You've just been told Peurova made an error in your favour and a tax rebate is on its way."

"No, it's better than that. Pin your ears back. John asked me sign a couple of professional indemnity forms but he also asked me how I was doing. I mentioned the Bluff problem and he said he knew something about the project but didn't know that I was involved in it."

Tony interrupted him,

"Is that all?

"No, Tony. Listen to this. He learned about it from a new chap called Davy Pringle who shared a flat with the guy who designed the job. It was none other than Torquil Knight. He found a major error he had made but the boss wouldn't listen. He was also abruptly removed from the project. He just handed in his notice and walked out into the street."

"Did you find out what the mistake was?"

"This is the best bit. David Pringle said Torquil Knight changed the system from steam to medium temperature hot water *and* had left in the pressure reducing valves!"

Tony scoffed,

"He can't have walked out. O'Casey said he spoke to him so, he must still be there."

"Not the case, Tony. John Pammis told me that Torquil Knight has left. His pal, David Pringle keeps in touch with him by phone at his parents' house in -

wait for it - Forres. He is definitely *not* still employed at Clark Chisholm."

"But, Douglas...that makes no sense. O'Casey said that it was Torquil who had insisted the design was not at fault!"

"Not so, Tony! Torquil Knight told his flatmate that the partnership wouldn't allow him to make the necessary changes. So he upped sticks and walked out in disgust."

Tony thumped his desk,

"O'Casey lied. Right! That's good enough for me Douglas. I'm beginning to like this young guy Torquil Knight. He seems to have the courage to act on his convictions. Allow me to write the next letter to Jarvis & Craig. I'll demand that they tell Jim Briggs the truth and stop this job in its tracks. I can see no point in continuing just because they think they have the upper hand."

"Thanks, Tony. Now that we have irrefutable confirmation of a cover up, what's my next move?"

Tony sat back in his chair, swivelled round and studied the trees outside for a minute. Douglas signalled to Mark to leave the room quietly then waited for his boss to explain his plan of campaign. Tony turned and spoke,

"Listen carefully, Douglas. This is what we'll do. Talk to Mark Trumann, phone the labour supervisor, Archie

McGregor and the site foreman, Angus MacLauchlan. Make a list of anything they're worried about. Let's get all the facts and use them as a battering ram against these chancers.

If they are truly ignorant of their mistakes or are actually trying to cover up everything that's wrong with this job, we'll have to use all of our resources to outwit them. We're not going to pick up the tab when it all goes wrong. These so called 'design consultants' will pay dearly. Come back in two days with the results of your digging. You and I will then organise our attack."

"Okay, Tony. This sounds like war."

"It is a battle, Douglas, and we will start to collect all the ammo we'll need in order to win it. If it becomes a war of attrition...bring it on! We can outlast, out think and outwit these clowns. Take the drawings and go over them with a fine toothcomb. Look for anything at all that's the least bit suspect. In other words, use your best knowledge as a consultant and designer to find any other flaws in Torquil Knight's design. While you're doing that, I've got a couple of things to get on with. First I'm going to drop our little letter to Jarvis & Craig using another of the contract clauses."

"Which one's that, Tony?"

"Paragraph 3.2.6.2 in the G.C. Works 1 contract."

"I must have missed that one. What's it all about?"

"My new way of telling them they are in breach of contract by forcing us to proceed to install this system."

"Nice one, Tony. Joe Hadshaw is going to just love that!"

"With Jarvis & Craig love doesn't come into it, Douglas."

"Yeah. I know what you mean."

Douglas left. Tony called Helen. He dictated,

Jarvis & Craig
15th Feb 1990
Attention of Mr J. Hadshaw
(By registered post)

Dear Sirs,   R.N.A.D. Bluff No 004)

Your letter dated 23rd January, enclosing a Variation order, instructs us to continue with the mechanical services installations under our contract with you at the above site. We have instructed our company lawyer to forewarn you that by issuing that order you have absolved us of any liability should the system fail as predicted by us and advised to you in our letter reference number 1990/ 003 dated 17th January 1990.

By that letter, we advised you of a problem with the design of the pipework. If you do not pass on that concern to your client you may be in contravention of the requirement of clause 2.0 of our contract with you.

We now advise you that we commissioned the Scottish Institute of Mechanical Engineering Research (SIMER) to design a computer software programme mimicking the fluid dynamics of the pipework at the

Bluff site. S.I.M.E.R. have advised us that there is a 95% probability that the pipework will begin to oscillate when put into operation, and eventually will 'self destruct'. We record that you declined our invitation to witness that important demonstration.

The safety implications in the Bluff armaments depot are ominous. There is likely to be a serious event at the site involving damage to MOD property and injury to personnel or the contamination of volatile fuels, hardware or electronic control systems for the nuclear and other armaments stored in the site.

Your instruction compelling us to proceed with this installation has denied us, ipso facto, the option of refusal. You are thus in contravention of Clause 3.2.6.2.of the G.C. Works 1 contract (a copy of this clause is appended to this letter) since, so far as we can know, you have not advised your client that there is a serious technical problem, which if not resolved, will most likely lead to some or all of the consequences indicated in this letter.

Since we have no other legal option but to carry out your instructions, we are proceeding with the work at site. It is within your power to rescind your instruction. Until you do, we will continue without accepting liability.

This letter will be founded upon if or when this dispute comes to court. We expect to be absolved of responsibility for any costs, delays, damage or personal injury claims.

In the fullness of time we shall present you with our claim for loss and expense attendant upon the serious disruption and delays (which are destined to occur) that we have clearly and responsibly advised you of in accordance with our obligations in our contract with you.

Yours Faithfully,

Tony Surtal,
Scottish Branch Manager
For: Franz Liseur, Scotland   *Ref: HT/TS*

cc	*Liseur Lawyer*	*McMeikle & Huggett*
cc	*Sir William North*	*Franz Liseur C.E.O. London. Great Britain*
cc	*Jules Dispard*	*Franz Liseur European Legal Council. Paris. France*
cc	*Fabien Le Maître*	*Franz Liseur Head of Engineering. Paris. France*
cc	*Thierry Le Jeune*	*Head of Fluid Dynamics. Basle, Switzerland*

Appendix: Clause 3.2.6.2. **GC Works/I Domestic Sub-Contracts, Scotland.**

3.2.6.2. If the Contractor performs any Work which it knows or should have known due to its experience, ability, qualifications, and expertise in the construction industry, that involves problems, conflicts, defects, deficiencies, inconsistencies, errors, or omissions in the Contract Documents and the work to be constructed and, any variances between the Contract Documents and applicable laws, statutes, building codes, rules or regulations, without prior written notification to the Architect/Engineer and without prior authorization to proceed from the Architect/Engineer, the Contractor shall be responsible for and bear the costs and delays (including costs of any delay) of performing such Work and all corrective actions as directed by the Architect/ Engineer.

"Right Helen that should set the moggy among the magpies, eh?"

"Very impressive Tony. I'm sure you all know what you're doing but I feel you are heading for a big fight. It's not just politics, is it?"

"Not at all. It's *mostly* politics but with a little mix of subtlety and subterfuge. Now see that goes by registered post tonight but first put a call out to Mister Pammis at the Peurova partnership; and keep it quiet. This is top secret."

"OK Tony. Mum's the word."

"Hello Mister Pammis. This is Tony Surtal of Franz Liseur here."

"Ah yes, the thief of Clydebank. I've just spoken with Douglas and he seems inordinately happy I am sad to admit."

"Well I may be a thief but I learned it from you six years ago when you robbed me of my best contracts manager."

"Alright, Tony I suppose we are even and I forgive you for now but don't hold your breath, he may yet miss the high life over here in Fife. Now, what can I do for you?"

"Actually I'm asking for your permission to speak with one of your staff. David Pringle may have important information about the Bluff project that would assist me greatly."

"I am quite happy with that, Tony. I'll get you transferred but first of all are you at liberty to let me know what it's about?"

"Actually it would be simpler if you got him on your intercom and listened in. That way you will be fully aware that there is no underhand stuff going on."

It took a minute or so to locate David and the conversation was short and informative. Tony made notes, thanked them both and hung up.

Half an hour later he got a call from Torquil Knight in Forres.

"Mister Surtal, my friend David Pringle advised me to give you a call. He said it could alter my present position. Is this correct?"

"Yes, Mister Knight. I feel from my recent experiences on the Bluff project that I already know you very well. In fact I am so well versed in the story of your dealings with Clark Chisholm that I would like you to come and join my firm and assist us with the project management of the job up there."

"Without an interview?"

"This is your interview. The job is yours. Will you start on Monday?"

"Yes."

"Fine, See you at 9.00am. Ask for me when you arrive."

"Right. And thank you. Mister Surtal."

"Call me Tony."

"Right, Tony. See you Monday."

Tony hung up and thought *I like him. His brevity and decisiveness are what is wanted for this job plus his courage under pressure. This can turn out well for him and us.*

Part 5
Fri 16th Feb 1990

Franz Liseur offices ~ Clydebank
Tony poured some coffee from the pot and sat down beside Mark in Douglas's office. He opened the discussion with some thoughts about the difficulties at Bluff.

"As domestic sub-contractors to Jarvis & Craig we have a problem. They are trying to prevent us from telling the MOD our concerns about the design. I only hope we're not too late. We need to stop (or at least delay) the work on site long enough to allow them to check their design and correct it before the installation reaches the critical point of no return."

"Are we getting anywhere with that, Tony?"

"No, Mark. It's like walking up a 'down' escalator. You've read my latest letter telling the builders we will carry on as instructed by the faxed letter of 23rd January from the top man, James Briggs. We have no choice but to get on with it. None of them is prepared to believe us when we say the current design will make the system destroy itself. I think they just don't care."

"So how can we get them to listen?"

"They will have got our letter number four yesterday. Their total silence speaks volumes. It's therefore time for you to send our fifth letter to the Jarvis. Demand a site meeting with the Supervising officer. If they ignore that or insist we continue with the installation we will take them the full road."

"What do you mean Tony?" Douglas asked.

"I mean we will augment the site teams, accelerate the work and get it operational as soon as we can. We then start it up and watch it destroy itself. When it falls apart, we put our fingers to our noses like they have done to us. After that we write letter number six asking a simple question...*please sir, what would you like us to do now?*"

But this is a nuclear site, Tony. We can't do that in all humanity. What if it all goes up?"

Tony shrugged,

"If them as owns it are as scared as we are, then surely they must eventually listen to reason. I hope they listen but there is not a thing we can do if they insist on being proved wrong. We will be held liable if we can't do that.

We can't just *say* you're wrong; we must irrefutably *show* that they are wrong. If that means blowing up their fucking depot at Bluff, then so be it. That's all there is to it, Douglas. It's a case of 'who blinks first', them or us. Now let's get on with our next bit."

Tony sat with Mark and Douglas to consider the many items Mark had compiled from his talks with the site foreman, Angus MacLauchlan and the labour supervisor, Archie McGregor. Some were minor niggles and were quickly discounted as not contentious within the contract.

A handful of observations could be argued as disruptive and costly but not in any way affecting the design. Such things as the additional cost of working outside instead of inside the security area would form part of a claim for loss and expense. That could be left till later. For now, the important issue was 'the efficacy of the Clark Chisholm partnership's design'. Besides the P.R.V question, there were three other serious issues that required to be advised to the builder under clause 2.0 of the contract.

The first one was *another* design fault to do with the expansion of the pipes that had the potential to cause the pipework to self-destruct. The second was about the use of Glycol and the possible pollution of the Moray Firth Estuary. Thirdly there was the matter of how the system was intended to accommodate the varying volumes of water as it heated and cooled.

They had been talking for nearly three hours when Tony brought the meeting to a close.

"Thanks lads. This has been very worthwhile. It means Douglas can now write to Jarvis & Craig and ask for an extraordinary meeting with the Supervising Officer to allow him to hear and judge our concerns. The M.O.D. and the consultant can be there if required but only as observers. We want the S.O.'s ear. Do not go into details at this time; just advise in general terms three further design problems that, if not addressed, will cause potentially serious or disastrous consequences. Send copies to inform our lawyers and the big guns in London, Paris and Switzerland. If the consultants think the P.R.V question is their only problem we will make them think again. Any final comments boys?"

"Let's go get them!" Said Mark.

"Let's bury the fuckers?" queried Douglas.

"Your letter will do that, Douglas. Work on it with Mark and let me read a draft before you send it."

Tony left the room. Douglas and Mark drafted letter number five. After Tony read it, his instruction was short and sweet,

"Excellent you guys. Get it typed and sent by registered post tonight. Oh, and bye the way chaps, I've hired Torquil Knight. He starts on Monday."

Mark and Douglas stood open mouthed as Tony continued,

"But he won't be going to the site for a while. I want it kept quiet from the builders and the rest. He is our secret weapon."

"I like it!" Said Douglas.

"Smart move!" Said Mark. "I'll get this letter typed."

Jarvis & Craig
16th Feb 1990
Attention of Mr J Hadshaw
(By registered post)

Dear Sirs,   R.N.A.D. Bluff (No 005)

Clause 2.0 of our mutually agreed contract requires that the Supervising Officer must be advised of any suspicion we may have of an error or omission relating to the drawings or the design of the systems.

We are thus obliged to advise you that our scrutiny of the design drawings has revealed such an omission which, if not addressed, will have serious (if not disastrous) consequences when the boilers begin to heat the water in the pipe system.

We have other concerns relating to two recent instructions from the Supervising Officer that we should (1) set the system controls such that the boilers operate only during working hours and (2) that we should dose the pipework with a 20% solution of Ethylene Glycol as a frost protection.

We would normally ask that you inform the Supervising Officer, on our behalf, of our suspicion of the serious implications relating to these items. In this instance we request a different approach. We suggest an urgent site meeting be arranged with the Supervising Officer. This would allow us to set out in specific detail our reasons for bringing our concerns to his attention.

We rely on this letter to free our company from any responsibility for any hazardous results from the failure of the Supervising Officer to discuss these items with a view to agreeing necessary and urgent action to rectify the problems. Failure by you to so inform the Supervising Officer is likely to place Jarvis & Craig in breach of contract.

Please advise your instructions within fourteen calendar days of receipt of this letter. In the absence of a reply we shall stop our work on the pipework systems until these technical issues are resolved. Any delays resulting from your inability to properly instruct us in this matter will be recorded by us as part of a loss and expense claim solely against your company. Please be clearly advised by this letter that Franz Liseur's accountants and surveyors will record any loss and expense from and including 2nd March 1990.

Yours Faithfully,

Douglas *Fairbairn*,
Scottish Branch Manager
For: Franz Liseur, Scotland   *Ref: HT/DF*

cc	Liseur Lawyer	McMeikle & Huggett
cc	Sir William North	Franz Liseur C.E.O. London. Great Britain
cc	Jules Dispard	Franz Liseur European Legal Council. Paris. France
cc	Fabien Le Maître	Franz Liseur Head of Engineering. Paris. France
cc	Thierry Le Jeune	Head of Fluid Dynamics. Basle, Switzerland

Part 6
Mon 19th Feb 1990

Franz Liseur offices ~ Clydebank
Torquil arrived just before nine. Douglas set him to work in his room to write a full report of his experiences with the Clark Chisholm Partnership and James Briggs.

There was a telephone call for Tony at nine fifteen.

"Hi. Tony Surtal here"

"Your pal is up to his tricks again!"

Tony recognised the voice and attitude of Joe Hadshaw but played dumb just for fun,

"I'm sorry. I don't have any pals who do tricks. You must have got the wrong number."

He hung up.

The phone rang again.

"Hi. Tony here."

"Don't hang up on me, Surtal. You know fine well it's me. I'm getting pissed off with your contracts manager's games. He's sent us another letter threatening if we don't arrange a meeting with the Supervising Officer, he'll stop the contract in fourteen days!"

"Oh, hello Joe. What about it?"

"What about it! He's way out of order writing more letters like that! You've got to put a stop to him threatening to stop the work at site. So what are you going to do about his latest letter?"

"Nothing, Joe"

"What! How can you allow this guy Fairbairn to write more letters like this?"

"Joe, it's very simple. You see, I instructed him to write the last letter. If you have any sense at all then you are best advised to arrange for the meeting; otherwise the work will stop in fourteen days. Do you understand what I am telling you?"

"I'm telling you, Surtal, you are not getting us to dance to your tunes any more. You'll get your site meeting with the S.O. You'd better have a good story this time or I'll ask the MOD for permission to terminate your contract. We'll get another crowd to finish it and you will foot the bill."

"Joe my boy, I think you should stick to bricks and mortar. Leave the engineering to us experts."

"Don't try to patronise me, Surtal! I am not, and never will be *your boy*. We can sort you out good and proper if you are wrong on this; and don't you forget it!"

"Mister Hadshaw, if you look at the distribution list in my letter, you will notice that I am assembling important technical personnel from around Europe. This team will establish our design expertise and technical credentials way beyond that of your friends from the Clark Chisholm partnership. So why don't you stop backing the wrong horse and come in with us.

"That'll be the day when we come into bed with you guys. Do you hear me?"

"Loud and clear. That will be your funeral, Hadshaw. We intend to discredit this design and the people who are culpable for spuriously defending it. You should make sure you are blameless because this project, if it goes any further on that site, is going to cost someone a lot of money to fix. I hope you choose the winning side. Don't forget that this is also a nuclear site. It might never be able to be fixed. Then where will you be my friend? Do you hear ME?"

There was silence for a few seconds. Joe Hadshaw was wracking his bricklayer's brain to think of a suitable response. He had long ago accepted that he was not up to competing with this arrogant sub-contractor and did not like *being* in such a position. Nevertheless, he had to try one last feeble ploy in an effort to have Tony realise how important were those professional people that his firm was castigating. He assumed a false mode of ingratiation,

"But, Tony, these consultants are clever people. They've declared their design to be right and that's why you've got the Supervising Officer's instruction to proceed. How can you not just accept what they say and get on with the work?"

"Joe, my friend. Douglas Fairbairn has just joined this firm after working for the last six years as a senior designer with The Peurova partnership; one of the biggest consulting engineering firms on the planet; He knows a thing or three about design. He is one of the few engineers in Scotland that know all there is to know about the design of steam systems."

"Well that's fine, Tony, but even I know that this is not a steam system."

"No it's not. But it used to be. Without any disrespect, Joe, I have to impress upon you that we now know why the system is faulty. In addition to the P.R.V difficulty, Douglas's letter refers you to a further design fault. We will only explain that problem to the Supervising Officer. If we are again told to go ahead, regardless of our observations and warnings, then we will do that. Then I assure you, you can stand back with us and watch an unholy nuclear disaster taking place."

"It seems I don't have any choice. I'll talk to Mister Jarvis and try to get that meeting arranged but I still think you lot are at it. I'll let you know."

"You do that, Joe."

Joe ran it all past Hugh Jarvis and within two hours he called back to advise Tony that a site meeting had been scheduled for 9.30 am on Wednesday, February the 21st. He and Hugh Jarvis would be there with Dean Chisholm, the Supervising Officer and the Clerk of Works. Tony brought Douglas and Mark in to brief them.

"This is an early morning meeting that may last all day. It is going to be contentious and there will be little or no assistance from the builders."

Douglas rubbed his hands,

"Our letter must have hit their soft spot, Tony. I'm looking forward to this."

He handed out copies of his list of points he would be raising at the meeting. After a short discussion it was agreed that with a couple of minor changes they would use it as their agenda. Tony warned them both,

"These things are going to upset the consultants. If their comments get personal, don't lose your rag with them in front of the S.O. Their anger will just indicate to him that they have run out of arguments."

"They haven't got any arguments to run out of!" said Douglas with a laugh.

"Don't be too sure of that. The S.O. will ask Clark Chisholm to respond. They will be well prepared for this encounter. I am looking forward to hearing what technical conundrums they come out with to save their reputation. But be damned sure they will try anything to discredit us and wriggle free."

Douglas laughed out loud,

"They can wriggle, Tony, but even The Clark Chisholm partnership can't alter the laws of physics."

"No. That's true. But in front of people who don't know these laws they will try to convince them that their design is watertight, if you pardon the pun? That's what we are up against here. It's them against us; engineers against engineers, but they have an officer's epaulets. To them we are common five-eight squaddies with no brains. They have the credibility with the politicians and we are expendable; people to be ignored. Let's hope the Supervising Officer is more 'engineer' than 'country gentry'."

Douglas stopped smiling and replied, quietly this time,

"I hope you're right, Tony. Otherwise we will be up against forces we can't beat. What's our next action?"

"That's easy, Douglas. Let Torquil know about our meeting and why he's not included. We'll get our heads together on Thursday when we get back from Bluff. I'll ask Helen to arrange dinner, bed and breakfast for us all tomorrow night in the Forres Hotel. We'll meet here in the morning at nine and go up in my car. Bring your jammies and toothbrushes. We will be fighting fit for them on Wednesday."

"Right, Tony. I'm ready for them now."

Part 7
Wed morning 21st Feb 1990

Site Meeting at R.N.A.D. Bluff
With government contracts it is convenient (and cheaper) for the Ministry of Defence to appoint one of

the project's professional team as the 'Supervising Officer'. On this project, the S.O.'s role was assigned to the Structural Engineer, Norman Keen of the Keen Parr Felt partnership. The protocol of this post requires that all other participants in the contract (with the exception of the MOD) must accept his authority.

Franz Liseur's five-man delegation entered the site office for the meeting. Tony had brought Douglas of course, together with Mark Trumann, Archie McGregor and he asked the site foreman, Angus MacLauchlan to join them. They were directed to one side of a long table, facing the builders, Hugh Jarvis, Joe Hadshaw and Terry Cordwell. Jarvis nodded to Tony and Douglas but didn't yet know who was who.

A second table formed a tee shape where sat the Supervising Officer and the Clerk of Works. Douglas caught Norman Keen's eye. They recognised each other from the James Briggs meeting from which Douglas was evicted. Neither made any sign of friendship or enmity.

When seated Tony and Douglas looked at each other mouthing a silent question. *Where were the consulting engineers?* The site hut door opened. They turned to witness Dean Chisholm making a swaggering entry. Sean O'Casey trailed behind him. Dean removed his coat and as if he were meeting two old friends, flung a loud and cheery greeting to the head of the table,

"Good morning Norman. Hello again George. Sorry if we seem a little tardy. Damned cook was late with our breakfast. How are you both?"

Norman Keen nodded a cursory welcome. Tony was not impressed and whispered the same to Douglas. This outburst of boldness by Chisholm was clearly designed to align himself with the people at the top of the table. Tony was even less impressed when the two consultants took their seats beside the S.O.

Norman Keen is supposed to be impartial, thought Tony. He was about to object but was beaten to it when Keen struck his knuckle on the table for attention. *He really thinks he's a judge. I'll wait for the right moment before making an enemy of this guy.* Keen addressed them like a schoolmaster,

"Good morning people. I am the Supervising Officer for this project. My name is Norman Keen of the Keen Parr Felt Partnership. We are structural engineers. My colleague on my left is the Clerk of Works for the M.O.D., Mr George Yeoman. Mr Chisholm and Mister O'Casey on my right represent the Clark Chisholm Partnership of consulting engineers. I believe most of the rest of you know each other. For the benefit of myself, the consultants and the Clerk of Works, please state your names, your firms and your positions."

Tony was now less than happy to be referred to as 'the rest of you' as if they were serfs; privileged to be in the presence of their betters. When all introductions were completed, he decided to open the meeting with a question.

"Mister Keen, I am slightly puzzled by our seating arrangements. Will you kindly explain why Messrs' Chisholm and O'Casey are sitting beside you at your bench?"

Norman Keen winced visibly. He had been about to open the proceedings by asking for calmness and respect for all parties present. He was aware of the contentious arguments that had been enacted in the past few weeks and was in no mood to be drawn into the middle of it all. As the S.O. his duty was to be not only impartial, but also to be seen to be so. This first shot across his bows came as a shock. He was clearly not used to the cut and thrust of the combative nature of site meetings. It seemed to Tony that Mister Keen would be more at home in a shooting lodge with his high-end clients than roughing it with the hoi polio.

Tony's use of only the Consultants' surnames was in Norman Keen's opinion almost beyond the pale. *Did these people have no respect for their professional superiors?* He tried to compose himself and find a way to put this Mister Surtal in his place. His gambit was slow and detailed but still curt and to the point.

"Mister Surtal, this *desk* (he emphasised the word 'desk' to nullify Tony's reference to 'a judge's bench') is for the design team."

Tony responded immediately before Keen could start another sentence,

"Then we are at the wrong meeting."

He got up to leave and waved his team to do the same. Keen banged on the table for attention, and shouted,

"What do you mean you are at the wrong meeting, Mister Surtal?"

Tony turned to face him. Their eyes met. For a fleeting second Tony noticed a hint of fear in Keen's eyes. It went away to be replaced with a smile, partly of derision and partly contempt. It was up to Tony to reinforce his dramatic action by issuing another dramatic challenge to the authority of the kangaroo court, from which he had threatened to exit,

"With all due respect to you, Mister Keen, I asked for a meeting with the Supervising Officer; not the design team. You seem to be wearing the wrong hat today sir. I insist that you take the proper role and get all others who are not supervising officers to vacate your table and either leave the hut or sit down beside us at this table as silent observers."

Norman Keen held Tony's gaze. His mind was adjusting to the realisation that Tony was absolutely correct. The purpose of the meeting was to hear criticism of the consulting engineer's design. He could not equitably adopt an impartial position while having the Clark Chisholm team sitting beside him. They were in fact opponents of Franz Liseur. He was finding it awkward to decide in favour of Liseur whilst at the same time having to climb down in the company of his fellow professionals. As he faltered, the decision was taken for him. Dean Chisholm stood up and signalled O'Casey to follow him. Without a word they walked round the top table to a new position, facing Norman Keen, at the far end of the "T" shaped table.

The S.O. thanked them for their courtesy. Chisholm nodded his assent. Keen looked at Tony with his eyebrows raised as if to say, *Well, Surtal. Are you now satisfied?* Tony read the look, smiled and turned, without a word, to look at the Clerk of Works who still sat beside Keen. To save the S.O. his blushes, George Yeoman stood up and moved to sit beside Joe Hadshaw. Tony sat down again beside Douglas. There was silence for a moment as Norman Keen collected his thoughts. Here was a man who had just tried to use his position as a professional engineer to subjugate the contractors by providing a protective shield to those whom he had assumed were his professional colleagues.

He had overlooked the obligatory rules of fairness he was supposed to adopt in a meeting such as this. Vivid ideas cascaded through his mind. *This manager of a firm with a fancy French name had embarrassed him. He did not like having to admit defeat in such an overt manner even before the meeting had started. He decided that this chap, Tony Surtal, had scored heavily. so, if he were not to be made to look a complete fool again, he would need to be very careful how he dealt with Liseur today. But he would exact retribution should the opportunity develop.* He coughed loudly and called the meeting to order,

"Let us begin gentlemen. The purpose of this meeting is for me to listen to observations from Franz Liseur regarding the efficacy or otherwise of the Clark Chisholm partnership design of the pipework systems for this project. I ask Mister Chisholm to make an opening statement."

Tony turned quickly and looked at Douglas with raised eyebrows. He felt like making another objection but relaxed slowly back in his seat smiling. *Let the big man say his piece. The more lies he tells the better for Liseur.* Douglas read Tony's body language and relaxed, knowing his boss's instinct for the fray. It may be that Keen and Chisholm had been in cahoots prior to the meeting. Chisholm had to be allowed to speak but he couldn't have any real defense to worry Liseur.

Dean Chisholm got up and placed his notebook on the table. He took out his spectacle case. With exaggerated dexterity he removed his eyeglasses and rubbed the lenses with a white handkerchief withdrawn from his waistcoat pocket. Holding, at last, the lenses towards the window he made large of checking for clarity, returned his kerchief to his pocket, donned the glasses, lifted up his notes and spoke slowly and clearly,

"As senior partner of Clark Chisholm, I advise that I and my staff have revisited all of our calculations for this project. That thorough re-visitation revealed no fault in any part of our design. I believe our friends from Liseur are being mischievous for the purpose of disguising the fact that they are behind programme with the work. As a result of their tardiness, they find it convenient to create trouble in order to divert the attention of their client, Messrs Jarvis & Craig, from Franz Liseur's contractual inadequacy.

Their criticism of our work is spurious, mischievous, unsubstantiated, rascally and unproven; not in the least in keeping with the high standards of etiquette we as a professional body have, for nearly half a century in this industry, enjoyed with many of Franz Liseur's more able competitors."

He sat down. Keen was not amused. He had expected much more than rhetoric. A bland blanket statement from Dean Chisholm and a disguised counter-accusation aimed at his challengers was wholly unconvincing. He sensed the whiff of a panicky undertone in Chisholm's utter rebuttal of all of Liseur's assertions; more especially since he was not aware of the sub- contractor's latest revelations. That seemed to him to be rather too convenient. He said so,

"Forgive me, Mister Chisholm, but the majority of the contractor's claims about your design are, as yet, unknown to the meeting. It is inappropriate of you to rebut these before you have heard them. It is surely possible that Liseur have some issues that will bear close scrutiny by me. Please bear in mind that I am not just a politician here; I am a qualified structural engineer with a fairly good grasp of the laws of physics."

Dean Chisholm harrumphed at that and sat lower in his chair. The S.O. turned and asked the builders for their opening statement. Hugh Jarvis responded by advising that they had nothing to say. They were there only as observers for the benefit of their domestic sub-contractor. Keen nodded and thought, *nothing wrong with that, they are stuck in the middle of this dispute. They have no idea how the engineering is supposed to work never mind understanding how it might be wrongly designed.*

He turned and invited Liseur to enlighten the meeting by making their assertions known. Tony did not get up. He had done his bit exactly as rehearsed. Douglas and he both knew the tricks of the trade. They had caught the S.O. out and gained the initiative rather well. Now it was up to Tony's man to show his mettle. Douglas opened his folder, lifted out some typewritten sheets and stood up.

"Good morning, Mister Keen. Thank you for giving me the opportunity to advise you of my misgivings concerning some design features of the pipework and some other extraneous items that bother me. For ease of understanding I have made a descriptive list of these items for you to peruse as I go through them. It should also assist when you come to compose the minutes of the meeting."

Dean Chisholm broke in,

"I would like a copy of that list if you don't mind.

Douglas rounded on him,

"You don't need it. You said there is nothing wrong with your work. We are here to discuss these things solely with the Supervising Officer. I would remind you, we have no contractual obligation to you or your firm."

"I have every right to see these allegations since they involve my professional integrity. Mister Keen, I insist on having a copy."

Keen was anxious to tread a fine line but retorted,

"You may insist all you like Mister Chisholm. It is not in my gift to give you them. At the moment they are part of a discussion between myself, as the S.O. and Jarvis & Craig, as the main contractor. Pass me a copy Mister Fairbairn and carry on please with your statement."

Tony was impressed. It had been a few years since he had seen Douglas in action. His friend had learned a few more moves since then. He sat back into his chair and relaxed; ready to enjoy his colleague's report and watch the reactions round the table. Douglas began,

"Firstly let me say we are continuing with this installation in spite of our advice that there is a ninety-five per cent chance that the system, when fitted with pressure reducing valves, will self-destruct when put into operation. The reason we are continuing is that we have been instructed to do so by our client across this table, Jarvis & Craig by their issuance of your written variation order Mister Keen."

"They are not pressure *reducing* valves they are pressure *regulating* valves!" Blurted Sean O'Casey.

"There is no difference," Responded Douglas. "The manufacturers tell us that the system will not operate with these items installed, no matter what you choose to call them. We have shown you the computer simulation, you must be blind if you don't see the problem!"

"There is no problem." Sean shot back. "We have advised the client how these will operate and the client has issued you with clear instructions. Get on with it and stop this nonsense!"

"I don't need you to instruct me, Mister O'Casey. I have just told the S.O. that we are following our client's instruction. The purpose of this statement today is to advise the S.O. that we are an international firm of mechanical and electrical engineers. We have the backing and the advice of the best people in our company that there is a clear danger in this design and we will not bear any responsibility when the system fails as in our opinion it will."

Sean O'Casey was by now quite red in the face with indignation.

"I don't care about your opinions, Fairbairn. It's our opinion that counts here, not yours or anybody else's."

Norman Keen had heard enough.

"I will have order now if you please, Mister O'Casey. There is no need for further discussion on this item. I have issued a clear instruction to the contractor to continue with the installation. My instruction is based upon Clark Chisholm's written professional and technical advice. The contractor has assured us that they will comply with that instruction. As far as the contract is concerned, that is the end of that matter.

As far as the Clark Chisholm partnership is concerned, perhaps I may be permitted to venture *my* opinion. Should Franz Liseur prove to be correct in their assertion about the use of pressure regulating or reducing valves, the Clark Chisholm partnership may be obliged, by law, to re-visit their *written professional and technical advice*. Please continue, Mister Fairbairn."

"Thank you, Mister Keen. Please note I am satisfied with how you dealt with that item."

"So noted Mister Fairbairn. Now, will you please proceed with your report?"

"Certainly, Mister Keen. The first item on my list is there simply to be recorded in your minute if you will allow it?"

"This is about your site establishment being outwith the actual security fence of the depot?"

"Yes that is correct. In the preambles of the contract documents, written by the Clark Chisholm partnership, it states clearly that we should have our site huts within the secure area of the depot. Being located outside in the builder's compound is causing our many operatives to use up valuable production time. They are passing through security, not twice a day as we allowed in our tender; but multiple times, sometimes four, six or even eight times per man per day."

"I see. I am reading the preamble and I agree with you. What would you have me do?"

"I request the minutes to record your acknowledgement of this inconsistency. If possible you may feel that an instruction should be issued that would allow us to recover the costs involved. You may also feel, since there is a penalty clause governing this contract, that an appropriate extension of time be granted under *force majeure,* clause 17. 2/a of the contract."

"I will do exactly that. You shall have it before the end of this week via Jarvis & Craig. Your costs could be recovered by using daily time sheets signed by my Clerk of Works, George Yeoman here?"

Yeoman nodded in agreement. Douglas was delighted. Tony sat looking up at the ceiling. His blank expression hid the pleasure he was savouring. Liseur were scoring all the points. Although he had expected some wins, he hadn't imagined it would be this good. The S.O. seemed now to be relieved that the consultants were at the other end of the table. Norman Keen was a surprise act to Tony. He had thought the M.O.D. and their design team would present a united front in solidarity against the contractors. Keen did not now seem to be that kind of man.

It was gratifying that the S.O was not about to condemn them before he had heard what they had to say. This was evident from the close attention he was giving to Douglas's comments. Perhaps some doubts were arising in his mind concerning the strength of Dean Chisholm's Defences? He had surprisingly hinted his scepticism of the consultant's explanation about the P.R.V issue by his reference to Chisholm's *written professional and technical advice.* It was apparent from that comment that if, as seemed likely, Liseur's dire prediction actually came to pass, Norman Keen would be a spectator when Dean Chisholm and Sean O'Casey, hand-in-hand, mounted the scaffold to be hanged.

Douglas had handled the issue of the site hut location beautifully. He could see that the clarity of Douglas's delivery was gaining respect from Norman Keen. *Let's hope he keeps it up. The next point on the list may result in more acrimony from Chisholm but should hopefully still end in our favour.*

"Thank you for that arrangement, Mister Keen. It is much appreciated. The next item concerns your instruction to run the system only during working hours instead of twenty-four hours per day as stated in the tender documents. For frost protection, we have been instructed to dose the pipework with Ethylene Glycol at twenty per cent by volume."

"Is that a problem Mister Fairbairn?"

"Not in itself but it becomes a problem in two attendant circumstances. First of these is that the system has a nominal water capacity of approximately one hundred thousand litres. That means the system will require twenty thousand litres of Ethylene Glycol. If it ever has to be drained for any reason, a significant amount, if not all of that glycol could be dumped into the drains and end up in the Moray Firth Estuary."

"What troubles you about that, Mister Fairbairn?"

Douglas handed the S.O. a copy of a letter.

"Can I ask you to read this letter from the Moray Firth Water Purification and Protection Authority? You will see they warn of prosecution if this were to happen. Glycol is toxic and heavier than water. It would sink to the bottom of the sea. All life on the affected seabed area of the estuary would perish. On the other hand, if a fracture of the welds occurred, the same volume of Glycol would pour out over the Bluff depot site. Since Glycol is highly flammable, this may be considered to be an unacceptable fire or explosion hazard in any location but more especially so in an armaments depot.

The nuclear implications are not known to us but presumably this would be of even greater concern?"

"It is plain that has to be avoided. You said there were two items of concern?"

"The second issue is that the pipes will burst in any case. There is no facility within this system to accommodate the excess water due to expansion during heating up. Well before reaching the design temperature the pipes will fracture. A hundred thousand litres of the water/glycol mixture will spill over somewhere on the site, find the drains and being flammable, will present the risk of explosions in the drainage systems possibly throughout the depot and beyond. Eventually the leakage will enter the estuary."

"What do you recommend Douglas?"

"Firstly I suggest cancellation of the instruction to use glycol for frost protection. I would instead use ultra-low wattage electrical heating tape around and in contact with the pipes prior to the application of thermal insulation.

Secondly I suggest the installation of a spill tank of around five or six cubic metres capacity complete with automatic controls, pumps and integral pipework and valves. This will capture the spill water, due to expansion as the system heats up and pump it back in as the system cools down. There will be no significant losses."

"Are you saying that there is no spill tank?"

"Yes. There is no spill tank or any other means of accommodating the expansion and contraction of the water"

"Is this true Mister Chisholm?"

"Forgive me, Norman. I shall have to confer with my colleague."

Norman Keen sat back and sighed audibly. He pondered for a moment; *Douglas Fairbairn has done his homework. He delivered precise details of the design fault and offered swift, well-constructed solutions to the problem. Why is this consultant not aware of this problem?* He leaned forward and voiced his exasperation, making not only his irritation clear but also that he had no wish to talk to Chisholm on first names terms,

"Mister Chisholm, your earlier short statement to this meeting gave me the clear impression that you had checked your design and all of your calculations for this project. Are you now telling me that you did not do that?"

"I had my staff do the checking and I trust their report, Norman. I shall allow Sean to respond to your question if you will bear with us?"

"Since you seem not to know the answers, it would be simpler if your Mister O'Casey responded to the questions in future."

Tony just loved this. The S.O. was justified in giving the chief consultant a red face. Dean Chisholm was floundering in his attempt to try on the 'old pals' routine. Norman Keen had succeeded in making him feel uncomfortable and seemed to be relishing having the big bumptious trout wriggling on his line. O'Casey eventually stopped thumbing through the notes in his leather-bound folder and looked up to speak,

"I am afraid I shall have to take notice of this item and give feed back at another time Mister Keen."

"Why?" Said Norman.

"I can't quite recollect what was actually specified I'm afraid."

"Well I'm afraid that is not good enough, Mister O'Casey. It seems that the contractor has found a glaring omission in your design. In spite of you senior partner's advice not ten minutes ago that you had scrupulously re-visited your records, you are telling me that you need to re-visit them once again. Perhaps this time you will do so more painstakingly if we are not to have our time wasted by your inadequate knowledge."

"Perhaps I can help, Mister Keen? I have a copy of that part of the preamble detailing the pressurisation unit."

"May I have a look at that, Douglas?"

The builders and the Clerk of Works were looking uneasy. It was unusual for an exulted consulting engineer to be pilloried like this, let alone the senior partner. Tony was not the least bit troubled...Quite the opposite in fact. The S.O. had addressed Douglas twice by using his Christian name. He had not used that civility with either of the two consultants and it looked as if he had no future intention of so doing. This was a roasting for Dean Chisholm.

Tony had promised that he and Douglas would *bury these bastards* but it was so much more fun to watch this astute Supervising Officer doing it on their behalf. Chisholm was being hung out to dry and Tony's man, Douglas, was pulling the rope. It was going to get tighter yet as they continued with Liseur's list. Norman Keen finished reading and handed the paper back to Douglas.

"There is no mention of a tank in the preamble. Is there a tank shown on the boiler house drawings or on the controls schematic by any chance, Douglas?"

"I have both of these here for you to look at. If you care to check, you will see there is no mention on either of the two drawings."

"Thank you, Mister Fairbairn. I believe I am safe in accepting your word for that. I will issue an instruction through Jarvis & Craig to obtain a quotation from you for the tank and controls for your pressurisation unit. I will rescind the order for glycol in favour of your excellent suggestion for the introduction of low wattage tracing tape around the entire pipework system including the boiler house. A separate instruction will be issued for that item. Are you able to anticipate these instructions and prepare your tenders for these items without any further delay, Douglas?"

"Yes Mister Keen, I have assembled the bulk of basic costs and can issue these to Jarvis & Craig in a couple of posts."

"Thank you. What is your next item?"

"There will be no cost involvement with this item Mister Keen. The preamble specifies that the gas safety shut-off valve in the boiler house must be held open by steel catenary wire. The Automatic Control Firms nowadays recommend updating and improving this method by the use of hard-wired electronic devices discretely attached to the gas shut-off valve."

"Why?"

"It provides a more reliable safety precaution. The old style piano wires need to be strung at head height on little pulleys throughout the plant room. The wires have fusible solder links above each gas burner on the boilers. These links melt in contact with fire. The wire is thus severed and releases a heavy weight attached to the gas shut-off valve. It falls and closes the shut-off valve. The tight wires present a hazard to people's faces and eyes."

"That sounds painful. I'm not sure I like that very much. Is there more?"

"Yes, the other problem is that the wires can get twisted and stick in their pulleys. In the event of a fire, the gas shut-off valve could remain open thus continuing to feed the fire. That mechanical method is not full-proof."

Dean Chisholm erupted with an impassioned shout directed at Douglas,

"How dare you say our design is out of date? This fire-valve cable system has been used as long as I have been practicing in this industry. I see no reason to alter it on your whim!"

Norman Keen ignored the outburst. Merely smiled and spoke directly to Douglas, picking up on the consultant's objection but almost in jest, included a barbed thrust.

"I can appreciate that modern technology is attractive these days but I'm sure you will understand, Douglas, that tried-and-tested ideas from the past do have a strong allure amongst the older generation of engineers. You said these old-fashioned catenary or piano wires can get stuck and the gas valve stays open. What happens with your new-fangled electronic system if there is a power cut?"

"The default condition in the event of a power failure, Mister Keen, is that the electronic fire shut-off valve closes automatically...every time."

"Well if that is the case it seems the electronic system removes an obvious personnel injury hazard and what is more important, guarantees protection at all times against fire. I shall instruct that the electronic system shall be fitted to replace the out-dated one. I note that this will be a 'no cost' item."

Dean Chisholm was furious. He jumped up from the table knocking his chair backwards with a clatter onto the wooden floor while spitting out an angry stream of vitriol at Douglas Fairbairn.

"Fairbairn! You insolent young pup! We've been in this business since before you were even on the planet. What right do you have to pick holes in our work?"

The room was silent. They all waited for a reply from Douglas who simply turned and looked at Norman Keen, expecting him to call for order. He was not disappointed. Norman spoke directly to Chisholm,

"If there were no suspicion of holes in your work then this meeting would not have been called. The fact that we are here today gives Douglas the right to say his piece. It also gives me the opportunity to prevent the Ministry of Defense suffering unduly from your flawed work Mister Chisholm. Please sit down and allow me to continue my work with Franz Liseur without further unhelpful and unsolicited input from you or your colleague, O'Casey."

Chisholm was speechless! Before he could muster another outburst, Norman Keen cut him off,

"I suspect that the afternoon session may prove equally enlightening. Since it is now eleven forty-five, I suggest we stop for an early lunch? We shall re-convene at one o'clock."

He got up and walked out past the Consultants. He had chosen to lunch on his own today.

Hugh Jarvis came over to shake hands and introduce himself to Tony and Douglas,

"How do you do Mister Surtal, I am Hugh Jarvis."

"Hello Mister Jarvis. I'm pleased to meet you. Wish it was in better company though."

"Yes I know what you mean. Your Mister Fairbairn here is surprisingly adept at poking holes in big balloons. My colleague, Joe has had some fun with him so far and I can see why you have him fronting this project. What I've heard today has opened my eyes to the tough times you have had to date with this design and those who have perpetrated it. Can it be sorted?"

"Well, Hugh I will leave the answer to that to Douglas here."

"It is going quite well towards a design solution, Mister Jarvis but if the consultant digs his heels in then it will become a battle of attrition for us all I'm afraid," said Douglas.

"Well now, if it's to be like that I will be very keen to see who will win. I guess it's early days yet but I'm keen to hear what this afternoon reveals. See you after lunch?"

"Fine," said Tony. "You are in for a treat."

"You mean there's more problems?"

"Yes, Hugh. Be assured you'll not be falling asleep this afternoon"

They went their separate ways but Hugh Jarvis was in a quandary. *At the moment Liseur seem to be the ones to win this contest. If they keep this up I should be able to pick the winning side. Time will tell. It's a bit early yet."*

Part 8
Wed afternoon 21th Feb 1990

Site Meeting at R.N.A.D. Bluff
The S.O. gave a brief summary of the morning's discussions and conclusions and called for calmness during the afternoon session. He made it clear that he would not allow any personal verbal attacks on pain of being asked to leave the meeting. When delivering this warning, he stared fixedly at the two consultants. Dean Chisholm was cleaning his spectacles at that exact moment; huffing his breath on them, rubbing them intently with his handkerchief and holding them at arms length up to the window to check for clarity. Norman invited any opening comments but there were no takers.

"Well, Douglas, it falls to you to continue with your list of items for my consideration. I see from your notes that there are pipe-welding issues?"

"Thank you, Mister Keen. There are three aspects that concern us about the testing of our welding. To begin with it seems from our foreman's reports that two out of every three welds are failing the ultrasonic testing. After three failures from any one of our welders, they are dismissed from the site. We have replaced five men in one month. I don't believe there are enough welders in Scotland to continue at this rate of attrition."

"Why are these welds failing?"

"Ultrasonic negatives of the welds are inspected by the clerk of works in a darkened room using a light box, just like doctors do in hospitals with X-Ray photographs. Mr Yeoman decides if the inclusions are acceptable or not."

George Yeoman was suddenly awake, sitting upright in his chair. His face showed a mixture of fear, alarm and panic. He seemed to be thinking, *oh no! Now I'm in the hot seat. After what Dean Chisholm has just been through, what will this man, Fairbairn, do to me about my work on the weld testing?* He did not have long to wait. The S.O responded,

"That seems simple enough to me, Douglas. Explain to us all what an inclusion is?

"It appears on the negative like an air bubble inside the weld where the metal has liquefied but not fused a hundred per cent together. The allowable bubble size has to be equal to or less than one quarter of the *weld* thickness. The pipe *wall* is four millimetres thick but when finished the *weld* is six millimetres thick."

Please explain the problem, Douglas? I am unfamiliar with this procedure."

"Well, none of our 'bubbles' has ever exceeded one point five millimetres in diameter. They should all have passed since they are all less than a quarter of the six millimetre thick *weld* and that complies with the applicable welding standard"

Norman, with his eyebrows raised, turned to face George Yeoman signifying he required his explanation. Yeoman coughed, leaned forward with his hands clasped and elbows on the table. Looking away from Douglas, he spoke directly to the S.O.

"The welds that failed have inclusions of more than one millimetre in diameter. They fail because they are more than a quarter of the *four* millimetre thick pipe."

"Well Mister Fairbairn. It seems you are both reading different testing parameters. Can you explain?"

"Yes I can. It is not complicated. Our pipes are four millimetres thick. Our welds are six millimetres thick. The inclusions should be measured across the *weld* thickness...not the *pipe* thickness. In all cases so far our inclusions have been less than twenty- five per cent of our weld thickness. All our welds should have passed."

"What do you say to that Mister Yeoman?"

"I've been told to use ISO 22825. That states that the wall thickness is to be used for measuring inclusions. Anything over one millimetre on a four-millimetre pipe is a fail."

"It seems you lose this one, Mister Fairbairn. Unless of course you have more to say?"

"Mister Yeoman is using the wrong standard. The contract preamble states that ISO 17640 is the standard that applies to our four-millimetre thick steel pipe meaning that the *six-millimetre thickness of the weld* should be used for measuring inclusions."

Norman Keen stroked his chin. He looked at the consultants and requested an opinion. He got an unhelpful response from Dean Chisholm, who, while staring out of the window, answered but didn't bother to turn round,

"Welding is of no interest to me or my colleague."

Norman Keen shook his head and answered him with a look of utter disgust,

"Well it should be, sir. Your specification for the project includes the welding standards to be used. Subject to checking this, I am nevertheless inclined to take a view. Before that I want to hear the other two points on this subject. If you would be so kind Mister Fairbairn?"

"Certainly Mister Keen. I regret that the next items concern the competence of the Clerk of Works. It would be churlish of me to proceed without asking for Mister Yeoman's agreement."

Norman Keen would have none of it and brushed the goodwill gesture aside,

"We don't need that. I want to hear what you have to say. If Mister Yeoman wants to leave the meeting, then he can."

Yeoman looked decidedly uneasy but remained seated.

"Please continue, Douglas?"

"Thank you. Also in the contract preamble is ISO standard 16809, which details the requirements for the equipment *and* the personnel to be employed when measuring inclusions. The inspector is required to have a current, valid ophthalmologist's certificate of compliance for his eyesight. It specifies that the measuring be done using a microscopic measuring device capable of reading down to one tenth of one millimetre. For instance, an engineer's micrometre screw gauge."

Yeoman sat with his head bowed over the table. He was not about to say anything but the onlookers heard his audible groan of despair.

"I take it you have some more to tell us about that, Douglas?"

"Yes. I am afraid the Clerk of Works was unable to produce such a certificate or the required measuring device."

"But surely he needed a similarly accurate device to measure such small 'inclusions' as you call them?"

"That is correct but it was not the case, Mister Keen, and I am slightly embarrassed to tell you. Mister Yeoman used and still uses a small, cracked and heavily abraded, Perspex ruler of the kind you would find in a school child's pencil case. The calibrations are in millimetres. He also wears spectacles.

Because of these shortcomings we have had all of our ultrasonic weld negatives inspected by an independent examiner. Many of them are well below one millimetre and not one is more than one point two millimetres."

Norman Keen looked at George Yeoman with some concern. Yeoman was still hanging his head, seemingly ashamed to speak. The S.O. waited for a moment or two before inviting him to give his account of his totally unacceptable technique. Yeoman looked up eventually, pointed to the builders and blurted out,

"It was Jarvis & Craig. They asked me to slow the contractor down by failing their welds!"

Hugh Jarvis had uttered not one word since the first statement in the morning. Now he ceased being an observer, spun round and bawled at Joe Hadshaw.

"Did you do that?"

"No!" shouted his manager. "I might have said something to our site agent, Terry Cordwell, but I never asked him to screw up the welds."

Yeoman was having nothing of it and was determined that if he was heading for the chop, Joe Hadshaw was going with him. He jumped to his feet shouting,

"You're a damned liar, Hadshaw. It *was* you! And you still owe me the money you promised you bloody skinflint!"

Hadshaw knew now that his time was up but tried one last gasp attempt to win a reprieve,

"Shut yer face ya stupid bastard. You'll get us baith hung!"

Hugh Jarvis sat still as a statue; his mouth hanging open in utter disbelief not knowing how to handle this infantile action by his manager. Norman Keen having heard enough stood up, thumped the table very hard and commanded,

"Stop this you fools! I will have order now! I have never in my life heard anything like this. Mister Jarvis, you need to remove your man from the meeting."

At that suggestion, Hugh jumped up,

"I'll do better than that!"

He grabbed Joe Hadshaw by his collar and punched him very hard in the face. Hadshaw fell to the floor like a burst tomato, blood oozing from his nose. Norman Keen, by this time had moved round the table to witness the bleeding form of Hadshaw struggle to his feet and head for the door followed closely by the sound of Jarvis's booming command,

"You're sacked! Find you own way back to Glasgow!"

Jarvis turned round momentarily to excuse himself from the meeting. Then, yelling expletives at the fleeing Joe Hadshaw, he darted out of the open door of the hut. The rest, as if turned to stone, simply watched the undignified departures of both men. Yeoman was in tears, head on hands, at the table. The S.O regained his seat, sighed and heroically tried to regain his composure,

"Well I never! I don't expect we shall see either of those two back in this hut today. As for you, Mister Yeoman, you can consider yourself suspended from duty. I should caution you that committing acts of sabotage within a naval establishment was at one time a hanging offence. Your conduct will be reported to James Briggs of the M.O.D. I expect you will very soon be honoured by a visit from the naval and civil police. Deposit your keys and pass to the gatehouse guards. Do not enter this site again. Be gone, you wretched man!"

Yeoman got up and slunk out without closing the door. The whole episode had lasted only a couple of minutes. No one could ever have expected such an outburst of violence. Tony whispered to his team to stay silent until the S.O. restarted the meeting.

"Will someone please close the door?"

The two consultants were nearest to the door but remained seated. They evidently felt, since lesser mortals were present, it was beneath their pay grade to carry out such menial tasks. Angus stood up, sauntered over and shut the door quietly. On his way back to his seat he whispered behind Dean Chisholm's chair so that all could hear,

"Ah don't mind showing the consultants how a door works Mister Keen."

Norman was discrete enough not to hear him, but showed by his downward smile he had secretly admired the foreman's wit. It lightened the mood from the recent unhappy scuffles. Now he could continue,

"I did say that this afternoon may be more entertaining, but I never expected this. In spite of all that, I am determined to continue. I want everything to be finalised before we go tonight."

Now, Mister Surtal, in light of the misdemeanours of the ex Clerk of Works, I authorise you to reinstate all of your welders. Subject to my satisfactory witnessing of your independent welding tester's results and a sight of the ISO standards Douglas referred to, I will instruct that your welds have passed.

I shall not require any further weld testing to be carried out unless you wish to keep a check on your own welders' quality. I expect, subject to simple calculation within your inevitable claim for loss and expense, that you will agree my action is acceptable and an end to that distasteful matter? Unless of course you may wish to pursue Jarvis and Craig for damages consistent with what we have just witnessed today?"

Tony was quick to agree and to thank the S.O. He expressed his regret for the untoward display across the table. Others might have interpreted the disturbance as an attempt by Liseur to cause trouble. He wanted to make it clear that his only motive was to secure the smooth, rapid progress and quality of Liseur's work.

"Thank you, Mister Surtal. Now Douglas, let us move on to your final item. Please continue."

"Thank you, Mister Keen. Our site doorman...sorry... foreman, Angus McLachlan, (no laughter was heard from the stone-faced consultants) brought to our attention the absence of flanges on the pipework. Pairs of flanges are often used to take up the pipe's expansion by the process known as 'cold draw'. It is not possible to use this method on this site, as the pipes form a straight line from north to south. That explains why there are no flanged joints on the pipes."

Norman Keen was interested in finding out why Douglas was actually complimenting the designer,

"It would seem in this instance Douglas, that you are quite happy with the absence of these items and have no argument with the drawings. Are you about to prove me wrong?"

"Perhaps Mister Keen. I do have an argument with the drawings but it is to show the consultants are wrong, not your good self. Cold draw can only be applied when a pipe changes direction. It can't be employed if the pipe is in a straight line. To that extent the drawings are correct in not having them."

"I am intrigued to hear what point you are making here. Do we need or not need flanged joints?"

"Let me say I believe we do need them. My reason will soon be understood. I studied the drawings to see how the design was intended to accommodate the inevitable *expansion* of these steel pipes. I saw no provision on the drawings or in the specification for controlling the huge expansion that will take place when these pipes are heated. That is a mistaken omission by the consultant who did the design"

"Any comment Mister Chisholm?"

Dean Chisholm forewent the display of cleaning his eyeglasses and answered without a pause,

"Yes of course. It's very simple. The pipes will hang on freely moving supports. As the pipes expand and contract, they move backwards and forwards on swinging drop rods. Seems that Liseur have tried again to cause trouble. This time I think we score the points. I rest my case Norman."

"Is it that simple Mister Fairbairn? Somehow I get the feeling that it may well be more complex. Please advise me?"

"Yes, Mister Keen. You are again correct. Mister Chisholm has just described a common mistake made by many designers. My simple calculation using the co-efficient of linear expansion of mild steel...."

He was cut short by Keen,

"Listen, Douglas. I am a structural engineer. I know how that works and I see where you are heading with this. Please continue however. Our esteemed friends from the Clark Chisholm partnership may find it educational."

Chisholm harrumphed loudly but said nothing.

"Thank you, Mister Keen. As you are aware we need only the pipe temperature and length for this calculation. The expansion along the full length of this site is over ten metres. There are no facilities to absorb such a huge increase in length.

There are no hairpin loops. There are no anchors or guides to cause the loops to compress and take up the expansion. Without those safeguards the pipes will lengthen by around five metres at each end of this seven-kilometre site.

Free-swinging supports will not accommodate that amount of expansion. The pipe supports will fail. Most of the branches to the thirty-five buildings will fracture and snap off.

The main pipework will self-destruct causing one hundred cubic metres of water at a hundred and thirty degrees centigrade to spontaneously flash into steam. The consequences of all of this disorder on a nuclear establishment such as Bluff are outwith my skill to speculate. I leave that to others."

Douglas sat down and closed his notebook. Tony slapped him on the back and whispered his congratulations. Norman Keen looked at Dean Chisholm. Dean Chisholm looked at Sean O'Casey. Sean O'Casey looked at the table. Norman turned to Douglas,

"I am certain you have a solution to the problem. Would you care to advise me and the consulting engineer?"

"I can suggest two ways to accommodate such massive expansion. These are quite simple but they are not cheap. The pipes require to be anchored to their plinths at strategic points, probably about thirty metres apart. In between each pair of anchors, a "U" shaped full-bore 'hairpin' type pipe loop would be fitted. I have calculated that it will take approximately four hundred of such loops in total for both pipes. Each one will take up between forty and fifty millimetres of the expansion. The overall length of the seven kilometres of pipe will not alter and the system will be stable, if it is well maintained."

"And the cost, Douglas?"

"For the pipes, flanges, supports, thermal insulation and attendant builders work I would suggest a provisional figure of about three hundred thousand pounds."

"Thank you, Douglas. Today I have listened to your cogent and compelling arguments for radical changes to the design of the mechanical services for this project. I congratulate Franz Liseur on their thorough investigation of this design as reported and discussed with us all today. I shall advise Mister Briggs of the M.O.D. of my opinion that I should be allowed to authorise the changes necessary to ensure the safe completion and operation of the mechanical services.

I shall also recommend that the Clark Chisholm partnership should be removed in favour of Franz Liseur to get this project finished safely using your indisputable design expertise. It is clear that there will be substantial time and cost penalties involved and these may, in my opinion, be recoverable in full by the mechanical contractor under a direct contract with the M.O.D."

Dean Chisholm grabbed his coat, dragged his associate from his seat and stormed out of the meeting. As he reached the door he made it clear to the S.O. that he was not amused.

"Now you listen to me, Mister Keen. You will not get away with this. I have powerful friends. You had better watch your back. This is by no means over!"

The door slammed. The meeting was over. Norman Keen turned to Tony and offered his hand.

"I'm glad that's over Mister Surtal. It seems that it's only those of us who know what they're doing are left. You and your team have done a thorough job today."

He turned to Douglas,

"Please let me have a letter with a copy to the builders giving me probable costs for putting this job right. I will recommend that the M.O.D. authorise the necessary instructions through me for the future of this job. How soon can you respond?"

"Well, Mister Keen...

Norman cut him off,

"Douglas, please call me Norman."

"Well, Norman, I don't know the exact cost at this moment. I can tell you that if you add up all I've told you today plus allowances for the builders, ten per cent contingency and a prolongation claim for loss and expense, I don't expect there will be much change out of two million pounds."

"Is that a conservative estimate?"

"No. It's a sum that I suggest would be sufficient to cover everything necessary to finish the job properly. It doesn't include any professional fees or other builder's work implications."

"Fine, if you would let me have that I will get ahead with the necessary permissions and instructions. I need you to set it all out in clear itemised sections. There should be no doubt in the mind of James Briggs just what an abysmal job these consultants have foisted on him Douglas. Nor what ways and means will be needed to put it right."

"I still have to gather a few costs, but I should be able to get the letter you want into the post within about a week. What about the P.R.V.'s Norman?"

"Oh yes, the P.R.V's. Chisholm is digging in his heels. The instruction from me still stands. Your reports today cause me to doubt the validity of my instruction to keep the P.R.V.'s in. It may vitiate the contract and I want no part of that. I will counsel Mister Briggs and urge that he come with me to watch your computer simulation... that is if you and Tony will permit it?"

"Of course he must come, Norman. If he isn't convinced now he will be when he sees what we've seen. He won't want to be hiding behind the consultants feeble smokescreen."

"Then it may even soften his attitude towards you, Douglas. How much notice do you need?"

"That may be. I don't expect he will chuck me out of this proposed meeting. We can arrange it with an hour's notice. You just let me know a time suitable to you both."

"Okay chaps. The meeting is over. Thank you all and good luck."

They all departed from a meeting that had been eventful, long, and fruitful and had come to an amicable end for those who remained. During their drive back to Glasgow, Tony gave his reaction to the events of the day.

"That was a major turning point in this saga lads. Douglas now has full authority from none other than the Supervising Officer of the Ministry of Defence to write the definitive letter that torpedoes that couple of clowns who call themselves consulting engineers. Are you quite clear Douglas about how he wants it presented?"

"Yeah Tony, it'll be short and sweet, just like the list I gave him. I'll summarise our opinions about the need for the suggested changes and stick the probable cost implications against each item."

"Make it clear it's all or nothing."

"Does that mean the removal of the P.R.V's, Tony?"

"Absolutely Douglas. Without that we will be building a job that is unsafe, will self-destruct and in doing that we will be breaking the law of the contract! Like Norman Keen, I want no part of that damned fiasco."

"I'm with you on that, Tony but it's down to Norman to convince the big guy in Edinburgh which side of his bread has the jam on it."

"I like that. If he chooses the wrong way he'll have jam on *his face*. I'm wondering if he has the authority to muster the cash needed to do what we want? After what he's done to the costs it may not be possible for him to go back for four times the amount he told London in the first place."

"Well Tony I hate to say it but...that's his fucking problem, not ours...and that makes a nice change, does it not?"

The other three guys were listening respectfully to this high level banter and their chorus of approval was well received by Tony and Douglas. Angus was particularly pleased with one aspect of the meeting,

"Ah must hand it to you guys for gettin' rid ae that daft George Yeoman. Ah told him he'd get done for the way he was failin' the welds."

Mark Trumann had a pennyworth as well,

"I could not believe that the S.O. started totally against us and then performed a summersault when Douglas put he facts in front of him. We certainly seem to have made an ally of Norman Keen."

"I couldn't agree more, Mark." Said Tony. "Did you notice at one point that he started to use Douglas's first name?"

"Yes I did, Tony but he always called you Mister Surtal. I think that means he loves Douglas but is still deciding about you."

Tony laughed out loud,

"That may be so, but I'd rather he liked Doug here than fall in love with me. Anyway, I don't fancy him. When we entered that lion's den of a site hut, I was convinced there were four groups against. Judging from Norman's about face, it can safely be assumed we need only worry about the other three; Clark Chisholm, Jarvis & Craig and the one I've yet to meet, Douglas's other lovely friend."

"You mean, James Briggs."

"Yes, Doug and I hope he comes to see our computer simulation. If that happens, it's almost certain we'll get him on our side."

"Don't bank on it, Tony. He is a consummate politician and slippery as an eel."

"I'm sure you're right, Douglas but I think it's our only means of stopping this disastrous installation from going ahead."

"Well, Tony I hope you're *right*."

"I *am* right. If he witnesses that simulation he's caught in a trap in this contract."

"How's that, Tony?"

"The conditions of this contract sometimes work in our favour."

"Tell me more. Tony?"

"Be patient. All will be revealed."

Part 9
Fri 23rd Feb 1990

Franz Liseur offices ~ Clydebank
Douglas called in Helen and dictated,

The Keen Parr Felt partnership
23rd February 1990
Attention of Mr N. Keen

Dear Sirs,   R.N.A.D. Bluff (No 006)

We thank you for the courtesies extended to our representatives during the site meeting of 21st February.

In line with your request, you and Mister Briggs can witness the computer simulation next Wednesday 28th February at the Scottish Institute of Mechanical Engineering Research. Let us know what time you intend to visit

The time and cost assessments you require from us are as follows: -

1. *We thank you for your instruction with regard to our huts being outside the security area. We estimate a loss of thirty per cent of our labour cost. Ten weeks of construction time was lost incurring a cost of £30,000.00.net to us.*

2. *The provision of an expansion tank, associated controls, pipework, insulation, testing and commissioning will cost of £33,000.00.net to us. A further six weeks of contract construction time will be needed.*

3. *The provision of 22,500 metres of Low wattage tracing cable plus controls on all of the pipework will cost £25,300.00 net to us. It will take an additional three weeks of contract construction time.*

4. *Fire valve cables changed to modern safety-conscious electronic devices will incur no time or cost penalty in the contract.*

5. *We appreciate your acceptance of the adequate standard of our pipe welding and your waiver on further ultrasonic testing. We confirm here that there will be no claim for loss of time or cost in this item. We shall continue to test our welders and keep the records for your scrutiny if required.*

6.   *To provide loops, guides and anchors to cater for the expansion of the pipework will require an additional 40 weeks of contract construction time.*

7.   *The installation of these items will cost, net to us: -*

450 Expansion Loops	@ £286.00 each	≅ £128,700.00
450 Anchors	@ £93.00 each	≅ £42,000.00
450 Pipe guides	@ £155.00 each	≅ £70,000.00
	Total	£240,700.00 net.

The pressure reducing valves need to be omitted but we are not yet in a position to offer an appropriate design solution or the time and financial ramifications of this. There will be an attendant loss and expense claim for prolongation of the contract. The extension of time may be measured in years rather than months.

We are at your disposal should you seek further clarification of this letter.

Yours Faithfully
Douglas *Fairbairn*
Contracts Manager
Franz Liseur
Scotland   *Ref: HT/DF*

cc	*Sir William North*	*C.E.O. Franz Liseur.*
		London.
cc	Hugh Jarvis	Jarvis & Craig.

CHAPTER FIVE:

Connivance

Part 1
28th Feb 1990 morning

Scottish Institute of Mechanical Engineering
Research ~ (SIMER)

Douglas and Tony were there ten minutes early for their
ten-thirty meeting. They sat chatting in their car while
waiting for the others so they could all go in together.
The previous week in a telephone call to Douglas,
Norman Keen acknowledged receipt of the cost report
he solicited at the site meeting. He also advised that it
wasn't easy but he succeeded in persuading James Briggs
to witness the computer simulation. Douglas had
misgivings about this meeting,

"I'm not eager to meet Briggs only six weeks after I was imperiously ejected from his meeting in Edinburgh."

Tony reassured him, "As the old saying goes, Douglas, it's wiser to face your foe than get stabbed in the back."

"Yeah, that might make sense if we knew how he was going to play this. He is partly, if not largely to blame for this fiasco. According to what Norman Keen told me, Briggs face didn't flinch when he read my letter. His only reaction was to command Norman not to issue any instructions until after he saw this computer simulation today. Maybe he is going to play silly buggers with us, Tony. My guess is he will steer a middle course until he is convinced we are able and willing to do a deal that keeps him in the clear. What's your take on this?"

Tony was intrigued. He didn't respond right away, just sat with his thoughts and stared out of the windscreen. The tranquillity of the almost empty car park with its islands of herbaceous borders, geometric manicured lawns and pristine, space markings was a far cry from the dramatic computer simulation they were about to show their powerful potential enemy; none other than the director of the M.O.D. in Scotland.

"Well, Douglas, he is an important man. Just take it as it comes. Play it by ear. Wait till Briggs declares his intentions. We can only do our best to get him agree with our proposed solutions. It'll be a different matter if he refuses to agree to our plans. Then you and me will need to apply more pressure to force him to acquiesce. What do *you* make of him Douglas? You've met this guy. Is he afraid of the costs?"

"I don't really know, Tony. He may be a bit worried or plain scared to death about the unavoidable approximate amounts listed in my letter. God knows what he will do when he hears that the whole job will end up costing about two million pounds. There's likely to be a bit of an earthquake."

"That could be the game changer, Douglas. If he's alarmed about the three hundred and thirty thousand in your letter, your two million will force him to look for a scapegoat. Otherwise it'll be him for the chop. Who do you think he'll have in mind?"

"I'm not sure, Tony. We now know from Torquil it was Briggs who forced him to slash the cost. That alone would prove that Briggs was the main culprit in the young consultant's panicked decision to alter the design. It could be that someone has leant on Briggs from higher up, someone in the Ministry of Defence in London perhaps? That won't hurt those guys in London. Briggs can't pass the blame up the way."

"I never thought of that angle. How do you think he will play this today?"

"Not sure, Tony, but if Briggs really is scared, it could work to our advantage."

"How do you figure that?"

"Briggs must be looking to blame *someone*. Norman Keen has shown him my letter. That only shows three-hundred-and-odd thousand pounds. I bet you a penny to a bucket of cow manure that Keen has told Briggs that these costs are about to double because of the P.R.V problem. Then there's the loss and expense claims from the builder and us; not to mention other costs and legal stuff we don't know about yet.

"How does that help us?"

"Simple Tony! He'll need to make friends with Norman Keen and Jarvis & Craig. They've done nothing wrong. He can't blame us. We haven't caused the problems; we've only highlighted them and listed the cost penalties."

"I take it, Douglas that you think we need to get into bed with the builders?"

"That goes without saying. We are part of their contract. Who are the ones being left out in the cold? And more importantly, who are the ones with professional indemnity insurance?"

It dawned on Tony what Douglas was getting at. His expression transformed from curiosity to a widening smile,

"Of course! The Clark Chisholm *Partnership*! He'll blame them, not Torquil. The boy has got no money. Briggs will try to use our technical arguments and sue Chisholm for recovery of all the additional costs! I like that. I hope Dean Chisholm has a big insurance policy!"

"So do I, Tony. It would be an elegant way out for Briggs. I hope we're right. Here they come, that's Briggs driving the car that just drove in. You introduce yourself while I stand back out of Briggs' reach."

They got out and walked towards Briggs and Keen. Tony shook hands with Norman and thanked him for coming. He turned to Briggs and offered his hand.

"Hello Mister Briggs. I'm Tony Surtal, Scottish Branch Manager for Franz Liseur. I'm pleased you decided to accept our invitation to look at our computer simulation."

"A great pleasure to meet you, Tony. Please, call me James."

"I believe you already know our Scottish Contracts Manager, Douglas Fairbairn? "

"Yes. Mister Fairbairn and I have met and indeed we have crossed swords, so to speak, but all in the line of duty you understand, nothing at all personal. I never take seriously what's said at meetings. After all, we are all bairns of that noble Scot, Mister Jack Thompson, are we not?"

Tony winced but said nothing as Briggs continued his monologue,

"The circumstances have changed since then of course. I'm sure Douglas and I will inter our proverbial axes and get along famously. His latest letter mightily impresses me. It raises some intriguing issues for which answers are to be sought and agreed. We are in great need of solutions. I understand from Norman that Franz Liseur, with their undoubted engineering excellence, might be persuaded to provide succour?"

Tony was guarded and ignored the implied leading question. He was not the least impressed by Briggs Scottish tweedy appearance or his pompous manner of communication. Without a word he gestured the group towards the entrance door of the SIMER laboratory where he saw Colin Thompson waiting to greet them.

On the slow progress across the car park, Tony exchanged pleasantries with Norman Keen while nursing thoughts about his new acquaintance; *Briggs is waxing very affable. It was shrewd of him to mention our solutions. That seems favourable. Maybe Douglas is right after all and Briggs needs accomplices to steer him safely through the complex battles to follow?* Briggs continued the charm offensive as they headed for the lab.

"Norman has given me a detailed account of the site meeting. Very alarming, I must admit, but we are here with open minds today to see and hear more from you splendid chaps. We must devise ways and means to get this project done and dusted. Agreed Tony?"

"You will find us very agreeable, James. My board has placed considerable resources at my disposal. How I use these depends upon our ability to recover our costs within this contract."

"Why do you say *within* this contract, Tony?"

"I have painful experience of recovering losses *outwith* contracts. It is more difficult and takes longer, James. In this instance my aim is to recover Liseur's considerable investment from within this contract or not at all."

The point was not lost on James Briggs. He had reacted immediately when Tony stated that Liseur had powerful resources. Should Liseur be abused on this contract in any way, especially financially, he now knew they were prepared to engage in a formidable campaign to recover all their costs. It went against his nature to keep up the pretence of friendship with Liseur, but he was the ultimate politician; you were not his friend even if you were the enemy of *his* enemy. He was also a realist. Behind him he had the might of the Ministry of Defence. Its power was based on its ability to threaten sanctions if some underling should rashly choose to challenge government authority. Bullyboy *tactics* were cheap and easy but for governments to spend substantial *funds* to fight battles was far from simple to arrange.

Briggs' brain was working overtime. He hoped to form a scheme, during today's encounter, to outwit the contractors and the professional team; *I've got the Defence Minister watching my every move. Bluff is more than a year behind and it'll be a lot more before it's finished. These technical problems will prove costly. I must find a way out without it costing the M.O.D. I need to keep in with these distasteful commercial people but I hate every one of the profiteering, quasi-legal shysters.*

They met Colin Thompson at the door and he ushered them into the laboratory. When they were comfortably seated he addressed them,

"Good morning to you all. Tony and Douglas have already seen the first computer simulation that I am going to show you. It has been produced using various algorithms that mimic, as closely as we can, the unusual dynamics of the Bluff depot pipework."

Briggs jumped in very fast with a direct question,

"Why are the system dynamics on this project unusual, Colin?"

"Hydraulic, or water-filled heating pipes systems are subject to changes in temperature and pressure. Common reactions take place; pipes expand and contract; pressures reduce due to friction of the pipe. Good system design seeks to control or moderate these changes. This system for the Bluff project has a major fault that was brought to our notice by Mister Fairbairn."

"And what might that *major fault* be, Colin?"

"It's to do with the laws of physics. The closed pipe system at Bluff depot cannot work with two different pressures in opposition. To get back to the boiler house the low-pressure return water from each building has to flow into the main pipe, which is at high-pressure. Violent reactions occur. As you are about to see in my computer simulation, the pipes dance up and down and break up. The sudden loss of pressure causes the high temperature water to flash into steam. Does that answer your question, Mister Briggs?"

Briggs showed no discernible emotion and his seemingly innocent tone made his next question sound bland.

"Have our illustrious consultants seen this computer simulation, Colin?"

Briggs was well aware that Chisholm's men had been to see it. The onlookers seemed by their silence, to sense that his question revealed a perceptible suggestion that he could lay blame elsewhere than himself. If Dean Chisholm *had* seen it then, in his effort to hide the truth, he was at fault for not notifying the M.O.D.

"Yes, Mister Briggs. They came along three weeks ago on the sixth of February. They were not very impressed I believe. Allow me start the computer for you?"

Briggs nodded and gave no physical sign of annoyance but his silence said a mouthful. Colin started the computer simulation and sat down. They watched in silence and a few minutes later Colin went over to switch on the lights. Briggs sat for a moment before voicing his reaction,

"I wish I had seen this three weeks ago. I would dearly love to have heard Chisholm's comments when he saw this remarkable demonstration. Why was I not invited?"

"But you were," Said Douglas. "We asked Jarvis & Craig to invite you along to see this computer simulation. They made no appearance and we assumed they did not tell you since you didn't come."

"I see. Thank you, Douglas. And I take it that Dean Chisholm and Sean O'Casey indulged their innate righteousness by disparaging the notion that they could conceivably be at fault for this whole thing?"

"Yes, they did, and in no uncertain terms. They stated rather boldly that their firm does not make mistakes. They pointed out that they had specified pressure *regulating* valves, not pressure *reducing* valves, so our simulation was utterly flawed."

Briggs turned to Norman Keen,

"You're an engineer, Norman. What's the essential difference between these two valves?"

"I'm afraid I am only a structural engineer, James. Hydraulics is not within my skillset" He turned to Tony, "Perhaps you could answer that?"

"Yes I could but the one who first spotted this problem might be the best one to answer your question Mister Briggs. Since he only recently joined us from the Peurova Partnership of international consultants, I will yield to his greater knowledge. Tell us the difference, Douglas?"

"There is no difference."

Briggs shot in with another question,

"Why then are there two names for the same valve, Douglas?"

"This special valve was designed for both *reducing* and *regulating* gas pressure in pipes. Your system at the Bluff depot was originally designed as a steam system. You all know that steam is a gas. For some reason Clark

Chisholm's engineer altered his design from steam to water. I still wonder why he did that. Could it perhaps all have been about cost?"

Douglas paused. He saw how quickly Briggs' expression had changed when he heard the phrase; *perhaps all have been about cost*. He knew something of which Briggs was as yet unaware. It was up to Tony to reveal that later at the appropriate moment. He made a mental note of the big man's reaction, *could it be that Briggs is showing signs of guilt and uncertainty?* Then continued,

"He changed the system from a gas viz. steam to a liquid viz. medium temperature hot water. The mistake was in retaining the P.R.Vs. The reason for that error being made is complex. Only the one who made the error can truly know the full story."

Briggs relaxed somewhat on hearing that. It was looking more like Dean Chisholm's firm would carry the can. He was keen to hear more and hazarded a further question,

"Complex or not, Douglas, I'd like to hear why this is a mistake?"

"I'm not inclined to bore you with a load of physics, at least not yet, but it's very simple really. Colin's computer simulation answers your question. You have witnessed a demonstration of what happens in a water system like this one when you attempt to vary the pressures with pressure reducing valves."

Briggs looked unhappy again and far from satisfied with that short answer. As he gathered himself to fire more questions at Douglas, Norman Keen cut him off,

"Thank you, Douglas, for that clear explanation. I didn't know it was quite so simple. What a pity our friends at Clark Chisholm can't see it and refuse to admit it. The man who designed this project was badly used by Sean O'Casey. Having seen this computer simulation today, I don't know why they are still insisting the design is correct?"

Without another word, Briggs stood up and went to gaze out of the window. It was evident that he had been strongly affected by the succinct report Douglas Fairbairn gave of the problem the P.R.Vs created. Tony went over to join him. Those two seemed to need a discrete huddle before coming back to look at the next computer simulation.

Douglas and Norman had moved to a small table on the other side of the room. Colin joined them carrying a fresh pot of coffee. After a few minutes Tony and Briggs re-joined them. While Colin set about preparing to show the next computer simulation he explained his reason for making it,

"Out of curiosity I examined the drawings to see if there was anything else in the design that might cause a disruption. At that time Douglas gave me a call. Like me he was curious to see if the pipe temperature might be significant. I adjusted the computer algorithm to consider only the effect on the system as it warmed up. When I saw the result I knew that Douglas would want to see it."

Again, Briggs was first with a comment,

"Colin, are you giving us good news or bad news?"

"It depends who you are, Mister Briggs. This simulation is based purely on the *temperature* of the steel pipes. Here's what it showed me."

He played the computer simulation. They saw the extreme ends of the pipes growing longer by about five metres. James Briggs gasped. The simulation showed the utter collapse of the pipes. Douglas shouted out,

"Colin! My calculation shows the same, about ten metres overall! There are no facilities on the drawings to take up and control that amount of pipe expansion. There are no expansion loops, anchors or guides detailed on the drawings."

"That's spot on. Douglas. Now we know that this system will self-destruct in *either* of these two ways, pressure fluctuations or temperature rise. What is certain is that it will definitely self-destruct with both. It's over to you gentlemen."

Douglas and Tony watched the now rather agitated James Briggs lead Norman Keen by the arm towards relative privacy of the window. The others could not hear a word but it was evident from Briggs pointing his finger at the S.O.'s face that he was issuing commands and wanted them obeyed. Norman kept shaking his head and turning away to break off the discussion; as if to say he would not comply.

Colin was quite certain that the man from the ministry would accept his predictions about the failure of the pipes. He was not sure what was going on between Briggs and the S.O. or what was going to happen next. Tony and Douglas sipped their drinks, waiting on the pair returning with their reactions to what they had seen. They hoped Briggs would say something dramatic and set their minds at ease. They were not disappointed. Briggs approached them, smiled broadly, clasped his hands and vigorously rubbed them together as if he had had a sudden and wonderful revelation,

"This is what we will do gentlemen. There is a fine restaurant in Glasgow that I often frequent. Let's all five of us repair to it now and relax with a splendid dinner. Nothing gets my mind round a problem better than a good juicy sirloin and they have never let me down. Agreed?"

"Who's paying James?"

"Why, Norman, you are the one getting all the fees. This one is surely on you my boy?"

"Not at all! Tony butted in, "Douglas will cover this one. I'll sign his expenses."

They left amid polite laughter. Tony was thinking *it's beginning to look like Briggs is mustering his troops for the war with The Clark Chisholm Partnership. He really has no choice. He either does it that way or his neck will be on the block with the MOD. I'll get Douglas to humour him till we find out what exactly is his game. Or maybe he doesn't have one and wants to pump us for a plan he can hang his hat on?*

Norman again shared Briggs' car. Tony followed in his with the others. Colin kept a discrete silence, listening closely as his two clients used their little bit of privacy to share their opinions about the meeting. Tony was clear about how the rest of the discussion should be handled over dinner,

"Colin, you just enjoy a free meal and don't be drawn into any cross-talk with Briggs."

"That suits me fine, Tony. I'm now fairly lost in the contractual niceties and happy to let you both do your stuff."

"Fine Colin. If you have to speak, just state facts. Douglas, if you get stuck on a point, just give me a glance and I'll take over. I'll do the same if caught. Okay?"

"Fine by me. Who takes what?"

Colin looked bemused but still kept quiet, fascinated to learn their conniving tactics, while Tony explained their code of conduct,

"Right Doug, You handle anything on money and design. I'll do politics, logistics and legalities. Okay with that?"

"Understood, Tony. What else and what about Torquil?"

"Yes, Torquil. Leave that to me Douglas. Don't bring it up like you nearly did earlier. We will not agree anything unless and until Briggs makes it clear that he will pay the bill; and I don't mean the dinner bill."

For that to happen needed Briggs allowing Norman Keen to issue official variation instructions in the contract. That way Liseur were guaranteed to recover their costs from the M.O.D. Tony came in with an afterthought,

"Oh and by the way lads, only soft drinks. Clear heads all round. We can't have any slip-ups now that we have the bear out of its cage. Okay you guys?"

All three were happy with the seemingly simple plan and sat back to enjoy general chitchat on the restful ride into town. But James Briggs would require skilful handling if he was to be manoeuvred into a vulnerable position. He had not risen to his lofty height in the M.O.D. without leaving a trail of victims behind him. Douglas was well aware of the man's tenacity when cornered. He was almost waylaid once by Douglas and escaped by bluster and misuse of his authority. Today he and Tony would need to gain the upper hand. It was not going to be easy but they had some advantages over the man from the ministry; plans, money, skill, men and, what Briggs was not yet aware of, they had Torquil knight. Now was the time for Briggs to squirm.

Part 2
28th Feb 1990 afternoon

The RAC Club ~ Blythswood Square ~ Glasgow
James Briggs was in good form during the meal, cracking a few little jokes about his prowess on the grouse moors. He had the same hyper-confident attitude that Douglas had experienced at their unhappy encounter six weeks before. This time though, the great James Bliggs was forced to be less aggressive needing to be everybody's friend. He refused to discuss the project while they were eating. When they were done he proposed they all have coffee and liqueurs in the lounge.

Once transferred, they began a tentative exchange of ideas on the best way to solve the difficulties they were all to a greater or lesser extent deeply involved in, Briggs more than the others. He was eager to resolve the complexities of this difficult situation with respect to allocation of blame as long as it was steered away from him. With a characteristic display of bluntness he initiated the conversation,

"Tell me Douglas, what will happen if we maintain our instruction to you to go ahead and finish the installation and then watch it destroy itself?"

Douglas looked at Tony as if to say, *did he really ask me that question?* Tony gave a slight nod as if to say, *I know it's a legal question but you answer it and just tell him the truth.* Douglas faced Briggs and began a quiet, precise answer,

256

"Nothing will happen to Franz Liseur, Mister Briggs. Both the contract and our letters of warning absolve us of any responsibility or penalty. We will cite you for vitiation of our contract in our legal proceedings to sue you via Jarvis & Craig for loss and expense.

Douglas noted just how cool James Briggs was. He had just been told he would be sued but his facial expression never flickered. Quite the reverse; he simply smiled and asked Douglas another question. He seemed to be indulging himself in some kind of irrational succession of hypothetical paradoxes,

"I see! Without any further instructions from me, how quickly could the work be completed so you could start your lawsuit?"

Tony responded to that,

"We have already begun to prepare our claim for damages, James. I assume, based on our earlier private conversation, your question implies that you are set on having the project completed, destroyed, repaired and finally made safe?"

"Yes, Tony. That is *precisely* what I mean."

"Well then, James it could take years to be completed, but don't take that as an offer. It all depends on what you are willing to do to help us."

"What exactly do you mean, 'help *you*'?"

Tony realised how quickly Briggs could turn things in his favour. He threw back a sharp retort,

"I didn't mean help just *us*. I meant *us* meaning *you* and us."

Briggs winced. He had taken a hit and it was noticed. It was clear to him that he was not dealing with a Torquil Knight. *This man Surtal is as capable as Fairbairn, both of them formidable combatants. I'll have to be careful not to antagonise them. It looks like I need them but they do not need me.* It was dawning on him that he could become the main target of Liseur and their formidable team of lawyers, designers and accountants. He altered his approach,

"Allow me to rephrase, Tony. We have to act *as a team* to get this job done. One way or the other, I am in a position to make this happen. You cannot get it done without my input. What do you need from me to get the project up to speed, properly designed and finished in a safe working condition?"

"As I suggested earlier, we would need your formal instructions to give Franz Liseur full design authority over the consultants. You will have to sack them."

"And if you got that...?"

"We will need you to issue instructions for us to implement Liseur's design modifications as detailed in our letter last week to the Supervising Officer. It will take us some time to procure all of the additional men, materials, tools and major plant items. There will be a lot of new builders work; hundreds of new pipe support bases will be needed. We will draw up a new programme of work. With all of that achieved we will make the project live and safe. I think that could conceivably be completed in around eighteen months from the date of your 'go ahead' to us."

"What do you mean? Are you saying you can't start it up without these instructions?"

"No I am not. We *can* finish the project in line with the present level of instructions. It would however, be criminally insane if you were to instruct that we should deliberately complete a faulty installation and then, knowing it would fail, switch it on and stand back to watch the devastation. We cannot, as responsible, safety-conscious contractors, countenance that approach. Sorry James. You would be responsible for all of the consequences I'm afraid."

"That's okay, Tony. I fully expected you to say that. So, if all instructions were issued next week for all of your suggested modifications, how would you answer then?"

"I'll let Douglas answer that one if you don't mind?"

"It's not that simple Mister Briggs." Said Douglas

"No Douglas, I somehow suspected that would be the case from you. By the way, now that we know each other a little better, I'd like you to call me James."

Douglas decided that he was not quite ready to allow Briggs to become too friendly and tailored his words accordingly, missing out his name entirely.

"Thank you. Our letter didn't show other costs for changes needed to allow the systems to be completed. I am talking about the P.R.Vs. We have received an official instruction to install them. We are thus contractually obliged to install them and to switch on an unsafe installation. We need your instruction not just to *remove* them but to make those other changes to give you a safely completed contract."

"Thank you, Douglas. If that instruction was denied, what would you do?"

"I would carry out your instructions. You, personally, would be responsible for all time penalties and costs when the systems fail in the manner we have demonstrated in our computer simulations and detailed in our letters of caution."

"How do you figure me to be liable? It is the Supervising Officer who issues the instructions."

Once again Briggs was attempting to confuse the Liseur arguments by diversion tactics. Tony, delighted by his quarry's schoolboy error, broke in and seized the moment to spring his trap,

"I am sorry, James. That is naïve. By coming to this demonstration today, you now *know* of the problem. By allowing the S.O.'s instruction to remain in place, you will be contravening your own clause 3.2.6.2 of G.C.

works 1-contract conditions. You will be liable for all loss and expense arising by allowing a procedure that you *now know*, or at least *suspect*, will fail."

Briggs was now struggling to maintain a show of bravado. He was beginning to feel the uncertainty of his own arguments. *It's simply not right that these lowly people should be harrying me in this way. The contractors are supposed to bend a little and assist their higher-ups to get out of situations like this. I'll make light of it and play for time. See what else they have in their armoury.* He tried a spot of levity,

"Well! Blow me down, Tony. You certainly know a thing or two about the contractual pitfalls. It's beginning to look like we don't have much wriggle room gentlemen. Douglas my boy, have you any idea of how long and how much it will take to finish the job properly so we can get the hell away from it?"

"Yes, as a matter of fact I do. It will take at least eighteen months, and you will be lucky to get change back from two million pounds."

Briggs spluttered into his coffee and grabbed for his napkin. He had not expected that figure. His mind was racing; trying to control his conflicting urges. He looked like he wanted to grab Douglas by the throat. At the same time he knew he needed to gain Liseur's backing if he was to escape the blame for this calamitous cost trap into which the Liseur boys had so cleverly steered him. He looked at Norman Keen and blurted out his frustration,

"Did *you* know it would cost that much, Norman?"

"Not officially, James."

"What do you mean, NOT OFFICIALLY man! You either know or you don't. Which is it?"

"James! Calm down please and listen. I was told off-the-record after the site meeting last week. It is not in the minute of the meeting and thus is entirely unofficial."

Tony jumped in at that to reinforce Norman Keen's remark about the cost,

"Yes! And it is *still* unofficial James. It is only a guess. If you procrastinate on this you might as well give us a blank cheque. Remember that the work is still going on at the site. Costs are mounting as we speak."

At this point, Colin Thompson decided he had heard enough. The young computer expert was a stranger to this kind of heated contractual cut-and-thrust. He got up to leave, making the excuse of needing to get back to some work in his laboratory.

"Tony, thank you for a lovely dinner. I'm afraid I'm not really comfortable in your discussion. I'll leave so you can sort this out amongst yourselves. I must get back to work if you don't mind. Nice to have met you all, goodbye."

Briggs, deeply depressed by the news of the probable cost, ignored the young fellow's graceful exit. Tony saw him to the door and slipped Colin enough money for a taxi back to his office,

"Thanks Colin, I think you're right to leave. I expect it will get a bit more intricate as the afternoon progresses but your work has been singularly important in helping us to unravel this fiasco to our advantage. Thanks also for that extra bit of work on the expansion of the pipes. The computer simulation was brilliant. Send me your invoice as soon as you like and we'll get you paid right away. May I have copies of the two computer simulations?"

Colin agreed, thanked Tony and left with a wave and good-luck wishes. Tony went back, taking a detour to the gents' washroom for a few minutes of thought. He needed to figure out where this guy Briggs' questions were heading. He was pleased with the way Douglas had dealt with the answers so far but Briggs was slippery.

He went back to the lounge with the intention of going no further with what they had so far told Briggs. He decided that the sensible course was to give not an inch unless the mighty James Briggs was prepared to deliver written assurances that Liseur would recover all expenses and losses. He returned just in time to intercept Briggs' next question.

"Assuming you don't intend to sue me, Douglas, who do you believe is responsible for this crazy situation?"

"Torquil Knight, James." Said Tony as he came to regain his chair.

"Do you two know him?" Asked Briggs.

Tony interjected, and gave the simplest of replies, "We know *of* him, James. His name is on the contract design drawings."

He didn't want Briggs to know the true answer to that just yet, or that he knew quite a bit about Torquil's sudden exit from Clark Chisholm. Briggs had to be kept in the mind-set that he was partly culpable along with Dean Chisholm's outfit. Tony had a very good reason to suspect that Briggs was fully aware of his part in causing the changes that ultimately damaged the integrity of the design. It was a lot to do with costs in the first instance. That was one of the main functions of the M.O.D., in the shape of Briggs, to keep costs to an absolute minimum.

Tony was intent on probing James Briggs further to try to get him to admit, or at least not to deny, his share in this sorry saga. Briggs was having none of it,

"That doesn't make him solely responsible, Tony. His senior people should have held his hand. Don't you agree?"

"No I do not. Signing a document makes you legally responsibility for what is in it; written on it or drawn on it by your hand."

"So, you would sue Torquil Knight?"

"No, James. There can only be two parties to an action. We would sue the builder who is the other party in our contract. Jarvis and Craig would sue you as their client. You would have to pursue Torquil Knight since you are his client. On the other hand you may choose to set your dogs on Torquil's mentors. But it would be wise to be cautious when considering that."

Tony had played Liseur's hand with skill and saw that Briggs was clutching at straws. *The man knows he is partially responsible. He must be feeling vulnerable having bullied the young consultant into agreeing to a ridiculously low figure for the project. He must know that the budget had given Torquil no choice. The young man had panicked under the pressure from his boss and from Briggs. He slashed the design and had unwittingly made classic errors.*

At this point Briggs was not certain whether Tony was just guessing or did he actually know Torquil had been misused? The only way to find out was to ask him direct questions. If Tony *was* guessing, he could relax.

"I don't follow your meaning, Tony. Please elaborate?"

"I can certainly elaborate but don't want to upset you, James."

"Listen Tony, two million pounds to finish the job! You can't tell me anything worse than that. Spit it out my boy."

Tony was about to disappoint him again,

"Okay, James. I do know Torquil Knight. In fact I know every detail of his dealings with his mentors. Clark Chisholm and Sean O'Casey gave the young man a steam project well within his design capability. It was his specialist subject in his thesis for his B.Sc. degree. What they failed to do was to mentor him in the negotiation skills needed to deal with a client who would bully him into accepting a ridiculously low cost restraint. Torquil was flung in at the deep end and left to drown in your pond while you held him under!"

Tony's last sentence was issued with tight-lipped anger. Briggs sat back in his seat looking shaken. *How on earth does this man know so much?* He wondered if Surtal knew more. *He can't possibly know of his dealings with me.* He tried again to steer the blame away from himself,

"So, they are responsible for his failed design. Bye the way, Tony just in case you hadn't noticed it isn't steam, it's a water system."

"Yes, James I had noticed. It was *originally* a steam system. The brief for the project was to replace the one at the site. Torquil Knight is an expert on steam systems. Sean O'Casey, an ex plumber, isn't! That is the real reason why he gave it to Torquil. Funnily enough Dean Chisholm has a degree in ancient history and totally ignorant of any kind of design."

"I didn't know that boy was so clever." Said Briggs.

"Well he is. Torquil went to the site, full of confidence and noted the design of the old worn-out, dilapidated steam system. That same old dilapidated system that today is still falling apart. It is literally corroding away on the hillside at Bluff; and is still leaking steam and hot water like a sieve all over your precious armaments depot. He designed a new system with all the modern improvements required to make it work properly, economically and above all, function safely for at least the next twenty-five years."

"I had no idea of the system details. All I knew was his cost budget was way over the top!"

"Yes, and that is when you decided to put undue pressure on him. The reason is that *you* were obsessed with keeping the cost to a minimum. That is why you hounded the young lad for well over a year. You finally screwed him so hard for cost savings that he made a fateful decision, in his trauma, to alter his design. He thought afterwards about what he had done and realised the seriousness of his mistake with the P.R.Vs. O'Casey wouldn't listen to him so, he resigned in disgust and walked out into the street."

James Briggs had listened with growing concern at the lecture he was getting from Tony Surtal. His face was becoming redder as the story unfolded with uncanny accuracy, recounting the unjust sanctions he was responsible for imposing on the young designer. His querulous expression gave away the reason for his response, and his feeble attempt to disparage all that had been said.

"You Liseur chaps are indulging in pure speculation about my dealings with that amenable young man, Torquil. I can't see where this idle speculation is leading. I want to assist you all towards a successful outcome on this job. All you're doing is putting me against you with these fairy tales. How do you expect any one to believe such nonsense? Only Torquil and I know the full story and he has departed the scene; probably never to be seen again after the crimes Chisholm allowed him to commit on this project."

"I am sorry to disappoint you, James, this is no fairy tale. He has not gone away. He is very much on the scene. It was he who communicated the full story to me. You see James, Torquil Knight joined the Franz Liseur staff two weeks ago."

Briggs was utterly shocked at hearing such frightening news. Liseur had harnessed the knowledge of the young man who could hurt him. His immediate reaction to this threat was to rubbish it. Without hesitation he shouted at Tony,

"It *is* a damned fairy tale! It's only Torquil Knight's word against mine!"

"Wrong again, James. It is proved by the first set of drawings showing the steam system and the final project drawings we are using on site. Torquil was wise enough to leave his office, armed with a full set of prints for both schemes and copies of the minutes of his meetings with you in Edinburgh. We have those locked up in a safe in our lawyer's office."

All this time, Norman Keen had sat quietly; absorbing the impressive details being given by the men from Liseur. He had been hoping to find out how they came by all this knowledge. They had cleverly debriefed Torquil Knight to put together the sad progress of the design and to verify the disastrous affect O'Casey and Briggs had on the final design.

Such unprofessional, bullyboy treatment of the young engineer was repellent to him. Dean Chisholm's vehement defense of the design was even worse. His blatant performance at the site meeting by fully approving a faulty system was utterly disgraceful. Norman's thoughts were now quite clearly formed as to his future alliances on this project. *Liseur can count on me in any action they intended to take against these charlatans. Taking the young engineer on to his staff was not only a very gracious act but also a Tony Surtal masterstroke.*

James Briggs stared at Tony in disbelief. He had a look on his face like a spider that had just got stuck in its own sticky web. He was trapped. Torquil Knight was Tony Surtal's secret weapon, a weapon that could be used to hang him out to dry. He had to think quickly or he was lost. There was one card left for him to play. Hopefully Tony was not going to spoil his idea by slapping an ace of trumps on it. He took a deep breath and spoke with a confident voice,

"Well gentlemen, it would seem, from your viewpoint, that there are three flies in the ointment; Dean Chisholm, Sean O'Casey and myself. There is very little blame on my part. I admit to having put pressure on the rookie consultant. That is what I do. It is my function. It is however, clearly the case that Knight's bosses are heavily culpable by not having properly directed him or checked the quality of his work."

Tony answered,

"You were the prime mover in the young fellow's demise, James. We are not here today to put blame on any of Torquil's persecutors; at least, not yet. Plainly though, Torquil Knight was mercilessly hounded by his employers and yourself. It's not our purpose to point fingers of blame. We only want to be paid. That's the bottom line. Whatever political way you want to play this, please know that we simply want time and money to finish this project properly and without penalty. Please advise me your opinion and intention, James?"

Briggs was visibly relieved at this unexpected and diplomatic suggestion from Tony. The fencing was over. This was his opportunity to avoid any personal grievance and to agree a way forward. The aggressive politician now emerged and spoke with and assured authority,

"My opinion is this. In my position with the M.O.D., I wield considerable influence to cause things to happen. I can also, in certain circumstances, find the means for their execution. A note of caution however gentlemen; there are occasions when I can do either of the two; but little likelihood of achieving both. There is no professional indemnity insurance involved in working for the government. The MOD cannot be sued. I am sure you know that for any project for the M.O.D., there is never a guarantee of payment. The only assurance you can have for doing government work is that you will be paid from *time to time.*

On the other hand, Clark Chisholm does have professional indemnity insurance. I believe it covers them for sums up to and including twelve million pounds. I suggest we come together, invite the builders to join us, and pursue the guilty party for the expense involved in putting a properly working installation into the Bluff depot."

While he spoke, heads nodded in respect for the clear way Briggs explained the extent of his considerable power. Since there was no other response to his suggestion he set out to reinforce it and promote a positive reaction from his attentive audience,

"This is my only offer. Remember I am at the tip of an iceberg called the Ministry of Defence. Even the considerable resources of Franz Liseur will find it impossible to come higher than second place in any dispute of this type with the MOD. Call me on Friday and let me know if you are prepared to proceed on this basis."

That was a definite end to Briggs input and drew a heavy line under all that had been said. It was time for Tony to bring things to a close,

"Thank you James, I shall do that. Your offer makes a lot of sense. I will run it past my chiefs in Europe. You will know on Friday what we intend to do with you."

Briggs recognised the disguised threat. He smiled and parried it with ease,

"Okay Tony, my thanks to you and Douglas. Let's go, Norman, it's a long way to Edinburgh."

But Norman Keen decided he had other plans that did not include the likes of James Briggs.

"Forgive me, James, but I am staying in Glasgow tonight."

Part 3
Thu 1ˢᵗ Mar 1990

Franz Liseur offices ~ Clydebank

During the morning, with Douglas in his office listening on the extension, Tony held group telephone conversations with his expert colleagues in Paris and Frankfurt.

Fabien Le Maître, their European Head of Mechanical Engineering, agreed that the case was rock solid in Liseur's favour. They could successfully blame and sue the consulting engineers for the poor design and inevitable collapse of the installation.

Their colleague, Thierry Le Jeune, Head of Fluid Dynamics in Frankfurt, Germany, shared this view. The only caveat he advised was that it was quicker and easier to sue a *firm* than to pursue a *government*. Going into partnership with James Briggs had some vague attractions but it was thought best to stick to the contractual protocols, i.e. proceed within the existing contract with Jarvis & Craig, taking only their instructions, whatever those might be. He had his team carry out checks on the pipework and agreed with SIMER that the system was bound to destroy itself on both counts, pressure reducing valves and temperature.

The European Chief of Legal Counsel, Jules Dispard, was very clear about how to proceed. In no circumstances should they enter into a parallel contract with James Briggs. They were to ignore and withdraw any offers to assist anyone outwith their contract with Jarvis & Craig. They should do no alterations unless accompanied by proper variation instructions and amended drawings from the Supervising Officer. Liseur's competent warnings about the design faults were legally in place in writing. Certain instructions have been issued. Liseur should get on with the work and finish it as soon as possible. Jules confirmed he would be starting on Monday to draft the frameworks for claims for the recovery of loss and expense due to *force majeure*. These drafts would be faxed to the Scottish lawyers, McMeikle & Huggett, within days.

His final observation was that the Scottish branch has more than six million pounds in its bank. He confirmed his conversation with Sir William North in London when it had been agreed these funds could be used to finance the speediest conclusion of the work. Douglas should then set it to work, have an array of cameras on the scene and record the disintegration of the installation. After that, they would be free to leave the rest to him. Jules will then advise McMeikle & Huggett, to issue writs on The Clark Chisholm Partnership, citing them as the cause while keeping Jarvis & Craig in the loop. Twenty-eight days will be given for them to respond. Tony thanked them for their advice, switched off the connection, turned to Douglas and whistled.

"And I thought that I was decisive, Douglas. These chaps are in a league of their own!"

"What do we do now, Tony?"

"Douglas, my boy! Let's bury the fuckers!"

Part 4
Fri 2nd Mar 1990

Franz Liseur offices ~ Clydebank
Douglas and Tony were deep in discussion about the
ethical problem involved in deciding which way to go
with the completion of the contract at Bluff. They had
made it clear to James Briggs, during their Friday dinner
at the RAC club, that there was no way they would
consciously build an installation they knew to be wrong
and was certain to fall apart. They had told him that
would be 'criminally insane'.

The startling advice from their top man in Europe,
Jules Dispard, was more akin to a set of instructions.
They should go against their instincts; finish the job,
film the evidence and then sue the responsible party. It
seemed so simple but it still went contrary to everything
these two guys believed in.

Engineering a project was like producing a work of
art. Even the humble welders on the site were artists in
their own right. *They* took pride in their finished
product. Tony and Douglas were being ordered to
destroy all the bonny work of their own tradesmen.
That did not seem fair, but fairness didn't come into
this. It was profit! There was no real option since there
was a lot of money being wasted. Their job was to make
sure it was not Liseur's money that was being
squandered. Now they had to make friends with James
Briggs to prevent that happening. Tony gave Douglas
the job of phoning their unwanted ally.

"Hello. James Briggs here."

"Hello. It's Douglas Fairbairn. How are you?"

"All the better for hearing from you, my boy. What the decision?"

"We are planning to muster as many fitters-welders as possible and to be on site within days to finish this project as soon as it is practical to do so.

"Do you need any further instructions from me?"

"Not at the moment."

"What is your anticipated programme?"

"We will require about thirty weeks including working three weekends out of four. That way we shall be commissioning by about the end of November this year."

"Excellent. Now what details are you using?"

"You will be pleased to know that we are using the current drawings and specifications in order to comply with the contract as it now stands."

"I am impressed with your decision on this. I will ensure that Bill Morgan, the new Clerk of Works, will give you all the cooperation you need to get this done. Norman Keen will do as he is told and will not issue any further variation instructions unless you specifically ask for them. This should turn out quite well, don't you think. Douglas?"

"It will for *some* of us. There are those of us who may need to run for cover."

"I am taking it that you mean The Clark Chisholm Partnership? My question was rhetorical, my boy. Now tell me, how will your additional efforts be financed?"

"There's no need to be concerned. We have the means to do what is required to get this to its conclusion. After that our lawyers will take the appropriate actions to recover our losses. By then we will be on some other, better designed but less interesting jobs."

"Douglas, my boy, it is my intention that your firm will be employed to clear up the mess of this project. It will need to be dismantled and properly designed and rebuilt. I can think of no other people I would want to do that. Please thank Tony for his help and take my apology to you for my initial run-in with you, my boy."

"I have forgotten it already."

"I know that you are being polite, Douglas. I had a job to do and at that stage was unaware of the quality of your firm and of your own skills. This project has taught me many things; one of which is humility."

Douglas knew when someone was trying to ingratiate himself. He was determined not to use 'James' when he spoke to Briggs. This big man was not the least bit humble. He was doing his best to become Douglas's pal, to be an ally of Liseur to fight the consulting engineers. He was wrong on two counts. Douglas chose his own pals and

Briggs was not on the list. Secondly, Briggs was not in the clear; he was very much in the firing line. The very least Douglas wanted was to have the head of James Briggs on a plate. He owed it to himself and to his new colleague, Torquil Knight. Douglas wanted to laugh down the phone but managed to give a response he hoped sounded sincere,

"I quite understand. I have learned some things as well. I'm looking forward to an amicable construction phase on this site at Bluff. With your help it should turn out as we have planned."

"Let's hope so, Douglas. Keep in touch."

"We can only stay in touch with you unofficially. We intend only to deal through the builders. I hope you understand?"

"Yes I do. Keep it straight down the middle, Eh?"

"Yes, Mister Briggs. Goodbye."

"Not *goodbye*, surely...?"

Faintly hearing the final salutation from Briggs, Douglas hung up, pointed at the receiver and thought, *No, Mister Briggs, but it soon **will** be.*

CHAPTER SIX

Construction

Part 1
Mid Mar 1990

Franz Liseur offices ~ Clydebank

Douglas had wasted no time getting things underway for the big push to have the installation completed in the thirty weeks he had estimated. Setting it to work sometime in a cold November would be ideal for optimum destruction. The cold weather coupled with the high temperature of the pipes would ensure the maximum expansion and buckling. That together with the oscillation caused by the P.R.V effects, promised to provide a fine spectacle for their cameras to record the mayhem; the vital evidence for the inescapable court case.

Archie McGregor had managed to assemble a sizeable team of men; eighteen qualified fitter-welders and sufficient labourers. Those twenty-five guys would be working to the directions of Angus McLachlan. A lot of overtime would be necessary but he was confident a squad that size would achieve the desired completion date.

Douglas directed Angus to keep the tradesmen in the dark about the expected destruction of the pipes they were working with such skill to construct. He expected that their subsequent anger would be short lived, offset by their much bigger pay cheques from loads of overtime up until November. Beyond that, things promised to be even more lucrative for these men and for Franz Liseur.

A lot depended upon Hugh Jarvis deciding whose side he was on. The very public on-site revelation of Joe Hadshaw's deceit against Liseur had damaged the Jarvis & Craig reputation within the contract. Tony was well aware how builders' minds sometimes work. If money was all he cared about, Jarvis might turn nasty with Liseur to save his face with James Briggs and Norman Keen. It was time to pin a tail on a donkey, so to speak. He hoped he would not miss and put the pin in Jarvis's *nose*. He had to convince the main contractor that his best interests would be served by joining forces with Liseur rather than continuing their early conflict.

During his tactical phone call to Jarvis & Craig, Tony was delighted that his gut feeling was correct. Hugh Jarvis was clearly very happy eating out of Tony's hand and had no hesitation in agreeing to the proposed plans.

"Yes, Tony. That all sounds good to me. We have no choice but to go along with you on this. After all's said and done, Briggs is the one we must satisfy. Am I correct?"

Tony was relaxed at this new show of goodwill. It seemed like the right moment to get rid of any other lingering contention between them. He wanted absolute clarity for the way ahead but must proceed with care. Builders were always slippery.

"You are quite right, Hugh. I am glad we can cooperate and I am counting heavily on your support. Is there anything you need to clear up before we get going with all this?"

"Well now, since you mention it, I think it only right that I should offer you my unreserved apology for the trouble caused by that rascal Hadshaw. He's gone and we can start afresh. Please let me know if you have recorded the amount that this weld testing nonsense has cost? I will reimburse you for any reasonable sum."

Tony was surprised at this unusual show of contrition, which was well out of character for a main contractor. He decided to avoid any untimely submission of costs.

"That is very kind of you, Hugh. Thank you for your apology. As far as cost is concerned, I prefer to include that figure as a part of our overall loss and expense claim. Our London-based claims experts are busy on this as we speak."

"Oh I see. Then you must allow me to lend you my two surveyors. They are doing the same for me. In this instance I believe they would prove useful to you since they know so much about our mutual dealings on this project."

"That *is* magnanimous, Hugh, but I'm sure you will need them more than me at this stage. Our London boys are well equipped to handle our claim, which I've just told you is well underway."

Jarvis was curious. He could not resist a probe,

"Is it a claim against us, Tony?"

"Only one of them is, Hugh."

"Do you mean you have two?"

"No Hugh, we are preparing three. One for you, one for the M.O.D. and one for the little boy who lives down the lane."

"You've got me, Tony. Who is this 'little boy'?"

"I'll say only this, Hugh. I hope they've got a fully paid up design indemnity insurance."

"Oh, I can guess who that is. Well good luck with it. Will you allow me to make you an offer just now to save you making a claim against me?"

"I always listen to any reasonable offer. Will it mean you will not be making any claim against me, Hugh?"

"No, Tony, I'll cancel ours. I can spot a winner and I'd like to go as part of your team. That leaves just the Hadshaw affair. If you agree then I'm willing to forego the two and a half per cent builder's discount on this contract. How does that sound?"

Tony reeled but kept his cool. It's not every day you get upwards of twelve grand from a builder without any kind of a fight. It was dawning on Tony that Hugh was truly contrite about the damage the Hadshaw affair had caused, not only to Liseur's progress on site but more importantly to the reputation of the building company Hugh Jarvis owned and had built from scratch. On top of all that, his and Douglas's performances and watertight arguments at the site meeting with Norman Keen had evidently impressed him deeply. Hugh's offer was one to be grabbed without hesitation,

"I will shake your hand on that, Hugh. Put it in writing and I will formally accept."

"I like the way you do business, Tony. Is there anything else I can do for you?"

"Yes. Get some more labourers onto site. You've got to finish these concrete bases for my pipe supports. We are forging ahead at some speed now and I want it all done ready for starting up by mid-to-end of November."

"Okay, Tony. I've got Terry Cordwell, my site foreman up there ramrodding the team to do just that. Hadshaw, as I just told you is no longer with us. Terry has been promoted."

"Yes, from the noise you two made at the site meeting I expected you would chop him. Tough on him but thanks for you help, Hugh."

"No bother at all, Tony. Maybe when this is all over you might care to join me on my wee boat for a sail round the west coast?"

"I didn't know you had a boat, Hugh but I'm not much into sailing. Golf is my real recreation. Maybe I can treat you to a game after our boat trip?"

"Okay then, you name the golf club and I'll choose the ports of call."

"That sound like a good plan. It's going to be next year at the earliest so there's plenty of time to make arrangements. I'll keep you posted. Bye for now."

Tony let Douglas know there would be no claim for loss and expense from Jarvis & Craig. Hugh's unsolicited gift of his mandatory discount was well in excess of what Hadshaw's impish games might have actually cost Liseur.

"It seems we have tamed a builder, Douglas. He's also invited me onto his boat for a sail. I must say I feel a little bit odd about all this. Don't you agree, it's very unusual?"

Douglas smiled,

"Yes it is. This is a double bonus, keeping their money and losing Hadshaw. Make sure you get it in writing, signed! And don't get shoved overboard."

Part 2
End Mar 1990

Franz Liseur office ~ Clydebank
Torquil Knight was out in the drawing office with Mark Trumann working on a report for the boss.

"That was a smart move on your part, Torquil to pinch copies of your drawings and calcs when you jumped ship from Chisholm and O'Casey."

"I thought so at the time, Mark but never dreamt they would become so important so soon after leaving that place. I still can't get over how lucky I am to be here cooperating with you guys. I feel secure seeing my project finalised and made to work. I look forward to it getting done properly."

"That's for sure, Torquil. If we can't sort this out then nobody can. We've got the best brains to pick from so, have no fear."

"I hope Clark Chisholm will 'get done properly' as well, Mark."

"I think you'll find Tony and Douglas are working on that so, let's just concentrate on getting this essay of ours finished."

"Good idea."

They were both were compiling a dossier of the reasons for the errors in Torquil's design. Prominent in it would be the name of the person most responsible for checking and mentoring Torquil's work during his time with the consultants viz. Sean O'Casey.

A précis of Torquil's meetings with James Briggs was also being prepared and attached to copies of the original minutes. They were intended for use in any subsequent court actions to prove Briggs' abuse of position and bullying tactics leading to the young man's blunders. They would form the bulwark of his case. He was put under duress and given only two options; to radically alter his design to comply with Briggs' unreasonable pressure and design to a cost of half-a-million pounds; or to resign. Hugh Jarvis was not yet aware that Tony was employing Torquil or that he intended to sue Briggs on the boy's behalf.

The Ministry codes expressly forbid adverse coercion of staff employed by the M.O.D. either directly or as outside consultants. Tony wanted at least to get Briggs the sack but there may also be some financial implication for his new engineer. The hope was to clear Torquil's name. If he then opted to stay with Liseur, his future within Douglas's team would be assured.

Things were at last beginning to move in Liseur's favour. Torquil's scripts would soon be passed to the firm's lawyers. Douglas and Torquil were busy finding ways to deconstruct the original "Humpty-Dumpty" design and produce elegant working solutions to put it back together again after its destruction at site. Liseur and Jarvis were in a strong position to make real money from this project.

Part 3
End Apr 1990

Bluff site ~ Forres
The harsh conditions of a bitter-cold March began to ease with the arrival of welcome spring sunshine. The welders and their mates still grumbled but generally they had started to relish the onset of some better weather. Progress out on the site was picking up in spite of the occasional shower of rain. Working outside underneath personal corrugated shelters, like miniature Nissan huts, gave the welders some cramped but appreciated protection. The constant humming of eighteen diesel generators supplying the direct electrical current for welding the pipes, lent an atmosphere of serious activity to this otherwise isolated location.

During their breaks the gangs chatted happily about the usual things; like who won on the horses; who had too much to drink; who slept with whom the night before or, who scored the goal. Often they talked about their satisfaction in constructing something that they knew was going to last. They could boast to their families, with the pride that only hard grafters on sites could honestly lay claim to; that they had worked for the government on this important project but had signed the '*official secrets act*' and could say no more about it. Who was to know how they were going to feel when they witnessed the calamity at the finish?

Douglas had been to the site twice since the fateful demise of Joe Hadshaw. He was enjoying the full cooperation of Bill Morgan, the new Clerk of Works, and Terry Cordwell, Joe Hadshaw's replacement. In a matter of five weeks, Terry had organised his squad of builders to complete the long, military lines of concrete bases needed for the pipe supports. Two kilometres of pipe had been installed since the start in January. Moving at this rate, the pipework had a very good chance of being completed by sometime in mid to end November. The boiler house was finished (with the additional expansion tank in place) and was ready to be started up as soon as the pipes were pressure tested.

Things were going well but Douglas, underneath his outwardly pleasant demeanour, was at times quite gloomy. He was angry and emotional at the prospect of seeing all this good and expensive work being destroyed in the name of politics. He confessed these feelings to Tony, who did his best to reassure him,

"Douglas, don't worry. We are not in the business of saving people who are so blind that they would rather see this happening than admit they have made mistakes. They had their chances to draw back and sort it but very soon it's going to be too late to stop it."

"Yeah, I know that, Tony, but it still feels wrong."

Tony knew it was time for some straight talking and a bit of fun as well,

"I'll tell you what we'll do, Douglas. We'll spend a million pounds adding expansion loops, take away the P.R.Vs and put in heat exchangers in all the buildings. It will work beautifully and be finished in eighteen months from now. Then we'll say to The Clark Chisholm

Partnership, *it was your entire fault. Now give us our million back for putting it all to work properly?"*

"Yes, Tony, I know. Fat chance we'd have of recovering our costs. We need hard evidence in order to win and get paid. Without proof beyond doubt we can't make them suffer."

"Correct, Douglas. Only by letting it go wrong can we blame them and successfully sue. Our losses will be small but Briggs had assured us we would be awarded the contract to put it back together again. That way we get our money back twice. Happy?"

"I know it's basically about profit and loss but sometimes there is a moral element that niggles at you. You are feeling the same. I can tell. But we only have the one option; we must bury the consultants."

"That's right, Douglas. They're the ones to blame...not us. We've got them in a box, now let's dig the hole and get it done.

"Okay, Tony. It was me who started all this in the first place. I'm away to get my shovel."

"Get two shovels, Douglas!"

Part 4
May 1990

Bluff site meeting ~ morning

Norman Keen decided that it was time to call a meeting at the site. There were numerous technical and financial considerations to be discussed and decided upon. In his position as the client, Mister Briggs of the M.O.D. was entitled to be made fully aware of the progress of the installation. It was essential that all parties concerned knew their responsibilities for completion of the work. Then Norman could legitimately steer the project to its dreadful conclusion.

He sat at the top table with James Briggs on his right and a stenographer on his left. The new Clerk of Works and the two consultants sat elsewhere. On the stroke of ten, Norman opened the meeting to the immediate clicketty-click of the typewriter taking down every word,

"Good morning gentlemen. It's good to see some fair weather arriving for the boys on site. The progress of the pipework is picking up nicely and in that regard I felt it favourable to call you here to bring everyone up to date. The purpose of this meeting is to discuss progress and to clarify several items brought to my attention by Jarvis & Craig and their sub-contractor, Franz Liseur. I intend to go through them sequentially. Before I begin I require a statement from the Clark Chisholm Partnership concerning their design. I will proceed on the assumption, Mister Chisholm, that your promised re-visitation of your files has been completed. Is there anything you wish to be entered into my minute of this meeting that alters any previous statements from you?"

Everyone in the room saw this opener as a clear invitation for the consultant to eat his words and admit his design was full of faults. They watched him in silence.

Dean Chisholm stood up and without hurrying, laid his notebook on the table. From his spectacle case he carefully removed his eyeglasses and rubbed the lenses with a blue, silk handkerchief drawn from his pocket. He lifted the specs, held them towards the window, seemingly checking for clarity, returned his kerchief to his pocket, donned the glasses, lifted up his notes and spoke,

"I can confirm that everything I said at the last meeting is the same as what I would say at this one. I have no need to alter the position of The Clark Chisholm Partnership, insofar as we totally disagree with the contention of these"...and he paused..."contractors." They are not the designers of this project. We are! We shall not be swayed one inch or millimetre by their so-called *dynamic computer simulation*.

As for their nonsensical expansion claims, we know the pipes expand by about one-and-a-half inches every 30 metres. Our design of swinging pipe supports is sufficient to accommodate that tiny amount. We refute all that they have said. They are profiteers out to fleece our esteemed client. When this farce is exposed, Mister Briggs will know how to deal with these scoundrels. In my humble opinion they should be banished from site and banned from any further work. It is high time they went back to France and left Scottish engineering to competent Scottish engineers!"

They all watched as he went through his spectacle rigmarole in reverse and sat down. He and Sean O'Casey shared looks of mutual satisfaction. Chisholm then turned to gaze imperiously down his nose at Norman Keen, as if to say, *Get out of that. I'm still here and there is nothing you can do about it.*

Norman ignored him and turned with a rather serious expression on his face to give a knowing nod to Briggs. James acknowledged the signal and looked down at the letter in his hand. The 'portcullis' logo of the House of Commons was discernable through the paper. He cleared his throat for attention. The smile left Chisholm's face. He thought, *what now? Clients don't speak at these meetings.* From his seated position, James Briggs began, in a sombre voice, to address him and to read the letter,

"Mister Chisholm, this letter from the Minister of Defence, instructs me to retain your services for the duration of this project till its conclusion."

Chisholm jumped up,

"I suppose this means that those Liseur people will be given the heave-ho and some responsible contractor will be called upon to finish the job without any further shenanigans! It's about bloody ti..."

James Briggs held up his hand to halt the outburst. Being stopped in mid word, Chisholm harrumphed and sat down. Briggs continued,

"The letter also instructs me to inform all parties to this project that they are to complete the work in accordance with the Clark Chisholm Partnership drawings and specifications."

Chisholm jumped up again,

"I knew it! Even the Minister thinks Liseur is a tuppenny-ha'penny outfit!"

Briggs again held up his hand. Chisholm sat down beaming a smile to his colleague. James Briggs then delivered what in Spain would be called the '*coup de grace*' but in the West of Scotland is known as, the '*Glasgow kiss*'.

"My final instruction from the minister is this. If the installation behaves in the manner described by Messrs Franz Liseur, then Her Majesties Government will sue the Clark Chisholm Partnership for all costs and losses suffered as a result of Clark Chisholm Partnership's intransigence, obduracy, incompetence and inadequate design capability."

"Then we have nothing to fear!" Shouted Dean Chisholm.

But James Briggs was not finished. He stood up, put down his official letter and lifted another page of typed notes.

"I am lodging this note from the Minister of Defence to be inserted together with his letter into the minutes of this meeting. It states his requirement that the minutes of this meeting are to be signed by all parties present and accepted by them as a true record. This minute, along with other relevant papers, will be produced in any litigation pursuant to the final outcome of the installation."

Briggs sat down and handed the letter and his typed note to Norman Keen. The supervising officer placed them beneath his notes. Knowing that Chisholm had just signed his own death warrant, he looked up and continued without a pause,

"My first item is to confirm that I have issued a variation order for the additional costs incurred by Franz Liseur due to having the location of their site huts outwith the secure zone of the Bluff depot. Mister Briggs has agreed this after consultation with the Minister of Defence. An approximate cost for the work has also been agreed as a provisional sum of thirty thousand pounds."

Chisholm shouted out, "Damned profiteers!"

Briggs turned and whispered something to Norman Keen that was inaudible to the rest. Norman listed attentively, nodding his agreement. Then he turned and smiled at Dean Chisholm.

"Mister Chisholm, you seem to be at variance with a decision made by a Minister of the Crown. Do you wish to withdraw your outburst or shall I allow it be included as a verbatim statement from you in my minute?"

Chisholm spluttered and out of his mouth came some jumbled words that made no sense to the others.

"I shall take it that you have withdrawn your outburst Mister Chisholm, but I must warn you, any further spontaneous remarks you make will be entered, word for word, into my minute. You are thus counselled to be mindful before you make a bigger ass of yourself than you have already."

This floorshow had begun to amuse the rest of the people in the hut, but the last remark from Norman Keen was too much to contain. It drew peels of laughter from them all, including James Briggs. Chisholm was far from amused. His face was like a ripe tomato as he harrumphed again, fighting to contain his indignation. Norman continued,

"My second item concerns the variation order, requested by the Clark Chisholm Partnership to introduce Ethylene Glycol for frost protection. That instruction is hereby cancelled. In consequence of that, the instruction to run the system only during working hours is also cancelled. An instruction to this effect will be issued for good order in the records. Are there any queries?"

Chisholm could not contain himself.

"On your head be it Mister Keen. Without our glycol solution the pipes will freeze!"

Norman instructed the typist to put Chisholm's statement in the minutes; then he continued,

"I have issued a counter instruction for frost protection by the use of an electric tracing cable. The Minister has agreed the cost for the work as a provisional sum of twenty-five thousand, three hundred pounds. Are there any queries?"

Chisholm sat quietly staring pointedly at Tony Surtal and Douglas Fairbairn. It began to dawn on him that this meeting was not going to end the way he had hoped. His expectation was that the S.O. and James Briggs would scoff at Liseur's attempts to rubbish his firm's design. Liseur by this time should surely have been sent packing and Chisholm given the courtesy, rightly due to a professional engineer of long standing, that he could not possibly be wrong. He glanced round at Sean O'Casey. His colleague seemed to have similar thoughts. Chisholm wriggled in his seat and fumbled for his spectacle case while Norman Keen continued the torture.

"The next item is my confirmation of the provisional cost for the new expansion tank and associated pipes and controls within the boiler house. It was set at no more than thirty-three thousand pounds. The work is now completed and I solicit the actual cost from Jarvis & Craig. Do you have that Mister Jarvis?"

"Yes I do. Here is my official offer itemised in detail, inclusive of builder's discount, in the amount of thirty-two thousand and two hundred pounds."

"Thank you, Hugh, I am recording my agreement of that sum in the minute. That figure can be entered as an item in your final account. Are there any queries?"

Dean Chisholm was not going to let this pass without his usual high-handed observation.

"And who, may I ask, will be responsible for the efficacy of the design for that item? It will certainly not be The Clark Chisholm Partnership, I can assure you of that!"

Jim Briggs was first to respond,

"Well Mister Chisholm, I can tell you for one that, considering some of the things I have been made aware of on this project, the M.O.D. will, like myself, be much relieved to hear you say so. Please Norman, enter Mister Chisholm's disclaimer in the minutes without asking for his retraction."

More amused looks were exchanged round the table. Tony whispered to Douglas,

"I'm amazed they haven't told the fat oaf to leave and let us get on with it. What do you think is going on?"

"It's easy, Tony. They've just very cleverly given him enough rope and he is now gasping for breath. It beats me how the big ass doesn't see it. He and his pal, Sean, must be completely nuts to still believe they are in the clear. This way everyone will get their money back except him. He's going to lose his shirt."

When Norman coughed discretely, they stopped their chat to allow him to continue,

"We have accepted Liseur's argument in favour of an electronic fire valve release mechanism. A variation order has been issued to cover this item. The contractor has agreed there will be no additional cost to the contract. Are there any objections?"

There was silence. Norman noted that in his minutes and continued,

"This next item is bound to be contentious since the argument from Mister Chisholm in his opening remarks is not accepted by me as a structural engineer. It concerns the expansion of the pipes for which the consultants have not made satisfactory provision in their specifications or on their design drawings."

Chisholm jumped up and thumped the table shouting,

"And who the hell are *you* to criticize *us*? *We* actually *do* know something about expansion?"

Norman Keen signalled Chisholm to be seated but the big irate blowhard remained erect still aimed his index finger at the S.O. as if wanting to shoot him in the face. Norman Keen was quick to answer him with an increasingly harsh tone,

"Mister Chisholm! Let me tell you something about the expansion on this project. It is cumulative. That means 40 millimetres for the first thirty metres, eighty millimetres for the second thirty metres and so on, giving a total expansion at the end of the site of nearly around ten to eleven metres. If you think your swinging brackets will accommodate that amount of expansion then you, Mister Chisholm and your smiling colleague, are arrogant and foolish amateurs. My words will be included in my minutes. Now, Mister Chisholm! Sit down!"

But Chisholm would not be silenced so easily. He clutched at what he must surely have known by this time was his last-remaining straw...James Briggs,

"Mister Briggs, I appeal to you, sir, in your capacity as my client. The M.O.D. sponsored me for this work and I ask you to severely rebuke this man, Keen. We are the designers, not him. I must crave your urgent intervention on behalf of my firm. This charade must cease or else I will be left with no option but to wash my hands of the whole affair and walk away!"

James Briggs, who had been rather stern-faced while listening to the S.O.'s harsh lecture, turned his gaze to the still-standing Dean Chisholm. His expression did not alter. Till this moment Briggs, although having seen the computer simulations, had not fully understood the seriousness of the expansion problem. It was now crystal clear to him. The consulting engineer was utterly exposed technically. There was no way he could help him even if he wanted to. He was simply dumfounded with his rising contempt for the big fat fool now begging for his life in the most despicable fashion.

It was time to tell this man that a schoolchild could understand the major problems on Chisholm's design. It was not credible that Dean Chisholm and his colleague were in total ignorance of the dreadful errors they had perpetrated on this project, let alone the impending calamity that was about to unfold. The blame for all that would soon be laid at The Clark Chisholm Partnership's door. Briggs asked Norman Keen for permission to speak. Norman nodded. Chisholm sat down. Briggs got up.

"I believe it is appropriate for me to advise you of the difficulty you and your firm have caused on this site. I will try to be impartial. Several times you have stated that you are the designer. The minutes of the site meetings and various letters from the contractors tell me that your design contains serious flaws. It is my intention, agreed by the Minister of Defence, that the project *shall* be completed to your design. Your design will, in the fullness of time, be shown to be a failure when the system self-destructs. I expect that to happen. You will then be removed as consultants. We shall pursue your professional indemnity insurance for recovery of all attendant costs and losses to put the system to rights. You will be commanded to return all of your professional fees awarded so far.

The MOD is unable and unwilling to assist you in your self-inflicted distress. The only person who can help you now is yourself. If you stubbornly choose to remain convinced of the viability of your design, we shall continue as I have described. You are now facing the axe Mister Chisholm. What do you have to say to the supervising officer?"

Dean Chisholm stood up again. He looked like a man hanging by a thin thread over a precipice. Sweat was glistening on his forehead. He retrieved his kerchief to wipe away the annoying dribbles and finished by rudely and noisily blowing his nose before he spoke,

"Mister Keen, I will stand by my firm's design drawings and all written work for this contract. The Clark Chisholm Partnership does not make mistakes. In spite of Mister Briggs and the rest of you having a different opinion than me, I am not convinced you have made your case. This will be in your minute and I shall sign it when this meeting comes to an end. Until then I shall not venture any further opinions. I shall watch with interest the outcome of your ambitious plan to destroy our work. I am certain it will be us who eventually will sue you all for the slanders and libels you have attempted up until now. Make no mistake, all of you, I shall have my day with you all!"

He sat down. Sean O'Casey slapped him strongly on the shoulder. The room was eerily quiet. After Briggs' challenge to Chisholm, they all expected an admission of some sort that would allow the mistakes to be fixed, the job to be finished in a working condition and the insurance company would pay up. They were stunned. How could these two intelligent men from a well-known and respected firm of consultants, fail to seize the 'get-out-of-jail' card that had been so transparently offered by Briggs? Tony turned to Douglas to question him with his voice hushed,

"You've been a consultant, Douglas. What do you know about their professional indemnity insurance? Could it be they don't have any?"

The answer was equally quiet,

"That's very unlikely, Tony. These insurance policies are automatically renewed. There's one thing I'm not sure about though. Maybe the insurers will not pay out if Chisholm and his associate *admit* they made mistakes. I think Briggs actually does know how it works. This is why he is keen to see the thing fail. Only then will there be a chance of all the costs being covered by Chisholm's insurance. That will keep Briggs and the MOD in the clear financially."

Tony listened intently and responded to Douglas in a much lower whisper,

"That makes sense, Douglas. Then *we* will go after *Briggs* on behalf of Torquil. I'm beginning to like the way this is panning out."

Norman Keen made sure the typist had accurately recorded the statements of Briggs and Chisholm. He wanted it in writing that Chisholm had agreed to sign the minute. Resuming his control of the meeting, he thanked Briggs for clarifying the reason they were all there.

"I see it is noon gentlemen, a convenient time to break for lunch I think. This afternoon I shall elucidate on my approach to the rest of the project based on the fact that Mister Chisholm is convinced there will be no failure. Essentially that means we shall build to their details but with some prudent omissions to minimise the repair costs when it becomes clear that the system requires redesigning and rebuilding. Thank you gentlemen. I expect you all to return in one hour. Mister Briggs, will you join me for lunch at my hotel in Forres?"

"Certainly, Norman."

Everyone left the hut in silence glad to be away from the consultants for at least the next hour. Chisholm and his man were left to their own devices.

Part 5
May 1990

Bluff site meeting ~ afternoon

Norman opened the meeting by thanking them all for their punctuality and hoping that each had managed a decent meal. The polite protocol over he delivered a sombre clarification of the purpose of that afternoon's gathering.

"Gentlemen, because the Clark Chisholm Partnership still maintain an unflinching defense of their designs, I took advantage of my private lunch with Mister Briggs to promote certain contractual suggestions. During his subsequent telephone conversation with the Minister of Defence, Mister Briggs secured agreement to my suggested ways to vary the contract. I shall elucidate these in a moment. The minutes will constitute a record of the decisions reached. By that means the contractors will have full authority to proceed with these changes without waiting for my formal instructions.

It is incumbent on me to advise all present that these variation orders will not be reversible. I shall however, at the end of the meeting, discuss with the contractors, and only the contractors, any of their suggestions for clarity of the wording I shall be required to adopt. Are there any questions so far?"

Dean Chisholm looked rather unhappy but didn't speak. Norman continued,

"That's fine. I shall start with the question of frost protection. Low wattage electrical heating tapes and suitable controls shall be used throughout this project. All necessary materials for this shall be procured and stored on site for use when required. This material shall not be fitted to the pipes until so instructed. Any questions?"

Dean Chisholm sat still and silent.

"Good. Now I turn to the question of thermal insulation. All necessary materials for this shall be procured and stored on site for immediate retrieval. This material shall not be fitted to the pipes until so instructed. Any questions?"

Dean Chisholm could no longer hold his tongue,

"What nonsense! There is no technical reason for leaving off these two vital items. The pipes will freeze in December and my firm shall be blameless."

The S.O. responded with an explanation and a warning,

"The reasoning is simple Mister Chisholm. When the pipes fail, as has been conclusively shown they will, the necessary repair work will be faster, easier and cheaper to carry out. The system shall be drained to prevent freezing. Work will then begin on the re-construction of the installations. That is the next item but please be aware, Mister Chisholm, that you are in this room by my courtesy. Unless you have anything constructive to add to these discussions, I expect your silent attention. Otherwise I will require your withdrawal from this meeting."

Dean Chisholm was not a man who was used to being bullied or dominated by any one. He was becoming very narked at this upstart treating him like an impish schoolboy. So far he was mystified as to why he had lost every one of his arguments with Norman Keen. He knew he was not paranoid but he appeared to be thinking, *why were all these people ganging up against me? I had better be careful but I shall have my little thrust,*

"I have no desire to leave your meeting, Mister Keen. You have my undivided attention. Please continue."

Norman ignored this display of foolishness,

"The third item is about the contentious problem of expansion of the pipes. It is clear that the means required to accommodate this have been omitted from the Clark Chisholm Partnership drawings. As agreed this morning we cannot alter or deviate from the consultant's drawings and specification. This leaves us to find options that do not interfere with those designs. The one we have adopted will be covered by my variation order bearing a *provisional sum* of four hundred and fifty thousand pounds.

This sum should be adequate to cover the Main Contractor and Liseur for the provision of approximately four hundred and fifty steel expansion loops, flange joints, concrete supports, pipe brackets, pipe guides, pipe anchors, extra thermal insulation and extra tracing tape.

These additional materials shall be procured and stored on site for immediate use when it becomes necessary to rebuild the pipes. It will be part of my instruction that pairs of flanged joints, set two metres apart, shall be fitted now, every forty-five metres along the pipes. They will be used for 'cold drawing' half of the expansion when the loops are fitted later...but not before."

At this point James Briggs spotted Tony in deep conversation with Douglas. He nudged Norman keen to point this out. Norman interrupted them to ask if it was an objection they wished to raise. Douglas responded,

"No, Mister Keen, if we could fabricate the expansion loops on site now we think it might be a good time saver. That way they will be ready as soon as they are required."

"An excellent idea, Douglas. The Variation Order will be worded thus; *Franz Liseur is invited to fabricate the necessary expansion loops on site ready for use at the appropriate time. Payments will be made within the monthly valuation certificates.* How does that sound Douglas?"

"That's bang on Mister Keen. Thank you. Have you thought yet about how the system should be rebuilt after it disintegrates?"

"Mister Briggs and I have discussed that but not at length. It seems appropriate that we wait till after November before getting into that side of things. It is likely we shall be devoid of a consultant at that time so an appointment will be required. Have you any thoughts on how this might be handled, Douglas?"

"Yes Mister Keen, we are at this very moment preparing a new set of drawings and a list of technical and physical alterations to Dean Chisholm's design. Doing it now means the whole thing can be put into operation with least time wasted. I assume that is the top priority for Mister Briggs?"

Briggs turned and gave a secret whisper to Norman Keen,

"Don't forget that Tony has taken Torquil into his employ. Be careful not to let Chisholm find this out."

Norman gave a wide smile to Tony as if to say, *you guys are way ahead of all of us!* He had to form an answer that didn't give the game away to Dean Chisholm

"Mister Briggs has just reminded me that you have a new designer at your disposal who knows the system very well. I expect with your expertise he will iron out these difficulties and find proper solutions. It is prudent to get these on paper sooner rather that later. I wonder if you and Hugh Jarvis might consider a meeting with us both in the near future to go over your suggestions and probable estimates of time and duration? Your new designer will be welcome to attend if you feel it will help?"

Hugh Jarvis immediately accepted that invitation and sat back to allow the S.O. to continue. Dean Chisholm got up and made for the door. Norman stopped him with a curt demand,

"Where are you going Mister Chisholm?"

"I have nothing more to contribute to your Kangaroo Court, Norman. You have just announced that we are to be dismissed from the contract. Up till now I have taken your insults like the gentleman I was bred to be, but enough is enough I'm afraid. We are now out of your sorry fiasco created out of nothing. I bid you goodbye. I shall see you all in court. That is where I shall obtain my satisfaction."

Before Norman could respond the strong voice of Hugh Jarvis was heard booming across the room,

"Aye! Right! They're a' oot ae step except wee Dean! You're blinded with your exalted position, man! You may have been bred to be a *gent* but as long as you have a hole in your bum you will never be an *engineer*! Let him go, Norman. We have no need for fools in here."

Chisholm strode over to strike Jarvis but Sean O'Casey jumped forward and halted him. Norman Keen leapt up shouting,

"Control yourself Mister Chisholm! I will not have a brawl started by you. You are not leaving my meeting without my say so. You may boast about your success in this project but you are dreaming. I believe your dream is becoming a nightmare. You and your colleague seem to be the only ones who cannot see that. If you leave now it is your choice but these witnesses will attest to your promise to append your signature to my minutes. You will receive a copy in the next post. Now... you *have* my permission to leave."

Dean Chisholm left. Sean O'Casey followed. The door banged. The meeting ended. There was a ripple of applause from everyone there including the stenographer.

Part 6
Mid June 1990

Franz Liseur offices ~ Clydebank

The Supervising Officer's invitation was fulfilled in June. They held their planned get together at a meeting in Liseur's offices at 11.30 am. Tony made Norman Keen welcome just before the arrival of Hugh Jarvis. He led the group up to Mark Trumann's desk where Torquil Knight was leaning over his drawing board, deep in conversation with Douglas. He appeared relaxed and confident. The introductions were made and Hugh Jarvis looked slightly bemused.

"Torquil Knight? That name rings a bell. Aren't you the consultant? Your name is on the drawings. What's going on Tony?"

"Well Hugh, Torquil's name will be on our drawings from now on. He is my engineer in charge of the re-design of the systems at Bluff. If you leave it at that for the moment you will be soon in the picture."

"This is a puzzle and no two ways about it but I suppose you all know what you are doing so I'll leave it to the S.O to carry on. Over to you Mister Keen."

Norman got straight to the point,

"Torquil, I know you have been advised of the impact your work at the Clark Chisholm Partnership has had on the Bluff project. We are told that you have found solutions to the problems. Can you explain your ideas to us?"

The young man looked at Tony and then at Douglas. They looked back at him waiting for his answer. He turned to Norman and spoke with a clear steady voice.

"Problem number one: P.R.Vs do not work on closed fluid systems because low pressure does not flow to high pressure. Problem number two; Pipes expand and the force of that expansion is so great that it cannot be ignored and has to be absorbed. A third problem has already been solved by the addition of an expansion tank beside the system pressurisation unit. These are the three main problems to overcome on your site."

The SO responded.

"That has become very clear to us all. Number three has been taken care of, Torquil. What do you propose for problems one and two?"

"The expansion will be catered for by expansion loops. There are other ways but using loops is by far the cheapest and, in my opinion, the best answer to this particular problem from the point of view of durability and minimal future maintenance costs."

"Yes, Torquil, but the pressure problem has not been solved yet, has it?"

"Well, in a manner of speaking Mister Keen, I would say it *has* been solved. These three problems were actually solved by me before I left The Clark Chisholm Partnership. The difficulty I had was their refusal to listen and help me to stand up to Mister Briggs at the M.O.D. He insisted the price be reduced. I tried hard to convince Sean O'Casey to listen to reason but he took me off the project. I felt I had no option but to leave. I genuinely hoped they would see sense and allow me to get them out of trouble. I see now I was wrong."

Tony stepped forward and put his hand on the Torquil's shoulder before adding his comment.

"You see, gents, this is not a silly wee boy let loose with a pencil and proceeding to reek havoc. Sure, he made errors but as soon as he spotted them he decided to own up and fix them to save the consultants from a major embarrassment.

He was trying to save the design, knowing he had been bullied by the top man at the M.O.D., namely Mister James Briggs, who in turn was probably being shit on from a great height by the Minister of Defence. Torquil actually had the answers but none of his senior colleagues would listen. They just ignored him and buried their heads in the sand. Neither was clever enough to realise that he was trying desperately to save his project."

Hugh Jarvis couldn't resist adding his bit,

"They never listened at the site meetings either. It seems your lad is cleverer than them. Well-done son. I would have punched their stupid faces!"

Tony laughed out loud,

"And where would that have got us Hugh? Much better if we do it our way. We are going to bury these clowns, aren't we Torquil?"

The lad pursed his lips but did not answer.

Norman Keen was still not convinced that they were out of the woods. There was still the problem of the P.R.Vs and the different pressures within the water system. He pursued Torquil,

"Tell me how we get medium pressure water into low pressure systems within thirty-five separate buildings and get it to come back out again?"

Torquil took the floor and in about three minutes explained in layman's terms how this could be achieved. It was not going to be cheap but it was a full-proof solution as elegant and simple as the invention of the paper clip.

Torquil had already told Douglas and Mark how this was to be done. They stood smiling at Hugh Jarvis and Norman Keen, waiting for their reactions. Jarvis shook his head,

"I'm just a silly bricklayer, Torquil. It's beyond me to understand the problem never mind your solution to it but it seems you are a better engineer than either of those two jokers who used to be your bosses."

Norman Keen was enough of an engineer to grasp the boy's cleverness in finding a simple answer to a complex problem. He voiced one regret,

"Well, Tony. It seems with Torquil's ingenious ideas we have the means to complete this project properly. It's just a pity we have to see it destroyed in order to repair it all again. Don't you think so?"

Tony smiled. It was reassuring to hear Torquil's confident account of the problems and his elegant solutions. How sad that O'Casey and Chisholm were so egotistical that they never saw or encouraged their young colleague. There were many things he could say in answer to Norman's question but he didn't want to cause Torquil any unease. Instead of a direct reply, he made an offer none of them could easily refuse.

"It is a shame, Norman. But I have an idea that might appeal to you. What do you say the six of us stop talking shop for an hour? Shall we go and enjoy a nice lunch?"

"That's a good plan, Tony." Said Hugh Jarvis, "but I have a better one, I'll pay."

"No complaint from me." Said Norman Keen.

"Or me." Said Torquil.

"Well, when you've all sorted out who's buying, I'll see you up there." Said Douglas, as he headed for the door.

Part 7
Mid July 1990

Franz Liseur offices ~ Clydebank

Douglas went into Tony's room and sat down. Tony looked up and smiled. Since Douglas had not spoken he assumed his contracts manager had some half-thought-out plan he wished to bounce off him. He waited for the words to come out.

"Tony, I've had a thought about what Norman Keen said last month. He said what a pity to have to destroy a thing in order to be able to rebuild it. Do you remember?"

"Yes."

"Well why not make the Clark Chisholm Partnership insurance company aware of what we intend to do. They might like what I want to tell them."

"What is that Douglas?"

"They will not want to spend a fortune by paying for a complete restoration job. Will they?"

Tony sat forward and commented,

"If somebody offered me the chance to save a lot of my own money, I would find it very attractive. What are you wanting to tell them Douglas?"

"Not so much *tell* them, Tony. More like *show* them. We invite them to see the computer simulation. We explain that the design is at fault. We tell them that after it is destroyed we are to fix it. We tell them it will cost them a lot but if we fix it before it fails, it will definitely be cheaper. They are bound to take the less expensive option, don't you think?"

"I like the sound of that but what if they don't believe the simulation. After all, their clients, Chisholm and O'Casey, will tell them it's rubbish and that their design is full proof. Some of these insurance guys wouldn't know the difference between a shaky bannister and an oscillating ten-inch pipe at Bluff. It will take cogent arguments to convince them to go against the consultants. After all, Clark Chisholm is their client."

"Yes Tony, I had thought of that. Here is the best bit. We take them to site with the consultants and show them the start-up of the system. When they see these pipes starting to go like the simulation they will be only too anxious to sign on the dotted line of a big fat cheque to us. Then we start dismantling and reconstruction of the system."

"Douglas my son, you've done it again. I expect Torquil will smile when you tell him what you're planning. Would you let him make the call?

"Nice idea Tony. It would be poetic justice, but I don't think Torquil is so spiteful."

"Yes, you're right. Leave him be. He's too young to be vindictive. You do it."

Douglas laughed,

"Oh! So, I'm the vindictive one here?"

"Yes Douglas. But that's only *one* of your endearing qualities."

With their joke shared, Douglas turned and went back to his office. He called the Association of Consulting Engineers to find out what insurer covered The Clark Chisholm Partnership. They were called Indemnity Protection and had a branch in Edinburgh. Douglas gave them a ring.

He made contact with a chap called John Smith who was amenable to talking about the project at Bluff but would not make any decisions till he spoke with his client. Douglas tried to dissuade him,

"If you call them, they will say we are wrong about their design. I would like you to come to Glasgow to view a couple of computer simulations made by the hydraulics experts at the SIMER laboratory. They made simulations of the pipes under the intended working conditions. You may be impressed by what they reveal."

"And what may I ask will they show me?"

"They will show the initial gentle oscillation of the pipes gradually increasing and leading to their violent buckling and final failure."

"But a computer simulation is not the real thing, is it Mister Fairbairn?"

"No it's not. You are quite correct Mister Smith. If you are not convinced that this will happen I will invite you to come to site in November this year."

"Will you have a better computer simulation at site in November?"

"No John, we will have the real thing. We are to make a digital record of the project starting up. I am sure you will be amazed by the size and scope of this major pipework installation. You will no doubt also be astounded to witness its total destruction. That record will be the basis of the lawsuit we are at this moment preparing for issue to your client on that very day."

"I see. I assume it will be filmed until it is totally destroyed?"

"Correct Mister Smith. You see this site is a Royal Naval Armaments Depot. The chances are that the pipes will so dangerously thrash about that no humans will be allowed to go in to stop them. Many of these buildings on the site will be damaged; buildings housing all sizes of live munitions, from rifle bullets to live torpedoes and nuclear missiles. The insurers will be looking at possibly ten or twelve million pounds in repair costs Mister Smith. It may be considerably more if these armaments react badly, especially the nuclear items."

"I see, Douglas. Now I'm getting the picture. You want us to pay now because it will be cheaper. Is that it Mister Fairbairn?"

"Not entirely. We want to change the design now and put the job in properly. The only problem is that these consultants are refusing to play ball. They will not admit their flawed design will produce the destruction that we say it will. It's not too late to fix it. We estimate about one-point-five million will cover it. Leaving it till November means what I told you *might* happen *will* happen. Then the cost will be much greater. It's up to you John, how you want to play this. For us it is a win, win situation. For you it's the difference between a big sum and a bigger sum; maybe six or seven times bigger."

"Right Mister Fairbairn, I will be in your offices next week to look at the computer simulations. Before that I will have spoken to the Clark Chisholm Partnership to get their side of things. It would seem that there is already a potentially high financial penalty for my company to bear. I am anxious to keep that to a minimum so, I shall not be pussyfooting around with these Chisholm people. I have no reason to be enamoured with folk who make expensive errors and leave us to pick up the tab. Thank you for the prior warning on this. I do appreciate it when people try to *save* us money."

"Right John. Good luck with that. Call me with an hour's notice when you want to come to look at the computer simulations. Bye for now."

Part 8
The following week

Franz Liseur offices ~ Clydebank

Torquil was sitting beside the boss's desk and stood up when Douglas came in with John Smith. After the necessary introductions, Tony gave John a brief history of Torquil's recent design difficulties with Clark Chisholm. The insurance man paid close attention to every word and expressed his irritation for the way the young fellow had been misused by the consultants.

"What a bunch! I've just left Chisholm and O'Casey. My frank exchanges with them got nothing but strong denials. I'm here to be persuaded that you are right and he is not, Torquil. I suspect I'll be convinced that what we are about to see will be in your favour so, gentlemen, shall we proceed?"

They watched the computer simulations in silence. Smith was visibly startled at seeing the effects of the pressure problems. When he saw the next one showing the calamitous expansion of the pipes, he sucked in air through puckered lips, folded his arms and sitting back in a pensive attitude, he stroked the hairs of his greying moustache.

Douglas looked at his two colleagues. They knew they were in the presence of a man who was no softie and waited for him to speak. They had been impressed that he had rebuked Chisholm in an effort to get him to admit the design faults.

That conceited man and his cohort would not budge even when John offered them two million pounds for alterations, right now, instead of later when the costs would rocket. Chisholm still refused to admit that he could be wrong. When John Smith had entered Tony's office he was not quite spitting tacks but it was noticeable that he was not on the side of Dean Chisholm. Douglas prompted him,

"What's on your mind John having seen our computer simulations?"

"Torquil, can you answer my question? Which of these two will cause the greater damage to the pipes; distortion by pressure fluctuations or buckling by expansion?"

Tony sat back and relaxed into his wing-backed swivel chair and clasped his hands behind his head. He smiled at Douglas who struck a similar pose in his carver. Torquil read the clear signals of confidence and began,

"It is not so easy to say which is worse. Either one will cause major damage. The pressure on the system will take time to develop into oscillations. The expansion will also be slow to develop since the heat will build up gradually. Either one will produce the same result, utter destruction."

"What's your point in asking this, John?" Said Tony.

"My thinking is this; the consultant would be liable if either one of these two faults was to happen. It would still cause damage to the pipes? Is it possible, Torquil to arrange that only the pressure *or* the expansion problem manifested itself? The destruction would be similar and the design would still be seen to be at fault?"

Torquil gave a smile of confidence,

"That's an easy one Mister Smith. The expansion only happens when the temperature is raised. All we have to do is leave the boilers off. The pressure will create enough of a drama as you saw from the computer simulation."

"Thank you Torquil, that's just what I was thinking. Gentlemen, I believe we have our answer. We will be there in November to watch the system dancing and undulating. As soon as that happens, it will take only a few minutes to satisfy me enough to underwrite your repairs. Are you able to minimise the damage Torquil?"

"Very simple Mister Smith. I will switch off the pumps, shut down the pressurisation unit and open a drain cock. The pressure will drop to normal in thirty seconds or less. There will be damage to the system but not catastrophic."

Tony stood up and patted Torquil's shoulder.

"Now that's a good idea. Well done you two."

Douglas congratulated the insurance man for his evident engineering knowledge and asked,

"How are you able to size up a problem so quickly and confidently, John?"

"Well, Douglas it's a common misconception that I am no more than a pen-pushing clerk or just a high-pressure salesmen but I spent twenty-five years in the Merchant

Navy as a first engineer. I have a reasonable technical knowledge of how hydraulic systems work and I know a little about high-pressure boilers as well. That background comes in very useful in a case like this."

"It certainly does, John. We are very glad that you are so quick to understand the problem and so keen to get it resolved with the minimum of pain and cost."

"It's to my advantage as *well* to take this attitude, Douglas. It looks like I can cut my firm's losses with this plan. I shall send you a letter-of-guarantee tomorrow underwriting your costs from the moment your system misbehaves as you predict it will.

Oh, and since you mentioned pain, I expect to raise the Clark Chisholm insurance premium. I may counter-sue for professional negligence. I think I can prove that Chisholm tried to conceal his knowledge of theses faults. My company will be grateful for your assistance in pursuing that, Tony."

"You shall have it John! Douglas, why don't you tell Mister Smith what *we* want to do to the Clark Chisholm Partnership?"

Before Douglas had time to reply, Torquil's very clear voice came from behind him,

"Bury the fuckers!"

There was loud laughter at Torquil's crude levity being so out of character but so appropriate in the present circumstances. The insurance man had taken to Torquil and expressed his solidarity with the Liseur team,

"You sound like you could have been in the merchant navy Torquil. I will be very pleased to assist you all in that endeavour."

He turned to Tony and Douglas,

"I've got a lot of moves to make chaps. Together we can make a good job of this. Thank you all for your assistance and for the clever work you have done. Might I make a suggestion concerning your men on site?"

"Be our guest, John. What's on your mind?" Said Tony.

"It seems to me that you must let them know of our intention when their primary work is completed. They should be aware that their skilled installations are to be severely damaged. Their cooperation is essential to carry out the remedial operations, not to mention their safety during the dangerous period of demonstrating the failure of the pipes and all the rest."

Tony and Douglas had already had a private discussion about this aspect of the job. He knew it was necessary to appraise the insurance man of their full agreement with him on the need for safety."

"Yes, John you are quite correct. We shall take extraordinary measures to ensure the safety of the men, the site itself and all attendant witnesses. I assure you that we have in mind a plan of operations that will allows us to do this dastardly deed safely. We intend to use the best means of walkie-talkie communication, split-second timing to minimise the damage and complete openness with the teams of men on site who will be fully involved in these organised procedures. The men will all be fully aware of our intentions and will be engaged for the remedial works till the project is properly completed and handed over."

"Well, Tony, I have every confidence that your proposals will be professionally carried out. Perhaps when you have finalised the details of your plans, you will allow me to comment?"

"Most certainly, John. I assure you that your valuable input will be much appreciated. Is there anything else you need from us?"

"Not at this moment. Let me say thanks to yourself, Douglas and Torquil here. It has been educational for me to see how you are handling the exceptional challenges on this unusual project. I'll bid you goodbye till next time."

They made their parting handshakes and John left. Their agreement with the insurers was a good result. Now all Liseur had to do was get the installation at Bluff completed for the big turn-on in November to create the dramatic demonstration. Tony had another issue to clear up before anything else. Torquil's planned redesigns would then be used to put 'Humpty Dumpty' together again.

"Are all your calculations and drawings done Torquil?"

"Yes, Tony. I'm sure of everything now and I want to be getting to the site to kick things off with Archie and Angus. What have you got in mind for me?"

Tony looked at Douglas and raised his eyebrows,

"How long has this man been working for us?"

"I don't know. Seems like just a few weeks but if he started in February then it's all of five months or more. Why are you asking?"

I don't recall any request for holidays. He must be due a break by this time don't you think?"

Torquil butted in,

"But I want to get this all done and dusted so, if you don't mind I'll get up to the site and brief the guys."

Tony smiled,

That's just what you will do, young man. Get away home to your folks for a couple of weeks. We will pull you in to the site for a day or so next week to do your bit with the men. But you do need to slow down and relax now that the heat's off, so to speak. What do you say, Douglas?"

"Couldn't agree more, Tony. Boy needs his holidays and I think there is a wee lassie who needs some of him too."

"Well that's all settled Douglas. Get John Logge to copy all the stuff Torquil will need to take with him. Okay?"

As Torquil attempted an ineloquent 'thank you' to his mentors, Tony turned to him saying,

"Oh! Are you still here? Bugger off home lad! And enjoy your holiday."

Part 9
Late July 1990

Forres ~ Torquil goes home

Torquil arrived at his mother's house on Saturday 21 July on the pillion seat of a 650cc Triumph Bonneville T100 motorcycle. Davy Pringle roared it into the drive announcing their arrival by skidding to a halt amid a spray of chips flying from the back wheel and scaring into grudging action a pair of lugubrious Afghan hounds languishing on the warm stones of the wide entrance porch. When they saw their young owner they loped towards the motorbike, stood up on hind legs and enveloped Torquil with the affection of faithful companions and protectors. They already knew Davy but he was not their leader so was ignored.

On hearing the commotion Missus Knight came out wiping her hands on a kitchen towel, yelling in delight,

"Torquil, Welcome home son. David, it's so nice to see you again. How are you?"

"I'm fine, Missus Knight. Your boy took me by surprise yesterday getting a holiday at short notice.'

"Will you be staying for the fortnight?"

"No, I've got work on Monday. I'd like to stay tonight and get away tomorrow morning if that's ok?"

"Oh good. You're always good company for Fergus. He just loves to beat you on the snooker table."

"Mister Knight must have had a misspent youth. He is too good for me and I thought I was not too bad."

Torquil giggled at their idle chatter,

"Come on, mum. Let Davy and me get these helmets off. We're hungry for some of your home cooking. Aren't we?"

David agreed with a smack of his lips. They made their way through the central doorway to enter the spacious hallway of the pink-sandstone Victorian villa.

"You two go upstairs and get cleaned up for dinner. It will be ready in about an hour so, you have time for showers if you want. Torquil's room is ready with single beds for you both. I'll give you a call at about half past seven, alright?"

"Thanks mum. Race you up the stairs, Davy."

They bolted away as his mother tutted,

"I do wish Torquil would use David's proper name. I so dislike this modern manner of informality."

She turned and saw her husband returning from his golf.

"Hello, darling." was his usual greeting to be repeated back as an echo by his good lady wife. "I see the boys are here. Are they getting cleaned up? I'm famished. When is dinner?"

"Seven thirty, Fergus. They will be down then so leave them to chill out, as I believe the modern saying goes?"

Fergus smiled, kissed her gently on the cheek and busied himself putting his golf trolley into the hall storage cupboard.

The dinner table was set for five people. Phillipa had joined them and the conversation ranged from idle pleasantries about their various careers to the latest films, pop culture and where the next holidays would be taken. After dinner they retired to the lounge for coffee and cake.

It was clear to David that Phillipa wanted to hear more about Torquil's prospects with Franz Liseur. He diplomatically asked for another thrashing from Mister Knight in the billiards room. The challenge was enthusiastically accepted and they disappeared along with Missus Knight who was polite enough to say she had to do the washing up.

"You must be nearing the end of that horrible Bluff place down there on the beach, Torquil. When is it to be finished?"

"It'll be a while yet Phillipa. We have to set it to work then see it fail after which it will take about a year to dismantle and reconstruct. Only then can we safely give it over to the MOD."

"So what happens when it is finally finished next year? Are you staying on with Liseur or do you plan to come home and work with us at the factory?"

"I haven't decided yet which way I'll go. The prospects with Liseur are very good. I feel secure there and my two bosses are good friends. They have given me a chance to get back my self-respect and I owe them so much. I'll have to wait and see what turns up."

"Well, what about us. We should be thinking about our future as well as Liseur's. To me ours is the more important, don't you agree?"

"I suppose you're right, but when you get a job like mine with the security and trust of your employer, it's very hard to just up and leave. Job satisfaction is very important not to mention the fun of solving the almost impossible and complex issues that crop up. It's very rewarding to work as a close team and get the buzz of the game. I'm not kidding. It's stimulating just going into that office and not knowing what's round the corner but I'm safe in the knowledge that whatever happens we can all get round it and solve it. Do you understand how good that is, Phillipa?"

"Yes of course I do. You seem to have found the perfect job with the best career prospects you could ever want. I see a different career for you that will give you the same security and allow us to live and work in the same town for the same employer. Can you understand why I think that will be better for us as a couple. If you decide that you want to marry me, Torquil I would not wish to be a weekend wife with you away down there in the south and me trying to raise a family, run a career and a house for what...to be horribly lonely all week?"

A silence fell between the two youngsters. They were both on the first rungs of fine careers ladders but the distance between their places of work would be too big a strain on them. They would not be able to make their lives work properly for themselves, their families or for their children, if they were able at all to consider having any.

"I don't want you to be lonely, Phillipa. I want us to be together. I want you to be my wife and I want to give you a good life. Please allow me a year to sort this out for us both. There is always a best answer to any problem. I've found that out in the past year. There is a best answer to this one. Please accept that we will get married and I will ensure that within the next eighteen months I will make the right decision and you will be able to say yes to my formal proposal. Is that a deal?"

Phillipa smiled the smile that he first saw when he met her in their secondary school class not four miles away from where they were sitting. It was enchanting then, and more so now that he was in his prime. She saw the effect it had on him and felt the same stirring of love and desire she always did when he adopted his serious manner of planning the way forward for them both. She knew that the love and respect she was feeling would never change. This was the time however for her to make a decision; not based on emotion but a hard and practical decision that would mean so much for them depending on how she responded to Torquil's offer. She leaned forward, held him with her palms over his ears, stroked his hairline on his neck and kissed him, ever so gently on his soft, warm lips. Then she whispered,

I will wait for you forever, Torquil. I love you and I accept your proposal."

Then she kissed him again before he was able to speak.

The next morning Davy was well fed at breakfast before taking his leave of the family and Phillipa, whom he kissed rather too well in Torquil's opinion, saying,

"It took you a long time to do what you should have done years ago my friend. See you soon, Torky. Enjoy the rest of your break. Goodbye all."

He roared away in a shower of flying chips scaring the dogs. Missus Knight could not contain her indignation'

"What a dreadful noise that machine makes, Torquil. Your friend, David is lovely but I do wish he would use your proper name."

The rest of his holiday was unremarkable except for his required site meeting with the men and the even more required interview with Phillipa's father. Missus Knight had cautioned that *formalities have to be observed, Torquil.*

Part 10
Wed 25 Jul 1990

Bluff site ~ Forres

Douglas had advised Archie McGregor to meet up with Torquil at his home in Forres and allow him to get to the site for a meeting with Angus MacLauchlan and all the men. Accordingly they were all assembled in the site-meeting hut with the seats arranged like a classroom. Torquil stood at a blackboard and opened his lecture,

"Hello guys. My name is Torquil Knight. I designed this installation. It is full of mistakes. I know what they are and I know how to fix them."

A hand went up.

"Yes Angus, I expected there would be questions. Go ahead."

"You've just told us you made all the mistakes. Is that right?"

"Absolutely correct! Any more questions?"

"Seems like you're no very clever, young fella." Said one of the Glasgow welders.

"Well sir, I'm the one standing here at the blackboard. Does that mean I'm daft?"

"No, but it seems as if you are honest and that's good enough fur me, son. Carry on if you don't mind."

"Right then. There are lots of politics associated with what I have to tell you but politics are not any of your business. What is of interest to you all is what is going to happen when this installation is set to work."

"Aye son, we'll all be out of a job for a while ah suppose?" Said his Glaswegian supporter.

"Not so. You will all be kept on site to do remedial work. That will probably take about another six months or longer to complete. Now I want to tell you why this is the case. You see, the installation will self-destruct when it is switched on but don't be alarmed. Remember I said it's only politics and that's none of your business. A state secret if you like and you have all signed the official secrets act. Am I correct?"

A murmur of assent tinged with incredulity was the pleasing response. Torquil continued and, using his chalk, drew an expansion loop on the board.

"You guys all know what this is and we will need a lot of these on this project. The reason is that none of these appear on the drawings and without them the pipes will buckle and break to bits. That is what I meant by self-destruct, okay?"

More sounds of assent.

"For all modifications I will issue my drawings. They will be self-explanatory to you chaps. I will be in constant contact with Archie, Angus and you men on site for any queries or problems until this all comes to pass some time in November."

He drew a circle and continued over the murmurs,

"The actual destruction will be allowed to happen under very close safety control and will only be momentary. Just enough to convince certain very important people that Franz Liseur is not to blame for the errors in design."

"But you said you are the guy who made the mistakes. Does that mean you're for the chop, son?"

"Not this time, my observant friend. Like I told you, it's politics and none of your business. You will be seeing a lot of me in the future but *other* people will get roasted. Any questions?"

Angus MacLauchlan had been listening intently to the details of Torquil's elegant delivery and all the backchat. He was as puzzled as the rest by the fact that here was the man who said he made the mistakes that would destroy the job and here he was, telling them all that he was the clever dick who would put it right. This did not add up. He had to ask a question,

"Mister Knight, did you leave out the expansion tank for the pressurisation unit in the boiler house?"

"Yes."

"Why did you do that and then suddenly we need one on site?"

"At the design stage it was not needed. Politicians made decisions that made it necessary, Angus. Okay?"

Angus thought for a couple of seconds before answering in his typically ingenious, streetwise manner,

"Ah see! If it was politicians I suppose that means it's none of my business then?

"Correct Angus."

Torquil turned back to the circle he had drawn earlier and continued to show with more sketches, his ideas for pipe brackets, guides and anchor points he intended them to use for the upgraded installations. His question and answer session lasted for another hour or so. Torquil was pleased to hear sounds of satisfaction as the tradesmen chatted on their way out of the hut.

He felt he had done a reasonable job of explaining the changes and gaining the confidence of the men. Archie's comment confirmed that feeling,

"Well done, Torquil. That was a very skilful way to let them into your secrets but keeping it at their level. Made my job a lot easier as well. Thanks for coming in during your holidays.

"No bother, Archie. It was a pleasure to meet you here with all your guys."

"You'll be away back home now. How's the holiday going?"

"It's grand to be up here again with my folks and my girlfriend. I'm hoping she will soon be my fiancé, Archie, but please don't tell anyone on the site."

"Congratulations, Torquil. Never fear; your secret's safe with me."

Torquil smiled and shook hands but something in the way Archie grinned and winked gave him the feeling the cat was out of the bag. Slightly bewildered, he mumbled,

"Cheers, Archie."

"You're welcome, Torquil. Come and I'll drive you back home to your lassie."

Part 11
Jul – Nov 1990

General

At the Bluff depot these were months of feverish activity. The pipes stringing their way along the hillside by the sea seemed tiny when viewed from a distance. The pipes from the boiler house joined them at the middle, to run both North and South along the elevated grassy coast. From up close at that point, the impression was of long, enormous fingers stretching away to vanishing points over two miles away in either direction. It was a pleasure to see the precision of the pipe support brackets sticking up from pristine concrete bases holding the two flow and return pipes running perfectly level to unseen points beyond normal vision.

The old dilapidated pipework looked shameful beside this fine workmanship. The old insulation was falling off in places. Leaks hissed steam and spurted hot condensate everywhere, ruining the grass and creating the musty stink of rusty iron and decaying vegetation.

Every two weeks Torquil visited the site to confer with Archie McGregor. That way he kept tabs on the progress, the aim being to gain maximum benefit from the diminishing time available. There were expansion loops to be made and left ready to install as soon as the demo was seen, filmed and accepted by John Smith. Other additional work inside the thirty-five existing buildings was to be done to comply with Torquil's ingenuous plan to solve the pressure differential problem. That work was well underway. Liseur's efforts would minimise the time needed to rebuild the system after the dramatic demonstration.

To see his design become real gave Torquil such a buzz as he watched his ideas developing and nearing completion. The good feeling an engineer gets only once in his life is to be there when his very first major project turns from scribbles on paper into solid, impressive reality.

His satisfaction was naturally tinged with regret. The fine workmanship of all the skilled tradesmen was to be abused because his mentors at the Clark Chisholm Partnership had been so pig-headed. They would rather see it destroyed than admit their shortcomings.

When he resigned and had walked out into the street he never dreamt someone like Tony Surtal would emerge and bring him back into the project. Here was his golden opportunity to make his previous bosses suffer for their obduracy in defending the indefensible. His amended plans were contributing hugely to making the project work properly. An additional pleasure was that the Clark Chisholm Partnership would be made to pay for it. Their insurance would cover it of course but there was the likely prospect that Mister Dean Chisholm would have other bills to pay.

Torquil had John Smith's letter in his file confirming the insurance company underwriting all the necessary remedial work. It was in that letter that he learned of Mister Smith's actual intention to counter-sue the Clark Chisholm Partnership for gross negligence. From Torquil's viewpoint it was starting to look like curtains for Dean Chisholm and Sean O'Casey...and not before time either.

Tony and Douglas were also aware of John Smith's strategic move on the consultants. The reason Smith was keen to help Liseur was not just because he knew they had an almost cast-iron case against the consultants. Smith also knew he had a better chance with Liseur's technical help to get his firm's money back. He had got them on his side and was using their best know-how to his own advantage. Working as a team they would make the Clark Chisholm Partnership squirm.

Tony hadn't long got the copy of John Smith's letter when another one came in from the Clark Chisholm Partnership. Tony laughed out loud when he read it and called Douglas and Torquil into his room to read it to them.

"Listen to this guys. That big bumptious bastard Chisholm is threatening to sue us for employing you, Torquil. He is claiming breach of his firm's confidentiality and non-disclosure clauses. He says we have *taken advantage of the young man's vulnerability to gain confidential information and data from copyrighted files and drawings that Torquil stole* when he walked out. They also want to sue Torquil for the one-month's notice that he never gave. What do you guys suppose I'm going to do with this lot?"

Torquil looked shocked. Douglas was smiling but on seeing the boy's face he turned to reassure him,

"Listen Torquil, You have nothing to fear from these people. You're one of us now, a team. Don't you worry; Tony and me will sort this out. Won't you Tony?"

"Absolutely right Douglas. I will send this to our lawyers and let them deal with it. I am going to instruct them to counter sue on your behalf, Torquil. I will offer Chisholm the chance to pay you a substantial sum. That will cover you for constructive dismissal, statutory redundancy, loss of use of offices during garden leave, severance pay, untaken holidays and unclaimed expenses for one month."

"Phew! You'll do all that for me?"

Tony and Douglas spoke at the same time,

"Yes."

The next day Tony instructed the lawyer to issue a writ asking for the amount of two thousand pounds to be in his hands within fourteen days. Failure to comply meant Chisholm and his lawyer would require to be represented at the Glasgow Sheriff Court in two weeks time.

Tony got a phone call from Dean Chisholm three days later,

"Yes Dean. To what do I owe the pleasure?"

Tony expected a blast of insults and protestations to come pouring out of the telephone, but that was not the case. Chisholm had plenty of time to think since storming out of the meeting on site in May. All the hard facts and accusations that were levelled at his firm regarding the Torquil Knight design work had him worried sick. He had carefully considered the additional, powerful points in Tony's letter.

He was also reeling from a stormy meeting with John Smith from the firm's insurance company. Because it was known that insurers don't pay for mistakes that are admitted, he obstinately maintained that their design was correct. Smith had disagreed but offered to cover him if he admitted the errors in design. He utterly refused to do that. Smith left in anger.

Chisholm's only remaining option seemed to be to find a scapegoat and Torquil Knight fitted the bill. The firm's reputation would thus be untarnished. He was clutching at any straw he could reach but these had virtually all but disappeared in the last few weeks. All he could think of was to get rid of this annoying writ. By adopting a softer line he hoped to reach a sensible agreement with the current monkey on his back, Tony Surtal. He purred,

"It's about young Torquil, Tony. I was not aware that the situation was as described in your letter."

"It was not *my* letter. It was Torquil's from his lawyer. Perhaps you should be talking to him?"

"I note from recent letters from your firm to the builders that Torquil's lawyer is the same one that represents Franz Liseur. Is that just a coincidence? If so then of course I will contact the lad directly."

"No Dean, it's not a coincidence. We are giving our engineer the protection of this company in his hour of need. During his short career he has never had that, until now. I assume you know that?"

"I take your point entirely Tony. Not my doing I assure you. I am very willing to accommodate him. If you are amenable I shall send you my personal cheque today in the sum of one thousand pounds. Will you withdraw the writ you have issued? I really don't want to have to go to court in seven day's time for such a small sum of money."

"That is very generous of you Dean. Of course I will withdraw the writ. I take it you will cancel your own plans to sue us?"

"Yes of course my boy. I will get the cheque written now and you shall have it this afternoon. A pleasure doing business with you my boy."

"Thank you, Dean. I will instruct Torquil's lawyer to cancel the writ for two grand and issue a new one for the one grand still outstanding."

"Now just a minute Tony. Where is your honour? I thought we had an agreement?"

"Well Dean, I've got to honour my agreement with my engineer. I promised two grand and two grand it will be."

"You are an unprincipled rogue, Surtal. I always knew that you were a scoundrel."

"It takes one to know one Chisholm, my boy. Will you pay or will I open Pandora's box on you?"

"You will have my cheque this afternoon for the full amount. Are you satisfied now?"

"Yes Dean, but my H.R. team tell me we still await Torquil's P45. Be sure your cheque appears on it as a tax paid bonus. If it's a firm's cheque I want two signatures. Okay?"

"Don't you trust me?"

"How high could I lift you Dean? Just be sure of one thing; if your cheque bounces I know where you live."

The phone was noisy when Chisholm slammed it down. At half past two a special messenger arrived with an envelope for the personal attention of Mister Surtal. Tony assembled the Liseur team in the drawing office. A photo was taken.

Tony turned in front of everyone to question Torquil,

"Where is your bank?"

"Sauchiehall Street. Why?"

"Does it have a branch in Forres?"

"Yes, Tony."

Right then. Take your cheque, get the bus home, put the money into your account and take that lonely wee girl of yours out for a slap up dinner. Don't come back till Monday.

A registered letter was sent out for the personal attention of Mister Dean Chisholm. It contained a photograph of a young engineer with a broad smile holding a small piece of paper with a very big number on it.

CHAPTER SEVEN:

Completion

Part 1
Mid Nov 1990

Bluff Site ~ the start-up.
All the fitters and welders gathered and cheered when
the final pipe connections were made to the heating
system of the last of the thirty-five buildings. The
pipework was then filled with water and ready for a
static pressure test to one-and-a-half times the design
working pressure.

The next week was spent finding and fixing any leaks
at flanges or fittings throughout the whole site. As far as
their work was concerned, these men were now done
with this original contract but were not in the least
disappointed. They could look forward to a short holiday
and then six months of solid dismantling, reassembling
and repair work to finish the job. First they had to 'finish'
this one by causing it to fail! The next stage was to start

the system's water pumps to demonstrate the pipe oscillations predicted by Colin Thompson of SIMER.

John Smith and the others were there to witness on the site what they had been shown in the computer simulations. Liseur had to convince everyone of the validity of Colin Thompson's assertion of disaster; otherwise they would be in very embarrassing financial trouble.

The site hut was buzzing with the chatter of the assembled interested parties. Norman Keen had laid on some tea and sandwiches for James Briggs, the Jarvis & Craig pair, Colin from the SIMER laboratory, Franz Liseur's team of four, plus Angus McLachlan, Archie McGregor, and of course John Smith.

Norman half-expected Clark Chisholm to be there or at least represented by someone from his office. Chisholm it seemed had acted smart and had sent along John Smith from their insurance company, *purely,* as they put it, *as an observer*; still not aware that he was there, in any case, because of his alliance with Franz Liseur.

The demonstration was set to begin at eleven sharp. At half past ten the group made their way through the guarded gates and into the site, heading for the best vantage point; the high ground on a grassy bank in the middle of the site. From there they could look in either direction, and have a clear view along the line of pipes. Torquil stood amongst them. The pumps would be started when he signalled to the men in the boiler house with his handset.

A team of fitters had been busy on site since eight o'clock in the morning and had completed the opening of all the branch connections to the various buildings. When the pumps started, the water, for the first time, would start to flow through the mischievous P.R.Vs.

Shortly after that, the pipes were expected to perform their peculiar ballet.

Douglas and Tony split up and began to walk in opposite directions along the pipeline. Their job was to oversee the four video cameramen they had hired for the occasion. It was ten minutes to eleven when they each, using their walkie-talkies, gave Torquil the news that the cameras were ready to begin filming. Torquil called Archie McGregor in the boiler house and gave the order to proceed. The starting up process began.

The pumps and pressurisation unit came online dead on five minutes to eleven. Torquil advised everyone in the group of observers that they now had a 'live' system. They stopped their conversations and turned their attention to the pipes. Nothing happened. Ten minutes went by and still there was no discernable movement. The video cameras were running. Tony phoned Douglas to ask if he had noticed any movements on his side. Negative. Norman Keen Looked at Briggs. The M.O.D. man was impassive. Torquil was becoming anxious. John Smith saw this and went over to reassure him,

"Be patient son. It takes a while to build up a dynamic response in a system as big as this. You're moving the best part of a hundred tonnes of water you know. Just give it a little time."

The young man appreciated the words of comfort but was still tense. Five more minutes passed when right beside them there was the tiniest little jump of the two ten-inch diameter pipes. Torquil's phones rang. Tony and Douglas shouted down the phones that they were filming a snake dance all along the site in both directions.

It was starting to cause the pipes to jump out of their brackets.

Seconds later the pipes beside the witnesses began to creak and clank alarmingly. The people nearest backed away as they watched the huge pipes repeatedly lifting a full six inches then clunking down on what now looked like flimsy supporting brackets. It was surely only a matter of minutes before the supports gave way and the pipes went tumbling down the embankment. John Smith shouted to Torquil,

"Tell them I've seen enough son. Turn the bugger off before anybody gets hurt."

It took about a minute for the system to regain stability. There were smiles all around and many a hard slap on Torquil Knight's back; accompanied by hearty congratulations Twenty minutes later Tony and Douglas arrived back with the four cameramen. Tony gave Colin Thompson a bear hug and grabbed his hand to shake it hard. Douglas shouted at him,

"Colin! You were right! You should have seen those pipes jerking and jumping man! It was frightening but so very pleasing. You're a clever little bugger. We've got fantastic pictures to show Chisholm. He can't deny his wrong design now. Can he?"

Colin merely smiled as if to say *I know*. They could now convince any one who doubted the validity of his computer simulations.

Norman Keen took control and steered them all back to his site office for an appraisal of what they had witnessed. When all were seated he whispered a few words to his shorthand typist and called for order to open the meeting,

"I have instructed my typist to make an accurate minute of all that will be said here today. In order to confirm everything we have seen at this extraordinary spectacle, I would like a statement from each firm represented. Please be brief gentlemen. I invite our client, Mister James Briggs of the M.O.D. to begin."

Briggs did not stand up to speak but quietly offered his apology to the others,

"Gentlemen, I am truly sorry that I, for the moment, have to adopt the position of an impartial onlooker. I have two separate interests in this scenario. One is the Ministry of Defence and the other is the firm of consultants that I have employed to design this installation. My honest and unprejudiced comment is that I am astounded to have witnessed in reality, what our mechanical contractor, Franz Liseur, many months ago predicted would happen using Colin Thompson's computer simulation. That is all I have to offer for the moment. Concerning repairs and financial concerns, I am eager to hear what the insurance company representative will say on behalf of The Clark Chisholm partnership."

Norman offered John Smith the floor. He sat as he spoke. His voice was clear and his words were measured and precise.

"Several months ago I viewed two computer simulations for this project. One showed the effect of pressure fluctuations. The other showed the effect of expansion due to temperature. Each one indicated severe destruction. In agreement with Franz Liseur, I asked that they demonstrate only the dynamic pressures for today's demonstration. That was to avoid or at least to minimise the possibility of severe damage and danger to personnel from falling pipes or pressurised water.

What I have seen this morning convinces me that the computer simulation from SIMER was an accurate prediction. I have no doubt that the other computer simulation relating to the expansion problem is also valid in its prediction that severe disruption would occur at or before reaching, the design temperature of this system.

By my letter to Franz Liseur in August, I committed my company to a provisional spend of one-and-a-half million pounds to put the design to rights and make this project safe and usable by the client. That offer was based solely on the understanding that what we have seen today would actually happen. I am pleased to allow this offer to be confirmed and recorded in the minutes of this meeting.

I await an accurate figure in due course from the main contractors, Jarvis & Craig. In the meantime I shall make funds available for immediate use by Franz Liseur. This will enable them to proceed with all speed to make all the necessary and I should say, pre-planned and already prepared, alterations to finish the work here. Thank you gentlemen."

Norman held his hand, palm upwards, towards Hugh Jarvis, inviting him to contribute. Hugh accepted and stood up.

"I have to say I was sceptical of the assertions that Douglas Fairbairn and Tony Surtal were making all those months ago. Today however, what I have witnessed has dispelled all of that doubt. We have had our differences with Liseur but I am impressed that they foresaw and warned us about these problems. It is sad that they could not convince the consulting engineers of the flawed design.

Mister Smith has obviously been in discussions with our sub contractor and I am glad this demonstration was enacted in such a way as to avoid unnecessary damage to our work and, more importantly to this rather sensitive armaments depot. On behalf of my company, I confirm my agreement to the financial arrangements as described by John Smith. Thank you John for underwriting the cost for repairing and setting to work. I expect that my company's costs will be minor compared to those of Liseur. I wish to record also my sincere thanks to the Liseur team."

He sat down looking very pleased with the outcome. Norman addressed the meeting,

"As the supervising officer for the project I have to record my admiration for the manner in which Messrs Liseur have struggled, not just in trying to bring these problems to our attention; not even just for their efforts to keep me advised of the severity of these serious design faults; but latterly by their cleverness in arranging this demonstration to cause the minimum of damage; just enough to convince the insurance inspector to accept the fault on behalf of Clark Chisholm. I offer the floor once more to my client, nay, our client, Mister James Briggs."

James stood up, walked to the other side of the table and shook hands with Douglas Fairbairn. Then he walked back to his place and spoke,

"I have just given my hand in friendship to a man whom, on the occasion of our first meeting, I ejected from my office. I am humbled by the commitment and strategic cleverness of Douglas Fairbairn and his colleagues at Franz Liseur. There were faults in the design and our professional consultants would not acknowledge that fact. They were the flies in our ointment gentlemen.

It has taken extraordinary efforts by Messrs Franz Liseur to convince everyone the faults were real and dangerous. I am glad the danger is over. Financial wrangles will ensue. It is comforting that our Mister Smith has shown great understanding and authority in arranging to guarantee the cost of reparations. As the ultimate client here today, I wish to pass my congratulations and thanks to you all for this happy outcome. Thank you all. Well done!"

He sat down. Tony and Douglas both noticed that he had not mentioned Torquil. Norman asked for a response from Liseur. Tony looked at Douglas who shook his head, turned to fix his gaze on Torquil and nodded that he should speak. His protégée looked surprised but rose to his feet. He looked at James Briggs and smiled. He had a lot to say to him but it would wait for another time.

Briggs did not hold Torquil's stare but hung his head trying to dispel some guilty thoughts; *I hope this rookie is not going to embarrass me. That would be bad form in a meeting like this when everything's going so well. Please, Torquil, keep it light and don't spoil the good day we are all having.* Torquil began,

"This is my project. I was the designer who visited site more than three years ago with a sketchpad, ruler and pencil and went back to my offices to invent an elegant replacement for the dilapidated steam system you can still see beside my new pipes. I intended to mimic the existing system with the addition of some modern upgrades. The probable costs I presented were realistic for what I felt was necessary to improve the installation.

My client said they could not afford that amount. I was compelled to reduce the design to achieve a cost that suited the purse of the Ministry of Defence. After two years of effort and stress, working with difficult colleagues and striving to satisfy my client, I altered my design to achieve the cost the client imposed upon me.

Shortly thereafter I realised in my panic to comply, that I had made some basic errors. My mentors at Clark Chisholm were not interested. They only cared about the fees. I was removed from the project and they went ahead blindly with the faulty designs. I offered to resign hoping that my protest would force my superiors to listen. They did not. For that reason I left their employ that day.

It was only by joining Franz Liseur's team that I was given the security, assistance and most of all the confidence to address the problems and to help Liseur deliver proper solutions.

I know what is wrong with the design. What's more important is that I also know how to put it right. Our men on site are already underway with the alterations to accommodate the pressure and the expansion problems. As we speak, they are draining the system to begin the installation of the pipe loops to accommodate the expansion. The P.R.V's will be removed and discarded. Are there any questions?"

There were none. He continued,

"Last week I had the men pressure test the existing heating pipes in each of the thirty-five site buildings. This proved that they were suitable for the higher working pressure and temperature of our new heating system. That means that we will have medium pressure and temperature within all of the buildings and will have no need for the P.R.V.'s. There will be no dynamic pressure problems to worry about in my new design. Thank you gentlemen."

He sat down and shuffled his notes into a neat pile in front of him. Douglas tapped him on the shoulder and whispered,

"Sit up and face the S.O."

He did so with a confident look. There was a question from Norman,

"If the temperature is going to be higher within the pipes in the buildings, Torquil does that present any danger to the personnel?"

"No sir. Any low-level heated pipe surfaces will be insulated and encased with aluminium cladding.

Radiators will be encased in protective wire mesh casings. This is the current health and safety practise to prevent injury to personnel.

"Thank you Torquil for devising these working solutions. What a pity you were prevented from doing so while employed by the Clark Chisholm partnership."

"I am afraid to say, Mister Keen, it would have made no difference. The cost would have prevented the M.O.D. from accepting. Mister Briggs would have cancelled the brief. The project would have gone to some other firm."

Briggs was on his feet.

"Norman, this must stop. There is a clear implication of my being responsible for the design of this system. If Clark Chisholm were too afraid to amend a wrong design they should not have gone ahead with it in the first place. Mister Knight must withdraw his remarks or I must censure the minutes and leave the meeting."

Tony Surtal was on his feet in an instant.

"We will not withdraw these comments. After all is said and done, Torquil Knight is the only one who actually knows this entire sorry saga. His stated opinions can be proved. We have copies of the M.O.D. minutes of the meetings chaired by Mister Briggs. It is clear from them that he forced the costs down. They also record his undisguised threat to cancel the project with Torquil's firm. He may amend or delete the minutes today but the written evidence and facts will be used elsewhere.

I assure you that Mister Briggs will very soon face a day of reckoning in a higher court than this."

Tony thumped the table and sat down. Norman called for order but was halted when Briggs jumped up and left without another word. There was silence for a few seconds until Norman Keen broke it,

"My meetings are certainly not dull affairs. Does any one have anything else to say before we all go to lunch at my hotel?"

"Great idea!" Shouted Hugh Jarvis. "Come on you lot, I'm paying!"

Norman Keen would have none of it,

"Not this time Hugh. I am on the bell for this lunch. Let's go and eat."

Part 2
Feb 1991

Liseur's squad ~ Bluff Site ~ Forres
Christmas holidays were over. The New Year had begun with positive attitudes all round. Liseur's squad of welders and mates on site were seasoned and working well in spite of the cold conditions. A year had passed since Liseur's men first started on the project. Every one of them was eager at the prospect of continuous work until the middle of the summer or beyond. The improving weather and longer daylight meant overtime

and heavier wage packets. It was well known that this was an insurance job. None of the men was unhappy about being on this financial 'gravy train'.

The finishing date for the project was set for mid June and it was looking likely that everything would be up and running like clockwork by then. The men were not at all concerned with what was going on at the site meetings with the bosses. The people who had the fancy titles and company cars could handle the politics. Like Torquil had told them, that was none of their business. These tough men had worked hard and earned the fun and banter in the site huts during their tea breaks. Angus McLaughlin was an old hand at keeping up their moral with his fund of stories.

"Ah once had a young apprentice sent to one ae my sites. He wiz only sixteen and one day in his third week he wiz looking a bit green."

"Must've been a Celtic supporter Angus?"

"Naw he wasnae. He'd ate a sandwich that had been lyin' in the hut for two days and he actually became sick as a dug. Ah phoned his mammy and she came on the bus to collect the boy. She was not pleased when she saw him."

"Mibbe she wiz a Rangers supporter, Angus and didnae want a green wean?"

"Shut it you. It wiz nothing tae dae with the fitba'."

"Whit happened, Angus? Did she take the boy hame?"

"Yes she did, but not before giving me a tongue lashing. She said she only wanted him to become an engineer like his daddy who it turned out was a plumber."

"That's no a tongue lashing Angus."

"Naw, that wasnae it. It was because ae what ah said about plumbers."

"Did you say something nice Angus?"

"Well no exactly. Ah said that a plumber wasnae and engineer."

"Whit's wrang wae saying that Angus?"

"It wasnae that. It wiz when ah said a plumber couldnae be an engineer because a plumber couldnae fit a nut intae a monkey's mooth. That's when she let fly wae the tongue lashing."

"Whit did she say, Angus?"

"Plenty! But ah couldnae repeat what that woman said. All ah could dae was haud my hauns over the wee boys ears. Right you lot, it's time tae get back tae work."

Amid laughter and grumbles the squad rose and headed back to the tough, windswept environment to continue with the seemingly interminable alterations on the pipework.

These were the men who were assembling the revised jigsaw puzzle according to Torquil's new drawings. Hardened site guys, working in all weather, using their special skills, generally feeling that, compared to them, the managers were having it easy sitting in their cosy offices. They had little idea of the long and complex back-story of this seemingly simple contract. In any case it was not for them to know or care how artfully Torquil Knight had participated in the intricate manoeuvres being enacted by Franz Liseur and the M.O.D.

Angus had learnt some of the background from his weekly phone calls with Archie McGregor. They discussed the progress and other essentials for the efficient running of the construction work. Every four weeks they met on site to measure the work for bonuses and to assess how much Liseur could claim from Jarvis and Craig for work done and materials on site. With all that done they invariably left the site to chat over a pub lunch. Angus would tease out of Archie some snippets of the bigger games being played by Liseur's men at the top.

"Who's this young fella, Torquil Knight, Archie?"

"You know who he is. He's the new engineer who designed the new system with expansion loops and all the rest of the modifications."

"Well ah know that much. Ah've seen his name on the drawings."

"That's right, Angus. So what else do you need to know about him?"

"Ah'd like tae know why he suddenly appeared out ae nowhere and gave us a lecture. Told us all how this job was badly designed by him and is to be severely modified. Then he says he's the wee boy that's gonnae do that. That disnae make any sense tae me. And another thing; his name is on the drawings that came frae Clark Chisholm. Dis that mean he's the consultant?"

"No he's not. He used to be but he left. He joined us and his ideas are the ones we are using to change the system so it works. That's it in a nutshell, Angus. All the rest is above our pay pokes."

"Ah still wonder how that a' fits thegither. We shouldnae complain since it's good work for us. But some of the guys are the same as me; they cannae figure it out. Torquil says it's politics and none of our business but if it's his business then ah'm glad ah'm a fitter-welder and no a politician. Ah can go home at night and forget my work but they seem to have it in their heads a' the time?"

"Angus, you're misjudging yourself son. You worry about your squad. You keep them right every day; listen to their problems and grumbles. That's the politics of the building site, isn't it? Do you think the office guys worry about those things?"

"No, ah don't suppose they do, Archie. Funny that, ah never thought about it that way. Glad ah brought it up."

"Me too. Now that's another worry of your mind. Fancy another beer?"

"Oh naw, Archie. Ah need tae get back."

"How's that, Angus?"

"Building site politics, Archie. None ae your business."

Part 3
Feb to Jun 1991:

General

The site squad worked steadily on; quite unmindful of those shenanigans taking place behind the scenes. Liseur's bank balance was better off by the injection of the promised funds, compliments of John Smith. Dean Chisholm was still smarting after forking out that ex gratia bonus of two grand to Torquil Knight. It would be a long time before he forgave Liseur for that insolent ruse. He had not altered the peculiar conviction that there were no faults in his firm's design for Bluff.

Unfortunately for him there was no one around now who could have told him of the successful demonstration of the system that took place in November. In fact, not a word had reached his ears since he stormed out of the site meeting way back in May last year. No one from the M.O.D. or Jarvis and Craig had felt any obligation to get in touch with him since he had been summarily removed from the project. He fully expected to receive an apology from the bunch of rascals who doubted his professional skill and integrity. *Then I shall sue those scoundrels for all they are worth.*

His anger against all of them, together with the certainty of his own innocence, served only to make his blood boil in frustration at having been entirely sent to Coventry. He was in this frame of mind, staring out of his upstairs bay window, when his secretary entered his office,

"Excuse me Mister Chisholm but these two letters have just arrived. Both are marked 'private and confidential'."

"Ah! Tracy. I wonder whom it is that needs to be so secretive?"

"I've no idea Mister Chisholm but I thought you'd like to see them right away."

"Quite right my girl, put them there on my desk while I fetch my spectacles. Will you be kind enough to bring me some coffee and one of those chocolate biscuits of which you always seem to have an inexhaustible supply?"

"Certainly Mister Chisholm. Won't take long."

His chat with the girl and the prospect of chocolate and coffee had cheered him. That mood changed radically when he read the first letter. His head reeled with resentment.

The Clark Chisholm Partnership
February 8th 1991

Attention of D. Chisholm Esquire.

Dear Mister Chisholm,   <u>*Ref: R.N.A.D. Bluff*</u>

In November last year we were represented at a site meeting at the above establishment to witness what would happen to the completed pipe installation when the pumps were running and the system was pressurised. We saw that Franz Liseur's alleged faults of your design were shown to be correct. The predicted oscillations of the installation were real, dangerous and frightening to all who witnessed this event.

We have awarded funding to Franz Liseur in the amount of one-and-a-half million pounds, pro tempore, to begin rectification of your design, to complete the installation correctly and set it to work at the earliest possible time.

Mister Torquil Knight has confirmed that he made you aware of this matter in the post-tender stage of the project. You failed to draw this to the attention of your client. We assert that you are thus in breach of the standard form of government contract between you and the Minister of Defence, represented by James Briggs of the M.O.D. in Edinburgh.

We cite the Clark Chisholm partnership as the entity liable for this whole occurrence. A prima fascia case will therefore be established against your partnership, ergo you personally since your partner is actually deceased, for gross negligence verging on criminal irresponsibility. We shall hold you to account for all costs of circa one point five million pounds plus fees.

You are required by this letter and by our writ being sent under separate cover, to be legally represented one calendar month from the date of this letter at: -

The High Court of Justiciary,
Justiciary Buildings,
1, Mart Street,
Saltmarket,
Glasgow,
G1 5JT.

Should you fail to appear or be legally represented, we shall arrest your income and freeze your various bank accounts.

We have sent a copy of this letter to the Association of Consulting Engineers with a recommendation that your firm be reprimanded for what we consider to be grave professional misconduct committed by you on the contract at Bluff.

Subject to the outcome of the action against you we shall review, and probably increase, your annual premiums should you require future cover.

You are also advised that we have copied this letter to: -

> *Mr. James Briggs of the M.O.D.*
> *Mister Tony Surtal of Franz Liseur*
> *Mr. Norman Keen of the Keen, Parr and Felt partnership*
> *Mister Hugh Jarvis of Jarvis & Craig*

The evidence of these parties will be put before the sheriff along with the affidavit of Mister Torquil Knight, detailing his experiences with your firm during the design stages of the project.

Yours Faithfully,
John Smith
Senior Claims Inspector (Indemnity Protection Insurance Company)

Dean Chisholm was stunned. When Tracy appeared with a tray she stood and looked at his face thinking he was about to die,

"Mister Chisholm! Mister Chisholm! Are you all right? You look as if you have seen a ghost. Can I get you an aspirin or something?"

Dean looked up from his reading still wearing the deathlike stare,

"No. No Tracy, my dear. I've just had some bad news with this letter you brought in. I'll be fine when I have some of your coffee. Thank you for your concern. Don't worry; it's nothing I can't handle. Off you go."

The girl was not too sure that she should go and leave her boss in that state. She left and pulled the door quietly closed behind her but lingered on the landing to hear if there was going to be the same reaction to that second letter that was still lying on Chisholm's desk. Her boss's condition did not improve when he read the other letter. It came from the M.O.D.

Clark Chisholm　　　　　　　　*From: James Briggs*
February 8th 1991　　　　　　　*M.O.D. Edinburgh*

For the attention of Mr D. Chisholm

Dear Mister Chisholm,　　　　　*Ref: R.N.A.D. Bluff*

I had a visit to the above establishment last November to witness a demonstration of the oscillations of the pipe installation. Last year Franz Liseur predicted this by means of a computer simulation. One of their project engineers, Mister Torquil Knight, made me aware that he told you of these faults in the post-tender stage of the project. You ridiculed his advice, refused to correct those errors and effectively gave him no option but to resign.

On behalf of my employer, the Ministry of Defence, I declare that the Clark Chisholm Partnership stands in

breach of the standard form of government contract between us since you failed to draw this matter to my attention.

Since the project is now well beyond the originally planned finishing date due to the problems associated with your shoddy work, I consider that it would, ipso facto, be inappropriate for you to request any further fees for this work. I shall also seek to recover all fees already paid. It is hoped that the Minister will have no difficulty in securing the return of past payments without the need of a writ.

My lawyers aver that your state of mind during the run up to the tender could be construed as 'animus nocendi'. Loosely translated this suggests that you authorized a crime while you had not only knowledge of its illegal content but also must have been aware of its inevitable consequences. I shall pass this notion to your insurers who normally cover you for genuine mistakes. Whether they insure against deliberate malpractice is not for us to judge. Regardless of that, we intend to pursue you for all other attendant remedial and reconstruction costs and fees when the work on site is concluded.

I take no pleasure in further advising, as a result of your performance on this project, that our tendering rules preclude your firm from any Ministry of Defence consultancy opportunities for a period not exceeding ten years.

For the absence of doubt I take some pleasure in further informing you that your firm is no longer associated with this project. You and all of your staff are refused permission to visit this site at any time; now or in the future.

Yours Faithfully,

James Briggs

Senior Administrator

The Ministry of Defence

Scotland.

Tracy was in no doubt that her boss was still alive. She hurried away on hearing him yell into his intercom,

"O'Casey! Get your backside up to my office at once. In thirty seconds!"

Chisholm was flabbergasted to find himself so comprehensively ensnared in these legal traps. He intended to waste no time finding his escape route. Prior to calling his firm's lawyers, he wanted to pin this all on Sean O'Casey,

Out of breath from running up the stairs, Sean appeared. Before he could speak, Chisholm was at him,

"You are in big trouble! Don't say a word to me till you have read these two letters."

Sean visibly shook while he took the necessary few minutes to digest what he read. His response to Chisholm was aggressive,

"What do you think your talking about? It's not me that's in trouble here. The letters say it's you! And they're right! You knew about this all along!"

Chisholm was red with anger. This had all suddenly got out of control and he was not going to let O'Casey off the hook. He practically stumbled around the side of his desk to scream loudly at his colleague,

"That is not the case! You told me there was nothing to worry about. You said you had it under control. You did nothing to help Torquil Knight! You just let it all go ahead. Now I know why the boy left. This is all your fault!"

O'Casey's mind was racing with confused thoughts. He had had enough. To argue was pointless. It was he himself who told Torquil that *'we don't make mistakes in this firm'*. But it was Dean Chisholm who gave that instruction. He just followed his boss's orders. Although he realised that meant little, he was determined to make Dean Chisholm eat at least some of the dirt. His brain worked overtime to retrieve appropriate answers. *My time in this firm is up! Chisholm should be the guy paying dearly for his arrogance. I won't leave without giving him some straight talk.* He spoke through clenched teeth,

"Now you listen to me! You had chances at the site meetings to put this to rights. You could have stopped all this from happening. But no! Not the great Dean Chisholm who can't see past his lofty position on top of his own dung heap. You stink. And I stink because of you. You decided to run with this hoping to get away with it. You are an ignoramus if you can't see that the boy was right all along. But no! You had to be the big cheese. You had to be proved right. You are like Canute; to deny the laws of physics and trying to outsmart engineers more clever than you'll ever be. You're a bloody fool and I hope they fucking hang you, but I hope they take you to the cleaners first."

He spun round and headed for the door. His parting shot left nothing to the imagination,

"And another thing you fat bumptious bastard! You can stick your job up your arse!"

The door slammed shut before Chisholm could respond. He stumbled round his bureau to collapse into his high-backed leather-bound armchair. His brain hurt with the effort of trying to replace reality with his disbelief. Reality won.

"I'm going to lose everything," He mumbled.

CHAPTER EIGHT

Comeuppance!

Part 1
Fri 13th Sep 1991

Franz Liseur ~ Dinner Date

Tony Surtal was in a good mood. His branch was doing well, his staff were contented and looking forward to autumn holidays in the predicted Scottish Indian summer or elsewhere in warmer climes. For the moment he was nursing a plot to reward the two people who took on and solved the Bluff job. He went out and asked Douglas and Torquil into his office

"Right you guys, get your coats on. We're going out to dinner."

They both looked at their watches in disbelief. Douglas said,

"It's only eleven, Tony. Either your watch is wrong or you are starving."

"Neither Douglas. We are goin for a ride in my car, a mystery tour. Dinner is more than an hour away so, let's put a jildy on, eh?"

With an invitation like that it took no time at all to get them on their way. Tony drove and took the scenic route from Kilbowie Road through Drumchapel to Milngavie via Bearsden. The Balmore country road led on to Kirkintilloch, Denny, Stirling, Bridge of Allen and Dunblane. His passengers had no idea where this dinner was to take place but Douglas had his suspicions.

"This must be a very special place we're going to, Tony?"

"Well, you two are special people. I want to impress you the way Franz Liseur treats its good guys. Especially you, Douglas; you mustn't believe that Peurova has the monopoly on fancy staff perks."

They were now past Auchterarder. Douglas turned to look at Torquil in the back seat. He pointed to the time on his watch and made another signal with his index finger that they were about to turn to the left. Then he winked. Torquil shrugged. He had no idea what this meant but seconds later all was revealed. They had entered the driveway of Gleneagles Hotel. And swung to a stop at the main entrance to be met by the military looking commissionaire.

"How about this lads? I could get used to this."

"Me too." Said Torquil. He jumped out to confront Douglas, "Now I understand what all your gesticulations meant. A hour exactly and here we are at the dinner place."

"You've not been here before then, Torquil?"

"To Gleneagles! Are you kidding, Douglas? This is the best. I could never afford to come here. Thank you so much, Tony. There's no way Dean Chisholm would ever take his employees to a *dinner,* never mind the most luxurious hotel in Scotland."

While they admired the imposing elegance of the hotel building the commissionaire took the keys and handed them to a laddie to park their car. Tony turned and rubbed his stomach,

"*Now* I'm hungry, Douglas."

"You're always hungry." Joked Douglas.

The Maître De led them to their table in the vast, high ceilinged, square dining room. Two adjoining walls, one facing north and the other facing east, consisted mainly of floor-to-ceiling French windows leading out to manicured lawns. The low September sun shone in from above the emerald green rolling skyline of the Ochil Hills giving the room an unreal, but soothing golden lustre.

The talk over dinner was relaxed and the time did not seem to matter. The job at Forres was done and dusted.

All that remained were pats on backs and the resolution of the costs. Douglas and Torquil both knew that there was a financial result due to be revealed. It was pretty certain that it would be good news; but how good was yet to be disclosed. Tony was toying with them today and he guessed they might be thinking, *maybe this is why Tony is splashing the firm's lolly on this expensive dinner? We must be in the money from Forres.*

He would keep them guessing for a little longer. It was his inclination to allow them the fun of reviewing the history and shenanigans during the Bluff contract. He wanted to savour their recollections and share the elaborate moves they made leading up to their ultimate success; politically, financially and on the technicalities of the job.

"Douglas, do you recall your first couple of letters to Jarvis and Craig?"

"Yes I do. It was just a try-on to win a bit of time, asking for setting out details from them. They hadn't a clue what was going on. That clown, Hadshaw was lost from day one. That little encounter with Briggs in Edinburgh allowed us to nullify the four-week penalty gambit from Jarvis. Briggs didn't have a clue what I was doing. I liked that.

I also enjoyed setting builders back on their heels. Making *them* feel insecure. My third letter was a cracker. The one about the P.R.V.'s."

Torquil butted in, "Oh, I only got involved when the error of the pressure reducing valves was raised. So, that was you?"

"Yes; and it was me who sent David Young up to see you to warn you about the schoolboy error you had made. I didn't know you then but I'd hoped you would get Chisholm and O'Casey to let you fix it before it was too late."

"O'Casey's answer was to take me off the project and tell lies to everyone. I wasn't strong enough to make him listen, Douglas. I wish I had been but it's water under the bridge now isn't it? I'm never going to get over that."

Tony saw the anguish in Torquil's face. He was clearly still wrestling with the guilt of his error made under extreme pressure from people above him as well as his deep dissatisfaction from not being allowed by O'Casey to fix it.

Even after all this time and the successes they had achieved on this project, the lad was still feeling the pain of his underachievement in the employ of Dean Chisholm. Tony was determined to lessen Torquil's remorse by explaining to his protégée some of the facts of life in general and business in particular. He leaned forward saying,

"Listen to me. There is a basic difference between an employer and an employee. When the Dean Chisholm's of this world need staff they just put the word out and a hundred youngsters like you turn up. You have one chance in a hundred. If you get the job, you're always thinking, *if I fail there are ninety-nine people waiting at the door to pinch my place.* The contract you have with any employer is very one sided. The boss has the power and you have no one but yourself to fight your battles."

"I appreciate what you say, Tony. But why would they not listen to reason? You chaps proved the P.R.V's were wrong with computer simulations that don't lie. They even dismissed it after seeing the films of it actually happening. I can't understand how these men could be so blinkered."

It was Douglas, who tried to answer that question,

"It's like this, Torquil. They weren't stupid; they were greedy. Look at it this way. Dean Chisholm pays you and all your colleagues a fiver per hour. He charges his clients forty quid per hour for every hour you all work for him. Thirty quid of that huge revenue pays for salaries, rent, gas and electric bills etc. He keeps the other ten for himself. That's a quarter of the firm's total income. He gets that big pay packet for what he is supposed to *know* and for making sure *you all* give a quality service to his clients under his supposedly *expert* direction.

"But I was the expert, not him or O'Casey. I *knew* it was wrong." Blurted the boy."

"Yes Torquil, we all know that now but Chisholm's reputation depends on reliable work. He is not paid to make mistakes. His clients pay him well for his professional knowledge. If he defaults he loses his reputation, then his customers and finally the considerable income you and your colleagues earn for him.

Now do you understand how he was in the same kind of trap as you? He had to bluff it out, no pun intended. It was because, like you, he had people on his back; his clients; his bank manager and his insurers. None of them would pay the cost for changing the design if he admitted the errors."

Torquil's face showed the enlightenment he felt from his mentors' revelations of the mysteries of capitalism; greed and fear...on both sides of the workforce.

"That's right, so he did, and Briggs was the same. He had the Minister of Defence poking him with a stick. I see that now. I am better off than Briggs, Chisholm and O'Casey because I was lucky to join up with honest people and we beat that lot at their own sad game."

Tony beamed at Douglas and offered him the chance to continue this line of discussion,

"Since its evident we are having a cheering effect on our comrade in the war of attrition with the clever dicks who caused it, why don't we savour what we now know of their fates? James Briggs for instance seemed at the end to have become a stranger to the site."

Douglas came in right away with his version,

"I think Briggs preferred his ivory tower in Edinburgh hoping it would all blow over and he would simply get back to his normal activity; lording it over his in-house subordinates; or anyone else who had the misfortune to come under his dictatorial power. One good thing he did for himself was his writ against Clark Chisholm Partnership to recover all their fees to date. That must have hurt old Dean in his lower abdomen, eh Tony?"

"It's even better than that, Douglas. Chisholm thought he'd got away with it when his insurers paid all the fees back to the MOD. His real shock was to be sued by the very same insurers to get it all back plus the best part of two million quid for the remedial work this year? Doesn't that sound good Torquil?"

"It sounds better if *we* are to be given that money so the MOD doesn't benefit. That means Briggs doesn't get any kudos from down south. I like the sound of that! Do we know how much was it, Tony?"

"Yes I do. The Ministry of Defence has no option in law. They have awarded Franz Liseur, the surrogate designers, all of the fees of fifty-eight thousand, four hundred and sixty-one pounds. This was done to the satisfaction of everyone except the Clark Chisholm Partnership and James Briggs."

Douglas and Torquil were mighty pleased to hear this for the first time and were anxious to hear more.

"Is there any news of the rest of the cash?" asked Douglas. Tony smiled and held both palms up to the two men,

"You will both love this. Back in February the case brought before the high court by John Smith for recovery of costs from Clark Chisholm Partnership was successfully argued. Torquil's affidavit was the main evidence along with our digital displays and the actual films from the site demonstration showing the dancing pipes."

"And what does that mean in financial terms?" asked Douglas.

"All costs were ordered by the judge to be recovered from Dean Chisholm and his partners and paid back to John Smith's firm. Now here's the best bit and the reason why we are all stuffing our faces with roast goose, prunes and Armagnac at Chisholm's expense. The judge has accepted our joint claim with Hugh Jarvis for loss and expense for the whole project. The insurers have just been instructed to distribute *that amount* to Jarvis & Craig and to Franz Liseur. Don't know how much yet but we are being paid in full for all loss and expense. Everything!"

Torquil spluttered his wine into his napkin and laughed out loud. Douglas slapped his back with a hearty belt of his hand,

"It seemed to hit a spot with this fellow anyway, Tony. I think we should give him the floor."

"That's fantastic, Tony. If all that has to be paid by Clark Chisholm then they must surely go out of business?"

"It has been paid. They have shut up shop."

"Hallelujah!" shouted Torquil. "I am so glad to hear that. Isn't that just fabulous? Oh, wait till I tell my pal Davy; and my mum and dad; and Phillipa."

Tony and Douglas were pleased to see the joy in the face of the young man whom, in the last five or more years, had been through so much. It looked as if there was nothing else anyone could do to make him any happier. But there was. Tony signalled the waiter. A few minutes later he whispered,

"Torquil, look who's over there."

He turned round to see Phillipa standing smiling at the dining-room door beside his father and mother. He looked back at his two friends. He was lost for words and trying to suppress his emotion. Tony patted him on the arm, handed him an envelope and whispered,

"This is your autumn bonus. Go and join your folks, go home and relax for a week. Come back ready for work a week on Monday."

"Tony, Douglas, you guys are just brilliant. How can I ever thank you for all this?"

"Don't think about work for a week." said Douglas

"Just don't be late for work." Said Tony.

"See you a week on Monday. Bye."

He walked over to embrace his parents. He made a brief backward glance as he led them out of the dining room with his right arm round Phillipa's waist.

Part 2
Fri 20th Sep 1991

Franz Liseur offices ~ Clydebank

Tony spent an hour or so with Douglas discussing issues with the rest of the contracts currently underway. There was nothing as significant as the Bluff contract on the books now, so it was a relaxed meeting. They turned to a more personal topic,

"I hope the lad is having a good break at home, Douglas?"

"Yeah, me too. He was really chuffed by what you did on Friday. He will be back next week raring to get going on something else he can get his teeth into. Have you got anything in mind?"

"No, not really. I'll leave that up to you. I still have a nagging feeling about not completely closing off the Forres job."

"How's that? It's all done and dusted now and running like the proverbial sewing machine."

"No, I don't mean the system up there. I'm not satisfied we've sorted the Briggs thing. We had to show him two faces in order to get the job done and paid for but he has not had to suffer for what he did to the boy."

"We can't make him suffer, Tony. He's Teflon coated. All the money has been sorted and he is off the hook.

Like I said last week, he's in his ivory tower and we don't have a ladder to reach him."

"I'm not so sure about that, Doug. We know a lot about him. Maybe we can go above his head. Get his bottom spanked. What do you think?"

"Above his head is the MOD in London. Do you know who his up-line is?"

"No, but I can find out. I'll have a chat with Jules Dispard. He's bound to know the strings to pull. If I get a name or title we'll write and spill the beans on Briggs."

Who's writing *that* letter, Tony? It has to be watertight or it won't stick to the wall."

"That's what I like about you, Douglas. You come out with great advice but your mixed metaphors are rubbish."

They both laughed.

"Right Douglas, you've got all the gen. Give all you know to our lawyers at McMeikle and Huggett. Get a draft from them for us to approve."

"Right, I'll get that done by tonight. When do you want their response?"

"As soon as possible but not more that a week if they can. Oh, and bye the way, I don't want Torquil to hear of any of this. If it falls flat then he'll not fret."

Douglas phoned Gordon McMeikle and outlined Torquil's treatment at the hands of Briggs who they believed misused his position of authority to bully the young engineer. Angus offered to search the Civil Service guidelines for senior civil servants in dealing with people under their control. If any breach of the rules was indicated, he agreed that a polite letter was required asking for a reaction and possible sanctions. Douglas would let him know the name of an appropriate senior officer of the Ministry of Defence. A draft for scrutiny was requested as soon as possible.

Within a week a draft letter arrived that Angus thought might be suitable. Tony and Douglas agreed it was a real shocker of a character assassination; skilfully couched in the language of the law. They admired the lawyer's excellent piece of legal lynching and Tony gave the go-ahead for it to be sent, unabridged, by registered post to London. Hopefully that would ensure a response albeit not necessarily swift.

He still chose not to tell Torquil in case the plan for revenge on James Briggs just fizzled out. It would not be kind to raise the young man's hopes. It was more likely that some civil service underling would push it under the carpet. That would be the way the ministry was usually expected to protect the reputation of the M.O.D. James Briggs, that self-righteous, pompous bully in Edinburgh, would perhaps never even know this letter had ever existed.

The Ministry of Defence
Whitehall
London
SW1A 2HB
United Kingdom.

McMeikle and Huggett
Solicitors
1, Park Circle
Glasgow
G4 1GA

27 September 1991

For the attention of the Secretary of State for Defence

Sir,   *Ref: Contract at R.N.A.D. Bluff,*
                                  <u>*Forres, Morayshire, Scotland.*</u>

We represent Messrs Franz Liseur, the contractor for a mechanical services contract carried out at the above base. They were sub-contractors but due to severe design difficulties, were obliged not only to re-design the project but also to finance it to the tune of nearly two million pounds in order to have it completed in compliance with their contract with the Builders, Jarvis & Craig Ltd.

Many problems arose because your senior administrator at the Ministry of Defence offices in Edinburgh, Mister James Briggs, severely, continually and quite unjustly, mentally abused a young consultant engineer from the Clark Chisholm Partnership. Over a period of two years he demanded that the cost be continually reduced to such an inadequate amount that the design was completely insufficient for the purpose on site.

We know from published records the original mechanical services budget for this project was two million pounds. It is palpable that James Briggs can be construed as culpable of self-aggrandisement by his insistence that the mechanical services cost be cut to half-a–million pounds. This may have been done to curry favour with his financial overseers in the hope of promotion. In so doing, he has in our opinion, broken a number of the British Civil Service established rules of behaviour.

A Government Civil Servant holding a supervisory post is obliged by those rules to take all reasonable steps to ensure the integrity and devotion to duty of all Government servants for the time being under their control and authority. It is clear from our discussions with our client that Mister James Briggs did not in this instance,

- *Maintain high ethical standards and honesty.*
- *Promote the principles of merit, fairness and impartiality in the discharge of his duties.*
- *Act with fairness and impartiality and not discriminate against anyone,*
- *Perform and discharge his duties with the highest degree of professionalism and dedication to the best of his abilities.*

The civil service rules also mandate that no Government Civil Servant shall, in his dealings with hired staff or with external consultants, force them to submit to his will, adopt dilatory tactics or deliberately cause delays.

It is patent in all of these instances that Mister James Briggs has singularly failed to maintain these required high and noble standards of etiquette and behaviour towards our client, Mister Torquil Knight, an erstwhile employee and design consultant with the Clark Chisholm Partnership for the above project. We do not seek damages in this instance for the pain and suffering of our client; nor do we seek any reward for loss of office due to his subsequent constructive dismissal. These have been secured by another route in another place.

We simply seek audi altrem partem; that everyone has a right to Natural Justice. I appeal to you sir, to act in accordance with your best principles within the rules that you know so well and those we have highlighted for good order, perhaps to censure the said James Briggs and consider his future within Her Majesty's civil service.

His actions against our client contributed to causing the above project to be extended by three-and-a-half years and involved the expenditure of considerable extra funding.

Perhaps you might take the time from your busy schedule to advise us of your proposed action, if any, in this unhappy matter? In the meantime we are at your disposal were you to deem it necessary to command further elaboration.

Yours Faithfully
Gordon McMeikle LLB St Andrews
Senior Partner,
McMeikle and Russell

Part 3
16th Oct 1991

Franz Liseur's offices Clydebank
Tony had Douglas in his office for a brief chat to prime him before inviting Torquil to join them.

"I thought you might like to be here when I show Torquil this letter from the Ministry of Defence?"

"Seriously? I had forgotten all about that. Keeping it secret by forgetting, you know?"

"Yep, I do that all the time. Here, have a read."

Douglas took time to read it making the odd 'hum' and 'gasp' before handing it back with a grin of sheer pleasure.

"That is some letter. How do you plan to let the lad know?"

Let's just call him in and I'll chat about Chisholm. I want to draw him out about his dissatisfaction that Briggs has got off the hook. Play a wee game with me. Disagree with things I say about Chisholm and I'll get Torquil to bring up Briggs, okay?"

"I'll follow your lead. This should be fun, Tony. I'll call him in and you start the ball rolling,"

"Hi Torquil. Come in and have a cup of coffee. We had fun at Gleneagles but I noticed you were overly delighted by what happened to Chisholm. I didn't think he was totally to blame for the fiasco at Forres."

Douglas, as rehearsed was not in agreement,

"Oh yes he was, Tony. He was his own worst enemy... away from the design of projects for so long that he must have lost all sense of reality...lived in a dream world in fact. Even my three-year-old son would have known the design at Bluff was wrong. O'Casey was just as bad if not worse, blindly sticking to the firm's dogma, *we never make mistakes*. Who else could be to blame but those two clowns?"

Tony was brief in answering the rhetorical question from Douglas. The Dean Chisholm ruse was going well.

"No one else is to blame I suppose. After all, Briggs was not at fault for the design."

Douglas was on him like a shot, bating Tony's tender trap of Torquil,

"He's not to blame for the *design*, but his treatment of Torquil here was very much to blame for it going wrong!"

"Yep! You're not wrong, Douglas. Wouldn't it be nice, Torquil if we could think of some way to get him slapped on the knuckles?

Torquil smiled. He was confident in the presence of his friends but was unsure how to respond. On one hand he wanted revenge but something inside of him felt that the big bully Briggs should get his comeuppance from people more able to apply it than him or his two bosses. When he decided to answer, his argument was elegant,

"James Briggs must have broken a lot of rules in his time. Men like him who gain high positions, always seem to wriggle out of trouble. If he's not stopped, he'll just do again what he did to me. I believe when the fellows in the Ministry of Defence realise the final cost on this project, Briggs will catch it, big time! They are better able to make him suffer that we are. I wish I could persuade them to do that! But it's hopeless, isn't it, Tony. Those people are too far above us to make them do anything. Look at the bother we had with Chisholm. He was small fry compared to that fellow Briggs, never mind trying to argue with the M.O.D."

Tony was pleased and surprised at what he was hearing but for a moment, was startled by the strong emotion in his young engineer's eloquent speech. There was a lot in what Torquil had just said that confirmed Tony's own attitude to Briggs. He thought, *Okay, Briggs is a bully but his treatment of Torquil had evidently affected the lad much more than I guessed.*

Now seemed the perfect time to show Torquil that Franz Liseur were *not* in a hopeless position to do damage to that big buffoon. He spoke in a measured tone,

"It may seem desperate, Torquil but I don't see why we shouldn't try. After all, we have just achieved the impossible on the site. The system has been properly fixed and is working like clockwork. None of that seemed very likely the day Douglas found your slip-ups and we all suffered as Chisholm and company denied what we knew to be true.

You two guys worked your socks off and produced cogent, proof positive arguments together with solutions to the types of problem from which lesser men would run.

What do you both say we don't run away from Mister Briggs? Do you think we can find a solution to shorten his continued existence in an exalted position and totally burst the big fat oaf's bubble! What do you say?"

The increasing volume of Tony's voice was such that, when he finished Torquil gave a wide smile and relaxed into using the boss's barrack room language,

"Yes please, Tony. Perhaps we could bury the fucker as well as Chisholm?"

"This is what I wanted to hear. And this is what I wanted to show you. Have a read at this, Torquil."

He handed him Liseur's letter to the Ministry of Defence. Torquil was flabbergasted when he read this denunciation of his onetime oppressor. He gazed up at both men with such a look of relief and gratitude that they had to look away. The young guy had been through such a lot at the hands of Briggs, Chisholm and his pal, Sean O'Casey. Tony and Douglas relished their attempt to hurt Briggs. It gave them a warm feeling in flexing the firm's legal muscle on behalf of their colleague.

"I don't know how to thank you for all you've done to help me to recover from the worst part of my life. Chisholm has been made to pay me and I guess that hurt him a lot. I hear from a former colleague that Sean O'Casey disappeared off the scene before they finally folded the firm. I don't know where he has gone but all I can say is I don't think many people will miss him. Do you think the M.O.D will do anything about Briggs?"

Tony handed him a second letter saying,

"Read this and see for yourself. It will answer your questions better than we can."

McMeikle and Huggett   *The Ministry of Defence*
Solicitors   *Whitehall*
1, Park Circle   *London*

Glasgow   SW1A 2HB
G4 1GA   United Kingdom

14 October 1991

For the attention Mr G McMeikle DCL

Dear Sir,   Ref: Contract at R.N.A.D. Bluff,
                           Morayshire, Scotland.

I am referring to your letter dated 27 September concerning the conduct of our Mister James Briggs at the M.O.D. in Edinburgh. Your complaint came as no surprise to this department for a number of reasons which I précis as follows.

1. The fiscal matters you alluded to have been advised to me since the start of the installations at the Bluff depot. It seemed inconceivable that a budget was reduced by almost eighty per cent and the project still went ahead.

2. It was, for a while, the belief that the original cost plan was faulty and Mister Briggs was indeed carrying out a sterling exercise in cost management.

3. We became concerned when the project went into a long delay but we were keen to maintain the attractive cost that was still pertaining for the work.

4. Mister Norman Keen, the Supervising Officer for the project, told us of the court case of Messrs Clark Chisholm Partnership versus the Association of Consulting Engineer's insurance underwriters at the High Court of The Justiciary

in Glasgow. We took a much closer look at the financial ramifications of this important project.

5. We have a copy of the minute of the last site meeting that Briggs attended and have used this as an accurate account of the difficulties experienced on this installation. It is required to enable disciplinary action to be initiated against this senior administrator.

6. The charges will be many and varied since his actions have been under scrutiny for some time. Those items in your brief but excellent letter will be included, inter alia, when this process is fully implemented and I assure you of our intention that it shall very soon become real for James Briggs.

That elucidation is what I feel you deserve. It is my honest account of the current career prospects of your client's alleged abuser. In normal events it would be left at that but considering the very important role played by your young engineering client in what must have been a most distasteful chapter of his early career, I shall speculate the following. It is my considered opinion that Mister James Briggs will be dismissed from the civil service sine die. He will not receive a full pension nor will he receive a customary parting golden handshake. On the contrary...he may be eligible for a short period of character-forming time at Her Majesty's pleasure.

You have gracefully waived your client's right to claim financial reward against Briggs. This is laudable, sir. It is however the case that Mister Torquil Knight has provided his services above and beyond what would have been expected of one having been so abominably treated.

It is because of his noble efforts that I have recommended he be given an ex-gratia payment for services rendered to her Majesty's Civil Service. As is traditional in such cases, it is a nominal sum. Please therefore pass to him the enclosed cheque in the amount of one thousand pounds from a grateful Minister of Defence.

I thank you and your client for bringing all of this detail to my attention. I will be grateful if you will please, now treat this matter as closed.

Your humble Servant
Sir William Maxwell-Grant
Minister for the Crown (Defence)

Tony got up and handed over the cheque and shook Torquil's hand warmly. Douglas did the same and said in a loud voice,

"Torquil! I believe the drinks are on you my boy!"

"Yes of course, Douglas. But we can also celebrate something else. This money will help me and Phillipa to get married next year."

That was good news but Tony made a worrying mental note. If he gets married next year, will he stay with us or disappear forever into the mists of far-flung Morayshire?

Part 4
Dec 1991

Franz Liseur's offices Clydebank

It was near to Christmas. Snow was starting to fall around the lowlands of Scotland. Tony had called for a get together with Douglas, Mark and Torquil to publish the details of their final account for the job at Bluff. Over a cup of coffee they reflected what had happened to Chisholm and Briggs. Tony showed no remorse for those two rogues by saying softly,

"Wasn't it just delicious to bring those two down?"

Both of his colleagues readily agreed and suggested the next time they met them they could pee on them. Tony responded with a giggle,

"Hear! Hear! But now let's have some fun seeing how much we got from them for satisfying the Ministry of Defence and putting Bluff to bed; which, after all's said and done is what we did. Agreed?"

"Yes, Tony."

He handed them each a copy of the draft final account prepared by their commercial manager. The list was long and detailed including the original contract amount plus costs for all the additional work, prolongation costs and extra moneys for accelerating the program to get it all done and working by the middle of 1991.

They also had the waiver from Hugh Jarvis of nearly twelve grand of builder's discount off the original tender. Jarvis too, had come out of it quite well since his additional builders work was all covered by the insurance company. Tony smiled at his team as they read the final figure,

"Well lads, it looks like we are picking up quite a stack of loot. The bottom line is one million, seven hundred and seventy-four thousand for us. Mark tells me that we should make over nine per cent net profit. Considering we are usually happy with three per cent, it has turned into a little cracker of a project. That's the big end of a hundred and sixty grand, lads. Well done us, eh?"

Douglas agreed,

"It's great to hear that but after all we've all been through, especially Torquil here, I think we only got what we deserved. We actually earned it, didn't we, Tony?"

"Yes Douglas. I said at the tender stage we should cut the price to get this job because I felt it would be a good little earner. Well! It looks as if I was right, but what a little bugger it was to get it done!"

"Yes Tony, but you have to admit, it was fun. Torquil and me are looking forward to the next one."

"Funny you should say that, Douglas. We've an enquiry in for a wee job at Machrihanish. It's a Royal Air Force base for the Ministry of Defence."

To the sound of running footsteps, Tony shouted,

"Douglas! Torquil! Come back!"

....

About the Author

Robert was born in 1942 among the slums of Glasgow. His father was a soldier killed in the war in North Africa that same year. His mother was 'in service' with one of the upper-class families of the town. The story of his childhood is told in his first book, *27, Raglan Street*. His secondary education was in Perthshire at Queen Victoria School for the sons of Scottish servicemen.

In 1959, he left there to begin his career in the building industry designing and managing mechanical services for commercial, public, medical and military establishments. During his 47 years in this field, he alternated between working with contracting firms as a project manager and in more elite positions with international architectural and engineering consultancy partnerships.

Robert's broad experience of the politics and in-fighting, as well as the endemic abuse of authority by some who were promoted, often beyond their capabilities, serves him well in creating the story for this, his second book, *Achilles Heel*.

Lightning Source UK Ltd.
Milton Keynes UK
UKHW011122060123
414937UK00001B/79